# SAMANTHA CHRISTY

Books Publishing Group

Saint Johns, FL 32259

Cover designed by Maria @ Steamy Designs.

Quiet
Beautiful
Things

Samantha Christy

# Note To Readers

To my valued readers: While numerous deaf sensitivity readers have been consulted during my writing and researching process, I've found that many things can differ based on circumstances. Please keep that in mind while enjoying this work of fiction.

# Chapter One

## Blake

Sometimes adulting sucks.

Like now, when I'm pushing a cart through the aisles of Truman's Grocery Store looking for things to make for dinner.

Okay, so technically, I've been an adult for a while. You'd think I'd have it down by now. But after four years of college—eating either take-out or dorm food—two years traveling abroad and visiting many of the world's finest wineries, then two years of grad school—where my roommate could have been getting a degree in culinary arts and not business—I've never really had to cook for myself, save the occasional bowl of pasta.

I study a package of steaks. Why do they always bundle them in pairs? Then some burgers—those come in a four-pack. I sure as hell can't finish all of those. I pick them up anyway. Maybe I'll invite my brother Lucas and his fiancée over for dinner.

Throwing them in my cart, I turn then freeze. Because across the store stands the most breathtaking woman I've ever seen. She's definitely not from Calloway Creek. I know everyone here. Or I used to.

She's in the produce section, picking up and studying various vegetables I don't even know the names of.

Vegetables. I need some of those, right? A pre-packaged salad I can douse with ranch and serve as a side to the burgers.

The woman puts something in her basket. Basket. Good. Maybe that means she's shopping for one. Hell, the only reason I have a cart is that I despise grocery shopping and the less I have to do it the better.

She brushes a piece of blonde hair behind her ear, and I can see her face even more clearly now. Holy hell, maybe this place isn't so bad after all. She's a good twenty feet away, but I swear she comes into focus as if she's right in front of me. She's gorgeous. And though I can't make out the color of her eyes, I know they are as beautiful as the rest of her. Her cheekbones are high and pink. Her lips rosy and full. And her body—if what's underneath her bright blue romper is anything like the rest of her… wow.

I will her to look up and see me.

"Hello, Blake," Mr. Truman says from behind the meat counter. "Haven't seen you around for a while. You back in town now?"

I face him. "Have been for about a month, Mr. Truman."

"Finally joining your daddy's business, eh?"

"You know it. I've been working at the winery full time since I've been back."

His head bobs up and down. "I suspect it's in good hands then."

"I appreciate the vote of confidence. See you later, sir."

"That you will."

Glancing over at the produce section, I'm disappointed that the woman is gone. It's just as well. I don't need any distractions. As the newly appointed Chief Operating Officer of Montana

Winery, all of my energy needs to go into impressing Dad—showing him I can handle things and letting him see I'm the responsible adult he always claimed I could be. He's worked for decades putting the winery on the map, and over the past several years, he's been handing over the reins. First, he made Lucas Chief Marketing Officer, then our middle brother Dallas, became Chief Financial Officer, and now me.

While he's still very much a presence there—he is only fifty-eight after all—he's due time off and an early retirement. It's our turn to run things now. Even our sister Allie has gotten more into the business over the past few years, running the tasting tours and organizing events.

I catch a glimpse of blue down the toiletry aisle. The mystery woman looks up. Our gazes collide and she looks at me the same way I do her. As if intrigued. Mesmerized. Entranced. If expressions could speak, hers is saying she likes what she sees. But it's also telling me she's hesitant, as if silently begging me to make the first move. Like part of her is worried I wouldn't be receptive.

However, I can't move. My feet are cemented in place just as my eyes are. I swallow. Because for the first time in my life, I'm at a loss on how to approach a woman. At a glance, I can tell this woman isn't like all the others. She's different somehow. Special. How do I do this? I have absolutely no fucking clue.

I think it's her eyes. I'm drowning in them. And I sure as hell don't want to be saved.

She looks at me like she knows me. There's no way she does. I'd have remembered a face like hers.

What she couldn't possibly know—because no way is my face as expressive as hers—is that in these fifteen seconds, my whole outlook on life has changed. Because of her. A stranger in a grocery store. She also doesn't know that this feeling inside me—this foreign feeling that once we speak, I'll never be the same—has knocked the wind right out of me. It literally causes my breath to hitch, and I swear I hear angels sing.

Mrs. Kendall, the high school choir teacher, comes around the corner humming a tune, and I laugh inwardly at my idiotic notion.

"Hello, dear," she says, stopping her melody.

"Hi, Mrs. Kendall."

"I didn't know you were back in town. You helping out your parents?"

"Yes, ma'am."

"Good boy," she says like I'm five and not twenty-six, then scampers off, resuming her humming.

When I turn back again, the mystery woman is gone.

I push my cart from aisle to aisle, searching for her. After all, we had a moment. Blake Montana doesn't have 'moments' with women. Flings. One-night-stands. Hookups. But never moments. And for damn sure never ones as intense as whatever the hell passed between us in those few seconds.

Maybe she wasn't even real. An apparition conjured up by my overactive imagination courtesy of my four-month dry spell.

Yeah, that's what it was. My mind dreaming up the perfect woman. Dark blonde hair that reminds me of a sandy beach at sunset, expressive eyes a man could get lost in, the face of an angel, a body that wars are fought over, and a voice that would shout my name when I nuzzle between her legs. Utterly divine.

But I'm not crazy enough to think such a creature exists.

I put her out of my head and stick to the job at hand. I fill my cart with the usual: Cereal. Snacks. Milk. Beer. And some healthy shit I'll probably never eat but get anyway in case Mom looks through my pantry.

Loading my car at the curb out front, my eyes are drawn down the street toward Gigi's Flower Shop, the place I spent summers and holidays working when I was an undergrad. Dad wanted all of us to have work experience outside of the winery. He said it would build character.

Maddie—the flower shop owner—steps outside carrying a bundle of flowers, and I wave. No, wait, it's not Maddie. It's the mystery woman. She looks behind her, confused by my wave. Then she smiles, and, holy shit, it's the biggest, brightest smile. I smile back. We have a moment. A *second* moment. Now I know I'm not imagining things. This girl is for real. And with just a look, we're connecting on some existential level I've never experienced before. Like we've known each other forever, even though I'm certain we've never met.

A horn blasts next to her. She doesn't even flinch. Her eyes never stray from mine, and it makes me feel like fucking Tarzan.

"Dude, you leaving? Some of us are in a hurry."

I look over my shoulder. Hawk McQuaid is glaring at me, waiting for me to vacate the prime spot right in front of the store.

"Park out back, McQuaid," I bark.

"Don't need to." He eyes my cart. "You're leaving. So hurry it the fuck along."

I put the final bag into my trunk and shut it, then leave the cart for him to take inside since he's so impatient.

When I look back down the sidewalk, the beautiful, stunning, perfect woman is gone, replaced by three pre-teens on skateboards who happily zip their way past me.

Without further acknowledgment of Hawk, I slip behind the wheel. I take the long way home, driving slowly by Gigi's, then the coffee shop, then through the roundabout the street was named after—McQuaid Circle. Apparently, since Hawk's ancestors founded the town, he believes that gives him the right to park wherever the hell he wants.

Then, *bingo*... I see her. She's walking toward the apartments set back from the park on the other side of the circle. As if she can feel my presence, she turns. Our eyes lock. There it is again, that feeling. What *is* that?

A car honks behind me. "Move your ass, Montana."

I peer in my rearview. It's my buddy, Dax Cruz. We grew up together, went to the same schools in Calloway Creek, then lost touch when I left for college. The rest of our families seem to despise each other, much like the Calloways and the McQuaids used to. Something about a feud surrounding our ancestors. But Dax and I never gave a crap what the rest of our relatives thought. And now that I'm home again, we're friends just as if I'd never left—something his brothers and mine aren't too keen over.

I stick my arm out the window and flip him the bird. He honks again, passes me, and yells, "See you tonight!"

*Damn.* The girl is gone once again. Vanished. Maybe she thought I was being creepy. But that smile—it said something else. I don't know her name. I haven't as much as spoken a word to her. But something deep down inside hurts at the thought that I might never see her again.

And somehow I know that would be a tragedy.

# Chapter Two

## Blake

When I get home, there's an unfamiliar car parked in the circular part of my driveway near the front door. Two people sit inside it. The driver gets out as I pull into the garage. I'm popping the trunk when a woman comes around the corner.

"Blake Montana?"

I try to place her but can't. She's not from around here. "Yes."

"I'm Trish Nelson." She pulls a business card from her pocket and hands it over.

I scan the card. "A private investigator?" My eyebrows shoot up. "Am I being investigated?"

"Perhaps we should talk inside." She glances into my trunk. "How about I help you with these bags?"

Refusing her help, I string the lot of them up both my arms. "Follow me," I say, reluctantly, wanting to tell her to get off my property, but at the same time, curious over why she's here.

She shuts my trunk and we head inside. I drop the bags on the counter and shove the cold food away in the refrigerator. Then I lean against the bar. "I'd offer you a cup of coffee, but at this point, I'm not sure if you're friend or foe. Mind telling me what this is about?" I nod to the front door. "And will your friend be joining us?"

"That depends," she says.

"On what?"

She walks behind one of the chairs at my kitchen table. "May I?"

I hold out my hand in a be-my-guest gesture. "Sure, why not."

I remain standing, trying to deduce what a private investigator could want with me. For a moment, I wonder if it has anything to do with Phoebe's and DJ's deaths a few years back. But it was evident Dallas's wife and son were killed in a carbon monoxide accident, so that wouldn't make sense.

"Mr. Montana, does the name Lucinda Wilcox mean anything to you?"

I narrow my eyes and nod. "Lucinda. Yeah, she was at NYU when I was an undergrad."

"You knew her well then?"

"I wouldn't say well. We went out a few times. But her name, it's unique enough that I'd remember it."

"You *went out* a few times? Can you elaborate?"

I pull out a chair and sit. "Oh, shit. Is she dead? Was she… murdered? Listen, I'm sorry, but I haven't seen her in five years."

"She's not dead, Mr. Montana."

"My dad is Mr. Montana. You can call me Blake. And if she's not dead, would you mind getting to the point, Ms. Nelson?"

"Trish, please." She places her hands on the table. "This is the awkward and typically shocking part where I tell you I've been hired to find the father of Miss Wilcox's child."

My eyes bug out and my stomach clenches. "Ah, damn. Really?"

"Before I go much further, you should know you're one of eight men who could be the potential father."

"Eight?" I scrub a hand across my jaw. "Jesus." A thought occurs. "Did she find out who my family is and decide I'd be a good meal ticket?"

She shakes her head. "It's not Lucinda who hired me. It's her parents."

"I'm confused."

"Honestly, Blake, I would be too were I in your position. I'm not at liberty to say much until the identity of the father is confirmed. Except I'll tell you the child is in danger of being placed in a foster home. In an attempt to avoid that, the Wilcoxes gave me full access to their daughter's phone and social media accounts. Through those, I was able to identify eight men she may have had relations with during the period in question. You are the sixth one I've been able to track down."

"What happened with the other five?"

"Three refused to take a paternity test. Two complied but have been ruled out as the father. I'm still working on locating the other two."

"You want me to take a paternity test?"

She motions to the front door. "I have a home health professional with me. All it involves is a swab of your cheek. The Wilcoxes have paid for expedited results which we should have within a week."

"Three others refused?"

She nods. "You have every right to refuse. However, if the father can't be identified based on those who volunteer, the

Wilcoxes will seek court orders requiring you and the others to take one."

"Why would I refuse? I mean, it'll help rule me out, right? And if by chance it… rules me in, well then it's my own reckless fault and I'll deal with the consequences."

Trish's head tilts, examining me as if taking measure. She's slightly older than I am, maybe even in her early thirties, but it's almost as if she's looking at me as a proud parent would. "That's mighty honorable of you. The other two took a bit more convincing."

"Yeah, well, I'm no saint. Lucinda wasn't the only one who slept her way through the student body at NYU. Guess maybe I wasn't as careful as I thought I was. It would be my own stupid fault. Takes two to tango. So the kid would be what, four?"

"That's correct. She's four. Five at the end of the summer."

I do the math in my head. It seems to work out. If I recall correctly, we met spring semester of senior year. Then I realize what Trish said. *"She?* Do you have a picture?"

"The child is a girl, but that's all I'm at liberty to say. Her identity is being protected as she's a minor. I'll have more information to share should you be a match."

"I guess let's get on with it then."

She stands. "I'll get the nurse. She'll need to see two forms of identification."

I pull out my wallet. "Not a problem."

She goes for the door and turns. "Thank you, Blake. You've made my job very easy today."

I nod, then run my hands through my hair as she fetches the nurse. Because, shit… thirty minutes ago my only problem was figuring out who the dream girl at the supermarket was. And now… now I could be a fucking dad.

# Chapter Three

# Ellie

I put away my groceries, arrange the bundle of flowers, then look at all the boxes still piled against the living room wall. Where do I even start? I should have accepted Mom and Dad's offer to help. But I wanted to do this on my own. This is my first real apartment—apart from the ones on various college campuses— and my first real job.

Yes, I've had lots of jobs before, but as a student teacher, or co-teacher, or a TA in grad school. Never anything like the one I'm about to start. And certainly never one that came with this kind of responsibility. But I can't wait to get started.

Outside the window, it's a beautiful spring afternoon, and I'm eager to explore the town. It's the polar opposite of where I grew up in New York City. Life seems slower here. More peaceful.

My little sister, Beth, was concerned I wouldn't have all the resources larger cities have to offer. I disagree. The school where I'm going to work is a wonderful resource. The rest will work itself out.

A jogger on the running trail that snakes behind my building catches my eye. I perk up when I see he's got dark, unruly hair like the mystery guy from earlier. My heart does a little flip just thinking of the encounter. Then I sigh when the guy turns and I see it's not him, the pang of disappointment in my stomach surprising me.

I sit on my couch, the only piece of furniture not covered in boxes, get out my phone, and type out a text.

**Me: I swear to God I just met my future husband.**

**Beth: Eeek! And you've only been there for one day. Tell me more.**

**Me: Okay, so I may have exaggerated. We didn't exactly meet.**

**Beth: I'm confused.**

**Me: Honestly, so am I. I was at the market. We saw one another from across the store. Our eyes locked on each other's and it was like... OMG, it was like there was this instant connection. And then I saw him again out front. And then again in his car.**

Beth: Ellie, are you sure the guy's not a stalker?

Me: It's not like that. I can't even explain it. We were drawn to each other. It was something out of a movie. I'm telling you, something happened. Something amazing.

Beth: So, this future husband of yours. If you haven't met him, you don't know his name. If you don't know his name, how can you ever expect to find him? Oh my gosh, Ellie. You could spend your whole life pining away for a guy you shared a look with.

Me: That's the good thing about small towns, sis. I'd bet my right arm I'll run into him again.

Beth: Well, if you do, don't stand there and drool like a sniveling idiot, get his name for crying out loud.

Me: LOL

Beth: How's the unpacking coming along?

Me: Slowly.

Beth: I could hop on the train and be there in an hour.

Me: You'll do no such thing. I need to do this myself. I love all of you. And I love how you support me. But I have to do this on my own. I promise once I get settled, I'll have you and Mom and Dad over for dinner.

Beth: You'd better. So other than Prince Charming, who you technically haven't even met, have you met anyone else?

I sigh.

Me: A few neighbors came to welcome me. I think I scared them away. Typical.

Beth: Fuck them.

Me: They're just not used to me yet. I'm sure we'll become fast friends. And if not, there will be plenty of opportunities for me to make friends at work.

Beth: You're going to need a life outside of work, Ellie.

Me: I've been here for twenty-four hours, Beth. Geesh! Give me a second.

Beth: Gotta go. I have class in thirty.

Me: Make me proud, little sister.

**Beth: Always. Bye.**

I toss my phone down and look over at the pile of boxes. One is marked 'Pictures.' I push off the couch, rip through the tape holding the box shut, and pull out framed photos of Beth and I, Mom and Dad, and all four of us. My favorite one, though, is the one of Dad and me when I was only two years old. It was the day he adopted me and officially became my dad. I've never seen him look so happy.

My biological father was never in the picture. Mom left him before I was born. Then later, when he found out about me, he wanted nothing to do with me when he learned I wasn't a 'perfect' child. I looked him up once, when I was eighteen. I didn't want a relationship with him. I just wanted answers. Or closure. Or... something.

I've never wanted for anything. Love, security, belonging. I've had all of it. But there's something about a parent not wanting their own child that sticks with you despite all that. It was a mistake, looking for him, finding him. He was just as bad as Mom made him out to be. No, he was worse.

I put all thoughts of Grant Lucas out of my mind as I search for a hammer and nail and hang the photo of Dad and me front and center on my living room wall. When it's perfectly centered, I run a finger across the frame, vowing to make him proud.

~ ~ ~

Hours later, half of my boxes unpacked, I put on my running clothes and jog back to McQuaid Circle. It only takes a few minutes to get there. I chose my apartment based on the close proximity to the school where I'm going to work. I'm happy to also be within walking distance of the small shopping district surrounding the circle. As someone who grew up in Manhattan, this whole area reeks of small town. But it'll be a nice change from the hustle of the city.

Earlier, I was so hungry—and then preoccupied with the mystery guy—I didn't get a chance to see anything but the grocery store and flower shop. Now, with no more distractions, I take it all in as I jog down the sidewalk and check out all the storefronts. I pass a coffee shop on the corner, then a bookstore, an ice-cream parlor, a diner, a nail salon, a hardware store, and a sub shop.

I think I'm going to like it here. People seem nice, the judgmental neighbors I told Beth about notwithstanding. And as I pass some locals—families eating ice cream, a couple walking their dog, teenagers scurrying around on skateboards—I know I made the right choice.

The far end of the circle is clearly where the nightlife is. I spot a movie theater and a bowling alley. I probably won't go to the theater, but bowling might be fun. I wonder if the school has a league. Next to those venues is a place called Donovan's Pub. I jog by slowly. Peeking in the windows tells me this must be the Friday night hangout spot for a lot of the locals.

*Locals.* I'm one of those now. I can almost picture myself sitting in a booth.

I jog around the corner, all the way around the back of the movie theater. There's a huge parking lot running behind the theater, bowling alley, and pub that leads back around to the park where I just know there must be a great jogging trail.

I'm delighted to see that the backside of the pub has an outdoor patio. It's tastefully illuminated by long strands of hanging white lights. Outdoor heaters stand tall in each corner of the patio, but they aren't needed on this mild spring evening.

My steps falter and I almost trip over my own feet when I see the mystery guy sitting at one of the outdoor tables, a beer in hand. But his entire demeanor is completely different from earlier. He looks like his dog died. He stares contemplatively into his beer, twisting the glass with his hand. Why is he so sad?

My heart sinks when I spy a second glass on the table. Is he on a date?

He looks up, right at me, shock unhitching his jaw. My heart pounds when he stands, looking like he might approach. I'm a good thirty feet away but I can see his expression clearly. The burning tether of his gaze lets me know he's surprised—and perhaps pleased—to see me.

He waves. I smile and wave back. He smiles. I like his smile. Despite the hint of sadness I detected a moment ago, his face now shines with an undiluted grin displaying what I imagine are perfect rows of teeth.

He turns away abruptly as if someone called his name. A man who bears some resemblance to him claps him on the shoulder and takes the other seat. *Not a date.*

I smile again, this time to myself. Then I whirl around happily and jog to the park.

# Chapter Four

## Blake

"Did you hear yet?" Lucas asks as soon as I answer his call.

I stop jogging, something I've been doing a lot more of this week after seeing *she* likes to do it, and I roll my eyes. He's called me twice a day for a week. I'm beginning to regret even telling him. I swore him and the rest of my family to secrecy. But I needed to tell them. We're all very close. Or we used to be, until Dallas lost his family and took off to a remote cabin upstate where he's been for the past two years.

"No, dickwad, I haven't heard. Don't you think I'd call if I had?"

"Either that, or maybe you'd drown yourself in the creek."

"I'm not going to kill myself if the kid is mine."

"Do you know how fucked up that would be if you had a four-year-old kid? What kind of woman keeps that information from a guy?"

"I suppose one who was so slutty she doesn't know who the father is."

"Have you thought about what you'll do if she's yours?"

"I suppose I'll write a big check every month and try to get to know her."

"If the slut allows it."

"You can bet your ass if I'm supporting the kid I'll be in her life. Even if I have to go to court."

"You know she's just looking for a meal ticket. Slap the name Montana on the kid and she'll be set for life. This Lucinda chick must know that."

"I told you, I have no idea what's going on. The private investigator said Lucinda wasn't the one driving this."

"Right."

I see someone walking ahead, a spark of recognition twinging in my gut. "Gotta go finish my run."

"Call me la—"

I hang up and jog ahead, plucking my AirPods out of my ears. "Hey!" I call out. It's her. I know it's her. That hair. That body. It's the dream girl I've been thinking about for six days. I've been running the trail in the park and jogging by the apartments every day after work hoping to find her.

She's far away so I pick up the pace. "Hey! Hello!"

I get close, but she doesn't turn. She approaches her building, punches a code on the keypad, and walks inside. Ten seconds later I'm pounding on the outer door, looking like an idiot as I shout after her. "Hey!"

I see her through the glass, but she still doesn't turn. *Damn it.* She must be wearing AirPods. Everyone wears them these days. Better luck next time.

At least now I know what building she lives in even if it does make me feel like a stalker.

My phone vibrates with an incoming email. I swallow barbed wire when I see who it's from. Trish, the private investigator, told me the paternity results would be emailed to me.

This is it.

*Oh God.*

I tap the email to open it. There's a lot of information I don't understand. Until I get to the very bottom where it clearly reads: **The alleged father is not excluded as the biological father of the tested child.**

While that might not be crystal clear, there's one thing that is.

The next line reads: **Probability of Paternity: 99.9998%**

*Holy shit.*

I lose my breath as swiftly as if I'd been kicked in the stomach. Tumbling onto the grass, I bend my knees and put my head between my legs.

*Holy shit.*

My heart races. I almost hyperventilate. Closing my eyes, I try to picture my life. The life that just got turned upside down with one swab of the cheek. One reckless night. One single email.

*I'm a fucking dad.*

~ ~ ~

Two hours later, Lucas, Allie, Mom, Dad, and I are sitting around my table with Ms. Duffey from New York Child Protective Services. I knew they'd be coming. Trish called and told me.

"Let me get this straight," Dad asks on my behalf. Probably because I'm still too stunned to speak. "This Lucinda is in drug rehab, the grandparents want to dump their grandchild on my son so they can sail the world on a cruise ship, and if my son refuses custody, the girl will go into foster care?"

"That sums it up," Mrs. Duffey says.

"Can we please stop referring to the child as 'the girl'," Mom says. "She must have a name. And do you have a picture?"

"Her name is Maisy." A picture is pulled from a folder and slid across the table.

Mom gasps. "My Lord. She looks just like you did at that age."

I study the picture. The girl is beautiful despite her unkempt curly blonde hair. And there is a definite sadness in her eyes. I raise a brow at Mom.

"I mean her face, Blake. Not her hair. She has your eyes. Your nose. The shape of your jaw. And I'm willing to bet, if she were smiling, she'd even have your dimples." A hand covers Mom's heart. "Maisy Montana. It has a nice ring."

"Let's not get ahead of ourselves," Mrs. Duffey says. "Legally, her name is Wilcox."

"Surely we can get that changed," Dad says.

"It all depends. While we're issuing Blake emergency temporary guardianship so he can care for her, there are still a lot of unknowns here. Such as what will happen when Miss Wilcox is released from rehab."

"And how long will that be?"

"Miss Wilcox is in a ninety-day inpatient program, after which she may have an extended stay in a sober living residential facility. I fully expect her to get visitation privileges after the inpatient program."

Finally, I speak. "As in, I'm babysitting for three months and then Lucinda gets to come back and do whatever she wants?"

She shakes her head. "You have rights as the father. She also has rights. But given the circumstances under which Maisy was taken away, the courts may rule in your favor should it come to that."

"What exactly are these circumstances?" Mom asks, lines of worry etching near her eyes.

"Neglect, mostly."

There is a burning inside me as I look at the picture. There is such sadness in her eyes. My kid—my daughter—has been raised and neglected by a drug addict. Surprise overcomes me as I realize how protective I'm being over someone I've never met. "Was she beaten?" I ask with a tight jaw.

"Maisy shows no signs of physical abuse. But sometimes neglect can have the same outcomes. She's shy. Reserved. And she doesn't communicate outside of pointing and drawing."

Mom gasps again. "She doesn't communicate? What do you mean?"

"Well, ma'am"—Mrs. Duffey looks at me—"it appears Maisy may be deaf."

A hand flies to Mom's mouth, covering her surprise. "Oh my gosh."

"What do you mean *'it appears'?*" I ask angrily. "She's four. How can you not know?"

"That's where the neglect comes in. There are no medical records to show she's ever been tested. Yet she's virtually unresponsive to verbal commands. I'd suggest the first thing you do is take her to an audiologist."

Dad pulls out his phone. "Roger Dullis is an audiologist and a good friend. I'll text him now."

My stomach heaves. I have a daughter. Possibly a deaf one. Definitely a neglected one. I feel utterly sick. "When can I meet her?"

Mrs. Duffey thumbs out the window. "I have a fellow social worker waiting with her in the car. Lucinda's parents packed her belongings."

I stand and go to the window. "She's *here?* And you want me to take her? *Now?*"

"Like I explained when I first showed up, Mr. and Mrs. Wilcox are leaving the country. Maisy was set to enter the foster care system and would have if your paternity test had come back differently. We had a judge issue the emergency temporary guardianship. It'll take time to get your name on the birth certificate, and, even then, there may be a custody battle ahead. But, yes, Mr. Montana, we'd like you to take her today. Right now."

I look around. "I don't have anything. I don't even know where I'd start."

Mom touches my shoulder. "I'll take care of it. Sweetie, there's a little girl out there who needs you."

Dad looks up from his phone. "Roger said he can come over and meet her. He'll be able to give you some preliminary information."

I nod. "Okay." My insides are shaking. "I guess… let's meet my daughter."

"I'll bring her inside," Mrs. Duffey says and heads for the door.

Dad clasps my shoulder as I take several deep breaths. "We're all here for you, Blake."

I nod.

Tension is building inside me, getting stronger every second, like a percolating pot of coffee.

*What if she hates me?*

*What if I don't know how to help her?*

*What if I can't be a father?*

It seems like forever before Mrs. Duffey comes back inside. When she does, she drags a large suitcase behind her, and her other hand holds onto a very scared-looking little girl.

My heart lurches into my throat. Everything the social worker said about Maisy's situation hits me like a punch to the gut. How could anyone treat such a fragile little girl like that? The lump in my throat makes it almost impossible to speak. Because, despite her disheveled appearance, this creature is the most beautiful sight I've ever seen. In one instant, one single heartbeat, I get it. I get what happened to Dallas when DJ was born. The immediate love, knowing she's a part of me. The intense need to be a protector, a provider, an emotional rock for her. To be *all* things for this small human.

Two hours ago, I was a bachelor without a care in the world.

But now, now there's Maisy. And suddenly my life has new meaning.

I vow, right here and now, to do anything and everything I have to do to make her childhood as happy as mine was. And to make up for anything she's been lacking.

I fall to my knees, trying to keep emotions at bay. I am, after all, a twenty-six-year-old man. Not knowing what to do, I simply smile and wave. "Hi, Maisy."

She looks from me up to Mrs. Duffey.

Mrs. Duffey gives her a nod, releases the suitcase, and gestures to the chair to my right. Maisy shuffles over as if she's been instructed to take a seat a million times before. She sits, removes her backpack, and pulls out a stuffed cat.

"What do I do?" I ask everyone.

Mom walks over to Maisy and points to the cat. "What a lovely kitten."

Maisy doesn't respond. She's not even looking at Mom. She's just holding the stuffed toy, her blue eyes sunken and distant. Every so often, I catch her sneaking side-glances at everyone in the room, as if she's somehow monitoring each of us to figure out who the biggest threat might be. And she keeps looking at the door. Perhaps she thinks it's her escape route if things go bad.

"This is all of her things," Mrs. Duffey says.

I tear my eyes from Maisy and regard the sole suitcase. "That's *all* of her things? How can that be?"

She shrugs. "I guess her mother only got her the essentials. Listen, I hate to drop her and run, but I have three other clients to see today."

I turn abruptly. "You're *leaving?*"

"Mr. Montana, Maisy doesn't know me any better than she knows you at this point. We'll check back with you in a few days. And we'll keep in touch about the progress of your guardianship. My advice is to hire a lawyer as soon as possible to get things moving along with regards to both the birth certificate and the future custody arrangements."

"Okay, well, I guess… thanks."

She offers a sad smile. "It's a lot, I know. But from what I can see"—she gestures to my family—"you have an amazing support system. That tells me this is the best place for her. You have my card. Good luck, Mr. Montana."

And with that, she's gone.

I turn to Maisy. "Maisy, can you hear me?"

She doesn't look up.

I crouch down and make sure she can see me. "Maisy, can you hear me?" I say louder.

She just pets her cat.

I reach out gently, hover my hand over the stuffed cat and ask permission with my eyes before I pet it. When she doesn't object, I run my hand along the animal's back. Then I smile and do it again. Maisy doesn't do anything. She just watches me pet her stuffed animal.

"This just won't do," Mom says behind me.

I look over my shoulder. She's got the suitcase open and is pulling out clothes.

"Allie," Mom says, snapping her fingers. "Be a dear and grab me a pad and pen. I'm going to make a list of necessities. You and Lucas will go shopping. I'll stay here with your father and Blake. Then I'll make a call to Janice Masterson over at the furniture store and see if she can arrange a quick delivery."

Allie hands her a pad and Mom starts scribbling. I notice Maisy watching Mom. "Mom, make sure you add crayons and paper to your list."

Mom looks up and smiles at me as her eyes get teary. "Look at you, Blake, you're already thinking like a father." She goes back to her list, mumbling, "She'll need clothes. Size 4T or extra small. And underpants." She rummages through everything. "I don't see diapers or pull-ups, so she must be fully toilet trained. That's good. Get socks. A few size ten shoes." She looks over at Allie. "Little kids ten, not women's ten. Tennis shoes, sandals, and Mary Janes maybe. She'll need toiletries. Gentle soap. Kids' toothpaste. Lots of snacks, but make sure some are healthy—applesauce and yogurt. Oh, I hope she doesn't have any food allergies." She scribbles more. The list is already a few pages long. "I'll get her a twin bed, so get sheets. She seems to like pink based on everything in her suitcase. And get one of those bed rails so she won't roll off." She chews on the pen and thinks. "Get her some toys. Just look at the age on the boxes. Barbies. A baby doll. Things like that. And a kick ball. And whatever else you can think of."

Mom hands the list to Allie along with a credit card. "Get going. This will take you hours. Target should have everything you need." They're almost out the door when Mom yells, "Get a car seat for a four-year-old!"

"Got it, Mom. Chill!" Lucas calls.

Mom gives him the stink eye. "We'll text you if we think of anything else." She gets her phone out of her purse and places a call. "Janice, thank God. I have a bit of an emergency." She walks into the other room, chatting away.

Dad and I look at each other, then at Maisy.

"I have no idea what I should be doing," I say.

He nods to the open suitcase. There are mostly clothes in it, but a few picture books. "Maybe try to engage her with one of those."

I pick out a book about a cat and sit on the chair next to Maisy. I point to the cat in the book and then to the stuffed cat in her lap. Again, she's unresponsive.

"I really hope your friend gets here soon," I tell Dad. "Maybe he'll have an idea on how to communicate with her."

"Well, son. If she really is deaf, I imagine you'll have to learn sign language."

I scoff, exasperated. "And until then? What do I do until then?"

He touches my shoulder. "We'll figure it out, Blake."

"What if she's hungry or thirsty? Or what if she needs to use the bathroom?"

"Why not give her a tour of the house?"

"Dad, I'm not even sure she understands that she'll be staying here."

"I'm not sure either. Maybe once the furniture is delivered, she'll understand."

"Maybe." I stand and tap Maisy's shoulder. She looks up and I gesture for her to follow me. "Come on," I say.

She hugs her animal tightly.

"You can bring him," I say. I point to the cat and gesture for her to follow me again.

She must understand, because she gets up off the chair. When we walk into the kitchen her eyes go wide. Maybe this kitchen is bigger than the one she's used to. I don't know anything about where she grew up and what she had. But based on her lack of possessions, I'd say it was no place as nice as this. Opening the refrigerator, I point inside and shrug. She shakes her head. Okay, not hungry then.

I step out of the kitchen and wave her toward me. We walk down the hall and stop in front of the guest bathroom. I point to the toilet and hold my hand out, asking if she needs to use it. Again, she shakes her head. At least I think she might be understanding. Either that or she's shaking her head because she doesn't.

I show her the second, third and fourth bedrooms which are not really bedrooms but a home office, a workout room, and a spare room I use mostly for storing winery stuff. I figure the last one will be the easiest to clear out for her since it only has a futon and some boxes. The final stop is my bedroom. I point to myself and to the bed. She stares blankly.

She follows me to the dining room and through to the family room, where she walks over to the large picture window overlooking my back yard. She stands and stares. I watch her and wonder what she's thinking. She's been taken from her mother. Neglectful or not, Lucinda may be the only person who's been a

29

constant presence in her life. And she may be the only person she communicated with. Then again, why is she not trying to use sign language?

Mrs. Duffey said her only communication is pointing and drawing. Has Maisy never been taught any signs? Maybe they have it all wrong. Maybe Maisy isn't deaf at all. She could be autistic. Hell, she could just be scared. But at this point, there's only one person who can say for sure. *Hurry the fuck up, Roger.*

"The furniture will be delivered by six." Mom rounds the corner and stops when she sees Maisy looking outside. "I'll order a swing set tomorrow. Every child should have one."

"Mom, we don't know how long she'll even be here."

"Nonsense. You heard what CPS said. She's been neglected. She needs you, Blake."

"A lot of good I can do. I don't even know how to ask her if she's hungry."

"You'll learn. I have faith in you."

"My job." I look over my shoulder at Dad, who's standing in the doorway. "I've only been COO for a month."

Dad laughs. "It's not as if I can't run the company without you, Blake. You'll work when you can. Maisy is your primary concern now."

The doorbell rings and I pray it's the audiologist. I look at Maisy. She's still staring out at the back yard, petting her stuffed cat. She didn't even turn when the doorbell rang. My heart takes a tumble.

A minute later, Dad introduces me to Roger.

"Your father told me what happened. Looks like you've been thrown right into the deep end."

"Feels that way, Dr. Dullis."

"It's Roger. Now let's have a look at this precious girl." He goes over to Maisy and taps her on the shoulder. "Hello, Maisy," he says. "How are you?"

As he speaks to her, he uses ASL, which I don't understand in the least. He turns to me. "I'm not proficient at signing, but I know enough to communicate with my patients."

"Maisy, are you hungry?" He points to her then draws his hands toward himself. With his right hand, he puts all his fingers together with his thumb and pulls them toward his mouth. "Do you want food?"

She doesn't respond. He points to her stuffed animal. "Is this your cat?" he says, using his thumbs and forefingers alongside his face to indicate whiskers.

He turns to me. "It doesn't seem she's been taught any signs at all."

She looks back out the window.

"This is a bit rudimentary," Roger says, "but bear with me." He stands behind her and snaps his fingers. Then he claps his hands. Then he says her name forcefully. She doesn't turn. He pulls something out of his messenger bag and shakes it right behind her head. It sounds like a tin can full of marbles. It's a horrible sound that could wake the dead.

Maisy doesn't flinch. *Oh, God.*

He pulls out a small cup and a ping pong ball. Then he taps Maisy on the shoulder. She faces him. "Can you throw the ball into the cup?" he says very slowly as he signs.

She looks at the ping pong ball then pets her cat.

"Maisy." He waves to get her attention. "Can you throw the ball into the cup?" This time, as he talks, he shows her what he wants her to do, tossing the ball into the cup. Then he gets it out and points to her and then the ball.

She takes the ball from his open palm and throws it into the cup. Well, she tries to, but misses.

Roger claps and smiles. "Yes," he says while moving his fist in a nodding motion. "Very good." He signs something that I assume means *good.*

"Maisy, are you hungry?" This time, he doesn't use the same ASL motions he did before. He points to her then to his mouth, then rubs his stomach.

She nods emphatically. It's the most emotion she's displayed since setting foot in the door.

He gestures for us all to follow him into the kitchen. "Do you have something for her to eat?"

I open my pantry. It's large—a room in itself. I invite Maisy inside. She wanders in, eyes wide as if she's walked into Willy Wonka's chocolate factory. Her gaze settles on a package of M&Ms. I go over and pick them up, pointing to her then the candy. She nods and makes a nasally 'ungh' sound. I turn to Roger to see if he heard. He did. I go to the kitchen table, open the package, and dump out a handful. Then I pour her a cup of water.

She puts her cat on the table, eats an M&M and then 'feeds' one to the stuffed animal.

I notice Roger stepping from the room to make a phone call. He returns a few minutes later.

"She's inattentive," Roger says. "She can't understand simple signs. She doesn't respond to her name. And she doesn't startle at loud sounds. She's also nonverbal. All of this points to profound deafness. But before making an official diagnosis, I'd like you to bring her in for an audiometry exam. It will test her ability to hear sounds based on intensity and tone."

"But you just said she isn't responding to loud noises."

"That's correct. It's possible she still has some residual hearing. Testing her in my office will let us know just how much, if any." He hands me his card. "Call my office first thing tomorrow. Tell them I've agreed to squeeze you in. It seems Maisy has gone over four years without any meaningful way to communicate. It's imperative you get started right away."

He hands me a second card with a name and number scribbled on the back. "I've arranged for you to meet with a mentor from the Deaf and Blind school. A person who will help come up with a learning plan, help you both learn ASL, guide you through daily life with a deaf child, and become an advocate for Maisy in her educational needs. A Dr. Stone has been assigned as Maisy's mentor. A home visit is scheduled for tomorrow afternoon."

"Tomorrow?" I run a hand through my hair, still trying to process everything. "All of this is happening so quickly."

"Time is of the essence," Roger says. "The best time to cram as much exposure to language as possible is from birth to age five. Maisy has missed out on almost all that time. By age seven, children lose the opportunity for grasping language and thought processing. Every day you wait is one less day of learning. I'm not going to lie and say it will be easy. It's going to be a long road. For both of you. The good news is that she has you. She has all of you. That's more than she had last month, last year, or even this morning."

I nod and thank him, then Dad walks him out.

"It'll be okay, honey," Mom says.

"Will it?" My heart sinks as I watch Maisy feed her stuffed cat and then herself.

"Yes it will. Sit with her. I'll make us all dinner."

Three hours later, twenty bags are scattered across my living room. They're full of clothes, toys, and a bunch of other stuff I didn't even know I'd need. Bedroom furniture is being set up in my fourth bedroom—the one with a private bath. As soon as the delivery guys leave and Mom makes the bed, I gesture for Maisy to follow me. When she enters the room that was once my storage area, she looks up at me, confused.

I point to her, then to the bed, then I put my hands up by my head like I'm sleeping.

She looks around the room. There's a dresser along one wall, toys in the corner, and new clothes hanging in the closet. She eyes it all and points to herself.

I nod. "Yes. This is your room now."

I'm not sure if she understands a damn thing I'm saying, but she understands enough to take her cat over to the bed and sit on it.

I smile at her and nod. Because for now, this will have to do. It may be a baby step. But it's a start.

"She needs a bath," Mom says, standing in the doorway.

"I, uh…"

Mom rummages through a bag and pulls out pajamas. "I'll do it this time. But only this time. Okay?"

"Okay," I say, more than a little relieved.

She shows the pink-flower-covered pajamas to Maisy, then points to the bathroom. Maisy puts down her cat and disappears with Mom.

I sit on her bed wondering how, in a matter of hours, this became my life.

Allie appears in the doorway. "I'll babysit anytime you need." She moves her fingers around into random positions. "Look, I even googled how to sign *Maisy.*"

"Show me?"

She cracks a smile, sits next to me, and teaches me the five letters.

Twenty minutes later, Mom emerges with Maisy, whose hair spirals in wet blonde ringlets that fall to her shoulders.

"She has the most gorgeous hair," Mom says. "You'll have to learn how to manage it. You can't just brush curly hair or it will frizz."

"I think I have more important things to learn than how to do her hair."

Allie scoffs. "Blake, you have to learn about her hair. Do not let her walk around with the rat's nest she arrived with. Promise me. She's so darn cute."

"Fine, fine. Geez. I'll add that to the five hundred other things I have to learn."

Maisy yawns and Mom hands me a picture book. "Put your daughter to bed, Blake. Then come have a drink with us. You've earned it."

I take the book, show it to Maisy, then point to the bed. She crawls up onto it, pulls her cat close and gets under the covers. She gets that she's sleeping here. Thank goodness for small favors.

Not knowing what to do, I simply read her the book as if she can hear. I point to the pictures. I lean down and make funny faces. She doesn't show much emotion. Maybe she thinks I'm crazy. Maybe she misses her mom. Maybe she has no idea who I am and what's happening to her.

She falls asleep after the second read through. I start to tiptoe out of the room and then shake my head at myself. I turn off the light in her room, but leave on the hall light, remembering how I was scared of the dark as a kid.

I have that much-needed drink with Mom, Dad, Lucas, and Allie. All of us are in disbelief. None of us knows what the morning will bring. I've never been more scared in my life. And that includes the time Dallas and I got stuck upside down on a roller coaster a hundred feet high and had to wait nearly an hour to be rescued and lowered to the ground by firemen.

The four of them are getting ready to leave after I refused Mom's tenth offer to stay the night.

Dad comes into the hallway just as I'm pulling the mattress from my futon near Maisy's bedroom door.

"What are you doing?" he asks.

"I'm sleeping here. What if she wakes up, gets scared, and wanders out of the house?"

Dad smiles and puts a hand on my shoulder. "Your mom and I raised you right. And I've never been more proud." Other than when Dallas's family died, I've never seen my father cry. But right now, tears coat his lower lashes. "You're already a great father, son."

He turns to leave as I absorb his words. I'm a father. I'm *her* father.

*Jesus.*

Settling in, I become very aware of just how quiet the house is. Almost eerily so. I lean back and recline on the futon mattress. Is this what it's like for Maisy all the time?

I hear the squeaking of a neighbor's garage door. A dog barking in the distance. The sound my feet make when I move them. No—I fear it's not what it's like for her at all. And I wonder, despite what Dad seems to think, if I'm capable of being any kind of father at all.

# Chapter Five

## Blake

*Profoundly deaf.*

The words roll around in my head as I watch Maisy across the living room.

*Profoundly deaf.*

She scribbles away with her crayons as I try to process what this will mean for her.

Dr. Dullis explained it. But it still seems so surreal. She can't hear anything. *Anything.* She has practically zero residual hearing. The only sound she's capable of hearing is a very very loud noise such as a gunshot or a jet engine. And even then, only if it's a few feet away.

She's so deaf, in fact, she wouldn't even be able to hear loud sounds with hearing aids. I scan one of the many pamphlets given to me by the audiologist. It's about cochlear implants. There are a dozen more for me to look through after this one. Deaf camps. ASL classes. Support groups for deaf and hard of hearing. Resources for parents of deaf children. A brochure from the local Deaf and Blind school.

I stare at the title of one of the brochures. 'Silent World.' In a flash, my heart lodges in my throat. Maisy's world is silent. She'll never hear birds chirping or people clapping. She'll never hear anyone tell her they love her. She'll never even hear the sound of her own name. I tilt my head and study her. Christ, does she even *know* her name? Does she know what's happening to her? Does she understand that I'm her father?

Maisy stops coloring and looks at me. All I can do is smile. Her face remains stoic as she points to the front door. She's done it several times today. I have no idea what she wants. When Mom was here, after she accompanied us to the doctor's office, she said maybe Maisy was trying to tell us she wanted to leave.

I wave my arms and look around the room then point at her. "This is your house now."

She just points at the door again.

I shake my head. "No. We're staying here. I'm so sorry. I wish I could understand what you want."

She stomps an angry foot over and over.

"Maisy, you live here. With me." I waggle a finger between us, hoping she gets that we have a connection.

Her lips pucker into a scowl and she pushes her papers off the table, scattering them everywhere, along with the glass of water that's now a shattered mess on the floor. She looks over at me, eyes filled with terror, then she screams and runs away.

"Maisy!" I chase after her but hit my shin on the coffee table. "Fuck!" I lean over, rub my leg, and check for blood. When I look back up, she's gone. "Maisy!" I go down the hall and look in her room. It's empty. "Maisy, where are you?"

I inwardly roll my eyes when I realize no matter how loud I yell, she won't be able to hear me. But that doesn't stop me from continuing to call her name as I go from room to room. Panic begins to set in when I can't find her. Jesus, is this what it's going to be like? How will I ever know if she's in trouble? How will she ever know when I need to find her?

I sit on her bed, feeling like a failure for the hundredth time today, when I hear a rustling from across the room. It's coming from the closet. My throat thickens when it dawns on me that in her attempt to hide, she has no idea she's making noise.

When I open the closet door, I find her crouched in the corner, her cat pressed tightly to her chest. She looks up at me, fear in her eyes. Damn, does she think she's in trouble for breaking the glass?

"It's okay," I say, trying to soften the expression on my face. "It's okay." I motion for her to come out.

She shakes her head over and over, hugging her stuffed cat as if it's the only thing protecting her. How can I tell her it's not? How can I let her know that *I'll* protect her?

I back away, leaving the door open, and sit on her bed. Maybe she felt threatened with me hovering in the doorway. A minute later, her head appears as she looks out, but then it's gone. More rustling as she settles back where she was.

A knock on the door ends my plan to sit and wait for her to come to me. *Shit. Is it four o'clock already?* I should have accepted Mom's invitation to stay and clean up.

I race out through the living room, eyeing not only the trash from all the stuff Allie and Lucas bought last night, but the strewn papers and shattered glass. It looks like a tornado came through here.

It's useless to try and pick anything up at this point, especially when I hear a second pounding on the door. I perk up on my way to answer it, realizing what this means. The cavalry has arrived.

This Dr. Stone will surely be able to help. He'll be able to communicate with her. I feel my day just got a whole lot better.

When I open the door, however, all I can do is stare. It's *her*. The dream girl from the grocery store. Those gorgeous eyes. And she's here.

"You," I say in utter disbelief. "What... uh... how did you find me?"

She's staring at me the same way I'm staring at her. As if she can't believe it's me. Both of us seem to be at a complete loss for words. Then, as if a curtain is drawn down her face, her entire demeanor changes. Her surprise at seeing me disappears, replaced by confusion as she pulls something from her pocket. She hands me a business card. It reads: **Dr. Ellie Stone**, along with a bunch of letters behind her name. Below her name is the name of the Deaf school, and more acronyms I don't understand.

I look up. *"You're* Dr. Stone?"

She shrugs and nods, a funny look on her face as if we're both being punk'd or something.

I step aside. "Please come in. I don't know how any of this works. I don't even think Maisy—"

My shoulder gets poked. I turn back to her. She moves her hands quickly. Oh, she's signing.

"Sorry," I say with a shrug. "I don't understand sign language."

She points to me, then her mouth, then her eyes.

It takes my feeble brain a second to catch up. My eyebrows shoot up. "You're *deaf?"*

Everything makes sense now. Why she didn't react to the car horn at the grocery store. Or to me shouting after her when I was jogging. But... how is this going to work? I don't know ASL. Maisy doesn't know ASL. And Dr. Stone is deaf. How will any of this work?

She gets a notepad from her bag, writes something down, and hands it to me.

*My interpreter is running late. She should
be here any minute.*

I breathe a sigh of relief. Interpreter. At least that's good. I give her a thumbs up and then grimace, feeling like an idiot. She's a doctor, not a kid.

A woman runs up behind her, signing with her hands as she speaks. "Sorry. Sorry. My last appointment ran over."

Dr. Stone sees me looking behind her and turns.

"Sorry, Dr. Stone," the woman says and signs.

Dr. Stone signs something, then the other woman approaches me and holds out her hand. "I'm Hannah, Dr. Stone's interpreter."

I shake. "Blake Montana. Nice to meet you."

Dr. Stone signs and Hannah starts speaking. "I'm Ellie Stone. I've been assigned as your daughter's advocate."

*My daughter.* It still doesn't seem real. *I have a daughter.*

"It's nice to meet you. Thank you for coming."

"Please look at me when you speak, not my interpreter," Hannah says for her.

"Right. Sorry."

A pained cry behind me rips my attention from both of the women, and I spin around to see Maisy on the floor, holding her bare foot. Ah, shit, she stepped on a piece of glass. I stride over and try to pick her up. She's all arms, thrashing at me and shoving me away while making high-pitched throaty noises.

"Maisy, I'm trying to help you!"

Dr. Stone appears beside me, gets down on her knees and signs to Maisy.

"She doesn't know sign language," I say to Hannah. "Tell her she doesn't know ASL."

*"You* tell her," Hannah says, stepping behind me so Dr. Stone can see her. "Speak to Dr. Stone, not to me."

"Maisy doesn't know sign language," I say as I look directly at Dr. Stone.

Her eyes scold me, and I can already tell this woman is a force to be reckoned with.

"Can she read yet?" Hannah asks on her behalf.

I shake my head.

"Then how do you communicate?"

I raise my hands up. "We *don't*. That's why you're here, right?"

I watch Dr. Stone's face morph into a scowl as her eyes follow Hannah's hands while she interprets my words.

She disappears into the kitchen then comes out with a wet paper towel, signing something along the way. "Band-Aids?" Hannah asks.

"I'll get one."

After I fetch my first aid kit, I stand by and watch Dr. Stone check Maisy's foot, wipe away the blood, and put the bandage on. Then Maisy runs away, back to her room, and maybe even the closet.

Dr. Stone looks at the mess, which now includes droplets of Maisy's blood. "I should call CPS," Hannah interprets. "Look at this place. She's living in filth."

I whip my head around. "What the hell?" I say to Hannah.

Hannah points at Dr. Stone. "Her. Not me."

I turn back. "What the hell are you talking about? CPS *was* called. That's why you're here." I motion down the hallway. "That's why *she's* here."

"This place is disgusting," Hannah interprets as Dr. Stone signs. "Maisy is four-and-a-half years old. She knows no sign language. You haven't begun teaching her to read. She's isolated from the whole world. You should be ashamed of yourself. And now that she's old enough to attend kindergarten this fall, you thought you'd dump her on the residential Deaf school and make her someone else's problem?" Her head shakes in loathing. "How do you live with yourself?"

My blood boils. "Lady, you don't know what the fuck you're talking about." I turn to Hannah. "Tell her I just got Maisy yesterday. Tell her—"

"Mr. Montana, please," Hannah urges. "Talk to Dr. Stone, not me."

I'm sure I'm red in the face when I turn to the woman I thought was my dream girl. But really it seems she's nothing more than a nightmare.

"Lady?" Hannah interprets. "Did you just call me Lady?" Dr. Stone looks pissed as she signs more forcefully. "It's Dr. Stone. Or just doctor. Or even ma'am."

"Fine," I say, my temple now throbbing. "Well, *doctor*. Listen up. Until yesterday, I didn't even know I had a kid." My arms fly around, gesturing to all the empty bags and boxes. "All this shit is here because Maisy was dumped on my doorstep with nothing more than a suitcase. I had to get everything. Furniture. Clothes. Toys. Shit kids eat. I don't know how to be a fucking dad. And I especially don't know how to be a dad to a deaf child. I'm doing my best, but I'm drowning here.

"And then you show up and accuse me of being a deadbeat. You don't know the first thing about me, so get off your high horse and quit judging me. You're here because I need help. Not because I want to *make her someone else's problem'.*" I shake my head. "Jesus, she's not a fucking problem. She's my goddamn kid."

Her expression softens as Hannah continues to sign well after I'm done speaking.

Dr. Stone lets out a long, frustrated breath and paces behind the couch as her hands begin to move. "I'm sorry," Hannah says for her. "I wasn't given any of that information. I was told it was an urgent case. I jumped to conclusions when I saw the trash and the broken glass. Let's start over, shall we? And please call me Ellie."

Ellie uses her fingers to slowly spell out her name. At least I assume that's what she's doing, all I've learned is *Maisy*. Then she brings an open palm toward her face, tapping her middle finger twice on her cheek. Hannah interprets, "This is my name sign."

# Chapter Six

## Ellie

*What the heck just happened?* I never go off on parents like that. Not to mention how unprofessional he must think I am. Why did I react so strongly?

I convince myself it's because of our 'moments.' It's because I had this image of him being a perfect guy in the perfect town, and that image was instantly shattered when I saw the messy house and the way Maisy reacted to him. Some PhD I am. *Oh, God, did I really call him a terrible father?*

I feel even worse when he explains how CPS showed up yesterday and handed over a child he didn't even know about. He's been thrown into the deep end, and he has no idea how to swim. I try to imagine what it must be like for him, finding out not only that he has a daughter, but a deaf one with whom he has no means to communicate.

This guy—this handsome, compassionate guy—is actually quite amazing. He may not be able to swim, yet he jumped in with both feet. He's trying to show her this is her home. He's not upset with her. Yes, he's frustrated with the situation, but it seems he genuinely wants to help Maisy.

"Again, I'm really sorry about before," I sign. I thumb to the hallway. "Mind if I go back alone?"

"Be my guest."

Though Hannah is here to interpret, I still focus on his lips. His full, manly, inviting lips. On average, deaf lip readers pick up less than half of what people are saying. I've taken numerous advanced courses and worked with countless professionals to become proficient at it. Still, even with my extensive training, I only get about seventy to eighty percent. With Blake, however, it seems to be more. Maybe it's his mouth. Or the way he enunciates. Or the shape of his lips. I look away, heat crossing my face as I realize I'm still staring at those lips.

I gather up blank pieces of paper and some crayons and head out on a quest to find Maisy.

Blake's house is nice. Especially for a bachelor pad. He must be even more well-off than all those empty, expensive-looking boxes indicate. I recognize a famous piece of artwork in the room that must be his office. I step in and run my hand across a wine rack that's holding well over a hundred bottles. I remove one and read the label. My eyebrows shoot up when I read **Montana Winery** across the bottom. His name is Blake Montana. Oh my gosh, I have a few bottles of his wine back at my apartment. This guy is a millionaire.

Not that it impresses me. In my experience, most millionaires are jerks, my own family notwithstanding. My dad inherited millions from his grandparents. Beth and I are pretty much set for life. Growing up, we wanted for nothing. Yet our parents instilled in us a good work ethic and a sense of philanthropy. It makes me wonder if Blake's parents did the same thing, or if he's just another trust fund kid.

I put the bottle back where I found it and leave the room. The next room I come to is obviously Maisy's. And now I'm thoroughly impressed. The guy just found out yesterday that he's a father, and yet this room is decorated as if Maisy has grown up here. Stuffed animals are piled in a hammock strung in one corner. Toy bins line one entire wall and are filled with Barbie dolls, books, miniature ponies, and a hundred other brand-new toys. A white, wooden-frame bed covered with a pink quilt is unmade. I can still see the indentation of Maisy's head on the pink pillow.

I look under the bed, a place some kids like to hide. But it's empty.

A flash of platinum blonde ringlets comes from the closet. She was peeking out at me. I sit at the small table in the corner and start to draw. It takes a few minutes, but Maisy's curiosity gets the better of her and she slowly exits the closet and looks at what I'm drawing.

Her eyes are glued to the paper as I do my best to depict a house. *This* house. I even draw a bed with a pink duvet cover on it. To the side, I draw two figures. A little girl with yellow ringlets in her hair holding a cat. And a man. I become acutely aware of a warmth spreading from my fingers to the rest of my body as I draw him.

Done with my masterpiece—I did take three semesters of art as an undergrad—I put down the crayon. I point to the house in the picture and gesture at our surroundings. I point at the bed in the picture and then over at her bed. I point to the little girl and then to her. Then I point to the man and gesture to the open door.

She follows all of my hand movements as if she understands.

I pick the crayon up and connect the man's hand to the child's hand. Maisy simply stares and hugs her stuffed cat.

My heart hurts. This precious little girl has virtually no means of communicating. I've seen children in the past who didn't know ASL, but at least they could read and write. There was always some form of communication, even if it was rudimentary.

I can't even tell Maisy what's happening to her. She must be so scared.

She picks up a black crayon and draws a stick figure. I'm quite impressed at her drawing skills. Then again, if she can't communicate in other ways, maybe this is how she's done it, which explains why she's better at it than most four-year-olds.

The figure is as big as the man I drew. She gets a yellow crayon and draws long hair. She joins the hands of the stick figure she drew and the little girl I drew. She looks up, points to me and then the stick figure.

I shake my head and she gets sad. She thinks I'm somehow part of the picture, and I fear she might bond with me more than her father. I'm here to facilitate their bond, not steal it. I'm going to have to tread carefully.

I lean over, get a bucket of blocks from the toy bin, and spread them on the table. Grabbing a fresh piece of paper, I draw a red square. I point to the square and then to the blocks. In short order, Maisy picks out four red blocks and builds a square.

I smile and sign, "Yes." Then I wave my hands at the wrists, the ASL sign for clapping. Some people call it jazz hands.

Next, I draw a large green rectangle. Again, she sorts through the pile, picks out six green blocks, and lines them up perfectly to replicate the shape. She looks up with expectant eyes.

I do jazz hands.

She smiles and does jazz hands back.

My heart lurches.

We play this game for a few more minutes, then I switch to something more difficult. I get a large pack of flashcards from my messenger bag. The cards have pictures of common objects on them. House. Shirt. Dog. Pencil. On the back of each card is the ASL sign for the object. I sift through and find the picture of a cat. I hold it out for her to see and point to her stuffed cat. Then I do the sign for "cat," using my thumbs and forefingers near my cheeks in an outward motion symbolizing whiskers.

I do this several more times, pointing to the picture and her stuffed animal.

I think she understands that the sign means cat, but she doesn't get that I want her to do it. I carefully reach out and touch her hands, put them to her cheeks, then release them and do the sign again.

Finally, she does it.

"Yes," I sign then do jazz hands.

I find the flash card with the house. I point to it, then to my house drawing, then I gesture around. Then I sign, "house," by outlining the simple shape of a house with my hands starting with a roof and then the walls. I do this over and over, then motion to her hands. She does the sign.

I do the same with "book," opening my hands as one would open a book. Then I point to a book. I only have to do this one once before she repeats the sign.

My smile is huge. So is hers. Her mouth opens, and I think she makes a noise. A happy one I hope.

We go through other flashcards, ones with the simplest signs that correspond to things I find around her room. The more we do, the more excited she gets.

We're going back over the signs when she stands and cups a hand over her crotch.

I motion to the bathroom, and sign, "bathroom." Then I take her to the toilet.

She doesn't need any help. But when she's done, she heads right back out into her bedroom. I tap her on the shoulder. When she turns, I point to the sink and rub my hands together. She stares blankly, looking at me as if she has no idea what I'm asking. Lord, has she never been taught to wash after using the toilet?

I stand at the sink and wash my hands. Then I point to her and rub my hands together. She washes her hands for two seconds, barely rinsing the soap from them before she's turning back to her bedroom. Before she can pull away, I grab her hands and help her rub them together for ten more seconds. Once done, I catch her gaze in the mirror and smile.

She dries her hands and runs back out to the table. I'm delighted she's eager for more.

Fifteen minutes later, the room lights flash off and on. I turn to see Hannah in the doorway. She tells me she has another appointment to get to—I swear they always overbook interpreters—but she also looks concerned as she gestures down the hallway.

"It's fine," I sign in slight irritation. "Blake and I can text. You go."

She waves and leaves.

Another fifteen minutes pass. Then another. When I teach her the sign for bed, she does the previous sign instead. *Food.* And when she does it over and over, it sinks in that she must be hungry.

I stand up and turn, then stop. Blake is standing in the doorway. How long has he been there?

He looks stunned. "Wow," he says as I look at his lips—far longer than necessary.

I shrug as I feel heat cross my face. We're staring at each other again. And butterflies dance in my tummy.

"She's hungry," I sign. I don't expect him to understand the sign for hungry, so I point to Maisy and then rub circles on my stomach.

He nods, indicating he understands, and says, "She's hungry," before he motions to the kitchen.

We follow him down the hall, and when Maisy pops up onto a barstool and looks at us expectantly, I pull out my phone and open the notepad app.

It's best to give her choices, I type. Do you have two things to offer?

He nods, opens the refrigerator, and pulls something out. Then he disappears into the panty for a moment. Walking over to Maisy, he holds up a box of macaroni and cheese in one hand and one of those Lunchables in another. He does a great job with his facial expressions as he looks from one to the other and then back at her, eyebrows raised.

Shyly, Maisy looks over at me then points to the Lunchable as if asking my permission, not Blake's.

He sets her choice down on the bar and peels back the cellophane. Then, he puts the box of mac and cheese away and grabs a cup of applesauce and a spoon, setting those down in front of her too.

I type into my app, It would be better if we could text. I open my contacts and hand him my phone. He promptly enters his name and number and hands it back. I tap out a text.

**Me: Maisy is quite intelligent and very eager to learn.**

He reads it on his phone and looks up in surprise.

**Me: Don't look so surprised. Deaf are just as intelligent as the hearing. Some of us have even tested at the genius level.**

His face cracks into a sexy half smile.

**Blake: I figured as much. I mean you are a doctor. Where did you go to medical school?**

**Me: I'm not that kind of doctor. I have my PhD in Critical Studies in the Education of Deaf Learners.**

**Blake: Ahh. That explains the long acronym on your business card that I didn't understand.**

I laugh silently.

**Blake: How can you tell she's intelligent after spending so little time with her?**

**Me: You don't have to text me if you don't want to. I read lips very well. I'll tell you if I need help deciphering your words. Maisy has already begun to understand a few signs. We**

**started with simple objects. House. Cat.
Book. Things like that.**

I pull out my flashcards and show them to him.

**Me: This will be a great teaching tool for both
of you as you'll be learning together. I'll warn
you now not to feel too inadequate if she picks
it up faster than you do. Children are sponges.**

He laughs.

There are very few times when I wish I could hear sound. It's
a silly thing to wish for, and I stopped long ago, but when I see his
eyes sparkle, his chest shake up and down, and his mouth open—
this is definitely one of those times.

"Tell me - - -" Blake says, speaking too slowly. "I want to help
her learn. I want to learn - - -"

I didn't pick up everything he said. He's over-enunciating,
something everyone tends to do at first.

**Me: Please don't speak too slowly or over-
enunciate. Just look directly at me and speak
in your regular manner.**

"I said I want to learn everything."

I raise my brows and send a text.

**Me: You want to learn ASL?**

He looks at me like I asked a silly question. "Of course, why
wouldn't I?"

**Me: Over 70% of hearing parents of deaf children don't learn how to sign. They pin their hopes on hearing-assisted technology. It works for some, but I'm glad you want to learn. Those devices don't always work out as planned and kids may miss out on a lot of communication which in turn may result in insufficient language input.**

His jaw drops. "Seventy percent? That's insane. Why would they not want to communicate with their children?"

**Me: It's not that they don't want to communicate. They just assume it's more beneficial for children to adapt to the hearing world.**

An irritated head shake confirms he isn't one of those parents. "So," he asks. "What do we do first?"
I roll my eyes, because where do I even start?

**Me: Blake, this will be a long and arduous process. It will come with a lot of frustration. You have to be patient with her. And with yourself. First off, here's a preliminary list of things NOT to do.**

I fetch a preprinted list from my bag. It's something I give all hearing parents of deaf children. It reads:

- Don't shout. It's pointless, and it will make you seem angry.
- Do not speak slowly or over-enunciate.
- Do not look at the interpreter while they are interpreting. They are not who you are having a conversation with.
- Don't call your child disabled. They need to understand deafness is more an obstacle than a disability.
- Focus on the myriad things your child CAN do rather than the few they can't.
- Don't turn down the lights. Deaf need to clearly see other people unless they are sleeping.
- Don't wear shirts with busy patterns, they are distracting when signing.
- Don't speak as if your child isn't intelligent. Your child simply speaks a different language than you do, same as if they were speaking Italian or French and you weren't.
- Don't ask a deaf person to read lips for you in an attempt to eavesdrop.
- And the most important thing… don't pity your child. Deafness isn't the terrible thing most hearing people assume it is. It's a culture, and a beautiful one.

Blake looks dejected as his eyes meet the floor. Guilt oozes from his expression. He speaks, but he's not looking at me.

I touch his arm, and I swear electricity jolts through me. His arm is strong. Muscular. Soft. His eyes snap to mine making me wonder if he felt the same jolt.

"Sorry," he says. "I said I've already broken so many of those rules."

> **Me: Well, you didn't know them. You get a pass. Now, I have an important question to ask you.**

"Okay."

I show him the sign for 'okay' as I silently mouth the word. He does it back and I smile. Our eyes lock again, and I swallow at the squishy feeling I get inside.

# Chapter Seven

## Blake

**Ellie: What are your intentions as far as school for Maisy? Technically, in the fall, she'll be eligible for our residential program where kids live at the school during the week and come home on weekends.**

I shake my head vehemently when I read her text, and I look up, disgusted. "Jesus, no. I mean, I'm sure it's a fine school, but I wouldn't want to only see her on the weekends." I glance out the window, then back at Ellie. "Honestly, I'm not even sure she'll still be living here in the fall."

**Ellie: Say that last part again.**

I realize I might have been mumbling due to my disappointment over it. "I said I'm not sure Maisy will still be living with me in the fall."

She studies me for a moment, starts typing, then deletes what she wrote. She wants to ask me more about that. More about why I just found out about Maisy yesterday. More about where her mother is and why she grew up the way she did. It's only natural to be curious about these things. But she doesn't ask.

> **Ellie: I'm happy you want her to live at home. While the school is amazing, I think the most important thing for both of you right now is to form a bond. Sending her to live at school would impede that. You'll still have many choices to make. She can go to the Deaf school, or she can go to public school. I've toured the elementary schools here. They have a few resources, and an interpreter would be provided should you request one. And then there's whether or not to try cochlear implants—a highly polarized topic in the Deaf community. And whether or not to teach her to read lips, which is not as easy as it might seem, by the way.**

My head cocks to the side. "You seem to do it very well."

> **Ellie: You just so happen to have easy lips to read.**

She blushes. Goddamn it. Every time she does that it's like there's a tether on my dick that gets yanked. The redness across her face brings out freckles on her cheeks. They disappear as she starts texting again.

Ellie: In general, deaf people comprehend about 30% of lip reading. Those who grow up with hearing parents and who have taken advanced classes can achieve far greater comprehension than that. I'm pretty good at it, but by no means perfect. We rely on body language and context to fill in the gaps. Which reminds me, you are expressive, which is good, but you need to be overly-so. Whereas I don't want you over-enunciating, I do want you over-expressing. It might seem strange at first and make you feel self-conscious, but it will be better for her. It will help her understand.

"Give me an example."
She chews on her lip as she thinks, then she starts typing.

Ellie: Use facial expressions. Raise your eyebrows when asking yes/no questions. Furrow them when asking a question that requires more of an answer. Widen your eyes for emphasis. SHOW your level of excitement. Talking should be a whole-body experience. Use your hands, posture, face, and eyes.

Ellie: Earlier, when I accused you of being a bad parent, I could tell how vehemently you thought I was wrong. You looked not only angry (you were obviously shouting, and your nostrils flared), but you looked hurt as well,

**helpless almost. Hannah was interpreting, but had she not been, I still would have picked up most of it. Passion tends to come through in body language. It was the moment I knew I had gotten you all wrong. I'm not one to pull punches, Blake. I've had to throw plenty of them to get where I am. But I also recognize determination when I see it. You've got it. And if I haven't said it before now, Maisy is lucky to have you.**

"Wow." I look up. "Now *I'm* the one blushing."

She laughs silently.

Maisy pounds on the table and we both look at her. I assume pounding is her way of getting our attention.

I want to ask her what she wants, but I have no idea how to do it. I expect Ellie to do it, but she just stares at Maisy with lifted brows.

Maisy pounds on the table again—harder this time. Is she frustrated? I look at her half-eaten food. Does she not like it?

Ellie doesn't seem as concerned as I am over Maisy's outburst. She texts me.

**Ellie: Maisy needs to learn to ask for what she wants. Even if she can't properly sign yet. As soon as she can communicate her needs, the tantrums will stop.**

Maisy pounds so hard, a bead of applesauce pops out of the cup and onto the table. Instead of wiping it up, Ellie surprises me by handing Maisy a napkin.

I touch Ellie's arm so she'll look at me. "That's kind of mean, isn't it?"

She shakes her head and goes back to staring at Maisy. Finally, Ellie points to the stack of flashcards she left on the table. Maisy looks pissed, as if she expects us to know what she wants without her having to tell us. Almost in defeat, she picks up the flashcards, goes through them, then holds one up. It's a milk carton with a glass of milk next to it.

*Shit.* I didn't give her a drink with her food. I jump up and stride to the fridge, feeling guilty once again at how I'm failing at this.

When I come back with the glass and set it in front of Maisy, she happily drinks it.

Ellie shows me the back of the card and teaches me the sign for milk. I must do it incorrectly because she reaches over, taking my hand in hers to fix the handshape of the sign. Yeah, okay, I just got a half-chub right here in front of my daughter. *Soooo inappropriate.* But damn her hands are soft. When she pulls them away and waits for me, I completely forget what I was supposed to be signing.

I can tell she's trying not to laugh.

Maisy does the sign for milk, and I'm stunned. "She's signing. That's incredible."

Ellie's face cracks into a wide smile, she lifts an eyebrow, almost in challenge, and sorts through the deck of flashcards. She holds up one of a cat and shows Maisy. Maisy wipes milk off her lip and then runs fingers across fake whiskers. Ellie turns the card around and shows me the sign. The same sign Maisy did.

Ellie then shows Maisy a house. Again, Maisy does the sign as it appears on the back. This happens several more times. Boy. Girl. Ball. Book. Eat.

The whole time, my heart is in my throat. Maisy can communicate. After less than an hour with Ellie, she can talk. Well, sort of.

I touch Ellie's arm and find it impossible not to let my fingers linger. "It's a miracle." I point at her with my other hand. "You're amazing."

She smiles. At my words? My touch?

It's almost like she doesn't want to pull away to text me. She likes my hand on her as much as I do. Eventually, when it becomes awkward, she retreats.

**Ellie: I told you, kids are sponges. She's going to learn quickly.**

My stomach growls and I check the time. It's nearly time for dinner. I get up, go to the pantry then the refrigerator, and bring back a few things. I stand in front of Ellie with a box of macaroni and cheese in one hand and two steaks in the other. I raise my brow. Actually, I over-raise it.

She smiles just for a second, but it's gone in an instant. I have to put the food down to read her text.

**Ellie: I appreciate the invite. But it's best I not eat meals here. It would give Maisy the wrong information. She needs to know this is your house. This is her house. This is not my house. I'm her advocate. Her mentor. If I eat here, she may come to believe I'm her stepmother or her father's girlfriend.**

I swallow what feels like a shard of glass and ask, "Does she know I'm her father?"

Ellie shrugs.

> **Ellie: I'm working on it. It'll come soon. She may suspect already.**

I pick up my phone, wanting her to understand clearly.

> **Me: You say you shouldn't eat here. How about at a restaurant? Not tonight, but maybe another day? I have family willing to watch Maisy.**

She seems to read my text more than once. And she doesn't look up, not right away. Is she contemplating it? Or am I an idiot for hitting on the woman who's trying to help Maisy. Ah, shit, maybe I've gone and fucked it up just when she was making progress. I tap the table with my fingers, and when she looks up, I shake my head. "Forget I asked. Not a good idea." I nod to Maisy. "Tell me what to do now."

Guiltily, as if she wanted to accept my invitation but thought it might be a conflict of interest, she types out a text.

> **Ellie: Play games. The memory card game would be a good start. Engage her in play with every opportunity. Use the flashcards to communicate for now. Draw lots of pictures with her. The next time we meet, we'll talk more about your options. We'll start to come up with a plan about school. With your**

blessing, I'd like to see her enrolled in Pre-K at the Deaf school at the very least. It's a half-day program that will immerse her in ASL, allow her to meet other deaf and hard of hearing kids, and hopefully improve her social skills, which are greatly lacking.

Ellie: If I can leave you with one bit of advice, it would be this: don't get so wrapped up in her diagnosis that you miss the milestones. It's not always about being deaf. Don't forget to enjoy your daughter.

I feel more inadequate than ever with all this information. Especially knowing Ellie is about to leave and I have no idea what will happen next. "When are you coming back? And will you be her teacher at school?"

Ellie: I'm not a teacher. But as her assigned mentor, I will have some one-on-one time with her on a daily basis. Pre-K is every day for three hours. I'll do home visits three times a week whenever it's convenient for you. We'll take her out into the world on some of those. Expose her to stores, restaurants, parks. I get the feeling she's lived a very isolated life. She's pale, shy, and only has her stuffed cat as company. I'm afraid your daughter has lived a life devoid of not only communication, but external stimuli. The more we can expose her

**to, while at the same time teaching her, the**
**faster she'll acclimate to her new world.**

Three home visits a week. My eyes re-scan that sentence. *Home visits. Here. At* my *home.* My stomach tightens at the notion of seeing her that often. I feel like a kid with a schoolboy crush on his teacher. His hot, curvy, sexy teacher.

Ellie holds out her hands as if asking, "what?" As I don't know the sign yet, maybe she is.

I shake my head. I've already been shut down. I don't need her knowing I've had fantasies about her this past week, before I even knew who she was or had a conversation with her. And now that I've seen her, talked to her, smelled her, those fantasies will not be going away anytime soon.

**Ellie: I can see you're overwhelmed. It's a lot**
**to take in. For now, let's concentrate on baby**
**steps. Learning to sign the basics. Focusing**
**on visuals. Using letter cards and picture**
**flashcards. Building her vocabulary.**
**Eventually the hope is to have her bilingual in**
**ASL and English.**

As Maisy finishes her milk, and then busies herself with drawing, Ellie gives me pointers on how to communicate when she's not here to help. She also urges me to buy Maisy a durable iPad, telling me there are lots of programs she can watch that will help her learn to sign.

**Ellie: Everything you do at this point should**
**be educational. But also fun. At bathtime for**

instance, get foam letters and make learning exciting and silly. Mealtime can be about counting peas. Clothing choices can teach her names of colors. Make her a part of it. Learn with her. Once you both learn signs, you should try and sign everything you say. And we should sign every conversation.

**Me: EVERY conversation, Ellie?**

She reads my text, then looks up at me as if she knew I texted it because I wanted her to be clear on every word.

I can almost see a shiver run through her as if the connotation behind my words sent tingles down her spine. And then... *bingo*, I see the blush. Good, I'm glad she understands I really would like to have more conversations with her that may not necessarily be centered around my daughter.

**Ellie: Every conversation that concerns her. Basically, every conversation that a hearing child would be privy to. And you'll need to help her feel included by letting her know about the sounds around her. Deaf people miss out on tons of audiological information throughout the day. We don't hear the sounds hearing people take for granted. For instance, tell her someone is at the door when the doorbell rings. Better yet, have a visual doorbell installed that will set off flashing lights when rung. Tell her the phone is ringing before you just get up and answer it.**

> Tell her you're going to make dinner as she won't be able to hear pans clanging, which clues hearing individuals in to what's going on in the other room. Tell her your girlfriend is here when you hear her car pull into the driveway. All of that is incidental noise. Dogs barking, a firetruck's siren in the distance, conversations going on around her that are clues into people's behavior. Be her ears and fill in the gaps. It will make her feel included and less isolated.

I smirk and look up from my phone. "I see what you did there, sneaking that in." I snicker. "I'm not dating, Ellie. There will be no girlfriend pulling into my driveway."

She shrugs as if she has no idea what she did. But I don't miss the small, satisfied grin she tries to hide. She stands, typing out another text.

> Ellie: It's time for me to go. The next time I come, Hannah won't be with me. I don't feel it's necessary after this initial meeting as long as you're comfortable with it. Since you seem eager to learn, you'll learn faster without someone speaking for me. We can text when needed. Like I said, I'm a pretty good lip reader. With instruction and lots of practice, Maisy can be too if that's what she wants. The goal is to introduce her to different ways of communicating and then she can choose what she's most comfortable with. I'm not here to

tell you or her what to do. As a parent you have choices. There is no one right way. Each child is different. When she's older, she may even change the way she wants to communicate. I'm getting ahead of myself. This conversation is for another day. We made good progress today. Maisy is a special little girl.

She swipes on her phone, and I get a glimpse of her calendar as she studies it.

Ellie: What days and times work the best for you? I'll work around your job.

"I'll work my job around this. Maisy is my priority."

She smiles, her whole face lighting up at my proclamation. And damn, my entire body hums at the authenticity of her smile. I have about a hundred things on my plate right now, but my dick is only concerned with one of them.

Ellie: Like I said, she's lucky. How about M/W/F at 4:00? We'll spend an hour or two together, the three of us.

Three to six hours a week face-to-face with the enchanting doctor? *Yes, please.*

Our eyes connect and I give her an affirming nod.

Ellie: We'll meet again this Friday then. We can go over more options then too. She can

start Pre-K on Monday if you're good with
that. We'll meet with a few administrators and
educators at the school to come up with an
IEP. That gives you a few days to do some
learning. Watch videos. There are some great
on-line programs that can teach hearing
people ASL. I'll text you some links. Your
homework—learn to sign Maisy's name.

I have a hard time not smiling when I use my right hand to
fingerspell M-A-I-S-Y.

Ellie's eyebrows practically touch her hairline, making me
laugh.

"My sister, Allie, taught me last night. It's all I know."

**Ellie: What's your sister's name? It looked like
you said my name.**

**Me: It's Allie.**

She fingerspells Allie's name and shows me the sign for sister.

**Ellie: You've gotten off to a great start, Blake.
And it's very encouraging to see a parent who
wants to be so involved.**

It's hard not to show my disgust over parents who would
simply ignore their child's deafness. I mean, I've only known Maisy
for one day and I already want to give her the goddamn world.

Ellie waves to Maisy and points to the door. Maisy looks upset
and shakes her head. Ellie picks up the flashcards and hands them

to me then points her finger between me and Maisy. Maisy seems to understand, but from what I can see, wants nothing to do with me. She wants Ellie. She hops off her chair, runs over, and hugs Ellie.

A pang of jealousy courses through me. Maisy is my daughter. She should be hugging *me*.

Ellie stares at me and the look on her face tells me she knows exactly what I'm thinking. She sinks to Maisy's level, points at herself, then at her eyes, then at Maisy, then she does a sign. I'm not sure what the sign means, but it looks like it might mean 'later.' If I picked up on it, I wonder if Maisy did too.

Maisy looks sadly at the ground, picks up her cat, and heads back down the hallway, presumably to her room, and maybe even her closet.

**Ellie: Don't worry. It'll come.**

Then she waves at me, gathers up whatever she didn't leave for us, and walks out the door.

I feel the loss when she's gone. Like I'm emptier somehow. I just wonder if it's because Dr. Stone—Maisy's mentor—just walked out the door. Or because Ellie—the woman—did.

# Chapter Eight

## Ellie

Blake's house is only a mile from my apartment, so I walk home. I haven't felt the need to buy a car yet. I guess that's the city girl in me. But the thought of having to Uber to some of my other clients' houses that are farther away isn't all that pleasant. The first time I ordered an Uber, I had to wait forty-five minutes. A far cry from the city where you can wave your hand and a cab magically appears.

Before turning the corner to head out of his neighborhood, I glance back at his house. Blake has the perfect family home and doesn't even know it. His yard is bigger than some of the others. His house appears larger as well. Interesting that in this family-friendly neighborhood, the bachelor may have the largest home.

He didn't seem the least bit cocky about it though. The guy must have serious money, or at least his parents do, but he didn't seem entitled. And I'm impressed at how much he wants to help the daughter he didn't even know he had until yesterday. I'm sure he could easily send her away. Pay for a boarding school. Hire a nanny to 'deal' with her so he doesn't have to.

The guy seems too good to be true. There must be something wrong with him. In my experience, no man is that handsome, well-off, and caring. Well, if you don't count my dad. A smile cracks my face knowing I'm going to see my parents and Beth tonight. They're coming into town to take me to dinner.

Hope flutters through me. I want so much for Maisy to one day feel about Blake the way I do my father. We have a long way to go, and I'm not exactly sure she even understands who Blake is to her. Who *I* am.

Maisy and I already have chemistry, that much is evident. But I need to be careful. She may see me as more of a parent than Blake. It's a fine line I'll have to navigate.

Maisy and I aren't the only ones who have chemistry, though. He asked me to dinner. Well, sort of. It's the only time in my adult life I've been tempted to accept a date with a hearing man. I've never dated one. Never wanted to. I was sure I'd never be able to have a connection with one. Especially one who doesn't even know ASL or the first thing about Deaf culture.

Then why do I feel this pull whenever I see him? Why do I get the sense we can communicate without spoken words, without ASL, without anything but our eyes? It's the strangest feeling in the world.

But he's the father of a client. There's a line. One I'm not sure I want to cross. No matter how much my body seems to want me to. Just thinking about him—his inviting lips, his electric touch, his chocolate-brown hair and how it falls perfectly back into place after he runs a hand through it—has dampness soaking my panties. What is happening to me?

A familiar SUV pulls up alongside me as I'm approaching my apartment complex. My smile is a mile wide when I see Dad at the wheel, Mom to his right, and Beth lowering the backseat window. Dad nods for me to get in the back, then angles the rearview mirror once I'm settled so I can see his lips. "Do you need to go home and change, or are you ready?"

"Let's go eat," I say and sign.

I sometimes speak verbally around my family. It's how I practice speaking. Though they tell me I sound great, I've been reluctant to speak in front of others for a long time. As someone who is profoundly deaf, I have no clue what I sound like. I know I have an accent. Many deaf people do. A lot of us have a thick monotone or guttural accent since we can't hear all the sounds letters make.

As a professional, especially one who advocates for deaf children, I know I shouldn't feel the way I do about speaking. But after being bullied about the way I spoke back in middle school, I simply just stopped using my voice except around those closest to me.

"Where are we going?" I ask.

"Dad made a reservation at Lloyd's," Beth says and signs.

My family are all proficient in ASL and most of our conversations are held that way. But in the car, like we are now, we SimCom—speak and sign at the same time—so nobody feels left out.

Mom turns. "Are you all unpacked?"

"I finished yesterday. I still need to buy a TV."

I've had my eye on a big screen, but I've been waiting for it to go on sale. Large screen televisions are really nice for deaf people as the closed captioning is much more visible, making it easier to both read and watch.

"We'll pick one up after dinner."

I shake my head. "I have a job, Mom. I can buy it myself."

Beth elbows me and signs without speaking. "She's been going crazy. You have to let her pamper you a bit."

I roll my eyes and sign, "She survived when I was away at Gallaudet all those years."

"You were in college," she signs. "That was different. This is you out in the real world. She's worried about you. But don't go feeling all special, she goes bat-shit crazy over me, too."

Mom waves to get my attention. "Hey, you two. Stop talking about me. I know you are."

Beth and I laugh. Mom hates it when we sign behind her back. When we were kids, we'd literally turn our backs and have ASL conversations with her in the room. She hated not being privy to what we were saying.

*Welcome to my world, Mom.*

Dad parks behind the restaurant and we make our way to the front. I stop and point left and sign, "The school is right down there."

"We know where it is," Mom says. "We toured it when you were younger."

My jaw slackens. I had no idea. "You considered sending me here? To live?"

She shakes her head. "We considered moving here. Research told us this was one of the best Deaf schools in New York. But you were adamant about going to a hearing school, so we dropped the subject."

"You would have moved." I point to myself. "For me?"

Dad wraps an arm around my shoulder and signs with his free hand. "Of course we would have."

We step inside and are escorted to the table. It's dark, and when the hostess speaks, Beth interprets for me. My family has always been great about making sure I don't miss out on conversations going on around me.

I watch the hostess, wondering if she'll assume I'm not intelligent—a mistake many hearing people make—but she simply smiles politely and tells us the name of our waitress. Maybe with the school just around the corner, she's used to deaf customers.

Once seated, I sign to my parents, "Thank you for not insisting I go there. It's a great school. But allowing me to choose for myself is one of the reasons I love you guys so much."

Mom reaches over and clasps my hands. She knows sometimes you don't need to speak to get a point across.

Beth looks at me, walleyed. She's the only person who knows what a hard time of it I had in school. But I was out to prove I could do whatever hearing students could—even if I went about it in the worst of ways.

I think my parents were the main reason I pursued my degree and this job. Giving me options and letting me participate in the decisions was paramount to my upbringing. I saw what happened to kids who were forced into environments they didn't want to be in. It's why I wanted to become an advocate for children who may not have been given the same opportunities I had.

After we order drinks, Beth asks, "How's work going?"

"Good." I find myself biting my lip and stop. "Really good."

"Oh my God," Beth says and signs. "You just blushed big time."

I roll my eyes.

She stares me down. Her eyes go wide as she lowers her hands so Mom and Dad can't see them and signs, "Are you fucking your boss?"

I'm pretty sure I guffaw audibly. I grab her hands so she can't sign, and I shake my head aggressively.

Mom waves her hand and scolds us for having another private conversation. "If the two of you want to speak privately, go to the ladies' room. It's rude to do it right in front of us."

She's right. It is rude. It happens all the time when you're deaf, people speaking right in front of you and not including you in the conversation.

"Beth asked if I was seeing my boss." I turn to my sister. "My boss is the president of the school. And she's a woman."

Beth snickers.

Drinks are placed before us, as well as a mouth-watering loaf of bread.

Dad slices the bread and passes us each a piece.

"Have you seen the hot mystery guy again?" Beth signs after shoving an entire piece in her mouth as if she hasn't eaten in days.

"What's this about a mystery guy?" Mom asks.

Dad puts down his bread, becoming interested in the conversation.

"Ellie met some hot mysterious guy right after she moved in."

"I didn't meet him. Not back then anyway."

"Wait, what?" Beth's eyes go wide. "What do you mean not back then? Oh my God. Did you see him again? Are you dating? Ellie, what aren't you telling me?"

"He—" I drop my hands before continuing. "Well, his daughter… is a client."

Beth's face morphs from surprise into utter fascination. "Hot mystery guy is a dad? Oh, please tell me he's a single father." She claps. "This story just got a whole lot better. Why didn't you say anything?" Her face turns into a pout. "You always tell me everything."

"Stop it," I sign. "I just found out today. I was walking home from meeting the two of them when you picked me up."

Beth shakes her head from side to side, her smile a mile wide. "Oh how I'd love to have been a fly on the wall when you two came face to face after having your encounter at the grocery store."

"Mind filling us in?" Dad asks, his protective instincts kicking into high gear.

I've always been super close to my family. They've been with me through the ups and downs of being away at college. The successes and failures. They are my biggest supporters, cheerleaders, and advocates. Yes, they tend to be overprotective at times, but still, I couldn't love them more.

I tell them what I told Beth about seeing Blake at the supermarket and having what I can only describe as an out-of-body experience when we looked at each other. And then how we were both surprised when I showed up at his door today. And how I accused him of being a terrible father.

Guilt sweeps through me once again when I think of how quickly I jumped to conclusions. Of all people, I should know better than to judge a book by its cover.

I leave out the part where he asked me out. I'm still not sure how I feel about it, so I don't need them slinging opinions on the matter.

"His little girl," I sign morosely. "She's sad and sheltered and… completely amazing." I have a hard time controlling my emotions as I think of her situation. "She's exactly why I wanted to do this job. She's the reason. She's the one deaf child that every deaf educator dreams of making a difference for. I just never thought I'd find her so quickly."

"It sounds like she's lucky to have found you as well," Dad signs. His proud smile overtakes his face. "Look at you already changing lives."

"I don't know about that. We've just met. There are mountains to climb with this one."

"Just be careful." Dad raises a brow in warning. "The job is new. You don't need entanglements and complications."

Mom swats his arm. "Says the doctor who fell in love with his patient." She winks at me.

Dad's body shakes with laughter, and he says something I don't understand. I narrow my eyes at him so he signs, "Sorry," then fingerspells the word 'touché.'

"It was almost instantaneous," Mom signs, "the connection I felt with your father. Even largely pregnant with you and scared I might lose you, it was there. We both felt it. We both tried to deny it. But I'm here to tell you, connections like that don't come often. When the signs are clear"—she laughs—"no pun intended, you have to read them."

Though the start of their relationship came with a lot of hurdles, my parents have the most loving relationship I've ever seen.

Warmth flows through me like a summer breeze. And I promise myself if Blake asks again, I might just consider it.

# Chapter Nine

## Ellie

What was I thinking not letting Mom buy this for me? I look at the large TV box as a worker from the store loads it into the back of the Uber XL I summoned.

I scold my idiotic determination to prove to everyone that I don't need any help.

*Anyone* would need help with this.

I slip into the back of the SUV, and as the driver pulls away from the store, he tries to make conversation. When I don't say anything and he catches me in the rearview, I point to my ear and shake my head. Then I write out a note for when we pull up to my apartment, asking if he'll help me move the TV upstairs.

He pops the trunk when we get there, and I hand the note to him. He reads it, gets out of the car, takes the TV out of the back, rests it against a tree, then gets back in the car and hightails it out of the lot.

Geez. So much for chivalry. I guess I should have slipped him a twenty with the note. I look down at the box and over at my building. I can do this.

*Maybe.*

Today's televisions are much lighter than what my parents had when I was young. How heavy can it be?

I eye the side of the box. It says it's ninety-five pounds. I sigh. If I can just get it to the building, I might be able to push it up the stairs along the bottom edge of the box.

But how do I get it over there? The door is at least thirty feet away.

I study the box. I have a PhD, surely I can figure this out.

I tip it onto the short end. The box is almost as tall as I am, but I grip either side of it and 'walk' it, one bottom corner at a time, slowly across the parking lot.

Halfway there, a car pulls in, and it can't get around me because I'm blocking the way. The driver looks annoyed at first, but then our gazes meet, and he looks a lot more interested. A cocky grin crosses his face as he opens his door and gets out.

"Need help?" the guy asks.

I nod.

He walks over and maneuvers the box so we're each standing next to a short end. "Ready?"

I nod harder.

We lean and lift. With him walking backward and me forward, we're almost to the door when he says, "You're new here."

I nod yet again, hoping he'll catch on.

"I'm - - -".

I don't understand his name.

I smile and nod.

"You're not much for words," I think he says.

I shrug.

"You're kind of acting like a bitch considering I'm doing you a favor here."

At least I think that's what he said.

With my hands occupied lifting the box, I can't tell him I'm deaf. I shake my head, not knowing what else to do.

The guy looks pissed. And just as we reach the door, he drops his side of the TV. Not sets it down—drops it. Then he looks behind me, spouts angry words that I can't decipher, and storms off to his car.

I set my side down and quickly look at the bottom corner of his side of the box. It's slightly crushed. I hope he didn't just damage the TV.

Movement catches my eye and I spin. The guy is still shouting out of his car door. But not at me. Then I see Blake, all sweaty in his running clothes, looking as handsome as he does pissed.

I've learned a lot about the heartthrob coming toward me over the past twenty-four hours. Word got around at the school that Blake Montana has a child and I'm the one working with them. No less than a half-dozen coworkers visited my office to fill me in on the guy who apparently slept his way through every co-ed in college. Looking at him, I see the appeal. I mean what red-blooded woman wouldn't? He carries himself with such confidence. And not in a cocky, *I'm all that* kind of way. More like a guy who knows what he wants and goes after it. Not to mention he's now entered sexy, single dad territory. Why that combination of dangerous and desirable brings a flush to my cheeks, I may never know.

As he approaches, he keeps a suspicious eye on the asshole in the car who's parking one building over.

I lean the box against the building and get my phone out.

**Me: What just happened?**

"I should ask you that. I was running by and saw that jerk yelling at you. Who was he?"

**Me: I thought he was a good Samaritan helping me move this up to my place. I Ubered it home from the store. He pulled up and offered to help. He got mad when I didn't speak to him.**

"He said some pretty nasty things. Does that happen a lot?"

I shrug. I don't want to scare him and tell him things like that *do* happen, and that Maisy will have to learn to have thick skin.

**Me: My hands were busy holding the box. I couldn't exactly convey that I'm deaf. It was my fault. I never should have bought this beast without help.**

"Well, you have help now. And, Ellie, it wasn't your fault. That - - - had no right to say the things he said to you."

I narrow my eyes, having gotten most but not all of what he said. "Say again," I sign.

**Blake: I said I'll help you. It wasn't your fault. And that douchebag had no right to say those things to you. I saw him drop the box. I hope**

**he didn't break it. If he did, I'll get you a new one.**

**Me: I have my own money, Blake. But thanks for helping.**

**Blake: Let's just get this up to your place and see what we're dealing with.**

With Blake's help, we're up the stairs and in my apartment in no time. "Thank you," I sign, not even sure he understands it.

I'm delighted when he says, "You're welcome. Where do you want it?" He pulls a key out of his pocket and uses it like a knife to open the box.

**Me: You don't have to do this.**

**Blake: Ellie, I don't see anyone else around who can help you lift it up. This thing weighs a hundred pounds. Over on that console?**

I nod and sign, "Yes. Thank you."

We spend the next few minutes unboxing it, removing the packaging, and peeling off the cellophane covering the screen. He secures the stand to the bottom, then together, we set it on the console. He puts the batteries in the remote, flashes his crossed fingers at me, and presses the power button.

When the SmartTV menu appears, I'm relieved.

**Blake: Good thing. I got the fucker's license
plate. I was going to hunt him down and
make him buy you a new one.**

I furrow my brows and text him back.

**Me: I thought YOU were going to buy it for
me. What did you say to the guy?**

**Blake: I simply told him he might be more
comfortable if he got out of my sight.**

**Me: I'm sure you said it just like that.**

He lifts a shoulder and cracks a smile.

I have a hard time containing my own burgeoning grin. Blake
was protecting me. Despite the rumors I've heard about him, his
actions toward both Maisy and me paint him as a stand-up guy. I
suppose, however, it's quite possible to be both a player and a good
human.

**Me: Whatever it was, thank you. I appreciate
your help. Can I offer you a glass of water?**

"That would be great."

He tinkers with the TV while I fetch him a drink. The whole
time, I find it hard not to peek at him. He's six-foot-something of
muscle and man-sweat. Why that turns me on confuses me.
Probably because I'm so used to being surrounded by cerebral
types. But Blake seems to have a good head on his shoulders too.
He's not just fun to look at.

I hand him the water, showing him the sign for it.

He repeats the sign, then says, "Thanks. I think the TV is okay. Want me to help you program it?"

I turn down his offer with an appreciative smile.

"Okay." He thumbs to the door. "I'll just go finish my run."

When I thank him once again, he winks and says, "My pleasure."

On his way out, he hesitates when he sees my family pictures on the wall. He studies them for a moment, glances back at me, then leaves.

I sink down onto my couch and sigh, knowing he's just given me even more to fantasize about.

# Chapter Ten

## Blake

*How do people do this?*

I run a hand through my hair and look around my house. It looks like a frat house on Sunday morning. Toys are strewn about the living room, a trail of them leading back to Maisy's bedroom. Half-eaten snacks lie on the couch and a table. Empty juice boxes litter the floor. A stray shoe sticks out from under the couch. I don't have the energy to look for its mate.

I pop the top off a bottle of beer and sit at the kitchen bar. She's one tiny person. I'm one adult. How have we made such a mess of things after only a few days?

Ellie is coming back tomorrow. I should clean so I don't get chewed out again.

The corners of my mouth twitch into a grin thinking of the reaming I got. The woman's got spunk, I'll give her that. And an uncanny ability to invade my thoughts when I've been so busy I barely have the strength to think.

Now that I've been in her apartment, my imagination goes wild. It smelled of coffee and cinnamon and I just know I'll be reminded of her whenever I inhale those particular scents. I recall her wall of family photos. Her tasteful furniture among a few random, unpacked boxes. And a stray pair of black high heels on the floor. It's those heels I can't get out of my head at the moment. Or more specifically, the image I've conjured in my head of her wearing them—and *only* them.

A wayward thought occurs. Who was she wearing them for? Because I sure as shit would have noticed had she been wearing them at my house the other day. I didn't see any pictures on the wall of what could have been a boyfriend.

*Mmm*, I grumble at the strange sensation inside me that feels like it could be… jealousy.

I try to banish the beautiful deaf doctor from my thoughts as I glance around the dirty room. Instead of cleaning, though, I slide my laptop across the counter, lift the lid, and continue the on-line ASL class I purchased. It's how I've filled every spare second over the past few days. Which hasn't been much considering I have a rambunctious four-year-old.

I look toward Maisy's room thinking how far she's come in a mere forty-eight hours. When she arrived, we had zero means of communication. Now, at least she can tell me when she's hungry or thirsty. Sometimes she just goes to the kitchen and gets what she wants—a fact that both saddens and enrages me. Was she left to her own devices? Did Lucinda expect such a young child to fend for herself?

Ah shit. That reminds me. I need to hire a family lawyer. I add it to the growing list of crap that needs to get done.

"Nice to meet you," I repeat back to the screen as I sign the words.

I straighten when I hear a noise down the hall. I pause the video and listen, but I don't hear anything, so I turn it back on.

"The brown dog is running," I say and sign as instructed.

It's interesting how a lot of signs are quite intuitive, making them easy to recall. The sign for dog, for example, is patting your flat hand against your leg as if beckoning a dog. What's harder to get used to, however, is the order of words. In English, you say 'the brown dog is running,' but in ASL, it's signed as 'dog brown run' because the subject comes before the verb or adjective. Additionally, as ASL is a visual language, there are no signs for 'and,' 'or,' 'the,' 'of,' and 'is.' Many of those words are just implied, and others are conveyed through movements of the shoulders, pauses, or other non-manual signals.

Then there's PSE. Pidgin Signed English. It's not a true language, but contains a mixture of ASL rules and English grammar. The signs are from ASL, but they're used in a more normal English pattern. It's used as a way to bridge the gap between native ASL speakers and native English speakers.

With English being my first language, it might make sense that I would gravitate toward PSE. But I have to let Maisy guide the way.

Another noise comes from the hallway and then Maisy appears from around the corner. She sees me and her eyes fill with fear. She runs to the front door, and, before I can stop her, she opens it and darts out.

"Maisy!" I stupidly call after her as I topple the barstool over in my haste to chase her.

A flash of her clothing catches my eye as she crosses the front yard barefoot. *Oh, Jesus.* Headlights bounce off her white pajamas as I race forward, praying I'll make it to her before the car does.

Screeching tires mingle with my pointless screams as I reach her and scoop her into my arms just as she reaches the street.

My heart pounds wildly as she squirms in my arms. Why is she trying to break free?

"Is she alright?" a woman asks from the passenger seat of the stopped vehicle.

I nod, unable to speak over the horrific scene playing out in my head of my kid sprawled on the pavement, bloodied and mangled.

Surprised my shaking legs have the ability to walk us back inside, I wish I was capable of asking her why she did it. Did she have a bad dream? Was there a bug crawling in her bed? Is she a sleepwalker?

Defeat squeezes my gut. I have no means of asking those questions, and even if I did, she doesn't have the tools to communicate the answers.

I carry her back to her bedroom and set her down. She glances at her bed, the terrified look still on her face.

It's now that I feel the wetness soaking through my shirt. I look down at her legs and see the discoloration of her pajamas. Then I stride to the bed, put my hand on the damp sheets, and I immediately know why she did what she did.

I close my eyes, guilt oozing from my every pore. I fucked up. I didn't make her use the bathroom before I put her to bed. This is my fault. And even if it wasn't my fault, she shouldn't feel bad. She's four. And in a new place with virtual strangers. It's understandable. Expected even.

She runs into the closet.

What the hell am I supposed to do now? She ran out of the goddamn house. Does she think I'm mad? That I'll punish her. *Fuck*, did Lucinda?

*My God.* What if I hadn't seen her run out? What if I'd been asleep?

I stomp out of her room and into mine, feeling like an idiot for not thinking of it before. I open the keypad to the security system and set it to chime when an outer door or window is opened. I turned the feature off when I got the house because it was annoying. Now, there are so many things I need to rethink. I should get deadbolts or chains installed that are out of her reach.

But I can't think of any of that right now. I can only think of the scared little girl cowering in her closet.

Grabbing the spare set of sheets from the hall closet, I go back to Maisy's room and turn on the light in the closet so she can see me. "It's okay," I say and sign. I've used this sign a lot over the past few days and I hope she's beginning to know the meaning.

She doesn't move.

I get her stuffed cat off the bed and hand her the peace offering with a smile on my face. "It's okay," I say again.

Still smiling, I show her the fresh sheets in my hand and point to the bed. It feels awkward to smile so big at this situation, but it's the only way I can let her know I'm not mad. "Come on." I wave a hand toward the bed as I back out of the closet, hoping she'll follow.

She doesn't.

I strip the wet sheets off the bed—silently thanking my mother, who had the good sense to put a plastic mattress cover under them—and make it up fresh. After tossing the soiled linens into the hallway, I flick the room light off and on several times to get her attention. Soon, her curls appear in the closet doorway. She peeks out and looks at me hesitantly.

I hold out a fresh pair of pajamas and underwear in one hand, and a book about a cat—I think it's one of her favorites—in the other. Then I sit on her bed and pat the space beside me. My face hurts as I uphold the smile that must look stupid as shit by now. "It's okay," I say.

She fully emerges from the closet, dragging her cat with her, takes the change of clothes, and disappears into the bathroom for a few minutes. When she comes back out, she timidly crawls up onto the bed, leaving space between us.

It makes me sad, the space. Will there always be space between us? Not just physically, but emotionally? Can we ever connect in a way other fathers and daughters do?

My phone vibrates with a text. I ignore it, keeping it in my pocket, and I read to Maisy. I do the signs I know as I read. But she's not looking at me or my hands. Her eyes are glued to the book. And once again, sadness washes over me knowing she's never been properly read to.

*Don't pity her,* I hear in my head. It's one of the rules Ellie told me. But she texted it to me. Why then, do I hear a voice in my head? A soft feminine voice that I imagine to be hers. It makes me wonder if she ever speaks.

I keep reading until Maisy drifts off. Then I slide out of the bed, secure the bed rail, and turn out the lights, thinking how horribly this evening could have ended.

Just as I'm shutting her door, the doorbell chimes. It... couldn't be Ellie, right? It's eight o'clock on Thursday. I know it's not her. But I'm willing it to be.

I push a laundry basket behind the couch on my way to the door. Opening it, I'm disappointed to find it's just my friends, Dax Cruz and Cooper Calloway. Dax holds up a case of my favorite beer. "If the rumors are true, we thought you might need this."

I laugh appreciatively and step aside.

Cooper enters first, glancing around my mess of a house. He chuckles. "You should have seen my place when I first got Cody." He grips my shoulder. "It'll get easier."

"From your lips to God's ears," I say.

Dax pulls out three beers, opening them as he hands one to Cooper and me. "I never thought I'd see the day when Blake Montana had a kid, but cheers to you for stepping up." He clinks his bottle to mine then Cooper's.

I glance down the hallway. "We need to keep it down. I just got her to bed."

Dax narrows his brows. "Uh, Blake, isn't she deaf?"

I look at the ceiling and sigh. "Shit. Yeah. I'm… still getting used to this."

Cooper sweeps a toy aside and sits on the couch. "Addy told me she can't even communicate. Is that true?"

"Your sister must have been talking to my sister." I take a drink and sit. "She's right though. Maisy doesn't even know her own name. I'm not even sure she understands that I'm her dad."

"That's fucked up," Dax says.

"It is."

"So what's up with Maisy's mom?"

I shrug. "I have no clue. All I know is that she's in rehab for ninety days. For all I know, Maisy will go back to her after that. I mean, I'm going to fight it. I would hope CPS wouldn't give her back to a woman who didn't ever bother to communicate with her own kid."

"So you really are stepping up," Cooper says.

"She's so small," I say. "And scared. She has nobody." I swallow hard. "Fucking nobody. Her grandparents abandoned her to go on a goddamn cruise." I stare down the hallway. "She's amazing. I know she is. How could she not be after what she's been through?"

"What are you going to do?" Cooper asks. "How do you talk to her? Can she understand anything?"

"We're working with a woman from the Deaf school. Maisy will start Pre-K there on Monday. I'm learning sign language. But for now, we mainly just play." I gesture around the trashed room. "As you can clearly see." I pick up some papers off the coffee table. "And draw." I show them a picture I drew of this house with Maisy and me inside. "I'm trying to help her understand this is her house and I'm her dad. But I have no idea if I'm getting through."

"Think of it like having a baby," Cooper says. "They have no idea what you're saying, but they learn. Just keep repeating it. Keep drawing it. She'll understand soon enough."

"When did you get so smart?" Dax teases.

"When I had to man up and become a father to Cody," he says. "Speaking of which, I could bring him over and introduce him. Better yet, I could bring my nieces, Ashley and Aurora, they're both four. Isn't that how old Maisy is?"

"Oh, man, that would be great," I say. "Ellie says Maisy lacks social skills. I bet having her around other kids her age would be amazing. I'll ask her about it."

"Ellie?" Cooper's brow shoots up.

"Maisy's mentor from the Deaf school."

"Ellie?" he repeats. "As in not *Mrs. So-and-so,* but Ellie? Already on a first-name basis with your kid's teacher?"

I snort. "I'm not gonna lie. She's all that and more." I picture her in my head. Sandy-blonde hair. Blue eyes. Inviting smile. Small hands that look so graceful when she signs.

"Dude." Dax elbows me. "You're hot for teacher."

"Yeah, well, it doesn't matter. She already shut me down."

Cooper laughs. "Of course you already asked her out. You wouldn't be Blake Montana if you didn't."

Guilt weighs on me like a ton of bricks. My reputation does precede me. But I'm not that guy anymore. Truth be told, I haven't been that guy since I graduated. I'm sure it'll take a lot more than my four-month dry spell to convince anyone else though.

My phone vibrates again, reminding me I didn't check my previous text.

I pull it out and feel my face twitch when I see who it's from. Ellie has been sending me links to ASL resources.

"You are completely fucking smitten," Cooper bellows. "It's from her, isn't it?"

"Fuck off," I snap, putting my phone away. "And who the hell says *smitten?*"

"Hey, you tell Dallas yet?" Dax asks.

"That I have a kid?" My head swivels sharply. "It's not exactly the kind of thing he'd be excited about considering he lost his own family."

"He's your brother, he'd want to know. Even if it's hard for him to hear."

"I suppose I'll have to tell him sooner or later."

"Better he hears it from you than through the rumor mill," Cooper says.

The security system chimes as my front door swings open. Lucas walks in, takes in the three of us, and barks at Dax, "Don't you have a McQuaid to hang out with?"

"Give it a rest, Lucas," I say, tired over the constant feuding between families in this town.

"Yeah, fuck off, Montana," Dax says.

I flash Dax a scolding stare. "I said give it a rest. Jesus, there are more important things than the two of you being at each other's throats."

Lucas studies me. "As if you don't hate his derelict brothers."

"No," I say staunchly. "I don't."

"Well you did last week. What the hell happened to change that?"

I glance at the hall. "A whole hell of a lot."

Lucas scoffs. "You found out you have a kid and suddenly you're the family peacekeeper?"

I sigh, tired of this conversation. "Lucas, is there a point to your visit?"

He gives Dax one final glare, then pulls something from his pocket and hands it to me. It's a wedding invitation. *His* wedding invitation.

I look up, surprised. "Lissa finally let you set a date? I thought she said she'd see hell freeze over first."

"I wore her down," he says proudly.

Dax snickers. "Poor girl has no idea what she's in for. Are you going to even make it to the church this time?"

While I may have a reputation as a player, my brother is the infamous runaway groom of Calloway Creek. He's left two women at the altar—the actual altar, with processional music playing and all. And he broke it off with a third mere weeks before that wedding was to happen. Lissa is the fourth woman Lucas has been engaged to. There are actual bookies taking bets on when and if he'll bail again.

Lucas points to Dax. "You're not invited."

Dax holds up his hands. "Thank God. You've just saved me from having to put on a suit and sit in a church wondering if you'll have the balls to show."

Lucas looks pissed. But I see Dax's point.

"I'll show. I'll fucking show. This is the real thing, fellas. Not that any of you would know."

"Hey," Cooper says in his defense.

"Okay, so maybe *you* know," Lucas says.

Once again, my mind turns to thoughts of expressive blue eyes, hair that darkens or lightens depending on the light, and a smile that would bring any man to his knees.

"Blake?... Yo, Blake."

I turn to see the three of them staring at me.

Dax scoffs. "You've got it bad, don't you?"

"He's got what bad?" Lucas asks.

"A case of blue balls apparently." Cooper chuckles.

Cooper fills my brother in on Ellie as I tune out their chatter because my phone vibrates again. It's another text from her. The zings shooting through my body when her name pops up confirm that I do in fact *have it bad*. Dax is right. I'm totally hot for teacher.

97

# Chapter Eleven

## Ellie

Walking up to Blake's house, I instantly notice the changes. There is a large swing set in the back yard, and I'm fairly sure his yard wasn't fenced when I came the other day. How does one get an entire fence erected in just a few days?

The lengths he's gone for her are truly astounding. My heart misses a beat and I scold myself. *You cannot fall for this guy, Ellie.*

I knock, and moments later, he answers, balancing an armful of laundry in one hand and a stack of stuffed animals in the other. "Come in," he says. "Make yourself at home. I'll be right back."

Following him inside, I look around his living room that was an utter disaster the last time I was here. On his way through, he leans down and picks up a pair of shoes, then disappears around the corner.

I take the opportunity to peek into the kitchen and family room. Both are far more organized. I wonder if he hired a cleaning service. One glance at the dining room table has me smiling. It's littered with drawings. Upon closer look, the drawings have been made by not only Maisy, but Blake. They're communicating through art. It's fascinating.

I inhale deeply. *Heart—stop it.*

The light flickers overhead and I turn, having a hard time not smiling. He's already getting the hang of things.

But then… then he does something truly astounding. He speaks with his hands.

"Ellie," he fingerspells then smiles.

I nod and do jazz hands.

"It's nice to see you," he signs. "Please come in."

I'm speechless. He learned those signs in just a few days. And he did them perfectly.

Trying to look unaffected by his impressive display, I look around, mildly confused by his words since I'm already inside. At the same time, I'm bowled over at the ease in which he signed. I've never seen someone pick it up so quickly.

I pull out my phone and text him.

**Me: I'm already in.**

He laughs.

**Blake: I know. I practiced signing it all morning and then my hands were full when I answered the door. But they were the only phrases I learned and I was determined to use them. Oh, and I learned the alphabet.**

He looks up proudly and starts signing ABCs.

God, that makes him even more alluring than before. Is there anything sexier than a man, a single father, who would do anything for his child?

Single father. *Is he?* I don't know the whole story there. He didn't know about Maisy until earlier this week. Was the child kept from him intentionally? Did the mother pass? He said CPS was called. Is she still in the picture? Will Maisy be the center of a custody battle?

A million questions burn inside my head. But I'm not here as a psychotherapist. And I really have no right to ask about his past.

**Me: Well, nice job. You're picking it up quickly. How have things been going? Where is Maisy?**

"She's getting ready. I told her you were coming."

My brows dip. He *told* her?

He takes my elbow and leads me to the far end of the table. The thoughts I'm having about his hand on my skin are not very professional. His large, firm hand that just spelled my name. He lets go and our eyes meet. He swallows and briefly looks at my neckline. Okay, so I'm pretty sure he felt it too—the electricity between us.

He rummages through the dozens of pictures on the table and hands me one. It's like some of the others: this house with Blake and Maisy inside; the back yard with them on the swings; the kitchen with them at the table. But this one has *me* in it. I know it's me because he drew me in just like Maisy drew me in the other day.

He taps my shoulder to get my attention and says, "All day yesterday, I drew pictures of just Maisy and me. But twenty minutes ago, I drew this. She seemed excited. I pointed to you in the drawing and then to the couch, hoping she'd understand. She must have, because she ran to her room and started going through her closet." He laughs. "You'd think she was a teenager getting ready for a date. She picked out several outfits. She must really like you, Ellie."

I'm fascinated by how much I pick up from reading his lips.

He told her I'm coming. *Him*. A man with zero experience with deaf children. Someone who, before Tuesday, didn't even know about her. And she understood.

*She understood.*

Amazing.

This time, my heart doesn't just skip one beat, it skips *all* of them.

He motions behind me, and I turn. Maisy is in the doorway wearing a pink dress with a white bow on the front. Soft blonde spirals frame her innocent face, and her expression doesn't look quite as distant as it did a few days ago. Her blue eyes are bright and her full lips curve into a smile. And I melt.

She races over and hugs me, and my eyes close of their own volition when her small body wraps around me. I force them open and look over at Blake. He's smiling too, but it's full of both happiness and sadness.

Maisy should be hugging him, not me.

I pull back, not wanting to steal all Blake's thunder. After all, he's the hero here. He's worked so hard.

My goal today was to try and teach Maisy her name. But now my goal has shifted. She needs to understand that Blake is her father.

I take Maisy to the table and gather the drawings showing her and Blake in the house. Then I get some things from my bag. A book I found about a single father to a little girl. Flashcards with men, men and children, and men holding babies.

I show her the book. On the cover is a man holding the hand of a little girl. Then I show her the flashcards. Then I point to the drawings. I put my finger on the flashcard of the man holding the baby, being sure she knows I'm pointing to the man. I do the sign for father. I point to the man on the cover of the book and do it again. Then I point to the drawing and the likeness of Blake and do it a third time. Then I point to Blake and do it again.

Maisy repeats the sign.

In my periphery, I see Blake trying to control his emotions. He pulls out his phone.

> **Blake: Do you think she understands? Or does she think 'father' is just the name for 'man?' Or maybe she thinks 'father' is my name.**

It amazes me that he asked the question. It shows just how much he's invested in his situation. More than likely, Maisy does think the sign for father is the sign for man, but we have to start somewhere. Who knows, though. I taught her the sign for 'boy' the last time I was here. Perhaps she understands the difference.

> **Me: It's possible she thinks that. With repetition, she'll come to understand. But she's signing. Let's celebrate the small victories.**

He nods. And I think he sniffs because I see his nostrils flare. His patience and empathy seem to know no bounds. I've met a lot of hearing parents of deaf children before. But never one as driven as this man. I wish I could bottle that resolve and give it to all my clients.

I spend the next hour trying to teach Maisy her name. It's a long, arduous, and in the end, a futile process. I need her to understand that she's a girl and I'm a girl, but while we are both girls, we have different names. For all Maisy knows, people don't have names. Proper names may be something she doesn't comprehend.

We take a break and offer Maisy a snack. While she's eating, Blake turns on the TV for her and tunes it to a cartoon.

I turn it off, grab her new iPad, and pull up a more appropriate video.

**Me: Mainstream cartoons are difficult for the deaf. We can't read lips of animated characters. Best not to confuse her further. I'm sure she's spent the last four years watching them. Everything she watches now should be educational. There are plenty of fun videos that will also teach. Are you still okay with her starting Pre-K on Monday?**

He nods.

**Me: There are some things I should prepare you for when it comes to introducing her into the world of Deaf education. Everyone has opinions. Doctors. Teachers. Administrators. Passion over something can be bad if they throw in judgment or superiority. Some will**

**believe one way of communicating is better than others. Well-meaning friends and professionals will give opinions and may become upset with your decisions. And they'll all look to you to make choices. What you need to know going in is that there isn't one way that's better. And you need to understand that whatever method you choose may not be the method Maisy adopts. Or she may be successful with one method now but choose a different one later. What you need is someone to guide you without bias, and that's why I'm here.**

I watch him as he reads. His eyes seem to glaze over. He's overwhelmed again. I'm information dumping, impatient because Maisy has missed out on so much already.

He looks up, and our gazes connect, and it's like I can read everything behind those caring eyes. Despite the complete and utter upheaval of his life, there is a sheer determination in his expression I've never before witnessed. And it takes my breath away.

It's hard to tear my eyes from his. It's like a tractor beam is holding us hostage to each other. Flutters in my gut make me acutely aware of the intensity of the moment. But I have to remind myself the passion in his eyes has nothing to do with me and everything to do with his daughter. Knowing this, I break our connection and type out another text.

**Me: Our ultimate goal is for Maisy to be able to communicate her thoughts and be**

**understood. That could happen in a variety of ways. Through speech, cues, signing, or a combination. My point is, take time to gather information before making any decisions. Meet other families with deaf children. Connect with deaf adults and teens. Over time, as she gets older, your decisions may change. The path may twist and turn as she grows and is able to weigh in on those decisions.**

Maisy tugs on my shirt and points at the swing set outside. I shrug my shoulders and gesture to Blake, letting her know it's not my decision. She looks at him and he nods. He points to Maisy's shoes.

I'm taken aback when she sits on the floor, puts them on, and... *ties* them. She's four years old and she ties her shoes. It makes me both happy and sad at the same time. Happy because it's another indication of how bright she is. Sad because, based on the little information I have about her past, she probably taught herself out of necessity. Surely a mother who didn't even bother communicating with her child wouldn't teach her to tie shoes.

Blake gets up and goes to the back door, unbolting a deadbolt that is much higher than where Maisy can reach. *Is that new?*

We move to where we can watch her. I tap his shoulder and sign, "She's doing a great job." Then I text it to him. I point to him. "You're doing a great job." I don't bother with a text.

His head jerks quickly left then right. "I feel like a complete failure. Yes, I'm learning signs and stuff, but with her, I'm doing everything wrong. She almost got - - - last night. I can't even keep her safe."

I furrow my brows, sign, "Say again," then text him the same two words.

"She was almost killed. She ran out of the house - - - and a car - - - I - - - her out of the way."

He's so frustrated that his words don't form clearly, and I ask him to text. He tells me the whole story of it. How she wet the bed. How she thought he would be mad about it. How he handled it. How he turned on the chime and had extra locks installed.

> **Me: Blake, you're doing everything right. Can't you see that? I'll petition the county for a road sign that will alert drivers there is a deaf child in the area.**

> **Blake: See, you know all this shit. I didn't even have the damn door chime on.**

> **Me: But you do now. You're learning just as she is. It's a process. It's not going to happen all at once. You're doing everything you can. Tantrums and outbursts are to be expected until she can properly communicate. Even then, they might continue as she's likely to feel isolated. One of the reasons deaf children act out is because people are always saying no to them. And no one is filling in the blanks. They are generally left to figure things out on their own. Remember the other day I said you should clue her in to things going on around her that only hearing people would know?**

**The more you do that, the more included she'll feel and the less she'll act out.**

**Blake: It's not enough. It needs to be more. She needs more. She needs a father. I need her to know who I am. God, I wish she could understand.**

I touch his arm. He looks at my lips. I look at his. I wonder if he can hear the air crackle between us. It's a sound I've read about in books, but I swear I can *feel* it at this very moment. Passion dances in his eyes. The same passion I feel in my heart. If passion makes a noise, I wonder what it sounds like. In my mind, it's how people describe the subtle undertone of an ocean breeze.

*Kiss me*, my heart screams.

Someone walks in the room.

Our trance is broken.

"Mom," he mouths, his eyes connecting with mine as if he's as disappointed as I am that our moment was interrupted.

I'm introduced to Mrs. Montana, who I'm delighted to see has also learned some signs. Boy, did Maisy hit the jackpot with this family.

# Chapter Twelve

## Blake

*Tap tap tap.*

I roll over in bed, searching for those last few seconds of sleep.

*Tap tap tap.*

My eyes open to find a tousle-headed little girl standing not-so-patiently beside my bed.

Sometimes while I'm sleeping, I forget I'm a father. It's all still so new. Less than a week ago, my biggest worry was the weather. Grapevines do best with full sun, seven to eight hours a day of it. Less light leads to lower fruit production, poorer quality, and fruit rot. In my position as Chief Operating Officer, I became obsessed with the weather. Yet now I realize I haven't checked it in days.

Maisy turns on the light and shoves a picture in my face. I smile, because although I've had to say no the past few days, today I get to say yes.

"Yes," I say and sign.

She squeals.

I love her squeal. It's one of the few sounds she makes.

Somehow, when she was here on Friday, Ellie was able to convey to Maisy that she'd be going to school soon. She made three pictures of a little curly blonde-haired-girl sleeping and the fourth picture was of the same girl sitting in a schoolhouse with other children.

Maisy seemed to understand the school part, but what she didn't quite get was the three sleeps. For the past two days, she's come into my room with the same schoolhouse picture. And for the past two days, she's thrown a tantrum when I said no.

I hate saying no.

It's not that I want to spoil her—okay, so maybe I do a little—but saying no when she can't understand why is really a ball buster. It breaks my goddamn heart. But it seems there have been a lot more 'nos' than 'yeses' lately, which is why I'm happy to see her so excited right now.

She runs out of my bedroom. I learned very quickly not to sleep naked, so I roll out of bed half-dressed in sweatpants, and follow her. When I round the corner to her room, she's already undressing and reaching for the outfit she picked. It's not one I'd have chosen. It looks like something a little girl would wear to church. But based on the wardrobe she showed up with, it was evident she never got to wear fancy clothes. So now, that's all she ever wants to wear, even though all we've done is stay home.

Until now.

Suddenly I'm nervous. What if she hates school? Will the other kids make fun of her because she's so far behind?

But I mask my anxiety and try to bask in the fact that, for the first time, Maisy seems happy. The only other times she isn't sad is when Ellie is around.

Hmmm, that may be something we have in common. I sure tend to be in a better mood when Dr. Stone is here.

We had another moment Friday night. I'm pretty sure it might have even turned into a profound one had we not been interrupted by my mother. The way her expressive eyes were looking at me, I just knew she wanted it as much as I did, despite shooting me down days earlier.

Maisy finishes dressing and drags me to the front door.

I laugh, but then she gets upset when I try to pull her back.

I do the sign for food.

She stomps her foot and pouts, not giving up her spot by the door.

I go to the dining room table and sift through the many many drawings we've been using to communicate when signs won't do. I bring two back to the door and show her. The first one is of us eating at the table. The second is of the schoolhouse—one of many Maisy has drawn these past few days.

I point to the first one, then the second.

She seems to understand, and, although not happy, she shuffles to the kitchen and sits at the bar.

I take my time making pancakes because school doesn't start for an hour. After we eat, I try to convey to her that I need to get ready. She wants nothing to do with it and goes to stand by the front door. I point to myself and do the sign for bathing, then pull out my phone and raise my brows.

There's a game on my phone that she likes to play. It's the only thing that keeps her occupied while I need to do things she can't participate in. Like showering. Or shitting. And she's only allowed to play it during those times.

She still sulks but takes the phone anyway and starts playing.

After I'm done getting ready, and she brushes her teeth faster than ever, I show her the school picture again and start to walk through the house, away from the front door. She's confused, but quickly understands when she sees my car in the garage.

She takes a few steps toward the car, stops cold, and runs back into the house. Damn, this was what I was afraid of, that I'd have to drag her kicking and screaming. But after her display of excitement, I was sure I wouldn't have to worry about it. She reappears a moment later carrying her stuffed cat. That old thing is her security blanket.

I smile and open the back door to the car, her gateway to our first outing. We haven't stepped foot out the front door since she arrived—if you don't count the trip to the audiologist and the time she almost got run over. It's the longest I've ever gone without leaving my house. I haven't run since Thursday. Haven't worked in a week. Dad has been amazing, stepping back into the role he only recently vacated. He hasn't pressured me in the slightest. But I'm looking forward to going out to the winery this morning, even if it's only for a few hours.

At the school, there is a line for drop off. But I park and walk Maisy inside. As soon as we go through the main doors, I see Ellie waiting. She looks relieved, as if maybe she thought we wouldn't show.

Our eyes connect. It's the first time we've seen each other since the almost-kiss on Friday. Did she somehow become more beautiful over the weekend? Her hair is pulled back into a clip, tendrils falling to her chin. The blue blouse she's wearing matches her eyes, and her black skirt clings to her hips. I've never seen her in anything but slacks. I'm tempted to stare at her legs, but that would mean popping this magical bubble we seem to be surrounded by where the world falls away and it's just us— staring... wanting...feeling.

When she finally shifts her gaze to Maisy, her lips curve into a smile as my daughter sees her and runs over.

A woman standing by Ellie's side says and signs, "Mr. Montana, I presume?"

"Yes."

"I'm Mrs. Kasey. I'll be Maisy's teacher for the rest of the spring."

"Nice to meet you," I say, hoping I got the signs right.

Ellie taps Mrs. Kasey's shoulder and starts signing. Mrs. Kasey interprets, "Maisy will spend three hours in Mrs. Kasey's class, then she'll meet with the speech therapist, then the four of us will convene for our first IEP meeting. Is noon good for you? We don't want to overwhelm Maisy on her first day by doing too much, but it's important that we get started with a plan."

"Noon. Right." I look down at my daughter then back at Ellie. "Do you think she knows I'll come back for her?"

"If she doesn't, she will soon enough. This will be the routine five days a week."

Right. Everything is about repetition.

I lower to my knees and get on Maisy's level. "I'll see you later," I say and sign, feeling guilty that she probably doesn't understand. I should have brought drawings showing her coming home after school.

At this point, though, I'm not sure anything I say to her will mean much. She's excited. Her eyes dart around to the other kids funneling in through the front door.

I look up at the two women. "Do I just leave?"

"We'll take good care of her," Mrs. Kasey says. And with that, Ellie takes Maisy's hand, and the three of them turn and walk away.

The father part of me is upset that Maisy is walking away so easily. Aren't kids supposed to have separation anxiety about going to school? Then again, she hasn't even known me for a week. And at this point, she seems much more attached to Ellie.

I don't even know if my own daughter likes me.

Maisy doesn't turn around. But Ellie does. She shoots me a look over her shoulder. A look that communicates she understands every emotion swirling through my head right now. She smiles and nods before the trio disappears around the corner.

I blow out a breath. Maisy has only been with me for six days. A better part of that time has been spent with her angry at me because she can't understand. And most of that time, I've been frustrated with her. With myself. But now, standing here after she walks away, I find myself feeling like a part of me is missing.

~ ~ ~

Today has been busy. Catching up on work. Maisy's IEP meeting. And then… wow, what a transformation. After only one morning in Pre-K, Maisy is a different little girl. It's as if her whole world has changed. She came home knowing more signs than I thought a four-year-old could learn in a day. Ellie said she was bright. I didn't realize just how bright until now.

Maisy asked about Ellie after we came home. Or rather, she pointed to the picture we use when 'talking' about Ellie. It's evident she wants to see her. At the IEP meeting, Ellie told me that between Pre-K and speech therapy, there wasn't time for the two of them to meet. She didn't want Maisy to be overwhelmed on her first day. And while Maisy did seem upset earlier that she couldn't see her, she ate her lunch and immediately went down for a nap.

The doorbell rings promptly at 4pm.

It's Ellie. She's swapped the black skirt for a pair of jeans, though she still wears the same blue blouse.

She walks in and looks around.

"She's sleeping," I sign.

"Big day," she signs back.

I love that we can already have short signing conversations without texting.

"The school is amazing," I say. "She seemed to love it. I told her she'd go back after one sleep, and she was excited. Although I worry what will happen come Saturday when she doesn't get to go and I can't explain to her what a weekend is."

"She'll learn," she signs.

A noise from behind me is all the warning I get before Maisy dashes by and wraps her arms around Ellie. It always hurts a bit when she does this. I'm glad she's bonding with Ellie, but at the same time, I long for those little arms to wrap around *me*.

Ellie senses my pain. She's very good at reading me. It makes me wonder if she knows just how much I'm drawn to her. How I think about her all the time. How, other than Maisy, *she* is who occupies my thoughts. Thoughts about how close we came to kissing the other day. About just how much I want to kiss her. About how I want that and more. How after only a week, I can't imagine her not being part of my life.

Maisy takes Ellie's hand and drags her to the kitchen, opening the refrigerator and getting out the milk. She does the sign for milk, then she points to a cup on the counter and does the sign for cup. Then she does the sign for drink.

I go to pour her a glass of milk, but she doesn't seem to want it, leaving me confused.

She continues to pull Ellie from room to room, enthusiastically pointing to things then doing the corresponding signs. My jaw drops. I know she learned new signs. But this... this is fucking astonishing. She knows signs for some barnyard animals. Pieces of furniture. Clothing. Even a few colors.

Ellie and I share a look as Maisy continues through every room, labeling what she can. Ellie's eyes flood with tears. I'm not the only one overcome with emotion as the floodgates of Maisy's life open and her world begins to make sense.

In her bedroom, Maisy does signs for toys, bed, and window. She stiffens, and points to the bathroom, skips across the room and disappears behind the door.

I turn to Ellie. "My kid is a fucking genius."

A tear slips from her eye. Her expression tells me she's in full agreement with my statement. Her head shakes from side to side as if she's never seen such a profound awakening before. Maybe she hasn't.

When I reach up and wipe a tear from her cheek, she grabs my hand and holds it against her. Our eyes lock onto each other, and I'm swept up with emotion when I lean in and lightly touch my lips to hers. Her soft, salty, inviting lips. I pull back slightly to see if she minded.

She most definitely did not.

Our bodies press together as our mouths collide more forcefully this time. With nothing between us, I can feel the thud of her racing heart. Or maybe it's mine that's pounding. Her hands weave through my hair then settle onto the back of my neck, holding me tightly against her. With one hand on her back and the other cupping the side of her head, I deepen the kiss. Our tongues tangle together, passion spearing my entire being as if this is my first kiss.

In a way, it is. Obviously it's not the first, but it's the most meaningful. The most anticipated. And definitely the most wanted.

The skin on the back of her neck pebbles beneath my touch. She rises up on her toes and leans even more heavily into me. I walk her backwards and press her against the wall, allowing us to be even closer. My dick comes to life when a throaty mewl escapes her. I'm not sure if it's been five seconds or sixty. All I know is I want more. I *need* more.

The magical moment ends when I hear the toilet flush. I step away, even though it's the last thing I want to do, and point to the bathroom. As Maisy appears, Ellie wipes her lower lip and blushes. Maisy grabs Ellie's hand, oblivious to what went on in her absence, and continues her way through the house, labeling everything she can.

Ellie turns, looks at me, and smiles.

Standing back and watching them together, I wonder if my life will ever be the same.

I fucking hope not.

# Chapter Thirteen

## Ellie

Every so often, Blake glances at me from the driver's seat. It's hard to have a conversation with him driving the car, so we sit silently.

It's been eleven days since our kiss, and we haven't kissed again. Not because we haven't wanted to. Oh, we have. The heated stares from him. The blushes from me. The accidentally-on-purpose touches from both of us. There just hasn't been a chance. But wow, that kiss. It's not the first kiss I've shared with a hearing man. But he's the only hearing man I've truly wanted a second kiss with.

Maisy starts getting frustrated in the back. She doesn't understand where we're going. Perhaps she thinks she's being taken back to her mother, which I'm not even sure how she would feel about. Does she love her mother? Is she even alive?

Driving down the freeway, there isn't much I can do to calm her. Blake looks stressed as he glances at her in the rearview mirror.

I point to the volume control for the radio. Blake shakes his head. I point to it again and do the sign for 'music,' but he looks confused. I suppose there isn't any reason he'd have learned that sign. I do the sign for 'up' then 'loud' hoping he understands one of those. He narrows his brows but reaches for the touchscreen, taps the audio settings and settles on a station.

"Good?" I sign. "You can hear?"

He nods and grips the steering wheel harder when the car wobbles out of our lane. He's not used to driving and talking with a deaf person.

"Sorry," I sign. I point to his eyes and then the road.

Then I put my hand on the speaker in the passenger door and turn up the radio until I feel the music. Then I turn it up even more. Blake's reaction is typical of what a hearing person looks like when something is too loud. He winces, almost like it's painful. Even after all these years of people telling me about it and learning about it in school, it's still amazing to me that sound can cause pain. How is that even possible?

I turn to Maisy, point to the speaker next to her car seat, and do the sign for 'touch'—something she's learned over the past week because we've taught her what she *shouldn't* touch.

She touches the speaker with her fingertips, and her eyes double in size. She lays her hand flat against it. Her mouth goes slack, and she looks at me, her face slowly morphing into a smile.

Maisy has the most amazing smile. It doesn't come out much because she's frustrated a lot of the time, but when it does, it lights up the room. Her alabaster skin, platinum blonde hair, and white party dress make her look like an angel. And I don't think I've ever seen such an incredible sight.

When we stop at a light, Blake turns to me and I sign, "She's beautiful."

He glances in the rearview and smiles. Then he points to me. "You're beautiful."

The light turns green. He lightly brushes his hand against my arm then begins driving. I look down at my arm, the skin still tingling at the memory of his touch, not to mention his words.

It isn't much longer when we turn down a road at a large sign reading **Montana Winery.** I've never been to a winery before so this will be exciting. And other than Maisy going to school, this is her first official outing. I wanted her to see where Blake and his family work. She's already met most of his family, so it shouldn't be too stressful for her. It'll be an easy outing compared to say, taking her to a mall, which is also on my list.

The list is long. Based on my interactions with Maisy the past few weeks, I've come to realize just what a sheltered life she's lived. My goal is to introduce her to all the things in life most people take for granted but that she's most likely never experienced. Parks, restaurants, a fire station, a pool.

My eyes are glued to the side window as we wind our way down the street. As far as the eye can see over the rolling hills, there are rows after rows of grapevines that look like short little trees. But they aren't full of grapes.

We're driving slow enough that I feel it's safe to sign. "No grapes?"

He turns his head enough to keep an eye on the road but also so I can see his lips. "It's spring. The vines have just - - - from - - -"

I'm not sure if it's the angle of his face or if he's saying fancy words, but I don't pick up most of them. I put a finger to his lips to stop him. I shake my head, shrug my shoulders, and hold out my hands, palms up.

He laughs, getting that I didn't understand a darned thing.

"Say again," I sign.

It's a sign he's become more than a little familiar with.

He pulls into a parking spot by what I assume is the main building and gets out his phone.

> **Blake: It's spring. The vines have just reawakened from dormancy. It's called a bud burst. Green leaves burst awake in preparation for photosynthesis with the warmer months. But it's a delicate time as the new growth is in danger of spring frost.**

I sign. "When do you pick them?"

He smiles, proud of himself for understanding. I can always tell when he gets what I sign because there's an added sparkle to his already amazingly bright eyes.

> **Blake: Grapes are picked in the late summer or early fall. If we pick them too soon, the acid levels will be too high and the sugar levels too low. If we pick too late, it will be the opposite.**

"Can you eat them?" I ask.

> **Blake: Wine grapes are edible, but they're not really meant to be eaten out of hand like table grapes. They have seeds and thicker skins and tend to be sweeter because the sugars will be turned into alcohol during fermentation.**

**Me: Thanks for the crash course.**

People emerge from the building looking strangely at the car. I silently chuckle when I remember the music must still be on. I turn it off and Blake cuts the engine, then nods for us to get out of the car.

Before greeting his family, he gets Maisy out of her car seat in the back. I love that his first thought is always of her.

Blake's parents, Chris and Sarah, and his sister Allie are here.

"Welcome," his mom says.

"Thank you," I sign.

She seems to understand. All of his family have been learning ASL. Not at the speed Blake is, but still, they're making a genuine effort. It's fortunate Maisy landed in such a good situation with people to help and support her. I swallow, knowing we have that in common.

I watch as she gets pulled into a hug by her grandmother. Blake stands next to them, a look of longing on his face. *Has he still not hugged his daughter?*

Allie takes Maisy's hand, and they skip happily up the front stairs and through the door.

I look around at all the buildings, shocked that there are so many. I like wine, but I truly know nothing about the process of making it.

"What are these buildings?" I sign, then furrow my brows and gesture around.

"This is our main building," Blake says. "It has tasting rooms and offices." He points. "Over there is our bottling facility. Next to it is our warehouse." He points in the opposite direction, still keeping his face toward me, which I appreciate. "That's our reception hall. We host events. Weddings and stuff. That's what Allie does. In fact, my brother will be getting married here soon."

"Can I see your office?" I sign.

The sparkle and grin tell me he knows what I said. "Right this way," he replies.

Allie and Maisy are nowhere to be found when we go inside. I assume Allie is giving her niece a tour. I'm sure there's a lot to see. I'd like to see it all myself.

Past the reception area and some private rooms with mahogany bars lined with countless bottles of wine, there is a hallway of offices. Blake stops and motions to one, and I walk inside. It's like any other office. Desk. Computer. A few guest chairs. But what strikes me in particular is the sole picture sitting on the desk. It's a framed photograph of Maisy. From what I know, he's only been coming to work for a few hours every morning. He must be incredibly busy during that time, yet he made a point of getting this picture.

"What?" Blake says in reaction to my look of surprise.

**Me: I'm impressed that you have a photo of Maisy here.**

He narrows his eyes. "Why wouldn't I? You should see my dad's office. You'd think it was a shrine to his family."

I smile because I'm sure that means he, too, has a picture of Maisy.

*Lucky, lucky girl.*

Blake gives me a tour, having to text most of the time because, well... apparently I don't speak winery. We eventually make our way around to where we started and meet up with everyone in one of the tasting rooms. A snack has been laid out, and Sarah offers me a glass of wine.

I give his mom a shake of my head. "I'm working," I sign.

She doesn't understand.

"She said she's working," Blake tells her.

Sarah gives me a dismissive wave of the hand. "Aren't we all." She pours herself a small amount, then raises a brow at me.

I roll my eyes and sigh. I hold up one finger and then sign, "Small."

She cracks a smile and pours me a little.

> **Blake: Don't mind her. She's suspicious of anyone who comes to a winery and doesn't do a tasting.**
>
> **Me: Oh, I didn't mean to be rude.**
>
> **Blake: You weren't. But thanks for placating her.**

I raise my glass to Sarah and taste. The deep robust flavor rolls around my tongue, bursting in my mouth and awakening my taste buds as if they've been as dormant as the grapevines.

"Wow. Good," I sign emphatically.

Sarah smiles triumphantly. Then she hands a glass to Maisy. I'm flabbergasted. I mean, I don't know anything about growing up in a winery, but do they expect Maisy to… *drink?*

Blake doubles over, his shoulders shaking with laughter. I still don't know what to make of it. I swat his arm and ask, "What?"

He must have said something to his family, because they all join in the laughter.

**Blake: It's non-alcoholic grape juice. Who do you think we are?**

Relief floods through me while at the same time I chuckle at my assumption.

Chris gestures to the bar top. "Please, enjoy some snacks."

"Thank you," I sign.

While Maisy, Sarah and I graze on food and I teach them the signs for bread, cheese, and grape juice, Blake and his sister talk in the far corner. I appreciate the fact that they don't talk right next to me when having a private conversation. Hearing people don't understand how rude it is to talk right in front of you when you aren't meant to be included. They just assume that because you can't hear them, it's okay. He gets it. He had the decency to move 'out of earshot' so to speak. Sometimes it amazes me how quickly he's picked up on Deaf culture.

Blake joins us, popping a slice of gouda into his mouth. He half-grins, looking all mysterious and sexy as he types out a text.

**Blake: Allie offered to babysit tonight. She knows I haven't been out in weeks. How about it, El, join me for dinner?**

*El.* He has a nickname for me. Butterflies dance in my stomach. I told myself I'd consider it if he asked again. It could be dangerous going down a rabbit hole I have no business going down. Especially considering who and what he is. Besides, what if I agree and we don't click?

*You know you do.*

What if we have nothing in common?

*We have Maisy.*

126

What if—
Blake taps my shoulder and nods to my phone.

**Blake: You have to admit we're electric together.**

I stare into his eyes before I reply.

**Me: Maybe that's exactly what I'm afraid of.**

# Chapter Fourteen

## Blake

I buzz the security intercom on her building. After a few seconds, I realize what an idiot I am.

**Me: I'm outside your building.**

**Ellie: You pressed the buzzer, didn't you?**

I laugh.

**Me: Are you letting me up, or what?**

She doesn't answer. It's not like I haven't been in her apartment before. I did help her move the TV up. But this is different. This is a date. Wait, she knows it's a date, doesn't she? I mean I didn't come out and say it was, but she knows… *right?*

I look around the complex and see a few familiar faces. Ah, man. Maybe she's afraid someone will see us together and it'll get back to her boss. Of course she's been hesitant to go out with me.

It could jeopardize her job. I shove a hand into my jeans pocket. I should have waited in the car. I quickly fire off a text to Lloyd's, canceling the reservation I made.

The door opens and Ellie appears. And... *Jesus.* Hell yeah she knows this is a date. Those luscious lips are pink and shimmery and totally kissable. Her jeans hug every curve and taper down to the beige wedges that bring her a few inches nearer to my height, though I still pretty much tower over her. A pink blouse that matches her lips is a little transparent, giving a peek to the tight tank top beneath. The twitch in my pants reminds me how badly I want to peek beneath.

She blushes under my perusal.

This woman. She's strong. Independent. A professional. She has a PhD for cryin' out loud. Yet when she blushes around me and those freckles appear, she seems so goddamn innocent.

"You look beautiful," I say and sign.

The redness on her cheeks doesn't abate. "Thank you."

She signs something I don't understand.

I cock my head.

**Ellie: You're not so bad yourself.**

I blow on my fingertips and shine them on my shirt collar.

She rolls her eyes.

We walk to my car. I hold the door for her, not losing sight of the fact that she's the only woman I've ever held the door for.

Once I'm inside, I face her. "Change of plans. I was going to take you to Lloyd's." I fingerspell the name of the restaurant. "But it's close to your work, and I don't want to get you into trouble or make you feel uncomfortable. Mind if we drive over to White Plains for dinner instead? It won't take that long."

"Okay," she signs, then takes out her phone.

**Ellie: It's not against the rules per se, but I agree with keeping work and private life separate. You didn't tell Maisy where you were going, did you? It might give her the wrong idea.**

The wrong idea? As in, Maisy might think I like Ellie? I do— like her. I like her a lot. But I get the worry. She wouldn't want Maisy to get hurt if this doesn't work out. My heart squeezes. Maisy isn't the only one who would get hurt. Damn. I'm not sure I like this feeling. It's odd. Different for sure. Confusing. But at the same time... warm.

I just shake my head to answer and then start the car.

The ride is silent, but not at all awkward. Which is also different. We share glances and smiles. I have the urge to hold her hand but surmise it's too soon. Or maybe I'm just afraid she'll pull away. *Wow... what in the ever-loving fuck is wrong with me?* I've never been so nervous, careful, and chivalrous around a woman. *Why her?*

In twenty-five minutes, we're in White Plains. I didn't make a reservation so I hope we can get into the French restaurant Mom's always raving about.

After I exit the car and hand my keys to the valet, I hustle around to Ellie's side. I don't take her hand, as I'm still unsure what she thinks of all this. I do, however, put a palm on the small of her back as we approach the entrance. She stiffens at my touch, then relaxes. The relief rushing through me is as immediate as it is unexpected.

Inside, the hostess asks, "Name on the reservation?"

"Ah, damn. I don't have a reservation. Coming here was spontaneous."

"We have a two-hour wait for walk-ins, sir."

"Blake Montana?" someone shouts behind me.

I turn to see a tall brunette who looks vaguely familiar. She's wearing a tight dress and is heavily pregnant.

She walks toward me sporting a smile. "You have no idea who I am, do you?" She rolls her eyes when she sees my deer-in-headlights look. "It's okay, we were kind of drunk that night. I'm Julie. From school?"

My eyes go to her belly and suddenly I'm terrified. I look at Ellie wondering if she's picking up any of this. She looks more than a little uncomfortable.

"Julie. Of course. Sorry about that."

She touches her belly and chortles. "Oh my god. You didn't think…" Laughter bellows out of her. "Shit, I think I might have just peed a little." A man comes up next to her. "Blake, this is my husband, Tim Hanson. Tim, this is Blake Montana. We took Business Analytics together."

I breathe a sigh of relief. I took that class two years ago. I do *not* need another surprise after what I've been through.

"This is Ellie," I say and sign. I turn to Ellie and fingerspell Julie and Tim.

"Oh," Julie says to Ellie. "You're deaf. Cool." She overdramatically waves at her.

"Mr. Montana?" the hostess calls behind me.

I wasn't aware I gave her my name. I turn and wait for her to continue.

The hostess smiles. "Your table is ready."

"What happened to the two-hour wait?"

"Your parents are some of our best customers," she says. "Right this way."

Not about to balk at the special treatment—after all, I'm trying to impress my date tonight—I say goodbye to Julie and Tim and motion for Ellie to follow the hostess.

We're seated in a nice booth by the window with a view of the sunset. Ellie sits across from me, and I wonder, if we became a couple, would she always sit across from me? It would make it easier to talk, but the thought of it makes me momentarily sad. Like I'd be missing out on holding her hand or pressing against her thigh.

"Hi. I'm Makenna. I'll be your waitress this evening." She hands us each a menu, and I stifle an eye roll knowing this is the kind of masochistic restaurant that only has prices on one menu—and they assume that one goes to the man. "Can I get you a drink?"

I look at Ellie and sign and say, "Do you want a drink? Wine?"

Of course I learned the sign for wine. I had to. But to an onlooker, it might seem like I'm swatting a bug off my face or something.

"Are you okay?" the waitress asks, following the motion of my hands.

"She's deaf," I say and sign.

"Oh." Makenna turns to Ellie and says very loudly and slowly, "WOULD YOU LIKE A DRINK?"

*Jesus Christ.*

I've done a lot of research into deafness and Deaf culture over the past few weeks, wanting to learn everything I possibly can about it for Maisy's sake and mine. One thing I've learned is that a lot of hearing people just don't get it.

"For fuck's sake," I snap. "She's not hard of hearing. And she's not stupid. She's deaf."

Ellie taps my leg under the table and shakes her head. Then she signs, "Wine. You pick."

"I'm really sorry, sir," the waitress says.

I sigh. "Yeah. We'll have two glasses of Caymus."

"Coming right up."

> **Ellie: A lot of people don't know any better. It's fine, Blake. You don't need to defend me.**

> **Me: Well, they should know better.**

> **Ellie: Did you?**

> **Me: Yeah. I suppose. I mean, I grew up in a town with a Deaf and Blind school, so maybe I know a tiny bit more than the general population.**

> **Ellie: It's annoying at times, but you learn to let it roll right off you. You'll have to for Maisy's sake. You don't want her to see you getting angry with people because she's deaf. That may give her the idea that being deaf is somehow a bad thing. It's not.**

Surprised by her words, I tilt my head and study her. "You really don't think it is, do you?"

**Ellie: If you're asking me if I mind being deaf, the answer is no. And with a little luck, Maisy will grow up feeling the same way. Like I've said before, if you treat her like she has a disability, she may come to think of herself as disabled. Deafness, while technically falling under the disability umbrella, is not seen as such by most of us. It just means we often need extra accommodations so we have access to communication. But most will agree it's definitely not a disability.**

Wine gets placed in front of us by a groveling waitress. She looks right at Ellie and nods to her menu. Then in a normal tone, asks, "Do you know what you'd like?"

It's a little dark in here, so I'm not sure Ellie can read the lips of a total stranger, but she knows what she's asking, and she points to something on her menu.

"Salad with that?" Makenna asks.

Ellie fingerspells, "Ranch," and I relay it.

"And you sir?"

"Surprise me," I say. "I'll have whatever she's having."

I see Ellie's amusement out of the corner of my eye.

**Ellie: If you're trying to impress me by bringing me to this place, it won't work.**

"Damn. You got me. What *would* it take to impress you, Dr. Stone?"

She smirks and studies me for a moment.

**Ellie: You have no idea how much you already have. The things you've done for Maisy. The way you've accepted her into your life. The effort you're putting into everything.**

**Me: Now I'm the one blushing.**

She looks up from her phone and laughs silently.

I wave a hand around. "Tell me why this doesn't impress you."

**Ellie: I grew up coming to places like this. Not all the time, but sometimes. My parents are wealthy.**

I furrow a brow at this new information. "What do they do?"

**Ellie: My dad is a doctor. An MD. But that's not where the money comes from. In fact he runs a free clinic in the city. He and his brothers inherited a lot from my great grandparents.**

"But you live in such a modest apartment."

"Your house is small," she signs.

"It is not."

**Ellie: Compared to the size of your bank account, or your parents' anyway, I'd say it is.**

**Me: Okay, fine. So neither of us goes around flaunting it. Just one more thing we have in common.**

"One more?" she mouths.

I love the way her mouth moves. It reminds me of our kiss. She rarely mouths words, but I catch her doing it sometimes when she's signing just a simple word or two.

"Well, let's see. We both live in Calloway Creek. We come from money but don't advertise it. And we both love Maisy."

**Ellie: I wanted to ask you something. I know you love her, even in the short time you've known her. But I see the way you look when Maisy hugs me or your mom. Do you not hug her?**

**Me: I want to. You have no idea how much I want to. I'm afraid I'll scare her. I'm not sure she wants to hug me. She's more standoffish with me than she is with you, my mom, and Allie. Maybe it's because she never had a father figure? I guess I was just waiting for her to want a hug, or initiate one, or whatever. Do you think I'm wrong?**

**Ellie: Actually, I think just about everything you've done is right. Do you mind if I ask about her past? What happened to her? Is her mom alive? What brought her to you? I mean, if you're comfortable speaking of it.**

I spend most of our meal explaining what happened. It takes a long time because I text most of it between bites. And by the time I'm done, I realize, aside from my family, Ellie may know Maisy and me better than anyone else.

**Ellie: I have one more question. I saw the look on your face when you were talking to that woman out front. Did you think the baby she's carrying was yours?**

I frown. Time to get real. After all, I just told her Maisy was the product of a fling.

**Me: I'm not going to lie. I was a bit of a player in college. Even in grad school. I'm sure eventually you'll hear things about me. It's a small town. Word gets around.**

**Ellie: I already have.**

My eyebrows go halfway up my forehead. "And you still agreed to dinner?"

She shrugs and dips her lobster in butter then plunges it into her mouth. A bit of butter remains on her chin, and I lean over and wipe it with my thumb. Our eyes lock and I'm taken back to the very first time I saw her in the grocery store. Electricity sizzles between us. No words need to be spoken or signed. We both feel it. Every time I touch her it's like all my nerve endings instantly come alive.

I've been with countless women. Even liked some a lot. But never, not once, have I felt the way Ellie makes me feel. I'm tempted to tell her, but I don't. I'll scare her away. But surely she knows it. My eyes tell the story, right? Just like hers do. She wants me as badly as I want her. She's thinking about the way I wiped her chin. The soft contact of my thumb against her face and the intimacy it suggested. She's thinking of how our lips fit perfectly together the one time we kissed. And about how we don't need words to convey our feelings.

One thing niggles at the back of my mind, though. Maybe all deaf are like this and I'm reading too much into it. Perhaps her expressive eyes, her comfortable silence, her easy demeanor, are simply traits deaf people acquire during their lives and I'm misinterpreting it for what... lust?

I definitely can't say anything now. She'd run for the hills and maybe even assign another mentor to work with Maisy. No, I'll have to keep my secret for now. The secret that I think I may have fallen for her.

*Jesus, Blake, what are you, a horny adolescent on his first date? Man the fuck up and quit acting like a lovesick puppy.*

I reach into the far corners of my mind for something I can talk about that will make her less appealing.

It's hard. Really really hard. Luckily, I end up not having to think of anything as she sends another text.

> **Ellie: Maisy and I are more alike than you know. We've both been hurt in some way by a parent. While I've never known the neglect she had to endure, I was abandoned by my biological father.**

I sit back and urge her to continue.

Ellie: I mean, it turned out to be a good thing because he hit my mom. She ran away when she found out she was pregnant with me. That's when she met my dad—the man who adopted me. He was her doctor. After I was born, my mom and biological father had a run-in where he found out about me. It's not that I wanted him to be my dad or anything, but I know in the back of my mind I may never truly understand how someone could reject a child for not being perfect.

"He didn't want you because you're deaf?"
She nods.
"He's a stupid fucker."
She narrows her eyes at me and signs, "Say again."
I fingerspell, "Stupid fucker."
She shows me how to sign it.
The waitress comes to clear our plates and offer dessert. Ellie signs, "It's late. We should go," so I ask for the check instead.
Someone's phone rings in the booth behind me, their ringtone a popular tune that reminds me of our car ride to the winery.

Me: Can you tell me about the music in the car? Did you think Maisy would be able to hear it? Because I was told it was unlikely she could hear much of anything.

Ellie: No, I didn't think she could hear it. But she could feel it.

"Like the vibrations?"

> Ellie: It's more than just that. Different frequencies and vibrations are felt through the cavities in the body. Tactile vibrations are especially felt through the soles of the feet and the palms of the hands. Music doesn't just land in your auditory canal, it flows through your body. It can affect your mood, even your heartbeat depending on the rhythm, harmony, and tempo of the music.

She snickers then bites her lip as she sends another text.

> Ellie: I'm sorry. I fear I may have created a monster. She may want to listen to music all the time now. Your poor neighbors.

"Poor neighbors?" I scoff with an amused snort. "What about poor *me?*"

> Ellie: I'll buy you some earplugs. Try to be accommodating. Just as music can be inspirational for hearing people, it can have the same effect on the deaf. Don't be surprised if you end up buying an expensive sound system that Maisy can sit on and 'listen' to.

"You feel it through the soles of your feet, huh?"
She nods.

"So then, maybe we could go dancing sometime?"

She shrugs, "Maybe."

Disappointment courses through me at the non-committal response.

Ellie looks down at her phone, brows furrowed.

I tap her foot with mine and when she looks up, I ask, 'What?"

**Ellie: For the past week, I've gotten a call from the same unknown number.**

I shake my head. "Spam."

**Ellie: I suppose. But miraculously, I've managed to keep my number off the spam lists. And this particular call seems to come right around the same time every day. But it's strange, because everyone who knows me knows I can't answer a call unless it's a video one.**

**Me: I'm sure it's a robocall. It's impossible to stay off the spam lists forever.**

The check gets delivered and after Makenna takes my payment tableside, I get up and offer Ellie my elbow. "Shall we?"

She appraises it longer than I hoped she would, but then she stands and weaves her arm around mine. Those same nerve endings come to life again, as if they're dormant unless she's touching me.

As soon as I start the car, I turn on the radio. Loud. And find a song with lots of bass. She cracks a smile and places her palm on the speaker.

Thirty minutes later, my ears ringing, I pull into her parking lot and turn off the music.

"Thanks for dinner," she signs, and goes for the door.

I put a hand on her arm, urging her to wait, then I get my phone.

**Me: You said you were afraid earlier. You're afraid of us being good together?**

She shakes her head. Then she shrugs.

I'm confused. Then it dawns on me that maybe she's afraid of falling for me.

I turn on the overhead light. "Ellie, have you been hurt by a man before? Other than your birth father?"

She shakes her head again.

"Have you had long-term relationships?"

**Ellie: I've had boyfriends. Never relationships really.**

What does that even mean? I'm not one to speak. I've never had one either. Did she sleep her way through school like I did? Or is it something else? She used the word abandoned when mentioning her father. Does she have abandonment issues?

**Ellie: Don't read too much into that, Blake. School was my sole focus for a long time.**

"Go out with me again," I say, putting my hand on top of hers.

She pulls away to sign, "Good idea?"

"Hell yes it's a good idea. Didn't you have fun tonight?"

**Ellie: I did. What I mean is do you think it's a good idea because of Maisy.**

**Me: Come on, El. You didn't get where you are today without taking chances. Go dancing with me. It'll be no big deal. We'll go back to White Plains. I promise it'll be fun. We'll go someplace loud.**

I put down my phone, plug my ears with my fingers, open my mouth wide, and blink my eyes.

She snorts quick bursts of air through her nose in laughter. "Okay," she signs.

"Yes!" I shout, turning away, embarrassed about my childish excitement.

**Ellie: Under one condition. You call Dallas and tell him about Maisy.**

It's something I've dreaded doing for two weeks. I didn't want him to hear about it from anyone but me, but I know it'll hurt him. Still, I know I have to. And Ellie is right. It's time. "Okay," I sign.

She smiles and nods.

"Can I walk you in?"

She shakes her head, waves, then exits the car. She looks back before she enters her building, hesitating, as if she wants to say something. She could, she's fully under the lights. She could sign to me if she wanted to. But she doesn't. She just stares. I'm sure she can't see my eyes through the windshield in the dark, but I swear they connect with hers anyway. And that feeling—that warmth—floods throughout me like a rogue wave.

This woman has no idea what she's doing to me.

And for that matter—neither do I.

# Chapter Fifteen

## Blake

At home, after getting the third degree from Allie and sending her on her way, I stand in Maisy's doorway and watch her sleep. As always, her stuffed cat is tucked tightly against her chest as if it will somehow protect her.

I think of calling Dallas, and I swallow hard. Maisy has only been in my life for a few short weeks, and I already know I'd be devastated if she died. Before she came into my life, I was just Blake, Chris Montana's son and heir to the winery. Now... now I'm Maisy's father—a far better title if you ask me.

I'm a fucking dad. My eyes get misty just thinking about trying to go back to how life was before my daughter came into it. Yes, it was simpler. But far less rewarding. She's my reason for... *everything* now.

Back out in the kitchen, I pop the top off a bottle of beer and sit at the bar. I go through the pictures in my phone and stop when I find one of Dallas, Phoebe, and DJ. DJ would be two-and-a-half now. He'd be walking and talking. He'd be coming over for playdates with Maisy. And I just know Phoebe and Ellie would have been fast friends.

It's been two years since they died, but honestly, how much time is enough time to get over losing someone you love? Losing *two* someones. I can't even imagine. And now I'm going to break his fucking heart by telling him I have a child. How could he ever be happy for me? Will he be able to be an uncle to her? Will he even want to meet her?

I drain my beer, open one more, and realize I've procrastinated long enough. I open my contacts and tap on his name.

He answers immediately. "So you *haven't* fallen off the face of the earth."

I get it. He's the CFO and I'm the COO. Even though he works remotely from his cabin upstate, we usually hop on a business call several times a week. But I haven't sent him any weekly stats recently. Haven't returned his texts. Of course he's wondering what's going on.

"Sorry. Just got super busy with life, brother."

"You decide the job's not for you? How come the reports are coming from Dad again?"

"So, about that. I want the job. But I've had to cut back on my hours for a while because... well, because something's happened, and well... I'm not sure, uh—"

"Spit it the fuck out, Blake. What's going on? You've never been one to be at a loss for words."

"Alright. Here it goes." I blow out a breath, hoping I'm not going to drive a stake into his heart. "A few weeks ago I found out I have a kid."

Silence. And breathing. I don't say anything else. I let him absorb the news.

"No shit?" he finally says. "You have a baby?" I don't miss the way his voice cracks at the last word.

"No. I have a four-and-a-half-year-old daughter. Her name is Maisy."

"What the hell? And you're saying you knew nothing about her until a few weeks ago?" He scoffs. "Wait, why the fuck did you wait so long to tell me? This is kind of huge news." I don't answer. "Right, you thought I'd freak out."

"Are you?"

"I… I mean it's a shock, and yeah, maybe it's going to keep me up tonight, but what's new. I barely sleep anyway. So how exactly did this happen?"

I hate to hear that he's still not sleeping. He told me once that when he sleeps, he dreams of them. So he hates to sleep. I have no idea what he does all night instead. He never talks to me about anything but business anymore. In fact, we haven't had such a personal conversation in a long time.

I tell him about the private investigator, the paternity test, the social worker, and Lucinda's neglect. "Dallas, Maisy is profoundly deaf. Lucinda didn't teach her any sign language. She basically hasn't had any way to communicate."

"Jesus, seriously? How are you dealing with it?"

"Luckily, the Deaf school is here, and they assigned a mentor to work with us. Maisy has already made so much progress. We're both learning ASL, and at least she can communicate her basic needs. But it's a challenge. Dallas, I'm not even sure she knows I'm her father."

"Wow. That's… messed up."

"And the worst part is that after Lucinda does her stint in rehab, she could petition for custody."

"The worst part. So you want full custody?"

"Hell yeah, I do. I don't want her anywhere near that woman. Who doesn't bother teaching their kid to communicate? We don't even know yet, she could have permanently inhibited Maisy's ability to learn."

"Hmm."

"What does that mean?"

"I suppose I'm surprised you're being so responsible. I never pegged you for the parenting type."

I laugh. "Me neither. Do you... want to meet her?"

He sighs. "Sure. Someday."

"Maybe when you come for Lucas's wedding?"

"You don't seriously think he'll go through with it this time, do you?"

"Hell if I know, but he's going through the motions. You're coming right? You know you'll be pissed if he actually goes through with it and you missed it."

"I guess I would. But, Blake?"

"Yeah?"

"I'm not sure I'll make a very good uncle. I'm happy for you if this is what you want though. And I'm happy to go stag with you to the wedding."

"Maybe. But, uh, I'm sort of hoping I'll have a date."

"A date? To Lucas's wedding? That's pretty significant. I didn't even know you were seeing someone."

"Probably because you never ask. And I'm not really. But I want to be. It's Maisy's mentor. Dal, she's fucking amazing. The way she is with her. And she's beautiful, and new to Cal Creek, and when I'm with her, I don't know, something just feels—"

I stop talking. Because, shit. His wife is dead. I shouldn't be telling him about this.

"Feels what?"

"Forget it."

He scoffs. "Blake, you don't have to wear kid gloves around me."

"Says the guy who hasn't returned home in two years."

"Listen, if you've got a lady and a kid, I'm happy for you. But, you should be careful. Honestly, you were probably better off before. Loving people can only lead to heartbreak."

How do I even respond to that?

"But you'll come to the wedding?"

"Yeah. Sure. Whatever."

"And you'll meet Maisy?"

"Just don't expect much, Blake. I'll do what I can do."

"I don't expect anything. I just want her to know her family because I'm pretty sure before this she had no one."

"Well, if you've got nothing, you have nothing to lose."

"Is that how you plan to live the rest of your life? With nothing?"

"Get off my back, little brother. I get enough of that from Mom."

He starts talking business. That's how I know he's done with this conversation. Business is all he's done since they died. That and whatever the hell he does up there in his cabin to keep himself busy.

We spend the next half-hour talking about the profit/loss statements Dad sent out last week.

After we hang up, I stare at the picture of Dallas and his family and think about his words. *If you've got nothing, you have nothing to lose.*

And they hit me square in the gut. Because in such a short period of time I've acquired so much that I can lose.

# Chapter Sixteen

## Ellie

"Maisy is really coming along," Patricia Kasey signs. "I've never seen anything quite like it."

"She's a special girl," I sign, looking at Maisy over Patricia's shoulder as she plays kickball on the playground with the other kids.

She kicks the ball, jumps up and down, sees me, and runs over, arms stretched wide. I accept her hug, but at the same time, I can't stop thinking about what Blake said the other night about waiting for her to want to hug him.

I turn to Patty. "Mind if I take her for the last thirty minutes? There's something I've been wanting to work with her on."

"Go ahead."

"Come with me," I sign to Maisy, delighted she now understands simple instructions.

My shirt is tugged from behind, and I spin around and look down to see little Bobby Miller. "It's Maisy's turn," he signs. But instead of fingerspelling Maisy or pointing to her, he does a name sign.

My heart gets stuck in my throat. Being given a name sign by peers is somewhat of a rite of passage for the deaf. And even if Maisy doesn't understand what a major milestone this is, I do. She's a part of something much bigger than her small world now. My throat thickens as I bask in the triumphant moment.

"I need Maisy now," I sign, using her newly minted name sign. "She'll play again tomorrow."

He nods and looks at her, waving goodbye.

Taking Maisy's hand, I guide her to my office and ask her to sit down while I gather what I need. I have a large folder full of drawings Maisy and I have done that help us communicate. I quickly make a few others as well, realizing what my mistake might have been before when I tried to teach Maisy about 'father.'

Sitting next to her, I spread out the drawings and flashcards. Like before, most of the pictures are of men with children or babies, and I take special care to make sure all of the children are girls. No need to confuse her further. Then there are the drawings of her with Blake. But what I add this time are pictures of men all by themselves. To simplify things and stick with what she already knows, I use the sign for 'boy' instead of 'man.'

I point to each man in each picture and sign, "Boy."

Then I point to the flashcard of a man holding a baby. I spread out my fingers, bring them to my forehead and tap my thumb twice against it. It's the sign for dad, daddy, or father.

I point to the drawing of Blake and Maisy and sign, "Daddy." I point to the other pictures of men with children and do the same. Then I motion for her to try.

She points to one of the pictures of a man with a child and does the sign for Daddy. But then she does it again when she points to the picture of the single man. I shake my head and go over the exercise again hoping that eventually she'll understand that all men are boys but that only men with children are daddies.

She stomps her foot, something she does when she gets frustrated.

I label all the men in the pictures again as 'boy.' Then, again, I only point to the fathers and do the sign for Daddy. I pull out my phone and show her the picture I took of her and Blake at the winery the other day. I try not to think about how I've looked at this picture far more than I'd like to admit.

"Boy," I sign, pointing to Blake. "Girl," I sign, pointing to her in the picture. "Daddy," I sign again at Blake.

I point to one of the single men. "Boy," I sign. Then I shake my head. "Not Daddy."

I again show her the flashcard of the man and baby and do the signs for boy, baby, and daddy. Then I go back to the single man, only doing the sign for boy.

I ask her to do it. She studies all the pictures. I'm fascinated at the way her nose crinkles when she's thinking. It's the same thing Blake does. Every day, I notice more similarities between them. The slopes of their noses. The shape of their fingers.

It's hard not to think about Blake. I thought about him all weekend. Maybe I even missed him. I was surprised when he didn't kiss me Friday night. I know I told him not to walk me to the door, but part of me wanted him to. Then again, if this is just some kind of fling, he wouldn't do that. But if it's a fling, wouldn't he have tried to sleep with me?

I had a video call with Beth later that night. She knew about the date. She also knows about his reputation. She told me to go for it anyway. After all, I'm not one for relationships and she knows it. She asked how bad could it be—having a few romps with the hot single dad.

Maybe all he wants is a friends-with-benefits kind of thing, although we've yet to 'benefit.' I mean, this is Blake Montana. Everyone knows his reputation precedes him. Oddly, I'm beginning to be okay with it. I'm just starting my career. I have enough to focus on without having to coddle a relationship—one with a hearing man no less. Yes, I'm perfectly fine with Blake and I being a pleasant distraction from other things in life.

I shake off the thoughts racing in my head when Maisy starts signing. She points to all the men, doing the sign for 'boy.' She studies the drawings and flashcards. She looks at the picture on my phone. She points to the man holding the baby. "Daddy," she signs.

I nod.

She points to the drawing of her and Blake. "Daddy."

"Yes," I sign, hope growing in my chest.

She points to the drawing of a man with a child. "Daddy."

"Good," I sign. I point to the single man.

She looks between all of them then signs, "Boy."

I do jazz hands.

She smiles.

Does she get it? I still don't know. She could have no idea what it all means, only that those are the signs I wanted her to repeat for each picture. But it's these baby steps that will eventually lead to big strides.

The Pre-K dismissal light flashes in the corner of my office and I motion to it. She understands that means it's time to go home.

I walk Maisy out, searching for Blake. He still parks and comes inside to collect her every day. I adore how protective he is of her.

Maisy spots him and stops. She points to him and signs, "Daddy."

Emotions flow through me as I lock eyes with Blake, his shocked and impassioned expression confirming he saw her sign. He races over, and for a moment, his arms open. But then they fall to his sides as he lowers to his knees in front of her.

*Hug him,* I implore in my thoughts.

But it doesn't happen. She does, however, see our excited reaction and do the sign again.

Blake looks up at me. "Did she just call me… Daddy?"

I nod and smile, my heart growing larger on the spot.

Maisy turns and points to another man collecting his child. "Daddy," she signs.

As Blake's expression deflates, I quickly retrieve my phone.

**Me: It's okay. She's learned today that all men are boys but that only men with children are fathers.**

"Ellie." He hesitates. "Does she know I'm her father?"

I shrug. Because I don't know. All I can do is hope. "Baby steps," I sign.

He nods sadly, stands, and takes her hand. "See you at four."

I watch them leave, sad for the man who desperately wants his daughter to know who he is. I find myself disappointed that he doesn't turn and give me one last look like he usually does.

When they're both completely out of sight, I go back to my office, scolding myself for being so selfish.

# Chapter Seventeen

## Blake

Ellie arrives at six. She reached out earlier asking to push our appointment back due to another client needing immediate attention.

"Everything okay?" I say and sign.

"Yes. Thank you for changing the time."

At least I think that's what she signed. I don't know the sign for change. I do the sign back to her and furrow my brows. She fingerspells 'change.'

I'm starting to pick up more and more signs. A lot of it is just filling in the blanks when I don't get it. I feel like it's the same with Ellie when she reads lips. Context is very important.

Maisy was acting out earlier. She's gotten used to Ellie coming every Monday, Wednesday, and Friday at four. Although I doubt she can tell time, she's gotten used to the routine. And when I fed her dinner *before* Ellie came over, she noticed and got visibly upset. She even hid in her closet for a bit until she smelled her favorite dinner—grilled cheese. She pouted the whole time she ate, pointing to the drawing of Ellie. I kept signing 'soon,' but either she doesn't understand the concept or is just super impatient like any other four-year-old.

I don't tell Ellie about Maisy's outburst. The last thing I want is for Ellie to feel guilty.

Ellie spends an hour teaching us today's lesson. Maisy and I learn the signs for many things you'd find outdoors: lake, tree, clouds, sun, rain, park, bench, sidewalk.

Maisy becomes disinterested and fussy more quickly than usual.

"She's tired," Ellie signs. "We should take a break."

She pulls out her phone.

**Ellie: Speaking of outdoors and sidewalks, did you notice the new road sign out front?**

"It's here?" I ask, surprised.

She nods.

I slide Maisy's iPad over and open a game. Then Ellie and I go out on the front lawn. There's a large yellow sign that reads **DEAF CHILD AREA** smack dab in front of my house. My mind skips back to the night Maisy nearly got hit, and I'm relieved drivers will now have a heads-up to be careful in the area.

Walking back into the house, I hear voices on the sidewalk. I turn to see three teens passing by the sign and acting like imbeciles. One drags a foot behind him like a zombie. Another holds crooked hands in front of his chest as if he's brain damaged. The third rolls his eyes up in his head and hangs his tongue out of the side of his mouth.

Fuming, I take steps toward them. "You little fuckers!" As I approach, they laugh and run away.

"What?" Ellie signs.

I get out my phone, my temple throbbing.

> **Me: Those kids. They saw the sign and were acting like stupid assholes. I should go after them and give them a goddamn piece of my mind. Who the fuck do they think they are?**

She puts a hand on my arm and shakes her head.

> **Ellie: I know that upsets you, but don't fight her battles. Especially when she didn't even see it happen. People are cruel. They think deafness is somehow associated with lower intelligence. But let me tell you, Maisy is bright. And stubborn. Soon enough she'll be able to fight her own battles.**

I look up. "Did you? Have to fight your own battles?"

> **Ellie: Did and do. There are stereotypes and misinformation about the deaf. Every day I get looked at as if I'm different. She will too. Try to accept that now, Blake. You can't change the world. The best you can do is educate people whenever you can.**

"I'd like to educate those little fuckers," I mumble.

"Say again?" she signs.

"Nothing. Let's go back inside."

In the house, Maisy has fallen asleep on the couch, her iPad lying by her side. I'm so fucking pissed about those boys. Is this what lies in store for her? Is she destined for a life of being mocked by ignorant people? I'll do anything to make it easier for her. I just don't have any clue how.

Ellie taps me on the shoulder. She gets how pissed I am, but she smiles anyway. "Guess what?" she signs.

"What?"

**Ellie: I forgot to tell you earlier. Something great happened today. Maisy got her name sign.**

I've read about name signs and how they are a shortened version of a person's name, usually representing a physical characteristic, personality trait, or hobby. "Name sign?" I ask, wanting to learn more.

Ellie's right hand comes up next to her hair, and with her pointer finger facing upward, she spirals it down the side of her head.

**Ellie: It's because of her spiral curls.**

"You came up with it?" I ask.

"No. Children at school."

I look at her sideways, trying to get a better grip on the concept. "*You* have a name sign, don't you? I vaguely remember you telling me so the first time we met."

With her palm open and facing toward her face, she taps her middle finger twice on her cheek.

"What does that mean?"

She fingerspells 'freckles' and does the ASL sign for it.

"Makes sense," I say. "Your freckles definitely come out when you blush. Your parents must have noticed that early on."

> **Ellie: My parents didn't give me the name sign. Name signs can only be given by Deaf, not the hearing. It's a rite of passage. I went to a public school where I was the only deaf student, so I didn't get my name sign until college.**

"Tell me how."

She rolls her eyes. Then she blushes, her freckles appearing as if to validate the meaning of her name sign. Oh, this is going to be good.

I raise my brows, waiting.

She scoffs, then starts texting.

> **Ellie: It was given to me my freshman year at Gallaudet. I had a professor who was very handsome. Younger than most. And every time he called on me, I'd blush. It didn't take long for me to be given the name sign. About Maisy, though, this is a big deal. It means she's part of the Deaf community. You should be happy her peers have taken to her so well. She's doing better than any of us anticipated.**

I look at my sleeping daughter, wishing she could understand just how proud of her I am.

I turn back to Ellie. "You had a crush on your teacher?"

She shrugs.

I laugh. "I completely understand. I seem to be having the same issue."

She blushes.

I laugh again and do her name sign.

I nod to Maisy. "She's had a long day. I'm going to put her to bed. Wait here?"

She signs, "I'll wait here," and raises a challenging brow.

I know this look. It means she wants me to sign. So I do. "You wait here."

Her satisfied grin tells me she's happy with that.

I wake Maisy enough to get her to use the toilet, brush her teeth, and change into pajamas. Once in bed, she's asleep before I get to page five in her favorite picture book.

When I go back out, I find Ellie staring at all the new drawings on the dining room table. Maisy loves to draw cats. She loves to watch videos about cats. She loves to play with her stuffed cat.

"She sure does love cats," I say. "I was considering getting her one. What do you think?"

"Good idea," she signs. "Teaches responsibility."

"I'm glad you like the idea. Will you go with us to the pet store? It could be a fun outing."

She shakes her head.

**Ellie: No. But I'll go with you to an animal shelter. You should adopt, not buy. She's too young to understand, but someday she will. Someone's unwanted pet is another person's best friend.**

I read her text several times wondering if the meaning is so much deeper. She herself was unwanted by someone. It's not the first time I've wondered just how much this affects everything she does. Too deep a conversation to get into right now.

"I should go," she signs.

"You don't have to. You could"—I start signing—"stay for a drink."

Her gaze goes to the door, then back to me as she contemplates my offer. She sticks up one finger.

Wasting no time, I smile and go into the kitchen for two wine glasses. Then I motion down the hallway and sign, "You pick the wine."

She looks amused and heads down the hall. Maisy's room used to be where I stored all my wine. But now, the wine racks have all been moved into my home office. Ellie flicks on the light and peruses the bottles. She pulls out and studies three or four before making her selection and handing it to me.

"You have great taste," I say, not telling her she picked the most expensive bottle in the lot. Not that she'd care.

It's interesting that Ellie and I both had the same type of upbringing. We were raised by very well-off families, sent to public schools not private, taught to appreciate our position, and brought up to respect money, not covet it. Yet sometimes I feel we're worlds apart. In an instant, it becomes my mission to close that gap.

Back in the kitchen, I open the bottle and pour her a glass. She sips it and groans audibly, as if she instantly knows it's of the highest quality. She licks her lips. That's it. I can't stand it any longer. I take her glass, put it on the counter and cage her against the refrigerator with my arms. "I should have done this the other night," I say, right before I lean in and kiss her.

Her lips part instantly for mine. My tongue darts into her mouth, knowing this kiss will be even better than the one before. Because today she tastes like my wine.

I moan into her mouth. She must feel the vibrations and her hands come up to grasp my neck. I snake mine around her back and hold her tightly to me as our tongues explore each other's mouths. We kiss until we're out of breath, then my lips trail down her jaw and the cords of her neck. She tastes divine.

She grips me harder, her hands tugging on my hair. I take the opportunity to work my hand around to her front, up the side of her rib cage and over her right breast. She gasps but doesn't pull away, breathing heavily as my lips capture hers again. With one hand back on my neck, her other runs down my arm and settles just above my ass. There's already nothing between us, but she presses firmly anyway. I like that she wants us closer even though we're as close as we can be.

Touching her over her shirt isn't enough. I want to feel her skin. See her breasts. Lick her nipples.

I grind my erection into her and whisper close to her ear, "I want to see you, Ellie."

*Shit.* I pull back, embarrassed that for a moment I forgot she can't hear me. I look into her eyes, gauging whether or not she felt my whisper on her ear. I don't think she did.

But pulling away has broken the spell. I can see it on her face.

"We can't," she signs. "Maisy."

"But you'd be okay if Maisy weren't in the other room?" I ask.

She bites her lip, shrugging.

Fuck me, that's a yes if I ever saw one. I get out my phone and make a quick call.

Ellie puts her hands on her hips, cocks her head, and gives me a questioning stare.

"Allie will be here in twenty minutes. We're going to your place."

# Chapter Eighteen

## Ellie

Riding in the passenger seat to my apartment, I'm all warm and tingly. And I can feel the dampness between my legs. Is this really happening?

Do I want it to? *Oh, my God, did I shave this morning?*

Second thoughts race through my mind. I'm crossing a line. Could we hurt Maisy?

Then Beth's words come back to me. *How bad could a few romps with him really be?*

I study him as he drives the short distance to my place. He is undoubtedly the most attractive man I've ever seen. But how much of that is based on him being a doting father?

I quickly make a list in my head of reasons why I shouldn't do what I think we're about to do.

1. He's a client.
2. He's not deaf.
3. He's no doubt got much more experience than I do.
4. …

Before I can get to 4, he reaches over and traps my hand against my thigh, his thumb rubbing circles against the side seam of my jeans. Just like when he trapped me against the refrigerator, I lose all sense of reason and decide there is no number 4, and that 1, 2, and 3 don't matter since this may well be a one-time thing. Even if it's a two-or-three-time thing, they don't matter.

Because all I can think about right now is Blake's hand on me. And if this one hand can cause such a visceral reaction, imagine what it will do when there aren't any clothes between us. When his hand is on my bare skin. My stomach. My thighs. My breasts. My—

The car stops, Blake turns with a wry smile and quickly exits the car, racing around to open the door for me before I can even gather up my things. He reaches in and grabs my messenger bag then extends his hand out to me. He's acting like this is a date when we both know this is nothing more than a hookup.

Then again, if this is how he treats all his past flings, I get why there have been so many of them. The man is beyond charming.

At the entrance to the building, I fumble with the code, having to enter it three times. I don't look to see if he noticed. He follows me up the stairs and into my apartment. The last time he was here, I still had unpacking to do. This time my place is tastefully put together and, thankfully, clean.

He glances around. "Nice," he signs. "How's the TV?"

"Good." I widen my eyes. "Big."

"It's bigger than mine."

"That's what he said," I quickly sign.

He narrows his eyes. He didn't pick it up. And I don't bother to explain. Instead, I tell him, "Good for closed captioning." I slowly fingerspell the last part so he understands.

His eyes concentrate on my hands. I'm not sure why that makes me feel all warm and gooey inside. Everyone concentrates on my hands when I sign. Maybe it's because I'm aware that his eyes will soon be focusing on much more than just my hands.

In an instant, I'm having more second thoughts.

He grabs my hand. "We don't have to do anything you don't want to. It's nice just being alone with you."

See—charming. It's that charm that has me wanting to jump into his arms and throw caution to the wind. Is he a jumping-into-arms kind of guy? We've spent a lot of time together, but I feel like I barely know him. One of the obstacles to being deaf is I'm not privy to all the information the hearing get. The overheard phone calls. The gossip in the coffee line. The side conversations. The under-the-breath comments. The only information we get is what others want to tell us. Nothing more. So there's always that question of—are we getting the whole story?

"Do you want a drink?" I ask.

He slowly shakes his head, his sultry stare burning into me.

"Have you eaten? I could make—"

He gives my hand a squeeze. "I don't want food or drink, Ellie. I just want you." He signs the last part.

My heart does three full revolutions inside my chest. No man has ever said that to me. It's sexy. And he doesn't know it, but I'm fairly sure I just became putty in his hands.

That caution?… I decide to throw it to the wind.

When I jump into his arms, he almost falls down and has to step back to steady us. He looks up at me, laughing. Oh, how I love the way his eyes crinkle when he laughs. And his teeth... What I want them to do to me has heat flushing my entire upper body.

This time, I'm the one initiating the kiss as my lips crash down onto his. With us holding on to each other, there's nowhere for hands to roam. There's no need, however, because our heated kiss says it all. That there's more to come. That this is just the tip of the iceberg. That what we're about to do to each other is everything we've both thought about for weeks.

Out of breath, I lean away. But with my hands gripping him tightly, I can't talk. I nod to the door on the right and mouth "bedroom."

I think he says, "Hell yeah." But I can't be sure. And since he's carrying me in that direction, it doesn't really matter.

My bedroom is dark. He puts me on the bed, hovers over me, then retreats. He turns the light on. It's a small gesture, but one that somehow etches him further into my soul.

"Do you want to keep the light on?" he asks.

I get out my phone.

**Me: Turn that one off but keep the door open. That way there will be enough light for me to see your face, but not enough so that you'll see all my imperfections.**

He reads the text then signs, "Show me imperfection," fingerspelling the last word.

I do the sign for imperfect, loving the fact that he's always eager to learn. There are a few parts to it as it really means inadequate, defective, or not perfect. I do it a few more times.

He repeats it. Then he says and signs, "Nothing about you is imperfect."

That's it. Stick a fork in me. My throat becomes thick with emotion. This man. This *hearing* man just called me perfect. I should get up now. I should run far away. Because I know, deep down, I'm falling for him. And falling for a guy like him can only lead to heartbreak. But damn it, the way he's looking at me right now has me cemented to the bed, my body unwilling to accept the facts that my mind has concluded.

So I do the opposite of run. I pull my shirt over my head, leaving him staring at my chest that's only covered by my nothing-special, didn't-know-this-would-happen bra.

"From now on, only my hands will take off your clothes," he says as clear as day, striding toward me.

He climbs onto the bed as my breath hitches at my racing thoughts. Thoughts of him removing my clothes. Of seeing Blake Montana naked. Of him touching me… everywhere.

"Same," I sign, making his smile appear once again.

"Whatever you want, Ellie." He does my name sign. Then he stills. "Is it okay if I do your name sign, or can only deaf people do it?"

I nod. "It's okay."

"Good. But don't be offended if—"

I don't catch the rest of his sentence in the dim light. I narrow my eyes. He retrieves his phone.

> **Blake: I said good, but please don't be offended if you see me screaming your name instead of signing it in a few minutes. I'm not sure I'll be able to help myself.**

He watches me as I read it. Then when I blush, he does my name sign and laughs.

"You are beautiful," he signs. "Beautiful Ellie."

I reach out, fist the front of his shirt, and pull him down to me. But this time, his lips don't crash into mine. They lightly brush them. Teasing. Taunting. He kisses one edge of my mouth, then the other. Then he kisses my neck, his tongue darting out to lick my skin. He works his mouth up to my ear where I feel his hot breath flow over my earlobe. I can't help it when my hips arch and press into him. I want him to touch me. I *need* him to do it.

I take one of his hands and press it to my chest, pushing down one of the cups of my bra to give him better access. He stares at my bare breast as his erection grows between us. I'm pretty sure he says, "Jesus," right before his mouth devours it.

My eyes close as I bask in the feeling of his mouth on me. His tongue toys with my nipple. His lips pucker as he sucks it into his mouth. His teeth ever so lightly graze it.

Vibrations dance in my throat. At the same time, Blake's head pops up, eyes wide. He's pleased that I moaned. Before he resumes what he was doing, he unclasps my bra and discards it completely. Then he looks down at his shirt and back at me.

I crack a smile and untuck his Montana Winery shirt. He ducks low as I pull it up and over his head. I almost mimic his word of praise when I see his chest. It's no wonder he has a gym in his house. The man is ripped. I trace a finger along the lower side of his pecs, then down along his ab muscles that ripple as I touch them. His eyes close briefly. Does he like the feel of my hands on him as much as I like his on me?

When his eyes open, there's a fire behind them I've never seen. A passion I've never witnessed. I swallow the fleeting thought that this could turn into more. I push it to the back of my mind and lock it inside a box along with other things I can never have:

closure with my birth father, and getting my virginity back from the asshole I gave it to.

I tense under him and he stills. "You okay?"

Instead of answering, I go for the button of his pants. He seems to like this reaction better anyway. What man wouldn't? He rolls to the side as I push his jeans down to his ankles. Then he toes off his shoes and wriggles them off completely.

He takes off my pants next. But not as quickly as I did his. No, it seems Blake Montana likes to see his women squirm. He slides them down slowly with his hands, his lips following the same route, stopping to kiss my bare thighs, the inside of a knee, my ankle. He discards my shoes and pants on top of his. Then he stares at my underwear. My plain, black, bikini undies that are surely drenched through.

Locking eyes with me, he touches the singular article of clothing, asking permission before taking it off. I nod. Of course I nod. Hell, at this point, I'd *beg* him to do it if he weren't already asking.

My panties come off far quicker than my jeans. I'm fully naked beneath his gaze. He stares. He stares *everywhere*. I'm fairly light-skinned, though I'm sure my entire body has turned a shade of red under his perusal. After what seems like forever, but has probably only been seconds, he looks up. "Show me perfect," he signs, fingerspelling the last word.

I show him. He devours my body with his eyes once again then signs, "Perfect."

*Thump.* My heart stops then restarts.

In an instant, I'm all too aware that I'm the only one naked. Not even asking for permission, I reach for his boxer briefs. In my haste to remove them, they get caught on his erection. I cringe hoping I didn't hurt him. But based on the way he's looking at me, I'd guess either I didn't, or he couldn't care less that I did.

Both fully naked now, I expect him to just hop on and get it over with. After all, that's what always happened in high school when the clothes came off. Heck, the clothes didn't all necessarily even come off back then, just enough to allow Tab A to go into Slot B.

He surprises me by not going right for it. Instead, he leans down and feasts hungrily on my breasts. He slips a hand between us and explores the apex of my thighs. He finds my opening, and I feel vibrations coming from his chest when he runs a hand through my wetness. Then he touches my clit, and... *holy god*... I almost come apart beneath him here and now.

It's not as if a guy has never touched me there. Most of them did, but only in passing on their way to Slot B. It's as if they didn't know the clitoris was the way to a woman's orgasm. Or maybe they just didn't care.

Blake, however, is taking his sweet time getting his fill of it. His thumb runs circles around it. His fingers draw up my arousal, making my clit slick and easier to manipulate. With his every ministration, I feel myself building higher and higher.

I'm reeling over how different this is from my other sexual experiences. What's happening now is like what I've seen in movies. Read about in books. It's everything I'd hoped sex was about, but doubted it existed. I suppose I was silly to think all of that was over-exaggeration. That all men were selfish and only after their own gratification.

In an attempt for *me* not to appear selfish, I reach for him. I'm no stranger to hand jobs. I gave a lot of them in my teenage years. Even prided myself on how good I was at it. Then again, I was handling sixteen-and-seventeen-year-old dicks. A light breeze could have gotten them off.

Deeper vibrations come from within him, making me smile. Perhaps I can give as well as I can get.

Stroking him is different than the others. He's a man. A strong, confident, competent man. Not a kid just looking to get his rocks off. Then again, who's to say Blake isn't just a strong, confident, competent man looking to get *his* rocks off?

At this point, though, I'm way too far along to care.

He stops what he's doing to me and pulls my hand away.

Okay then, maybe I *don't* know how to do this properly.

He says something I don't quite pick up.

He reaches for his phone that he left beside the pillow, wipes his other hand off on the sheets, and sends a text.

> **Blake: El, if you keep touching me, I'm going to come, and this will all be over in a matter of seconds. If this is heading where I think it is, the only place I want to come is buried deep inside of you.**

While I read his text, he gets a condom from his wallet and puts it on the bed next to him.

His penis is erect and engorged. And… *sigh… completely incredible.*

I toss my phone aside and crack a smile. I expect him to go for the condom, but he leaves it untouched, instead, kissing his way down my body. His lips move from my neck to my breasts and down across my stomach. I shiver in anticipation of him doing to me what no man has ever done. He's entering uncharted territory here. Beth has told me about it. She says it's amazing and the only way she can orgasm with a man.

Thoughts race through my mind. What will he get out of it? How will I taste? Did I wash myself well enough? What if I *don't* come?

But all thoughts cease when his tongue darts around my clit. *Oh. My. God.*

If I thought his fingers on me were divine, this is—

Wow, I have a PhD, yet I can't even think of any words to describe this.

As his tongue works on my clit, his fingers slip inside me. In and out. In and out. He crooks them and I feel myself croon, hum, sing, or... *something*. These are new vibrations coming from within. Something I've never felt before. Whatever sounds I make simply drive him to work harder.

Soon, my insides coil tightly. I'm no stranger to the feeling. I do have a drawer full of personal devices, after all. But never in my life have I been brought to these heights by a man. I'm on the precipice of explosion and one more push of his fingers has me detonating beneath him.

I buck and squeeze and groan and writhe and swirl and fall and fly. It's as if heaven and hell erupted. Good and evil collided. And he just keeps touching and rubbing and pressing until every last quiver is done.

I'm languid. Completely spent.

Before I can recover and remember my name, he's putting the condom on. He hovers over me, asking permission. As if he needs to. After what he just did to me, I'd give him anything. The thought both excites and terrifies me.

I swallow and nod. Then I observe his face as he pushes into me. His eyes close, his expression one of pure delight and complete pleasure as if the most decadent dessert has been placed on his tongue and he's savoring every morsel.

He moves slowly inside me until he's fully in. Then he opens his eyes, locking gazes with me while we make love. If that's what we're doing. I'm not sure what to call it when two… *friends?*… sleep together. It seems too crude a term to call it fucking. It doesn't feel that way either. It feels like we're connecting.

I'm taken back to the first day I saw him. When we stood and stared. When I had an out-of-body experience over a man I'd never even talked to.

The way he's looking at me. Does he feel it too? Or do all men have this look when having sex? I never bothered to look at any of the others.

He bites down on his lip. Hard. Is he coming? No, he's still moving. His thrusts come more quickly now. I reach behind him and run my hands down his back then settle them on the globes of his ass, encouraging him to go harder, faster. He thrusts and holds it there, his eyes scrunching shut as things come off his lips that I can't even pretend to understand.

He slumps down on top of me, sweat squishing between us. His breathing is hard and his heartbeat fast. He stays this way for quite some time, the only movement being his thumb brushing the side of my head over and over. Finally, he rolls to the side. It looks like he has trouble rising onto an elbow. But he does it anyway, making sure I have a clear view of his mouth when he says, "Wow."

# Chapter Nineteen

## Blake

*Holy shit.* Maybe it's that I've gone almost five months without sex—an eternity in my book. Perhaps it's because she's more beautiful than any woman I've even been with. Could be that the build-up and anticipation since the day we laid eyes on each other in the grocery store made it even more intense. But, damn, that had to be the hardest I've ever come in my life.

It's dim in here, but I just know she's blushing as I stare at her.

Is now the time I tell her I'm falling for her? Hard? Or is after sex not appropriate timing? She did, after all, fall apart beneath me in the best of ways. Maybe watching any woman come spectacularly like that would have me feeling like this.

I decide to wait. With my history, I'm not at all sure I trust myself. And with my reputation, she sure as hell shouldn't be trusting me. Besides, I get the idea Ellie Stone isn't easily impressed by words. I'll have to show her with actions.

She shows no intention of getting up or kicking me out, so I take the opportunity to get to know her better.

"What's it like being deaf?" I ask.

When she doesn't answer, I realize the light is now behind me and there's no way she can read my lips. I fish around the bed for our phones, setting hers on her bare chest before sending a text.

**Me: What's it like being deaf?**

She studies me before answering. Then she signs, "Big question."

**Me: Call it research.**

She nods and starts typing.

**Ellie: How about you try to tell me what it's like being able to hear. Describe noise to someone who has never heard sound.**

As I read her text, the profoundness of it hits me. There's just no way.

**Ellie: You can't do it, can you? If you can't describe noise to someone who doesn't know what sound is, how can you expect me to describe the lack of it? Although it's probably far easier for you to imagine being deaf than for me to imagine hearing since I have no basis on which to draw my data.**

**Me: That's a very clinical observation, doctor. I've been wondering about something else**

lately, ever since Maisy had a bad dream the other night. How do deaf people dream? Is it even possible for her to dream since she knows so little language?

Ellie: Deaf are visual mostly. Her dreams would be in pictures, like a silent movie.

Me: Fascinating. And what about thoughts? Do you think in English or ASL?

Ellie: People who were born deaf most likely think in ASL. The only way to describe it is that I feel myself signing in my head, which I'm told is similar to the 'inner voice' of the hearing. Thoughts are images, not sounds. Though I'm aware that some deaf think in written language. Want to hear something funny?

I nod.

Ellie: When I was young, I thought hearing people spoke in letters. As in they would spell out each word in letter form. I thought they would say C – A – T instead of CAT. It wasn't until I started intense lip-reading training that I learned how a word is made up of many sounds connected together. Learning about syllables made it a bit easier.

**Me: How hard is it to learn to read lips?**

**Ellie: Hard. If you're asking if Maisy will be able to do it, I can't answer that. Especially considering the delay in her core communication learning. Imagine this... find an uncaptioned video of someone speaking Japanese, turn off the sound, and try to teach yourself Japanese that way. It's difficult. But not impossible.**

**Me: Wow. I honestly never thought of it that way. You're a great teacher, Dr. Stone.**

She does a sign, then texts me the word *teacher*. I do it back, but based on her expression, I must have butchered it. But I'm no idiot. I know that every time I mess up a sign, she's going to touch me. She takes my hands in hers and positions them properly. Damn, we just had sex and I still relish every second of her hands on me. She releases me, I do the sign, and she does jazz hands.

**Ellie: Something else you might find interesting is how deaf people are surprised to find out almost everything makes noise: lights and refrigerators hum, air conditioning whirs, even wind makes noise. This is why it's important for you to tell Maisy these things. Everything makes noise. What you think of as silence is actually far from it. I had a hearing professor once who said part of his training was to sit in a quiet room that was padded by**

so much noise absorption material that after a few minutes he could hear his heartbeat. He said it was the closest he'd ever come to being able to understand the profoundly deaf.

**Me: I'll never think of silence the same way again.**

When she's glued to her phone, but doesn't type out an answer, I put a hand on her arm.

She angles her phone, showing me an incoming call.

I reach over and turn on the bedside lamp. "Is it the same number as before? The one that calls you every night?"

She nods, looking back at her phone. Her eyes narrow as she studies it. After a bit, she sends me a text.

**Ellie: They left a voicemail this time, which makes it obvious they don't know me, but what concerns me is that the transcription is worrying. VM transcription sucks, but it says something about my sister, and my dad, and trying to find me. Is it talking about Beth? Do you think something's happened to my family?**

She shoves her phone at me, and I read the super long, mostly incoherent transcription and shrug, handing it back to her. But she doesn't take it. She taps it to play the voicemail and she watches as I listen.

"I've been calling for a while but didn't have the guts to leave a message until now. I don't know what you know about me or even *if* you know about me. My name is Sierra Lucas. My father is Grant Lucas. I'm your... I'm your sister. Well, half-sister. I'm twenty-six years old, same age as you, but I'm six months older. You might wonder why I've waited all this time to find you. The answer is that I didn't know about you until a few months ago when I was helping my parents move and found a box containing papers about a divorce from Alexa Lucas and others about forfeiting paternal rights of his child, Ellie Kessler. It took me a while to track you down with the adoption and the name changes. I didn't even know my dad was married before. He's... well, he's difficult, and not your typical father. Anyway, if you didn't know about me, I'm sure this comes as a shock. If you did know about me, I'm wondering why you never tried to find me. Maybe you don't want anything to do with someone related to a man who would give up his rights to you. I don't know, and I surely can't ask him about it. And my mom, she's... well that's a story for another day. I'm terrified over making this call. I hope you get this and decide to call back. Don't hold what our dad did against me. I don't have any other siblings. I... I'd really like to..." She sighs. "Please, just call back. All we have to do is talk. You have my number."

*Jesus.* She has a sister she didn't know about? I get why the transcription was so butchered. The girl seemed very anxious. She was stuttering at times and speaking very quickly at others.

I look at Ellie, unsure of where to begin.

"What?" she signs. "Tell me."

I tap her phone to play it again and text her the conversation. She doesn't even wait for me to finish, she watches over my shoulder as I type into my phone, her hand gripping my leg harder and harder with each word.

Tears cloud her vision. One drops on my skin, rolling down my chest.

Once I send the text, she reads it over and over, head shaking. Finally she looks up. "I have an older sister?" she signs.

"Pretty intense."

"I..." Her hands drop into her lap for a second. "I wonder if my mom knew."

> **Me: Your birth father's last name is Lucas? I kind of hate that.**

"Your brother," she signs, and I nod.

> **Ellie: I have to meet her.**

Warning bells go off in my head. My protective instincts kick in and I quickly type out a text.

> **Me: Hold on there. What if Grant is using her to get to you?**

> **Ellie: Why would he? He wants nothing to do with me. He made that perfectly clear when he gave up his parental rights, and then again when I sought him out after my 18th birthday.**

"You found him? You talked to him?"

> **Ellie: Not to seek out a relationship, but I had to see for myself what kind of man would abandon his child. He laughed at me. Said derogatory things about me. Everything my mother warned me about was true. He'd have**

**no reason to use Sierra to get to me. I want to meet her, Blake. I have to.**

I stiffen. Her father abused her mother. Who knows if he's abusing Sierra. What if she's reaching out to Ellie for help and getting involved would put Ellie in harm's way? I have a bad feeling about this. But who am I to tell her what she should or shouldn't do? I can tell by the look on her face she's going to meet Sierra whether I agree or not.

"I'll go with you," I sign.

Her face scrunches as if what I said was ridiculous. She shakes her head.

"Ellie," I say forcefully and with a determined expression. "I'm going with you. Just in case. I'll keep my distance, but I have to make sure you're safe."

**Ellie: This isn't your problem, Blake. You have enough to deal with.**

**Me: Not my problem? I care about you, El. Humor me. Text Sierra back and set up a meeting outside of Calloway Creek. I'll get a sitter. I promise not to butt in if everything goes okay.**

**Ellie: Fine. I suppose it might be nice to have some moral support. Besides, I may need an interpreter.**

I laugh. Both of us know I have mountains to climb before that could happen.

**Ellie: What did she sound like?**

**Me: Nervous. Like you are now. Now go ahead and text her back. But after this, the next time I get a sitter will be because I'm taking you dancing.**

She cracks a smile. Then she swallows, a look of determination crossing her face as she types, erases, types, erases, types some more, then finally sends off the text. She sets her phone down and lets out a huge sigh.

"It's going to be okay," I sign, hoping the words are true.

I sink down to lay next to her, draw her close, and wrap my arms around her. I hold her tightly. Smell her hair. Revel in the feeling of her body against mine. I take in every second, because I know in a few minutes, I'll have to leave.

# Chapter Twenty

## Ellie

After finding out about Sierra, I confronted my mother. She admitted she knew Grant had a woman on the side. She said that once during an argument, he even mentioned a kid, but that it was a very emotional time with her and my dad, Kyle, the divorce, and Grant rejecting me—which she's still grateful for to this day. She had no idea if he was being truthful about having another child, or just spiteful. And that over time, she just forgot. She said it was unfair of her and apologized, asking me to forgive her.

I did. Because she's been the most amazing mom. And well, she was trying to protect me.

But now, I can only smile. I have a big sister.

Sierra and I sit and drink our third cup of coffee. She's fabulous. She grew up in Chicago but left home right after high school graduation to live in a van in Colorado with a friend. There, she learned to ski, and worked her way from hostess to lift operator to ski instructor in three years. Now, she follows the snow, traveling to the southern hemisphere during our summer to be an instructor in places like New Zealand and Chile. As it's late April and the season just ended in Colorado, she's taking a little time off before heading south.

I catch Blake watching us from his table in the corner. After joining us for the first few minutes, and presumably deciding Sierra wasn't a threat, he excused himself to let us get to know one another and has been working away on his laptop.

That was two hours ago.

Sierra's eyes brim with tears. "I still can't believe it."

I'm delighted her lips are not difficult to read. Maybe because we have the same mouth and when I was learning speechreading, I'd practice for hours a day watching myself in the mirror.

It goes beyond just the mouth. Her hair is the exact same shade as mine, albeit a bit wavier. We're the same height. And her face, though more suntanned than mine, is stunningly familiar.

She looks down at her phone and frowns. "Can you excuse me for a minute?"

I nod, and she gets up from the table and walks outside, phone to her ear.

Blake takes the opportunity to text me.

**Blake: I did a double take when meeting her. I knew at first glance that you were sisters. In fact, the resemblance is so close, in the right light, you might be able to pass for twins.**

I'm not sure how I feel about that since it means we both got a lot of traits from Grant.

I look at Sierra, pacing outside the coffee shop as she chats on the phone. She looks stressed. I hope she isn't getting bad news.

> **Me: I'm sorry we're taking so long. It's just that she's amazing and I want to know everything about her.**

> **Blake: Don't be sorry. I'm fine. I'm getting some work done. And my mother says she and Maisy are having a great time at her house. Apparently, Maisy likes to play hide and seek. And believe me, with over 12,000 square feet, there are lots of places to hide.**

Sierra sits down again. She's not as happy as she was moments ago.

> **Me: Is everything okay?**

> **Sierra: Sorry about that. I had to take the call. It was from my mother. She has no idea I'm here. I honestly don't know if she knows about you. She's never said anything to me about you or even about my dad being married before. And I didn't want to get her into trouble.**

That last sentence sends chills down my spine.

> **Me: Why would she get into trouble?**

Her shoulders slouch and she picks at her napkin, unaware of how her body language speaks volumes.

We haven't talked about the reason we're sisters: Grant. We've talked for hours, yet neither one of us has mentioned him. I thought it was because she presumed I hated him for disowning me. Now, though, I'm wondering if there isn't a different reason.

**Me: Sierra, does Grant treat your mom the same way he treated my mom?**

She reads the text, looks up, and our eyes meet. She doesn't need to say or text the answer. It's written all over her. I reach out, put my hand on hers, and give her an encouraging nod.

**Sierra: I didn't want to ruin our meeting by talking about him. It's been so nice getting to know you.**

**Me: You won't ruin anything. It's okay if you want to talk. I'll understand. If you don't mind me asking, are your parents still together? I find that quite unbelievable if he's doing to her what he did to my mom.**

Her head lowers in shame, as if whatever is happening to her mother is her fault.

**Sierra: They've been married a long time. My mom was very young when they got together. She has no marketable skills. She's been a housewife and mom for twenty-six years.**

Even after I was gone, he didn't want her getting a job. I promised her when I left I'd make a lot of money and someday the two of us would share a house. Whenever I bring it up, she says I'm being ridiculous. Still, I'm scrimping and saving where I can, but it's never enough.

Me: Does she want to leave him?

Sierra: She's never said as much. But I think it's only to protect me. Our dad was never much of a father to me. Always gone. Never attentive. I think my mom preferred it that way. If he wasn't around me, he'd never have the opportunity to do anything to me.

My heart sinks thinking of two sisters who lived very different childhoods.

Me: She does have marketable skills, you know. 26 years of cooking, cleaning house, mending clothes, doing laundry, and raising a child could get her a job as a housekeeper or a nanny.

Sierra: She won't come out and say it, but I think she's afraid of leaving him.

Me: She should be, based on the stories I've heard from my mother.

Sierra: I'm going to help her. One day, when I've saved enough, I'm going to get her out. Even though she didn't ask, and even though she doesn't believe it will happen, it will. I have to.

Me: I'm sorry. I wish I could help.

She wipes a tear. "I'm the one who's sorry. I went and spoiled this."

Me: You spoiled nothing. In fact, we should do this again. How long will you be staying in New York?

Sierra: A week maybe. I have a few friends in the city I intend to visit, but I mainly came because of you. I can't tell you how happy I was to get your text. I booked a plane ticket that very night.

I instantly feel guilty that I have a fat bank account and a huge inheritance and she's struggling to save money to get her mom out of a terrible situation. Yet she spent money on a plane ticket and most likely an overpriced hotel to see me.

Me: I have an extra bedroom. Come stay with me.

Sierra: I can't put you out.

**Me: You wouldn't be. I work a lot, so you could take the train to town and see your friends. We could spend all weekend together. We'll invite Beth and have a girls' night. It'll be fun.**

Her face lights up. "Could you teach me sign language?" I smile and nod.

**Sierra: My hotel is just around the corner. I can be packed and back here in thirty minutes.**

**Me: What are you waiting for? Go?**

She jumps out of her chair so quickly it almost falls over. As soon as she's out the door, Blake joins me.

"Where did she run off to?" he asks.

"To get her stuff," I sign. "She's going to stay with me this week."

His eyebrows go skyward. "Do you think that's a good idea?"

I pin him with a scolding stare. "She's my sister."

He holds his hands out in surrender. "Right. I know. I just want you safe."

"You protecting me?" I sign with a crooked grin.

"I guess I am."

**Me: It's just for the week. She'll be flying off to New Zealand soon.**

I spend the next half hour telling Blake everything I've learned about Sierra. Including what she told me about Grant and her mom, Tara.

"You have to be careful," he says. "What if he finds out?"

**Me: What if he does? The man wants nothing to do with me. This isn't about him. It's about Sierra and me.**

Sierra appears with a suitcase and a smile. She's as excited about staying with me as I am about hosting her. We load into Blake's car and drive back to Calloway Creek.

Sierra and I text the entire way.

# Chapter Twenty-one

## Blake

"Very good," Ellie signs.

Maisy's face lights up. She loves pleasing Ellie.

Maisy is learning faster than any of us expected. This week, she's come to understand that people have names. That *she* has a name. That she's not just 'girl.' And I'm not just 'dad.'

*Dad.* That's another thing she seems to finally know and understand. That I'm her dad. And it brings me more joy than I'd ever imagined. Then again, I *can* imagine more. The elation I'll feel when she hugs me. When she wants to snuggle with me instead of just lying next to me, barely touching shoulders, when I read to her. When she wants to run up to me and jump into my arms after she's had a great day. Or when she seeks out my comfort when she's sad instead of running to the closet with her stuffed cat.

Ellie checks the time, something she rarely does when she's here. She's normally super focused and excited to work with us. But today she's... distracted.

**Me: You don't have to be here. I know you'd rather be with Sierra. She leaves next Wednesday, right?**

**Ellie: I DO want to be here, Blake. This is my job. Sierra and I will have all weekend together. And she's not at my place anyway. She's in the city having dinner with a friend.**

As Maisy normally does halfway into our two-hour session with Ellie, she takes a break, having a small snack and then playing on the swing. I take the opportunity to tell Ellie about the family we met earlier.

**Me: Maisy and I met Krista Lancaster and her parents today. You know her from school, don't you?**

**Ellie: I do. Krista is in third grade.**

**Me: She has cochlear implants. Her parents are both hearing, and they were encouraging me to get implants for Maisy. I know we haven't talked about it much. What are your thoughts?**

**Ellie: I haven't brought it up yet because I thought you needed time to talk to people, do your own research, and form your own opinions. I'm not here to tell you what to do.**

"I'm not asking you to tell me what to do. I'm asking your opinion on them, El. How come you don't have them? Are you opposed?"

> Ellie: I'm not opposed. But I don't push for them either. I've been well-educated on both sides of the argument. And both sides hold merit. It's really up to the individual. As I said before, you'll find widely polarized opinions on cochlear implants. I'd be lying if I told you there weren't times in my childhood I longed to hear. When I was little, my mother chose not to get me the implants. When I got older, she left the decision to me. But before I could decide either way, the choice was made for me. When I was nine, I fell off my bike and hit my head pretty hard—and just an FYI here, many deaf and HOH have issues with vertigo and balance. When they did an MRI to check for brain damage, they found a pineal gland cyst on my brain. It's benign and doesn't cause me any issues, but I'm still monitored yearly by MRI to make sure nothing has changed. MRIs are contraindicated if you have the implants. There are ways around it, but it didn't seem worth the trouble for something I wasn't sure I wanted anyway.

"If you could though, would you get them?"
"Honestly?" she signs. "I don't know."

"Are you just saying that because you don't want to influence me?"

She raises a non-convincing shoulder.

> **Ellie:** The fact is some people will benefit from them, some won't. But implants won't FIX our hearing as some people have come to believe. They don't work miracles. Even with the implants, the deaf have to learn to hear. Our brains have to be trained to process sound. And sometimes that just doesn't happen. For some, the implants work exactly as intended. For others, the sound confuses their brains instead of enhancing their lives and they end up having them removed. It's widely debated among the Deaf community. I'm not here to give you my opinion. I'm here to educate you so you can do what you think is best for Maisy in your situation.

> **Me:** You should be a politician, El. You're really good at not answering direct questions.

> **Ellie:** Just doing my job.

"I have one more question," I sign. "When are we going dancing?"

She chews the inside of her cheek for a second. "A week from Friday?"

"Did you say a week?" I look outside, feeling all kinds of impatient. Maisy is busy doing signs to her stuffed cat, so I tug Ellie toward me. "I've missed you."

Her gaze centers on my lips long after my words leave them. Then her hands come up between us and she signs, "You see me almost every day."

"That's not what I mean, and I think you know it."

She glances outside, then back at me, then she grips my shoulders and pulls me away from the window. When she leans up on her toes and kisses me, I'm amused by how much I like this bold side of her.

My hands weave through her hair and settle on her neck, keeping her lips against mine. The fruity smell of her hair permeates through me. The taste of her lips reminds me of being in her bed last week. My growing erection tells me how hungry I am for more. It's an urge I feel will never be satisfied. I could never get enough of her. When she's not right in front of me, she's still with me. In my head. My thoughts. My dreams. I'm fucking drunk on Ellie Stone and I have no desire to get sober.

The back door opens, and I pull away. Looking down at my tented pants, I quickly sit on the couch and pull a throw pillow over my lap.

Ellie laughs and I get out my phone.

**Me: To be continued next Friday.**

She licks her lips then smiles. It's the purest smile I've seen on her face. And it tells me that just maybe, she's a bit drunk on me too.

# Chapter Twenty-two

## Ellie

Beth texts me that she's here and I buzz her up. It makes me a little uncomfortable when Sierra notices the high-end bottles of champagne Beth has brought with her.

We haven't exactly talked about the disparity in our families' economic status. Then again, if Sierra used a private investigator to find me, she might know everything.

Sierra and I have learned a lot about each other over the past few nights, sitting on my couch and texting until well after midnight. But one thing is clear, we dance around the subject of our father.

Sierra and Beth become instant friends, which relieves some of my worry. Beth and I have always been more than sisters. We're best friends. She always had my back growing up. Still does. And

I'll always have hers. But I wasn't sure how Beth would handle the news that I have another sister.

I get a text that our dinner is here, so I buzz up the delivery guy and pay for our pizza.

Beth inhales. "Twenty-dollar pizza with two-hundred-dollar champagne. Does it get any better?"

I shoot her a scolding glance.

"What?" she asks.

Sierra's gaze bounces between us.

"Don't mind her," Beth says and signs. "She's had a stick up her ass since she moved here. I think it has something to do with not being able to bone the hot single dad who is the father of a student."

My jaw goes slack.

"What?" Beth looks at me like I'm the one who's crazy. "It's true, isn't it?"

I roll my eyes.

"Oh my God," Sierra says, Beth interpreting so I don't miss any words. "It's Blake isn't it? So he's not just a friend?"

Now Beth is the one rolling her eyes. "Oh please. She told you he's just a friend?" She laughs. "Our sister is drooling over the guy who may or may not be known as one of the foremost players of Calloway Creek."

Sierra's lips poke out in a pucker. "Why is it always the bad boys who are the most appealing?"

"He's not bad," I sign in irritation.

"Hey," Beth says. "I don't fault you for it. I've been with a few myself. They are always the most fun. Just make sure you know the stakes."

"Stakes?"

"As in, don't be surprised if after the two of you fuck, he loses all interest."

Sierra giggles and asks Beth to show her how to sign *fuck*. After she's proficient at the sign, Beth turns and eyes me. She studies me as I take a drink, the crinkle in her nose making an appearance before her eyes grow larger in realization. "Holy shit, you already fucked him, didn't you?"

The champagne in my mouth is immediately sprayed all over her. Flustered, I choke on what little is left and sign, "I... no."

"Liar." Beth wipes her face, laughing. "You did the deed with the hot single dad. It's written all over you." A slow smile overtakes her smirk. "Wait. It must have happened before you met Sierra, and he still went with you? Oh, my God, Ellie, he must really like you. How many times?"

I shake my head, having forgotten how Beth can read me like a book.

She grabs my arm. "Spill."

Both of them stare me down. I'm hesitant to say anything, because if I do, I might actually be admitting that I have feelings for him. Feelings I shouldn't be having for a guy whose only claim to fame—other than his family name—is bedding women.

"It's not a big deal. It was just the one time."

"It is a big deal," Beth says. "He practically popped your cherry."

Sierra looks like she just saw an alien. "Were you... was that your first time?"

I shoot Beth another look of disgust. Must we share *all* my secrets with Sierra so soon?

"It wasn't my first time," I sign, as Beth interprets. "But it was the first time in a long time."

"She was a bit slutty in high school," Beth says, revealing what I didn't.

I smack her arm. "I'm trying to make a good impression here."

"Not to worry," Sierra says. "Nothing wrong with being a bit slutty from time to time."

"But you want more times, right?" Beth asks me. "And based on the fact that he insisted on going to the city with you to meet Sierra, I'd bet he does too." She claps and bounces on the sofa. "There's nothing like a good old friends-with-benefits fling."

Sierra and Beth high-five each other, which is good, because it means they didn't pick up on the huge sigh that just escaped me.

*Friends with benefits. Fling.* The words bounce around inside my head as I begin to embrace the idea of it. After all, Blake and I could never be anything more. The sooner I accept that fact, the better off I'll be. But that doesn't mean I'm not tingling with anticipation over our impending dancing date next weekend.

"Teach me more dirty signs," Sierra says.

*Here we go.* I inwardly roll my eyes. If I had a nickel for every hearing person who asks this, I'd be richer than my father. But this is my newly found sister, so I decide to give her a pass.

Beth and I—but mostly Beth—spend the next ten minutes showing her the arsenal of curse-word ASL. Like most people, Sierra is surprised that ASL has such a rich vocabulary of profanity.

By the end of the night, we've taught Sierra how to spell her name, sign *nice to meet you*, and most importantly—for her anyway—how to invite a man to bed. I get the idea my new sister may be even more slutty than I was in high school. It would make sense. My limited training in psychology tells me enough to know that girls who grow up without strong father figures are more likely to seek unhealthy attention from men. So it seems the long-lost sisters both sought out attention from guys, but for very different reasons.

Sierra looks down at her phone and her smile completely disappears, being replaced by a pained grimace.

"What's wrong?" I ask.

"It's my mom." Her shoulders droop and she sinks into the couch. "Forget it. I don't want to bring down the vibe."

"Sierra," Beth says. "What is it? You can tell us."

After a long pause, and more pained stares at her phone, she says, "She drunk texted me."

Both Beth and I look at her, confused.

"It's something she sometimes does after… after—"

"After the bastard hits her," Beth says, having zero filter as usual.

Sierra shrugs as if afraid to admit it.

"This is a safe place," I sign. "You can tell us."

She picks at the sofa. "My dad… uh, our dad—"

"Not her dad," Beth says angrily. "She has a father. I get that the two of you are sisters, but I won't have our dad disrespected by calling that asshole her father."

Sierra nods. "Fair enough."

How I love Beth right now. She could have been threatened by a new sister coming into my life. But she's done the opposite, welcomed her with open arms. Still, she's not going to sit by and have our close family bond diminished by a wife-beating asshole. Besides, she said exactly what I've been thinking for days but haven't said.

"Grant is a captain at Chicago PD," Sierra explains. "He worked his way up from uniformed officer to detective, sergeant, and lieutenant. And now he's the commanding officer of his division. Mom was sure that when his role went from being out on the streets to mostly administrative, his stress would decrease and the... *punishments* would too."

"What does she get punished for?" Beth asks.

"Bad choice of words," Sierra says. "My mom does nothing wrong. She bends over backwards to make sure everything is right. That dinner is always ready. That his clothes are always pressed. That she keeps herself fit. When he acts the way he does, it's because something went wrong with his day. It has nothing to do with her. But unfortunately for my mom, his promotion to Captain came with a whole lot of unanticipated stress."

"Why hasn't she left?" Beth asks.

I tap her arm. "You know why. Mom has told us plenty of times how she couldn't leave."

"But she did," Beth says. "She left eventually. And maybe we can help."

Sierra's gaze falls to the floor. "My mother is a proud woman. She won't accept charity."

"What if she got a job?" I sign, Beth still interpreting for me. "Surely our dad can get her something at a hospital somewhere."

Sierra shakes her head sadly. "It won't work. He's a cop. He'll find her. As soon as she earns her first paycheck, he'll be able to trace her social security number and find out who's paying her. Mom only tells me things when she's been drinking. And she told me once that he said he'd kill her if she ever left."

"What if we found her a job that pays her under the table?" Beth asks.

"Not likely. Few employers would take the risk. Believe me, I've looked into it."

I touch Sierra's arm. "But you told me you promised your mom you'd live together without him once you saved the money."

"I know," she says sadly. "And it'll probably never happen. Because I suspect I'd have to disappear right along with her."

Beth and Sierra continue to talk, but my mind is somewhere else. I get an idea. A really good one. I hesitate to say anything until I can work out the details. But the thought of anyone living in fear, like my mother had, has my blood boiling. I have this new sister. Hopefully we'll have a relationship like I do with Beth. I would do anything for Beth. I should be willing to do anything for Sierra.

I shoot off a quick text, hoping my boss can meet with me first thing Monday.

Then, with renewed excitement, I pop open a fresh bottle of champagne.

# Chapter Twenty-three

## Ellie

Monday afternoon, I drive up to my apartment in a brand-new Toyota Camry. It's not *my* Camry. It's a rental. My nerves are shot, and it's been hard to work today with all the research and planning I've done. Hopefully it all pays off.

I go up to my apartment to find Sierra watching skiing videos on her laptop.

**Me: Your flight isn't until Wednesday night, right?**

She shakes her head.

**Sierra: Actually, I wanted to talk to you about staying a few more days. The airline reached**

out looking for volunteers to be bumped to a later flight. There's one Friday night instead. If that's okay.

Me: That's even better. I was worried about you getting back in time and missing your flight.

Sierra: Getting back in time from what?

I put the key fob on the table next to her, still nervous. She looks up. "What's this?"

Me: Don't get mad. Yes, I'm meddling. But it comes from a good place.

Sierra: Did you buy me a car? I'm leaving the country, Ellie. I'd have nowhere to keep it.

Me: It's a rental. Be patient. This is a long story.

She motions to the chair next to her. I sit and try to sum it all up in one quick text.

Me: The car is so it can't be traced back to you. You're going to drive to Chicago and get your mom. You're going to bring her here. I know it's a long drive, but you don't want to risk flying. He'd be able to track you. I got her a job. It's only temporary, but it's something.

If you're careful, he won't be able to find her or know it was you who helped.

Sierra: Ellie, I'll give you points for originality, and I applaud you for wanting to help, but she can't take a job. He'll find her. And I'm not going to have her living with you. That would put you in danger. I just found you. It's a risk I won't take.

Me: She won't have to live here. My boss agreed to give her a job in laundry and housekeeping at my school. And they won't be paying her. There will be no record of her employment. They will be letting her live there. It's perfect. It's the last place Grant would look. If he suspects you had a hand in it at all, he'll probably think you took her with you to New Zealand.

Sierra: She doesn't have a passport.

Me: That's good. Maybe he won't suspect you then. I have a plan. If you leave tonight, you can get there after he goes to work tomorrow. Go in disguise in case he has security cameras, which I suspect he does since he's a cop. Put on a wig and a ball cap so he can't see your face. Better yet, try to look like a man to throw him off. Wear different clothes. Stop at Goodwill on your way out of town to pick things up. If you know where the cameras are, do not glance at them, that would tip him off to it being you. Throw only what she needs in a suitcase—get one of those from Goodwill too in case he sewed tracking devices into all of theirs. Leave her cell phone there. Change her appearance as much as you can as soon as you leave the house in case he has posters made for a missing person. Maybe pick up a wig for her at Goodwill too. And clothing that is unlike anything she'd normally wear. Don't park in the driveway. A good camera might be able to pick up the license plate. Park around the block if you can. Leave quickly to put as much distance between you and Chicago before he gets home. Bring her back here. But then don't change your routine. Call or text her as you normally would so that he sees you're trying to get in touch with her. Maybe even ask if she's okay or if your dad has done something—but only if it's a question you'd ordinarily ask. And send photos when you get to New Zealand if that's something you'd do.

She looks over at me, stunned.

Sierra: You've put a lot of thought into this. Why? You don't even know her.

Me: I think of what would have happened to my mom. What would have happened to ME, if she hadn't had the courage to leave. If a complete stranger hadn't intervened when he saw her in trouble.

Her eyes become glassy. "I don't know what to say. Thank you. I'll leave tonight."

Me: Don't thank me yet. The job is only temporary and a huge favor from my boss. She's sympathetic and confessed that her own sister was once in a similar situation. But technically, if the IRS came snooping around, the school would get in trouble for offering room and board in lieu of wages, which isn't exactly allowed. But I get the feeling she'll let Tara stay until we can figure something else out. One more thing. If you think your dad tracks your phone, leave it here so you can't be placed in Chicago when she goes missing.

Sierra: I have my own plan, but I'm going to leave it here anyway, just in case. Better to be safe than sorry. What did Beth and Blake say about all this? It's pretty hard core, Ellie.

Me: Only three people know about this. You, me, and Candance—she's the president of the Deaf school. Nobody else can know. From my research, I learned that the more people who know, even if they are trusted, the greater chance of slip-ups and repercussions. This has to stay between the three of us and your mom. It's the only way it will work.

She wipes tears from her eyes. Then she breaks down sobbing. I scoot next to her and wrap her in a hug. I don't know if she's terrified of what her father will do if they get caught, or relieved that there's a plan to get her mother away from him. She cries on my shoulder, her body shaking. Finally, she stills and goes back to her phone.

**Sierra: Do you really think this will work? And if it does, how can I in good conscience leave her here alone to go to NZ?**

**Me: She won't be alone. She'll have me. And she'll have you. We'll get her a new phone so the two of you can be in constant contact.**

I get a wad of cash out of my purse and hand it over.

**Me: Use this. Not any credit cards. Not even for gas along the way. Your dad could trace your cards and find out where you used them and piece it together. You can't leave any breadcrumbs for him to find. If you have any belongings still at your house from your childhood, leave them. No matter how sentimental they are. If he notices anything but her clothes missing, it could point to you. The last thing we want is for him to come after you as well.**

She holds the money in her hand, staring at it in disbelief. "I can't believe you're doing all this for me."

**Me: This is what you do for family.**

Another tear escapes her eye. "I love you, Ellie." She pulls me in for a hug. I let her hug me long and hard. Then I teach her how to sign the words in ASL.

# Chapter Twenty-four

## Blake

Maisy sits impatiently on the couch. She's learned the routine. She knows when to expect Ellie. Every few minutes, she grunts and points at the door.

"Soon," I sign.

I think she understands, but she's four. Any four-year-old would be restless waiting for something they're looking forward to.

There's no use in trying to distract her with a game. I've done that enough times that she's caught on and it simply irritates her more. It seems my daughter is a force of nature, and when she has her mind set on something happening, she's not about to accept anything less.

Which is why I'm concerned that Ellie is ten minutes late.

Thank goodness Maisy can't tell time or she'd likely throw a tantrum.

I stand behind her, watching as she holds her stuffed cat, eyes glued to the front door. And it occurs to me that she hasn't thrown a tantrum in days. Or has it been a week? Ellie said they would abate as she became more able to communicate her needs. But there's still so much she doesn't understand, and sometimes I feel I walk on eggshells waiting for the next time she'll lash out. At just forty inches tall and a mere thirty-eight pounds, my kid can have an outburst like a two-hundred-pound drunken sailor.

There's a knock on the door.

I touch Maisy's shoulder. When she turns, I smile and point to the door. "Ellie."

Maisy's entire face lights up. She drops her stuffed cat like a hot potato and runs to the door. I'd already unlocked the deadbolt so Maisy could open it. When she sees Ellie, she barrels into her, almost knocking her over, and the two embrace.

Ellie looks at me, guilt on her face.

I can't help being jealous every time my daughter doles out hugs. Because she still hasn't given one to me. She'll never know how I dream of the day her face lights up when *I* walk into a room. That every day, I wake up hoping today will be the day she decides she likes me as much as Ellie. Allie. My mom. That one day she might even love me as fiercely as I've grown to love her.

That one day we become the family I never knew I wanted.

Thoughts of becoming a family send my gaze right back to Ellie. I remember what it felt like to lie next to her. To hold her. To be inside her. And—knock me over with a feather—I know I want her to be a part of it.

As usual, Maisy drags Ellie to the dining room table to show off her latest drawings. And as usual, Ellie gushes over them. If there is something Maisy has drawn that she hasn't yet learned the sign for, Ellie always takes the opportunity to teach her. Today, she learns 'sidewalk.'

When Ellie goes to pull materials from her bag, I wave an arm, getting her attention. "Did you forget?"

She scrunches her eyes.

I motion to Maisy and sign, "Cat."

Her expression tells me she *had* forgotten. We had planned to take Maisy to the pet adoption center today.

"We can go," she signs.

Maisy picks up on it. She knows what 'go' means. She looks between us, excited to go on another excursion. Over the past few weeks she's been introduced to quite a few new places. In addition to going back to the winery a few times—allowing me to get more work done as Mom is always around to occupy Maisy when we show up—we've taken her to the park, a restaurant, and the supermarket.

With the exception of the winery, Ellie has been with us every time, there to teach both of us the signs for everything we encounter. Our vocabularies are growing by the day.

Taking Maisy to Truman's Grocery was surreal. Her eyes went buggy at the aisles and aisles of food. When we went down the snack aisle, she stood staring at the rows of snacks as if she'd never been to a grocery store before. I had mixed feelings about the whole thing. I was excited to provide her with a new experience, but saddened at the thought that it was possibly the first time she'd ever been. Thoughts of what Lucinda had done kept popping into my mind. Did she leave her home alone when she did her shopping? Did she hire an ignorant babysitter who may have mistreated her? Was Maisy watched by the awful grandparents who would rather sail the world than be there for their grandchild?

I shake away a frightening thought—one of Maisy hiding alone in a closet when her mom would leave—and re-focus on the things I have control over. Things like getting Maisy a cat.

I haven't told her. I'm not sure I'd even know how. Maisy draws herself with a cat all the time. Her stuffed cat. I doubt she'd understand if I tried to explain we were getting a real one. And it's probably best I didn't, just in case it doesn't happen. I've never been to an adoption shelter before. I'm not exactly sure of the process.

> **Me: I haven't told Maisy a thing. There is a large box in my garage full of stuff I picked up at the pet store just in case.**

Ellie reads my text and nods. I thought she'd be more excited about this.

> **Me: We don't have to go. Is everything okay?**

> **Ellie: Everything is fine. And of course we're going.**

~ ~ ~

The animal shelter is just outside the town limits. Not as far as the winery, but farther than the park or grocery store. People turn and stare when we pull up. I laugh and switch off the blaring music, cursing myself for getting the upgraded stereo system when I bought the car. It's all Maisy wants to do when we go for rides. In fact, I keep a pair of earplugs in the cup holder.

It makes me think of the dancing date Ellie and I will go on in four days.

Since when have I ever counted down the days until a date? I turn and gaze at Ellie, wondering—not for the first time—what sort of spell she's cast on me.

I pat Ellie's hand. Normally, when I do things like that, there is a spark in her eyes. Not this time, however. And it's now that I realize we drove the whole way here without our usual heated glances. Our typical fleeting touches.

What happened over the weekend? Sierra's still staying with her as far as I know. Did they go out? Did Ellie... *meet someone?*

The way my chest squeezes like my heart is in a vise lets me know I'm in over my head much farther than I recognized.

She looks over and cracks a smile, but it doesn't go all the way to her eyes like it usually does.

I get Maisy from the back. When we go up the walk, there's a large sign with the shelter name, and under the name is a carving of several animals: dog, cat, duck, even a raccoon.

Maisy signs something.

Ellie stops walking, looking at her in surprise.

I tap her. "What did she say?"

"She said *farm,*" she fingerspells the word farm, then she shows me the sign for it. She turns to Maisy and signs, "No farm."

**Ellie: Damn. I wish we were at a farm so I didn't have to tell her it was wrong. She wouldn't understand what an animal shelter is. But I'm impressed at how she's putting things together. You should be proud.**

I nod, because I totally am.

"Come on," I say and sign.

Maisy still seems excited.

Inside, I introduce myself to the worker behind the counter. "I'm Blake Montana. This is my daughter, Maisy, and this is Ellie. They're both deaf. We'd like to adopt a cat for Maisy."

"Awesome," the teen worker says. He shoves a clipboard my way. "Fill these out then I'll take you back. All the cats have been fixed and vaccinated. You'll just pay an adoption fee, and, if you want, you can also leave a donation." He looks embarrassed to have said it. Then he adds, "Sorry, my boss makes us say that."

"Not a problem. And I'd be happy to make a donation."

I hastily fill out the paperwork knowing Maisy is restless and wondering what we're doing here.

Once done, the teen motions to a side door. "Come through there."

As soon as we're through the door, I hear barking. Instinctively, I look to Maisy to see her reaction, then I scold myself for it.

"The dogs are all out there," he says, pointing to another door. "Cats are this way."

We follow him past a row of offices. Then, as we pass some half-height walls that enclose individual pens, Maisy catches a glimpse of a family sitting inside one, where a young boy is playing with a large fluffy cat. She stops in her tracks and rests her chin atop the wall, staring. I don't know if she's ever seen a live cat before. We saw some dogs in the park. She even got to pet one. But she didn't seem half as excited as she is now.

I look at the size of the cat and ask the worker, "Do you have any kittens?"

"Not really. By the time people decide they don't want them, they're usually grown."

"Okay, well, let's go see what you've got."

He opens a door. Inside is wire cage after wire cage, each small enclosure housing an individual cat. There must be at least thirty of them. He gestures to the laminated sign attached to the front of the first one. "You can see how old they are and what breed. If our vets could tell, that is. Sometimes it's just an estimate.

If there's a red mark on the sign it means the animal is aggressive." He looks at Maisy. "Best not let her near those."

The guy tends to mumble and is making zero attempts at facing Ellie as he speaks, so I text her what we're talking about to keep her in the loop.

I point to a date on the sign. "Is this the birth date?"

"That's the date we acquired them. It lets us know how long each has been here so we can, you know, keep track."

He shifts uncomfortably. I did my research. There are very few no-kill shelters anymore. There are just too many abandoned animals.

"How long can you keep them, before… you know."

"As long as we have space." He shrugs and looks behind him like he's not supposed to talk about it. "But we run out of space a lot. Over seventy percent of cats that enter shelters are never adopted."

*Ah, shit.* I glance around at the eclectic array of cats. Fat and thin. Fluffy and hairless. Skittish and friendly. And most of them will probably be euthanized in a matter of weeks.

I want to look at all the acquisition dates and try to steer Maisy to the next one on the bubble, but I don't. I want her to pick the one she wants.

Maisy is stunned. She blinks, mouth agape, and looks from side to side at all the different cats. She leans over and sticks a finger through a cage to touch one. Thankfully, it's not one with a red mark on the sign. She looks up at me. I motion around to all the cages, not knowing if she has any idea I'm asking her which one she wants.

Ellie and I keep a close eye as Maisy goes to each cage, assesses the cat inside, leaning occasionally to put her fingers in.

Some of the cats come close, wanting the attention, while some shy away and head for the far corner.

When we come upon one of the aggressive cats, I point to the red mark and shake my head, guiding Maisy to the next cat. She understands and skips the next cage she sees with the red mark.

Some cats get more attention from her than others. I make a mental note of which ones.

The worker follows behind. "If you want to take one out and see how they get along, I can put you in a playroom."

"Sure," I say. "Just give her a few minutes to look at all of them."

At the end of the first row, Maisy falls to her knees in front of a cage with a kitten. I turn to the worker. "I thought you said you didn't have kittens."

"Yeah. I forgot about this one. You won't want him, though. He has a, gen, uh, genital defect."

I furrow a brow. "A *genital* defect."

"You know, something that was there when he was born."

I laugh. "You mean congenital defect."

"Yeah."

I watch intently as the kitten wakes, sees Maisy, then rises and hobbles over to her. I look at the kitten's details on the laminated sign. He's been here almost a month. Longer than most of the others. It says he's four months old and a 'mixed breed.' The kitten is almost fully yellow with one white streak along his left side, as if a painter dipped a brush in white paint, went to paint a stripe, then got distracted and messed it up. It looks almost like one of those heart monitor stripes, a horizontal line that then goes haphazardly up and down along its side. I've never seen one like it. Apparently neither has Maisy. Either that, or she prefers a kitten.

The teen doesn't miss Maisy's reaction either. He gestures across the way. "If she's interested in smaller cats, we have a six-month old over there that might suit her."

I get Maisy's attention and point to the other cat, who still looks a bit kitten-ish, seems to have a perfect gait, and is standing at the edge of the cage as if anticipating Maisy's arrival after having seen her greet all the others.

Maisy ignores my gesture and goes back to the yellow kitten. Ellie elbows me. "She wants this one," she signs.

Unsure, I ask the worker, "Can we get this one out?"

He cocks his head. "Really?"

I can almost hear the thought in his head: *you want this damaged one?*

"Yes, really," I say, maybe a bit too harshly. "She wants to see this one. Is that a problem?"

"Uh, no." He opens the cage, retrieves the kitten, who looks more than happy to be getting sprung from captivity, then asks us to follow him.

Maisy doesn't give any of the other cats a glance. She skips along next to the teenage worker, keeping an eye on the kitten, watching over him protectively as the worker leads us back through the door and into a playroom.

I'm not sure Maisy knows what's happening. I point to the floor. "Sit down," I sign. "You hold."

Her eyes bulge. She bounces up and down then plops down cross-legged on the floor. Excitement flows out of her as the teen places the kitten in her lap. I'm a little scared for the furball when Maisy pulls him tightly against her chest, but the cat purrs, seeming to love the attention. Maisy must feel the vibration. She looks surprised and then her hands run up and down the kitten's body.

Ellie and I look at each other and smile.

A vet comes and talks to us while Maisy plays with the kitten.

"I'm pleased to see someone interested in this one," she says.

"Maisy is already in love," I tell her. "Can you tell me about his leg?"

"He has an angular limb deformity. Present at birth most likely, but as it became more pronounced, I suppose the previous owners didn't want to deal with it."

"Will he be okay?"

"He's a happy, well-adjusted kitten. It hasn't hampered his ability to walk and play, but as he ages he'll most likely be more sedentary and he may develop arthritis. Other than that, he's like any other kitten." She turns to Maisy. "You like this one, young lady? I can tell he really likes you."

When Maisy doesn't look up, I tell the vet, "My daughter is deaf."

Surprise crosses her face for an instant before it's replaced with a smile. "A match made in heaven then."

I regard Maisy and the cat. *Is it?* Is that why she chose this one? Because he's 'different' like her?

"We're getting this one," I tell Ellie.

She nods. She understands. No more words are needed.

The teen brings me more paperwork to sign, and a half hour later, we're ready to go.

"Let's go," I sign after tapping Maisy to get her attention.

She looks down at the kitten, her face morphing into a deep frown. A tear sits in the inner corner of her eye as she holds the cat out to the teen worker.

I face Ellie. "She doesn't know we're here to take him home. She thinks this was just to play. Like a petting zoo."

I sit down next to her and put the cat back in her lap. I sign, "We take."

I thought she knew 'take,' but she seems confused.

Ellie pulls a drawing pad from her purse, quickly does a sketch, and hands it to Maisy. It's the typical drawing of my house, Maisy and me inside, with Maisy holding her stuffed cat. But Ellie drew another cat, a small yellow one, down by Maisy's feet. She even made one leg slightly shorter than the others. She points to the yellow cat in the drawing and then to the kitten. "You take," she signs.

Maisy's eyes dart from the drawing to the kitten then back to the drawing then up to me. She raises a brow. She does that a lot now. I guess it's her way of asking my permission.

"Yes," I sign. "We take him home."

I'm not sure if she still doesn't understand, or if she's in shock, but she goes completely still. Then, my entire world changes because she puts the kitten on the floor and climbs into my lap, her little arms snaking around me.

I try to hold it together as I get the very first hug from my daughter, but emotion overcomes me. I bury myself in her curls and let the tears roll down my cheek. I must look like a certified pussy. Thank God Lucas and my friends aren't here to witness my ridiculous display.

When I look up, Ellie is crying too.

After Maisy gets off my lap, I pull out my phone.

**Me: I swear to God, I'm going to give that girl the world.**

Ellie sniffs back more tears, then she smiles as I hand over my credit card and make a very fat donation.

# Chapter Twenty-five

## Ellie

Watching Maisy and the kitten is surreal. I swear they both had that same distant look in their eyes, but now that they're playing together, the look is gone, replaced by something else. Sheer joy.

"Cat needs a name," I sign to Blake.

"I'll let Maisy name him."

> **Me: She may just call him cat. Proper names are new to her. It might be easier if you pick one.**

He shrugs and watches the two play. Tilting his head to the side, one way then the other, he works his chin with his fingers. "How about Bolt?" he fingerspells the name.

I look at the white streak on the kitten's side. It does kind of look like a bolt of lightning. "Perfect," I sign. I don't have to fingerspell it. He knows the sign. And based on the intense, lustful look he's giving me, he knows I know he knows. I feel myself blush.

Maisy and Blake spend the next half hour learning the signs for all the cat supplies. We decide, in order to simplify things for Maisy, we'll call the litter box the cat's toilet.

**Me: You should make it her responsibility to do something for Bolt. Feeding him maybe. Keeping his water bowl full.**

**Blake: Isn't she a little young for that?**

**Me: Not at all. Kids are capable of doing a lot more than most parents assume. It'll be good for her. She needs to feel like she's contributing. I know you want to coddle her, Blake. You see her as this fragile little flower. You said you want to give her everything. But you can't spoil her because she's deaf. Too many parents make the mistake of trying to overcompensate. Even my own parents were guilty of it from time to time.**

**Blake: I'm not going to spoil her because she's deaf. I'm going to spoil her because it makes her happy and making her happy has just become my life's mission.**

This man. How is it that whenever he says something charming like that, especially when it concerns his daughter, it's like he's shooting a tether straight into my heart.

If I wasn't aware of his unsavory past, I'd say he was a keeper.

**Me: Well, Bolt seems to make her happy all right.**

I can't help but think back to the hug. The hug that was more than a month in the making. I feel it was just the beginning. And I hope Blake realizes that Bolt isn't the only one in Maisy's life making her happy. I see the bond Blake and Maisy are forming. It's getting stronger by the day. It's becoming palpable. Maybe it takes an outsider to notice because it wasn't the insta-bond one would hope for when meeting their child for the first time, but it's happening. Slowly and surely. Day by day. Moment by moment. They are becoming a family.

Blake gets out the bag of cat food and a measuring cup. He shows Maisy how to scoop the food up and pour it in the bowl.

I'm amused at the lengths Blake went to prepare for having a pet. The food and water bowls have cat paw prints etched into them. They both nestle into an intricate metal stand that is elevated off the floor by a few inches.

Maisy dumps a scoop of food into the bowl on the left, looking up at Blake for approval.

He nods, then hands her the second bowl and points to the kitchen sink. She scurries over, climbs up on the stepstool in front of it, and fills the bowl smack dab to the very top. Water sloshes out with each step she takes back across the room. When she realizes what a mess she's made, her smile fades and she looks up at Blake, frightened.

As soon as he sees her face, I know what he's thinking. Mostly because I'm thinking the same thing. *Did she used to get in trouble for making messes?*

He gets a dishrag, wipes up the spilled water, then smiles and dabs the end of her nose with it.

She relaxes and sets the bowl carefully into the stand. But the stand is angled, so some water trickles out. She tries to take the dishtowel from Blake, but he doesn't release it, and they start playing tug-of-war. Soon, they're both smiling and laughing. I stand back and watch them have this moment, not underestimating the significance of it.

Today has been a turning point in their relationship. All it took was one unwanted kitten to bring father and daughter together.

"Dinner?" Blake asks sometime later.

I look at the clock on his living room wall. It's way past the time when I normally leave. I wonder if it's because I've been enjoying watching Maisy so much, or if I'm trying to pass the time so I don't think about Sierra.

"I should go," I sign.

**Blake: No, don't. I know you think eating here will send Maisy the wrong message. But I'm not ready for you to leave. Stay. Not because it's your job, but because you want to. I'll feed her a quick dinner. We can just talk.**

I give in, happy for the distraction.

While he whips up a quick dinner of grilled cheese, broccoli, and applesauce, I study a map on my phone. The drive to Chicago is twelve hours. If you account for stopping for gas and food, it may take as many as fourteen. Her plan was to get there before Grant leaves for work, park around the block, and watch him go. That means she's most likely left New York by now.

Anxiety crawls up my spine. Have I made a mistake getting involved in her family business? Have I just gone and put her in danger? What was I even thinking? Having second thoughts about all of it, I text her, hoping to catch her before she goes. Maybe we need to think about this some more. I stare at my phone knowing the lack of response means she's already gone. And I don't have any means to get in touch. No way to know where she is, if she even makes it out with her mom, or how they're doing. I should have asked her to stop along the way and check in with me. Better yet, I should have bought her a new phone so we could communicate.

A hand lands on my shoulder.

"What's wrong?" Blake asks.

I don't say anything. I just stare at Maisy and watch how she won't even put down the cat to eat. She holds him in her lap, eating one-handed.

**Blake: I know something is bothering you, El. I've been flirting with you all afternoon and it's like I'm not even here. Is there something you need to tell me?**

I swallow. I should tell him. I should tell *someone*. But then I think back to what I read earlier. About how with every person told, there is an increased chance of abuse victims being located by their perpetrators. I can't tell him. No matter how much I want to.

**Blake: Seriously, what's going on? You are definitely not your usual self. Have you met someone else and are afraid to tell me?**

My head shakes vehemently. Maybe too much. I dial it back.

**Me: It's not that.**

**Blake: Good. Because I can't tell you how much I've wanted to kiss you all night. That shirt looks really good on you. And now that I know what's underneath...**

It's hard not to smile as my face heats up.
"There she is," he says, his shoulders shaking as he chuckles.

**Me: Sorry. I've just been distracted.**

"Work?" he asks.
I shake my head.
"Sierra?"
I must hesitate a moment too long.
"It's Sierra, isn't it? Did something happen? Did she leave?"
I shake my head again, even though it's a lie.

**Me: I guess I'm just feeling a bit over-whelmed. New town, new job, new sister, new everything.**

He raises an eyebrow. "New *man?*"

I sigh. Why does he say things like that when he knows what we have isn't going beyond the bed?

Bolt skitters off Maisy's lap and she traipses off to follow him.

Blake settles a hand on my forearm. Maisy isn't watching, so he leaves it there and runs his thumb across my skin. Goosebumps form at the feel of his touch. He said he's wanted to kiss me all night. He has no idea how much I've thought about kissing him. How every night since we were together, I think about being with him again. How I wonder if it will be just as incredible as the first time.

Simultaneously, though, thoughts of how it will end bombard me. I'll just be another notch in his belt. Which is fine... or it *was*.

*When did it* stop *being fine?*

# Chapter Twenty-six

## Blake

Maisy falls asleep on the couch right after she eats, Bolt still in her lap.

*A match made in heaven.*

"I'm going to put her to bed," I tell Ellie.

I carefully extract the cat from Maisy's arms, but when I pick her up, she awakens and immediately searches for him.

"Bedtime," I sign as best I can with one hand.

"Cat," she signs.

I turn to Ellie. "I think she wants the cat to sleep with her."

She shrugs and holds out her hands as if asking *why not?*

I suppose it will be okay. It's not like Maisy is an infant who can be suffocated. It's probably Bolt that I should worry about. But he's done well and seems to be completely happy with her smothering.

I lean down, grab him with my free hand, and put him back into her arms.

In her room, I put Bolt on the bed and point to the bathroom. Maisy knows the whole bedtime routine by now and is good at getting herself ready. I even let her brush her own teeth, though I help her in the mornings to make sure it's done properly, something I'm quite certain wasn't accomplished tonight since she's running back across the room and hopping on the bed in record time.

"Did you brush your teeth?" I ask, doing the motion.

She bears her teeth and shows them to me. I'll take that as a yes.

"Did you wash your hands?" I ask, mimicking the task.

She puts a hand up to my nose. I can smell the fruity scent of the hand soap.

"Good girl," I sign.

She snuggles Bolt the same way she has always snuggled her stuffed cat every night when we settle in to look at a book. The poor ragged toy sits perched against the wall, forgotten. I almost feel sorry for it. It makes me wonder if it ever had a name or if Maisy thought of it as 'cat' as well. Then again, she didn't even know what 'cat' was back then. She didn't know *anything* had names. She didn't know about letters and words. Her whole life was about pictures.

How lonely it must have been for her to live inside her head when she couldn't even think in words.

Maisy pats the book a few times to get my attention. Of course she picked one about a cat. I think we must have about twenty of those now.

She becomes sleepy, yet there's still a hint of a smile on her face. I hear Bolt purr and understand why. Just like the music in the car, Maisy must love the vibrations he produces when he's happy. I look at the two of them, each a misfit of sorts. Not because of any limitations, but because they haven't found their place in the world. Well, Bolt has found his. And I hope to God, Maisy has found hers.

It saddens me every time I think about the possibility that all of this could be a short-term thing. About Lucinda being released from rehab and wanting Maisy back. My only hope is that she'll see how well-adjusted she's become and not pursue custody. Maybe Maisy can live here permanently.

Would I be opposed to sharing custody if Lucida agreed to step up and meet Maisy's needs? Yes, I think, looking down at my sleepy daughter, I sure as hell would be opposed. I want to be the one to read books to her. The one who takes her to school. The one who… eventually, will even walk her down the aisle someday.

I love her. I love her so goddamn much. I want to tell her. I know the sign. But she won't understand the meaning. She's smart, but she still has so much to learn. Emotions are hard to explain to a kid who has a limited vocabulary. But I long to tell her. Tell her I love her and that she'll be safe here. That I'll always be here for her. But until the words and the sign mean something to her, it would be pointless.

I look at the open door, remembering who's waiting for me in the other room, and for a moment I wonder if Maisy is the only one I long to sign those words to. *Jesus Christ*—that thought just slammed into me like a ton of fucking bricks. Could I really be in love? It's a ludicrous thought. We've only known each other a short time. We've only gone on one date.

But still, I feel it. Like I do with Maisy. I swear I can feel it all the way down into my soul.

I put the book away. Then, since Maisy is half asleep, I do something I've never done—I lean down and kiss her forehead. Her soft, smooth, small, amazing forehead. I linger for just a second so I don't scare her. When I pull away, her eyes are open.

She shifts Bolt to the side and leans into me, her hands snaking around my neck.

Maybe she's still thanking me for the cat. Maybe she thinks that's just what you do after someone kisses you. Or maybe... maybe she's beginning to feel about me the way I feel about her.

"Goodnight," I sign without speaking. Because right now, I'm fairly sure no words could get past the happy lump in my throat.

I turn off her light and watch from the doorway as she snuggles Bolt in what seems to be a very reciprocal hug. And for the first time, I know I can do this. I can be a good dad. I can even be the father she needs.

I'm ready.

~ ~ ~

After pulling myself together in my bathroom—because I'm trying to impress Ellie, not send her running from the overly-emotional manchild—I walk back out to the living room.

Something is definitely wrong. She's staring blankly at her phone. She's been way more reserved than she usually is. Distant. Yet it's after seven o'clock and she's still here. She never stays late. That's got to mean something.

After a few long moments, she sees me standing in the room and sets her phone down. "You want to talk?" she asks.

"I don't know the sign for what I want," I say. I stride over, hover above her, and then lean down, trapping her on the couch with an arm on either side of her. "So I'll just show you."

My lips come down on hers. She's hesitant, but then her mouth opens and she returns the kiss with fervor. I settle my body between her legs, my knees on the floor, and we kiss like this for a long time. I can't ever remember a make-out sesh quite like this one. I sure as hell hope it's the first of many.

I grip her thighs, pulling her to the edge of the couch until her good parts meet my good parts. She doesn't seem to mind that I'm dry-humping her right here in my living room. If I had to guess, I'd say she's enjoying it as much as I am.

I love the throaty mewls that come out of her. I wonder if she knows when she makes noise. A question that's burned in my mind for a while finally percolates out of me. I lean back and look in her eyes. "Have you ever tried to speak?"

Her mouth becomes a thin line and she looks over at the wall. She's irritated that I asked. I immediately get out my phone.

> **Me: I'm sorry. I didn't mean to pressure you or anything. I'm not even sure if it's rude to ask. It's just that there are all these amazing sexy sounds coming out of you. I wondered if you knew they were happening. The question just popped out.**

She blushes.

> **Ellie: I can feel light vibrations. But I wasn't aware the noises were audible. Sorry.**

> **Me: Are you kidding? Don't be sorry. Those noises turn me on big time.**

She looks up at me as if I'm crazy. I gesture to the front of my pants, the outline of my erection clear. She blushes harder.

**Ellie: I speak around my family. But that's it.**

Surprised that she speaks at all, my jaw goes slack. "You *talk?*"

**Ellie: All deaf can learn to talk, Blake. It's just a question of whether or not we choose to.**

"Can you talk to *me?*"

She shakes her head forcefully. It's the most deliberate, expressive movement I've seen her make, alerting me to the fact that I've totally overstepped some sort of forbidden boundary.

I don't ask again. If she were comfortable speaking, she would. And she's obviously not. I try not to be offended that the gorgeous woman in front of me may not feel the same way about me as I do her.

"Enough talking," I say. "More kissing. Wait. Show me the sign for kiss."

She brings her fingers up to her mouth, touching it before she moves them up and touches her cheek.

I do the sign back to her.

She nods her seal of approval.

Silently, I sign, "I want to kiss you."

"Very good," she signs with pride like a bonefide teacher.

"What's my reward?" I ask with words.

She studies my lips, licks her own, then leans forward. I love how she can read my lips. She seems to be able to read mine more than most. *A match made in heaven*, I hear in my head as I wrap my arms around her and kiss her.

Part of me wants more. Wants what we had the other night. But oddly, another part of me is perfectly content with this. Her lips. Our closeness. Being right here with her in this moment. Savoring every minute we're together.

Unfortunately, the part that wants more is painfully throbbing against the fly of my pants.

I lean away, wiping a finger under my mouth. "Should I call Allie?"

She considers it for a second, then shakes her head. "I have to go," she signs.

**Me: I'm saying all the wrong things tonight.**

**Ellie: It's not you. I'm just not in a very good headspace right now. Stuff on my mind.**

At least after our marathon make-out, I'm fairly sure the *stuff on her mind* doesn't have to do with me.

I stand. "See you after school tomorrow?"

"Yes." She glances at the hallway. "I'm happy for you and Maisy."

"Me, too. She hugged me again. Before she went to sleep."

She does the sign for clapping and smiles brightly. Then she signs, "Amazing."

**Me: YOU'RE amazing. None of this would be happening if it weren't for you.**

**Ellie: Someone else would have been just as helpful. I'm just doing my job.**

I stare her down.

**Me: Is that really true, El? Did you stay late tonight because it's your job?**

**Ellie: I really do have to go.**

"Friday?" I sign.
She does a little jig dance move that makes me laugh.

**Me: I'll be counting down the hours.**

She cocks her head as if it's a foreign concept. As if a man can't possibly look forward to something as much as a woman.

As if she's obliviously unaware of these intense feelings I have for her.

# Chapter Twenty-seven

## Ellie

I stare at the clock in my office. 3:30pm.

It's been almost forty-eight hours since Sierra left. I was sure she'd be back by this morning. All kinds of scenarios play out in my head. What if Grant didn't go to work yesterday as expected? What if he came home when they were trying to leave? What if he followed them and made good on his threat to kill Tara if she ever left? What if I've lost my sister before we even got the chance to *be* sisters?

What if I just made the worst mistake of my life?

Movement by the door catches my eye. Seth Kingsley, another teacher here, is perched in my open doorway. We crossed paths at Gallaudet years ago when I was a freshman and he was a grad student TA.

"You okay?" he signs.

I nod.

He motions to a chair across from my desk and I invite him in.

"You know what you need?" he asks.

I shut my laptop. "What?"

"Tacos."

"Tacos? It's not Tuesday."

He laughs. "Still. Donovan's Pub makes the best shrimp tacos I've ever had."

"I haven't been there yet."

"How long have you lived here?"

"More than a month."

He stands. "Nobody should go that long without trying Donny's famous tacos. I was thinking of heading over after work. Come along? They have killer margaritas too."

I've accepted exactly one work invitation for drinks since moving here. And that was from my boss the first week I was on the job. Seth and a few others have asked, but their days end at four and mine don't end until six. Which reminds me, I need to start preparing for my appointment with Blake and Maisy.

"Work," I sign. "I'm on my way out to see a student. I'm sure you'll have fun with the others."

"You work too much." He stands and goes for the door, turning to tell me one last thing. "To be clear, I was asking you on a date, Ellie. There aren't any others."

*Oh.* I scrunch my nose guiltily, feeling stupid that I haven't picked up on any vibes from him. He's single. He doesn't have any exes in rehab. No children from past relationships. He would seem the safe option. He's tall, dark, handsome… and deaf.

He's perfect for me.

So then why do I feel nothing when I look at him? I shrug. "Sorry."

He clutches his chest as if I've mortally wounded him. Then he winks and walks away.

My desk vibrates and I look down at my phone. Blake is... *calling?* I pick up the phone and stare at it. Why would Blake call me? My heart races. Has there been an emergency with Maisy? I go to text him, but before I can compose it, a text from Blake appears. And a picture is attached.

**Blake: Look what came in the mail!**

I zoom in on the photo. It's Maisy's new birth certificate. And it lists Blake Montana as the father.

**Me: Wow! I'm so happy for you.**

**Blake: Hopefully the next step will be changing her name. Listen, I thought instead of our regular session at my house you could join us for a celebration. I was thinking Donovan's.**

Okay. Wow. Two invitations by two hot men. To the very same place. Yup, Calloway Creek is definitely a small town.

It's probably not a good idea, having a meal out with Blake and Maisy. It's been my goal not to send her the wrong signals. She's finally settling in with him. They're becoming a family. Sharing a meal with me might be confusing.

Why, then, do my fingers seem to take matters into their own hands and text him back before my brain can protest?

**Me: Sounds great. What time?**

~ ~ ~

I walk up to the pub thinking this was exactly what I needed today, something to keep my mind off Sierra and her mom. It's been too long, and I know it. If they aren't home by tomorrow, I'll have no choice but to go to the authorities. Sierra is flying out of the country on Friday. Surely she needs time to prepare. If she's not back, it's because there was a problem. And not the flat tire kind of problem. The life and death kind.

Entering the restaurant, I do a visual sweep, happy I don't see Seth. That might have been all kinds of awkward. But then a different awkwardness slams into me when I see Blake and Maisy sitting at a large table with family and friends.

*So Blake wasn't asking you on a date.*

This thing with Sierra has me misreading all kinds of signals. Of course he'd want to celebrate this with more than just me. Heck, inviting me could have been an afterthought.

Maisy sees me and her mouth opens. She must have squealed or something as everyone at the table stops what they're doing, looks at her, sees her looking over here, and then all eyes are on me.

It doesn't escape me that Sarah and Allie share an amused look when they see me approach.

Allie hops up and offers me her chair which is directly across from Blake's. I'm introduced to several people I hadn't met before: Cooper Calloway and his wife, Serenity. Dax Cruz. And a bunch of Montana cousins, along with Blake's aunt and uncle. The last person I meet is Lissa, Lucas's fiancée.

I get my phone out.

**Me: Tell Lissa congratulations on her upcoming nuptials.**

When Blake relays the message, Lissa turns to me. "You should come."

Not sure I read her lips correctly, I flash Blake an expression of uncertainty.

**Blake: It seems you've been invited to the wedding.**

"Me?" I point to myself. "Why?"

**Blake: I think she assumes we're dating. I think a lot of people here assume that, El.**

*Oh?* I look around to see most people watching me. I sign, "I guess you should—"

A hand touches my knee under the table.

**Blake: I should, what? Tell them they're wrong? Come on, go with me. It'll be fun. The event of the year.**

Lissa says something to Blake, but her head is turned away, so I don't pick it up. But I do pick up his response. "Ellie says thanks for the invite and she'll be happy to go."

I kick him under the table. "Seriously?" I sign.

He responds with a cocky smile.

I roll my eyes.

Allie grabs my attention and starts signing, showing off her new ASL skills. I'm impressed by how much she's learned.

Plates and plates of food are placed on the table, and I'm shoving a second taco into my mouth when I look over and see Seth Kingsley walking in the front door followed by fellow teacher Jake McSweeney. Seth stops walking when he sees me. He shakes his head, looks away, then sits down in a booth across the restaurant, his back to me.

I feel about two inches tall. I told him I had to work. Technically, I am on a 'home visit.'

"Excuse me," I sign to Blake, and get up.

I cross the restaurant on the way to the bathroom and stop at Seth's table. I say hello to Jake, then tell Seth, "Sorry about this. I am working. Sort of. There was good news concerning Maisy and I was asked last minute to come here and celebrate."

"You don't owe me an explanation," he signs.

"I didn't want you to think this was something it's not."

"So you aren't dating Blake Montana?" He raises a brow.

I look behind me. Blake's eyes are glued to me. Or more precisely, to Seth. I turn back and shake my head. But I must not be very convincing.

"Watch out for him," Seth warns. "He has a reputation. Having a kid he didn't know about dropped on his doorstep should tell you what kind of man he is."

I raise my hands to defend Blake, but decide against it, wondering if Seth is simply watching out for me, or if he's... jealous. The way Seth glares past me to where Blake is sitting clues me in to the latter. If that's the case, nothing I say will make any difference. "Enjoy your dinner," I sign, then walk to the restroom.

When I emerge, Blake is leaning against the wall opposite the ladies' room. He nods to a door on his left, opens it, and waits for me to follow. We end up in the restaurant office.

"Who is that guy?" he asks.

"He works at school."

"He didn't look happy."

I shrug. "He asked me on a date."

He narrows his eyes. I did a sign he doesn't know. I fingerspell, "Date."

He backs up. "He asked you out?"

I nod.

"Just now? When you're here with *me?*" He forcefully jabs a finger at his chest.

**Me: To be fair. I'm not here WITH you. I'm part of a large celebration for Maisy. But no, not just now. He came to my office earlier and asked me.**

"And what did you tell him?" He crosses his arms, waiting.

It's hard not to laugh or even smile. Is this Blake being jealous? I didn't think that happened to… guys like him.

**Me: I told him I'm not dating. Anyone.**

It's a lie. I didn't tell him that. And I'm not really sure why I even said it.

"Semantics," I think he says. "Not dating, but…" His lips stop moving and he does the sign for 'fucking.'

My jaw drops and I swat his hands.

"What?" he says. "It's true. Or it was last week. I'm hoping it will be true again on Friday."

Why is it that every time Blake talks about sex, my cheeks flame?

He smiles and does my name sign.

"I'll take that as a yes." He steps toward me, presses me into the wall, and leans down for a kiss.

His lips are firm, warm, and inviting. And completely wrong for me. The guy in the booth—*he's* the one who's right for me. He's the one who gets how frustrating it is when hearing people don't include you in conversations. He's the one who understands how vulnerable I feel when using my voice.

But as Blake's mouth devours mine, how come all I can think about is how much *this* man gets me?

Movement to my right startles me. Cooper Calloway walks in the office. He holds his hands up. "Sorry." Then he backs out of the door.

**Blake: Caught red handed. I guess there's no going back now.**

I'm staring at his text, wondering what that even means, when I'm reminded of the call I got from him earlier.

"Why did you call me?" I sign.

He looks guilty, and he may have said a curse word under his breath.

**Blake: It was a stupid mistake. I was so excited to share the news about Maisy's birth certificate that I forgot. I didn't realize my**

mistake until I heard the robot voicemail greeting.

Before I'm done reading the text, he sends another.

**Blake: I mean, I didn't forget you were deaf, El. I just... shit... I'm sorry.**

**Me: It's okay. Sometimes I forget you can hear.**

He looks up. "You do?"

**Me: I spend all day signing to colleagues and children. So, yeah, sometimes I forget that when I get home, not everyone is deaf.**

He chuckles. "I thought that you just liked to challenge me with complicated ASL conversations."
I laugh. "I do."
"So, we're good?"
I cock my head.

**Blake: We're good? As in I'm the only one you're 'not' dating?**

I roll my eyes.

**Me: Yes, Blake. You're the only one I'm NOT dating.**

He leans in for one more kiss. It's just a peck, but it has me wanting to speed up time so I can NOT date him on Friday.

"You should have brought Sierra."

And, now reality strikes again. I'd almost gone five whole minutes without thinking of my new sister.

I shrug and sign, "Let's go."

He takes my hand like it's a habit. Then both of us look down, surprised at his gesture. He releases me and smacks his forehead with his palm as if to say 'what was I thinking?'

I swallow, because for a moment, I didn't want to pull away. Then I see Seth's warning in my head and know pulling away is exactly what I should want to do.

# Chapter Twenty-eight

## Ellie

Blake drops me off at my apartment. It would have been pointless to turn down his offer and walk home. After all, I've been in the car with him and Maisy a lot.

I turn and blow a kiss to Maisy. She blows one back.

Just before getting out of the car, I notice the blue Toyota Camry parked next to my building. I fall back into the seat, relief punching me in the stomach. Even if Tara isn't with her, the presence of the car means Sierra is here.

Blake's hand rests on my shoulder. "Are you okay?"

I close my eyes and nod.

**Me: I think I just might be.**

I send off the text and hop out of the car. When I don't see the reflection of his car pulling away in the building window, I turn. The car isn't moving. And Blake is staring at me. Then he blows me a kiss just as I had Maisy. I roll my eyes, spin back around, and go inside.

At my front door, before I open it, I say a little prayer that there are *two* people in my apartment. When I step inside, it doesn't exactly go as I expected given there is a gun pointing directly at me.

I hold my hands up, because… well, that's what you do when a gun is pointed at you, right?

The woman holding it goes pale and lowers the weapon as my heart pounds so loudly I'm sure she must hear it.

Sierra steps into view, touching the woman's arm. Both of them look at each other, relieved.

My hands are shaking terribly, making it hard to text.

**Me: This is Tara I presume?**

Sierra motions for her mother and me to sit.

> **Sierra: I'm sorry about that. She's really on edge. She's barely eaten in days.**

> **Me: Is there a reason for her to be? Did he see you leave? Did he follow you? And where did you get the gun? Sierra, if you bought a gun, Grant will find out.**

She shakes her head. "I didn't buy it."

Sierra: It's my dad's. He has an arsenal back home. Most of it is in cases, under padlock, but Mom knew he kept one for easy access next to his side of the bed. It was in a combination lock box. With nothing better to do on the drive, Mom tried about a thousand numbers before it finally popped open.

Me: So it went down as planned? He didn't know you were there?

Tara traces the gun with her index finger. It makes me squeamish. Does she even know how to use it? My dad, who is vehemently against guns, once took Beth and me to a shooting range to learn how to handle one in case we ever found ourselves in a situation where we needed to. Wow—what a difference between him and the man who raised Sierra.

Sierra: Like clockwork. I got there early, around seven. I parked around the corner like we talked about and waited. He left at quarter to nine. I waited another forty-five minutes just to make sure he wouldn't come back. Then I pinned up my hair and put on the wig, baseball cap, and aviator glasses I bought at Goodwill, along with a pair of overalls and boots with platform heels. I don't think he'd ever suspect it was me. I knocked on the door, not wanting to walk right in. I didn't know what her reaction would be so when she cracked the door, I handed her a note. I knew if she heard my voice, she might hug me, and I didn't want that on any security cameras. She did exactly as I asked, not showing any emotion toward me as she packed a suitcase. We drove for four hours straight, not stopping until we had to for gas. At the gas station, before she left the car, she changed into different clothes that I'd brought for her and put on a dark wig. Ellie, it was almost too easy.

Me: The hardest part may be over, but you've still got a mountain ahead of you. She can't let down her guard. I don't mind telling you I've been twisted in knots these past few days wondering if I'd steered you wrong. With no way to contact you, I was going crazy.

Sierra: She was super stressed out and had a panic attack. So I thought it was best to stop for the night. I used the cash you gave me for a hotel. We were careful to go in and out in disguise. When we arrived here, I cut and colored her hair.

I look at Tara, the crown of her hair still damp, and wonder if this was the way my own mother looked right after she left Grant. Like a scared little girl. Like she's stepped into a whole new world she doesn't think she belongs in.

She looks just like Maisy did the first time I saw her.

Tara's eyes are dark and distant. Her demeanor guarded. She's a small woman. I'd be surprised if she weighs more than a hundred and twenty pounds. I know how big Grant was when I saw him eight years ago. It disgusts me that someone that large feels the need to prey on someone so helpless.

Her hair is reddish-brown and doesn't match her skin tone, making me think she may have been blonde just a few hours ago. She's shorter than both Sierra and me. And she won't take her eyes off the gun.

> **Me: Please tell her it's nice to meet her. Someday, I hope to be able to introduce our mothers. But for now, nobody else can know. Is she good with that?**

She nods, having a conversation with Tara that I only pick up bits and pieces from.

> **Me: And tell her I'm sorry, but she can't take the gun to the school. It's a federal offense to have one on school property. I'll keep it locked up here. The two of you can stay in my guest room until Friday morning. Early, before school, we'll move her into the residential quarters. She can relax here and get some sleep while we figure out how all this will work. I'll pick up a phone for her tomorrow. Do you think she'll be okay on her own there? I really think it's for the best that you go to NZ as planned. Just in case Grant suspects anything. She will be able to text me**

anytime. But only you and me. Nobody else, unless it's to communicate with others at the school. There is a hearing woman in charge of all the janitorial staff. Nobody at the school except my boss will know the arrangement. Everyone there will think she's just another worker getting paid just like them. There are four other workers who live in the residential unit as well, all women. Tara needs to understand that even if she makes friends with them, she cannot say anything. You need to come up with a new name, and a backstory.

Sierra and Tara have another conversation. Tara's hand tightens around the gun. Then she releases it reluctantly and slides it across the table. Sierra pulls the lock box out of a backpack and tells me the combination.

Sierra: Mom wants me to thank you. She admitted to me on the drive that she has been contemplating suicide for a while. She said I was the only reason she hadn't gone through with it. She was waiting for me to get older so I would be able to deal with it better. She told herself that every time she thought of it. It makes me wonder if we got to her just in time. How can I ever thank you, Ellie?

Me: Not so fast. We still have a lot of work to do.

**Sierra: Whatever happens, we're both grateful that you had the guts to make this a reality.**

**Me: It's the least I can do for family. You're my relative, and she's yours. That qualifies us all as family in my book.**

Tara, who has been reading our texts over Sierra's shoulder, comes around behind me and wraps me in a hug. It's long and hard and full of unspoken sentiment. This is one of those times when words just aren't needed.

# Chapter Twenty-nine

## Blake

In Maisy's IEP meeting a few weeks ago, it was decided she's coming along so well she doesn't need three home visits a week anymore. While that means progress, I wasn't exactly excited to find out Ellie would only be coming over once a week.

Add that to the fact that Maisy doesn't want me walking in to pick her up anymore—a request she was actually able to convey—and I haven't seen Ellie nearly as much as I'd like lately.

Not to mention she postponed our dancing date. *Twice.*

Something's been going on with her, and I hope it doesn't have anything to do with the guy at Donovan's that night.

Bolt rubs against my leg as Maisy finishes her dinner. Then he hobbles over to his food dish, gives it a sniff, and walks away. I regard him for a minute. Does he know he's different? Does he see other cats walking around gracefully and get upset that he doesn't have four fully functioning legs?

My focus shifts to Maisy. I've spent many sleepless nights wondering similar things about her. Does she know what Lucinda did to her was wrong? That kids shouldn't be locked up and hidden away just because they aren't perfect in their mother's eyes?

We've been communicating a lot more, and not just through drawings, but signs. Short and simple conversations.

I give the table a little shake—my way of getting Maisy's attention—and point to Bolt. "He's hungry."

She hops off the chair, takes her plate to the sink, then feeds Bolt and plops down next to him while he eats. She always sits next to him while he eats, protectively hovering.

I know the feeling.

When the house lights flash five times, Maisy stands and runs for the front door. She knows Allie is coming. I stride behind her and undo the upper lock.

"Cool," Allie says, accepting Maisy's hug. "I saw the lights from out here. Doorbell strobe lights."

"I had them installed last week."

Allie looks intrigued. "You're really in this for the long haul, aren't you?"

I snort. "What gave it away? The cat that has become a permanent fixture in this house? Or the playground cemented into the back yard?" I see the way she's staring at me. "Wait. Do you think I'm not cut out for this or something? Is that what people are saying behind my back?"

Maisy drags Allie over to the kitchen where Bolt is still eating.

"Don't get your panties in a twist," Allie says over her shoulder.

I follow them in. "What *are* people saying?"

"Do you remember the gossip that went around when Hawk McQuaid found out he had a kid?"

I stiffen, feeling a bit green. "Yeah."

"Well, it's nothing like that." She giggles at her attempt at a prank. "In fact everyone is impressed with how you've stood up and taken responsibility."

She turns to Maisy. "Show me drawings," she signs.

Maisy claps and races into the dining room to collect them.

Allie and I share a satisfied smile. Because it was just a few short weeks ago when my daughter wouldn't understand such a simple request. How *all* our worlds have changed lately.

~ ~ ~

**Me: I'm here. Buzz me up?**

I wonder if, like last time, she'll come down and meet me. But I've been up to her place since then. And honestly, if she thinks she's fooling anyone, she's not. People have seen us together all over town. Even if there wasn't anything going on between us, the rumor mill would have everyone thinking otherwise.

The door latch clicks in release, making me smile, and I climb the stairs to her apartment. Her front door is cracked open, so I enter.

**Ellie: Give me a minute to finish getting dressed.**

I take the opportunity to study the pictures on her wall. Family portraits mostly. I see only a slight resemblance between Ellie and her mom. What a shame it is that she must look more like the asshole. A new photo of her and Sierra is off to one side. It still amuses me how much they look like twins.

Ellie comes out from her bedroom looking... fucking amazing. She's wearing a short flowy blue dress that has pleats near the hem. I can almost see her twirling around as it catches lift from beneath. And those shoes. How women can dance in five-inch heels, I'll never understand, but damn, her legs look even more shapely than usual.

"You look..." Then I sign, "Wow."

She smiles. "You learned a new sign."

I flash her an arrogant grin. "I've learned a lot of them." She's standing right next to the photo of her and Sierra on the wall and I motion to it. "If you ever wanted to fool anyone, the two of you could switch places. She could pretend to be you and then eavesdrop on all the conversations going on around her."

**Ellie: That's sinister. Besides, I don't really want to know what people say about me behind my back. If they can't say something to my face, it's not worth knowing.**

**Me: Geez, El, that's so... healthy. You are definitely a bigger person than I am.**

She comes over and playfully squeezes my bicep. "No I'm not," she signs.

Her touch sends zingers right to my cock. She seems to understand this, and tortures me even more by adjusting her dress and rewarding me with a tiny flash of cleavage.

**Me: I'm not sure I'm okay with you going dancing in that dress. If I spin you around, others might see what's beneath it. And**

**believe me, I'm the ONLY one who's going to see what's under that dress tonight.**

Her freckles make an appearance. Then she lifts the bottom of her dress to show me it has shorts underneath. She does a sign I don't know then fingerspells, "Romper."

I don't do it back. That is one word I don't need to know how to sign.

"Good," I sign. "How's Sierra?"

She pages through the photos on her phone and hands it over. There's a picture of Sierra decked out in ski gear on top of a mountain, her goggles pushed up on top of her head, holding skis and poles at her side. Her smile is easy and comfortable. She must really be in her element.

"She looks happy."

When I look back down at her phone, a text notification pops up. I can't help but read the first line.

**Brooke: I'm doing wonderfully, Ellie. Please don't feel like you have to check on me every—**

The notification disappears.

"Who is Brooke?"

Ellie looks caught off guard. Scared even.

I hold out her phone. "Someone named Brooke texted you."

She takes her phone and reads the text. Then she does another sign I don't understand. She fingerspells, "Client." But, oddly, she does it while looking at the wall behind me.

It makes sense. But something isn't right. She was caught off guard by my question. And she *always* looks at me when she's signing. If I've learned anything about the deaf, it's that they are very visual. They never look away from conversation. Not unless they're mad. It's something I've learned Maisy does if I tell her anything she doesn't like. I think a deaf person turning away is akin to a hearing person sticking their fingers in their ears.

And Ellie never averts her eyes. She's lying.

*But… why?*

She points to her clock and raises a brow.

"Dinner is at eight," I sign. "Dancing after." I step closer. "Then…" I tug her toward me. She's too close for me to sign, so I say, "Then I'm going to take off this dress and everything under it and do things to you that'll have you screaming my name."

She stiffens in my arms. I replay the words in my head and understand why.

"Shit," I say. "I didn't mean—"

A finger comes up over my lips.

"Sorry," I sign.

She nods politely. But I can tell my slip up affected her. "Wine?" she asks.

"Of course."

I follow her to the kitchen. I've only been in here once before for a glass of water the night we were together. In one corner, there's a small desk with a computer monitor that's turned on its side, long side up. That's odd. I point to it. "What's that for?"

"Phone calls," she signs. "Deaf like video calls."

"Really?"

I shouldn't be surprised, knowing how visual they are. It makes sense that they would want to see each other sign versus read texts. It still baffles me sometimes that English is Ellie's second language. It'll be Maisy's second language too—when she learns it.

**Me: Good to know. When Maisy goes off to college, I'll make sure we each have a large monitor for video calls.**

Ellie smiles. Is she thinking what I'm thinking? That I hope I still have Maisy in thirteen years when it's time for her to go off to school?

She gets two glasses from her cabinet and a bottle of Merlot from her pantry. I raise an amused brow. It's one of ours.

"You like my wine," I sign.

"Really good," she signs emphatically.

I take the bottle from her. "You like me."

Her eyes roll. "Not bad," she signs.

I laugh, walk her back to the counter, and press her into it with my thigh. "I'll show you not bad."

When I set the bottle behind her, it knocks into something. I glance over her shoulder and see a spilled jar of fortune cookies. I palm one and show it to her. "Why all the fortune cookies?"

"My parents like them."

She's pleased that I understand.

"May I?" I hold it up.

She shrugs.

I remove the cookie from the plastic, crack it open, and pull out the tiny slip of paper, laughing when I read: ***Wise man never plays leapfrog with unicorn.***

I show it to her, then say, "Your turn."

She fishes her phone from her pocket.

**Ellie: I don't do fortune cookies. I just keep them around for my parents. They have a somewhat unnatural affinity toward them. It's**

kind of nauseating. But also romantic in a way.

I stare her down. "Humor me."

Her eyes don't avert from mine. We're having a silent battle of wills. It must last an entire minute before she caves. She sighs, rolls her eyes, and reaches for one.

She reads it and tosses it aside. "Stupid," she signs.

I pick it up and read: *The fortune you seek is in another cookie.*

I chuckle and hand her a second one. After another slightly less intense stare-off, she accepts it. I think I see the hint of humor in her eyes as she reads the second one. Then she shakes her head and balls that one up.

I smooth it out and read the crinkled paper: *Error 401: Try again later.*

**Me: I'd call that an UNfortunate cookie. Try another.**

She shakes her head.

"Why not?"

**Ellie: Because they're silly, and—case in point—they have nothing to tell me that I don't already know.**

**Me: That's deep, El. Are you saying you have your entire life planned out?**

**Ellie: Are you asking me what I want to be when I grow up?**

"Maybe I am."

**Ellie: I could ask the same from you. Maisy is thriving. Are you thinking of going back to work full time?**

**Me: Way to pivot the conversation. And, yes, I've been bouncing around the idea. My mom thinks I should get a nanny.**

She raises a brow and chews her lip. Do I detect a hint of... jealousy? I could swear I do. And it makes me stand a little taller. Ellie Stone holds her cards close to her chest. I don't know if it has anything to do with her deafness, or if it's just a random character trait. Sure, it seems she likes to kiss me, and she didn't seem to complain about me in bed, but I honestly have no idea how she feels about me. Or I didn't until now.

**Me: Don't worry. I'll make sure she's old and ugly.**

Ellie giggles, an almost imperceptible sound escaping her throat, and shows me the signs for old and ugly.

"I have an idea," she signs.

"If it involves you and me and your bedroom, I'm all for it."

She blushes. "Signs only tonight."

"You don't want me to talk?"

"Not with your mouth." She holds a finger to my lips as if to punctuate her words. "Or your phone."

**Me: What if I use a wrong sign and unknowingly call you a dirty hooker or something?**

She laughs and shows me the signs for dirty and hooker.

"Start now," she signs.

I crack a smile, thinking this is a game.

But once we get to the restaurant and I go to speak to the host, she puts a hand on my arm to stop me then places a finger against her lips and shakes her head.

Oh, so when she meant no speaking, she meant *at all*, not just with her.

"How?" I sign.

She shrugs, maybe liking this game a little too much.

The host is staring at me, waiting. Maybe he has a piece of paper. But I don't want to reach over the podium and just grab something. That would be rude.

Some men standing next to us shake hands, and one of them hands a business card to the other, giving me my answer.

I get out my wallet, fish a business card from the inside pocket, and give it to the host. He eyes me strangely. When I point to my name and then to his iPad, he puts two and two together. "Right this way, Mr. Montana."

"Than—" I stop talking before the word is out, leaving the host even more confused.

I simply nod and smile when he seats us and hands us the menus.

"Awkward," I fingerspell.

She shows me the sign.

"Hello," a woman says, coming to our table. "I'm Michelle, I'll be your server tonight. May I start you out with any drinks?"

"Drink?" I sign to Ellie.

"You pick."

"We'll—" I stop, roll my eyes, and find my selection on the wine menu, pointing to it before holding up two fingers.

Yeah, not awkward at all. The waitress now knows I can talk.

She looks between Ellie and me, like she's wondering if we're pranking her. When she looks at me again, I sign, "Thank you."

The waitress scurries off, not knowing what else to do.

Ordering drinks and dinner turns out to be the easy part. Sitting across from Ellie without being able to say everything on my mind is torture.

Ah, shit. Unexpectedly, I get a taste, however small it may be, of what Maisy must have felt like when she couldn't communicate. How she still must feel only knowing how to ask for basic needs and use simple words.

Part of me wonders if this is an exercise, part of an education plan for me to learn how to sign better. Another part wonders if this is Ellie's way of showing me just a little bit of her world. Probably a little of both.

It takes us ten minutes to have a simple conversation about the weather because I have to fingerspell a lot of it. And if there's one thing I can't do fast, it's fingerspell. I feel like this date is going horribly. I can't be my usual charming self if I can't talk. Is she even going to want to go dancing after?

The sultry glances and subtle toe taps she gives me are reassuring, however, and now I can't wait to have her in my arms. Plus, my hands are cramping. It'll be nice to give them a rest.

By the end of dinner, I know that no matter what I do, I could never even begin to know her world. Because even though I didn't speak, I could still hear everything going on around me. Gossip from the ladies at the next table. The platter of food that crashed loudly on the tile floor of the kitchen. The distant clap of thunder that warns of a brewing storm. But somehow, in all this silence, I feel closer to her than ever.

# Chapter Thirty

## Blake

Dancing with Ellie is surreal. The only thing that would make it better is if I could feel what she's feeling. The vibrations of the music. The pounding of the baritone. But no matter how hard I try to feel the music instead of hear it, I fail.

I don't want to be deaf. I just want to understand it better. And I fear I'll never be able to. Not really. Even people who aren't born deaf, but lose their hearing later, have some sense of sound. When they 'feel' the music, they can recall what it sounded like. When they see a bird, they know what sound it makes. When their lovers mouth the words 'I love you,' they can imagine what it sounds like.

To have been born deaf, however—*profoundly deaf*—with no exposure to sound whatsoever, there's just no way for a hearing person to truly understand what it's like.

I can't say how often I've thought about the time Ellie asked how I would describe sound to someone who can't hear. Obviously she's well educated. She knows the concept of sound.

But she'll never know if what she thinks of as sound is actually sound at all.

One thing is true. Ellie is proving you don't have to hear to dance. Because, holy shit, the way she presses against me during slow songs. Watching her sexy moves during fast ones. Letting her take the lead and following her sway. All in silence, while the music blares around me. And when we're close—like we are right now—my arms around her, with no use of our hands for speaking, it's like this entire last hour has been nothing but intense foreplay.

When I can't take it any longer, and my entire being screams for the unspoken promises she's all but guaranteed me with the movements of her body against mine, I lean back, reluctantly letting her go so I can use my hands to talk. I swipe a thumb down her jawline then sign, "Should we drive home?"

Her face cracks into a grin, then she covers her mouth and full-on laughs.

I furrow my brow and hold out my hands, palms up.

"You said *ride mustache*," she signs, slowly fingerspelling the last words. I can see the blush overtake her face even in the dim light. Then she proceeds to show me the difference between ride and drive, and then home and mustache.

I see where I went wrong. But can you blame me? I'm hornier than a three-peckered Billy goat. In the state I'm in, it would be difficult to speak my first language let alone sign.

Now *I'm* the one laughing. I wink and sign, "Happy to grow a mustache." I have to fingerspell *grow* because I have no idea how to sign it.

She shows me of course, and damn, my erection is what's growing now as we stand here and talk about this. "Leave now," I sign, then take her hand and pull her behind me to the door.

A short while later, having driven faster than usual back to her place because of the situation in my pants, I pull into her lot, park, then turn off the car. But despite what happened a few minutes ago, I don't get out. I don't want to presume anything no matter how much I want to follow her upstairs, strip off her clothes, and have a repeat of three weeks ago.

Three weeks of knowing what it's like to be with her and not being able to has been pure torture.

Three weeks of dreaming, fantasizing, and masturbating. A whole lot of masturbating.

Three weeks of being incapable of getting this silent beauty out of my head.

I sit back, look at her, and stretch an arm across her headrest. *Ask me.*

Dr. Stone is intelligent. She's driven. She's always taking the upper hand. Except when it comes to me. When it comes to me, or more specifically, sex, she's as shy as grapevines in winter. Sometimes I wonder, though, is it really shyness, or is it something else? She once said she had dated a lot of guys, but never really had relationships. It makes me wonder if she's just shy with me, or is it all men? Or am I mistaking shyness for apprehension? It must really do a number on a person to find out they're unwanted by another human.

Maybe what I perceive as shyness is really armor. Walls she's erected to keep from getting close to anyone.

I stare into eyes that I know are blue even though it's dark and I can't see them clearly. I stare into them knowing I want to break down those walls. Remove that armor.

"Good job tonight," she signs by the light of a streetlamp.

I hold out my hands and bow my head in pride even though I know my signing is still very rudimentary.

She's waiting for me to ask her. *Ask me.*

She chews her lip, a sure sign of nervousness. If I've learned anything from Ellie, it's how to pick up on non-verbal cues. I'm glued to my seat watching her teeth work her lower lip, the twitch in my pants proof of how much I'm enjoying the show.

She huffs out a breath and I try not to smile.

"Did you have fun?" she asks.

"Always fun with you," I sign. Or at least I think I do. I'm a bit unsure of the word always. *Ask me.*

She swallows, glances out her window, and then back. "You want to"—she hesitates—"ask me something?"

I throw her signs right back at her. "You want to ask *me* something?"

It's funny how I've learned to put emphasis on a single word merely by changing my expression. Yeah—she's a good teacher.

Another audible huff.

Why her uncomfortable awkwardness makes me even hornier, I have no clue. *Fucking ask me.*

I'm about to give in to this standoff when she bites her lip once more and signs, "Come up?"

"Show me *never*," I fingerspell the last word, not knowing the sign.

She looks taken aback for a moment, then goes in full-on teacher mode and shows me the sign, doing a half circle in the air with her flat palm then ending in somewhat of a karate chop. The sign resembles something like a question mark.

Finally I smile. I smile big. Because I just tricked her. "Thought you'd never ask," I sign.

She's an expressive person, and I see relief cross her face right before she playfully slaps my thigh. I trap her hand and hold it against me. She goes to sign with the other, but I reach out and stop her.

"No words," I sign. "Not with mouth or hands. Nothing."

She stares into me with dark, revealing eyes. She gets me. She forbade me from speaking. Now I'm forbidding her from signing. There will be no talking at all. What on earth will we ever do?

Surprising me, she climbs over the console and onto my lap, lowering her head to crush her lips against mine. *Holy shit, I'm a fucking genius.*

Having her in my lap brings back all the feelings I got on the dance floor and more. I'd unzip my fly and push her panties aside right here if we weren't parked underneath a streetlamp. Or maybe if I were five years younger. But Ellie Stone is not someone you bang in the front seat of a car. She's someone you take your time with. Someone you worship. Someone you make love to, not fuck.

And for the first time in my life, a girl is sitting on me and making my dick hard, and I'm thinking of her, not me. Not my needs. Because this woman needs a man who isn't like her birth father. She needs a man who accepts her for everything she is. A man who won't leave her. One who will always tell her how special she is. Not because she's deaf, but because she's amazing.

I open the door and carefully slip out, keeping her in my arms. She looks up at the light and wriggles out of my hold. I let her go, but only because I know in sixty seconds, she'll be right back where she was. Where she belongs.

She may have removed herself from my arms, but I still grab her hand. I grab it tightly even when she tries to pull away. She looks at me. I challenge her with my silent stare. She shakes her head, relaxes her hand in mine, and pulls me along. *Quickly.* Because she doesn't want anyone to see the handholding? Or because she can't wait to be straddling me again?

My question is answered when we enter her apartment and she throws down her purse, unaware it came open sending its contents dancing across the floor. Then, she's back in my arms, staring into my eyes, conveying everything she wants me to do to her without a single word, motion, or sign.

On the way to her bedroom, she taps on my shoulder, pulls out her phone and nods to the kitchen counter. I set her down, take my phone out of my pocket, and hand it over. She leaves both of them in the kitchen.

When we enter her bedroom, she leaves the light off and shuts the door. We're in total darkness with the exception of a small glow coming from a streetlamp outside her window. Wow, she's really going all in with this. Dark *and* quiet.

My cock hardens knowing this night is going to be all about touch. Touch without signs or words. Touch without anything else. I wish I had earplugs with me. Something to mute the ambient sounds of faraway traffic. Of the occasional voice coming from the sidewalk. Of dogs barking in the distance. I want to be immersed in only her.

We carefully navigate our way to the bed. She leads the way as there's not even enough light to see the outline of furniture. The box spring squeaks as she sits on the bed. I extend a hand, searching for her face. I cup her chin and lower my mouth to hers, capturing her lips with mine as I press her back against the mattress.

I'm so completely aware of every little noise. Our clothes rustling. Her breath hitching. Hell, I can almost hear my heart pounding. But Ellie isn't aware of any of that. She's surrounded by both darkness *and* silence, a circumstance that would scare most people. But not her. Or maybe she is scared but trusts me enough to be okay with it. The thought has me reeling. I want her to trust me. I *need* it.

"El—" I start to say when I pull back to catch my breath.

I freeze, my voice echoing in my head. I hope she didn't feel me speak.

Hungry hands running down my back tell me she may have been too preoccupied to notice. I vow to remain silent. To immerse myself in this experience that is already unlike any I've ever had.

Kissing her again, my hands snake across her body, feeling every curve over the silky material of her dress. After palming her breasts and pinching her stiff nipples, I work my way down, push the fabric aside, and find her pussy drenched. I moan, then realize my mistake and go still. She puts a hand on mine and presses it firmly as if begging for more. Okay, so moaning is allowed then. Encouraged, perhaps.

When I touch her clit, she moans herself. It's a soft, muted, high-pitched mewl that makes me feel all-powerful. I glide a finger inside her and she arches against me.

I can't take it anymore. I need skin against skin.

When my hand pulls away, a pouty huff escapes her, making me smile. She's as needy as I am. I feel around her back for buttons, or a tie. I find a zipper. I lower it and wait for her to remove her arms, sliding the dress down her legs and off completely, taking off her heels in the process. Then I kiss my way up her legs and remove her panties, inhaling her intoxicating scent as I go.

Before I can put my mouth on her, she's all hands, trying to remove my belt, but it's stuck. I undo it, then let her tug it out of my jeans. It snaps back and thwacks me in the head. She has no idea it did, and I don't tell her.

In no time at all, I'm naked next to her, my clothes and shoes strewn somewhere across her floor.

My hands waste no time getting back on her. First, the curve of her neck. Then her collarbones. Then her breasts. My mouth joins the party and I tongue an erect nipple, the taste of her skin nearly sending me tumbling over the edge. And her scent, the one that tells me she wants this, is overpowering.

It's surreal how not using your other senses seems to amplify the ones you *are* using. We're not hearing. We're not seeing. So suddenly, touch, taste, and smell are ten times more powerful.

Her hand grips my cock and I groan in pleasure. I know she felt it. She works her hand up and down, increasing the pace. I'm at a total loss here. I'm about to come like a thirteen-year-old with a nudie magazine. If I push her away, she might get the wrong idea.

A finger gets pressed against my lips. Did I make another sound? No. Then why did she…

*Jesus.* I lose all train of thought when her finger leaves my lips and reappears down by my balls. She's pumping me with one hand and the other is lightly teasing my ball sack.

Maybe she knew I wanted to say something. Something like last time when I told her I'd come too soon if she touched me. That was her way of letting me know she knew what I was thinking, but she was going to get me off anyway. Her putting a finger to my lips was her taking control.

*Fuck, that's sexy.*

Either way, I'm too far gone now, so I commit myself to the task and lie back to enjoy the impending detonation.

All I hear is the sound of her breathing and the noise her hands make as they bring me closer to God.

My butt cheeks clench tightly, and I stifle a prolonged groan right before I feel my hot, wet cum spilling across my lower abs.

My head falls back hard against the bed, my body languid as I recover. The need to talk to her, to thank her for one hell of a hand job, almost has me turning on the light. But I don't. Instead, I revel in the feeling of her snuggling next to me, waiting patiently for her turn. And what a turn I plan to give her.

Waiting for my energy to return, I'm disappointed when she pulls away. Then a moment later, I feel something swiping against my lower abs. She's cleaning up my mess. I take the tissues from her and finish the job. Then I toss them... somewhere... and get to work, vowing to make her scream my name even if she doesn't want to.

Palming her soft, silky skin has my dick twitching even though I just came. Still, I'm not about to sink myself inside her until, one: I've given her an orgasm she'll never forget, and two: I'm hard as a rock and ready to fuck like Superman.

I don't go right for the kill. I trail wet kisses across her breasts, down her rib cage, and along her right hip, bypassing her core altogether. She squirms under me as I tease her inner thighs with my five o'clock shadow. As I tongue the inside of her knees. As I kiss all the way down to her bare feet.

Working my way back up, still ignoring her wet center, she grabs my head and puts it where she wants it to be.

*That-a-girl.*

I work my tongue in and out of her, making love to her with my mouth as I taste the sweet tang of her arousal. I pull away, fearing I might sprain my tongue in my enthusiasm, and replace it with a finger. Then I add another. I feel her arch into me as I rub the inside of her, crooking my fingers to find the spot that will drive her wild.

I know the moment I find it. Her walls tighten slightly, and another faint sound escapes her. I smile, knowing she's mine until I extract every last quiver. Adding my tongue back into the mix, I tease her clit. I run it in circles. Then side to side. Up and down. I lightly suck it into my mouth and she explodes under me. My fingers get tightly squeezed, her orgasm pulsating against them. My tongue continues to work her clit until she urges me away, too sensitive to receive any more.

I roll to the side and wipe my mouth with my forearm. Then a hand lands on my chest as if a dead weight had dropped onto it. I chuckle and grab it, holding it in mine as I listen to her breathing become calm and slow, envisioning her limp body basking in afterglow.

I'm fully hard again and ready to roll. But I'm struck by the question… does she want more? Do I break character and ask her? I want to see her. I want to see her eyes. But she chose to have it this way for a reason, so I remain still and wait for a… sign.

Her hand disappears and her weight shifts on the bed. Then her hand is back in mine, a little square package nestled between our palms. I'm not sure if I'm happy or bothered by the fact that she has her own supply of condoms. I choose to believe she bought them recently in anticipation. But curiosity has me already composing a text in my head to tactfully ask her how many guys there have been. And then another text telling her that there won't be any more. Not after me.

I search for her face, careful not to poke her in the eye, and put my hand to her lips to see if she's smiling. She's not. Then again, I don't think I smile after a good orgasm either. I just lie back and savor the moment.

Her lips capture one of my fingers, sucking it into her mouth as if it's another part of my anatomy.

That, paired with the condom, is all the permission I need. I hastily pull my hand away, rip open the package and slide it on. She reaches for my dick and gives it a few tugs. Is she making sure I'm hard? Or checking to make sure I put it on? I momentarily wonder if she trusts men at all after what her wife-beating father did to her.

Pushing the thought aside, I move to get on top of her, but she pushes me back down. I feel her climb on top of me and guide me inside her, slowly at first, as if testing the waters. Then she comes down harder, fully seating my cock until I can feel the end of her. As she rides me, I only have my imagination to guide me in what she might look like. Is her head angled back? Is her mouth slack? Are her breasts bouncing with every movement?

Her hands explore my chest as her thighs do all the work to keep her sliding up and down my shaft. I grip her hips, helping with the motion. It's not enough. I need to feel more of her. I cup her breasts. I work her nipples between my fingers. I feather my thumb across her clit to find it engorged again. I want her to come with me inside her. I need to feel her orgasm clench my cock and milk it until we're both completely and utterly drained.

She moves faster. So do I. I lightly pinch her clit between my thumb and forefinger and she drives down onto me even harder. So I do it again. And then again. And once more, until she stills and spasms on top of me. I pump up my hips three more times, her name echoing off the walls as I join her in ecstasy.

She collapses down onto my chest and I wrap her in my arms. We lay this way, only beads of sweat between us.

Is there even a way to tell her she's the best I've ever had? Once could have been a fluke. It *had* been a while. But twice? And this time was even better. It was an out-of-body experience. More intense than anything I've ever felt.

Is it because it was just us in the silence and the darkness?

*It's because you love her.*

Still lying on my chest, she takes my hand in hers, places her other hand against my open palm, and... *spells something?* When I don't react, she does it again. I focus all my energy on the tactile sensation and try to feel the letters. There are only three of them. W-O-W.

*Okay, yeah. I definitely fucking love her.*

I swallow at the thought. It's not the first time I've had it. But it is the first time I've known it to be unequivocally, undeniably, indisputably true. Something flows through me. A lava river reaches the end of every finger and toe. It weaves through my body, warming every nook and cranny. Like a hand, it works itself right around my heart and squeezes. It squeezes hard. Because for the first time in my life, I fear I'm in a position I never thought I'd be in. I'm in love with someone who may not love me back.

The vulnerability of that slams into me like a bullet from a gun. I gently roll her off me and go into the other room.

*Fuck.* The word rolls around in my head as I pad out to the kitchen, still completely naked. I find a glass, fill it, and stand still, silently chugging water, hoping to calm the voices in my head.

I spy the fortune cookie container on the counter and wonder if it has any wise words for me.

Couldn't hurt to see.

Reaching in, I swirl my hand around as if picking the next tribute in *The Hunger Games* and pull one out. I open it.

**Your heart knows the right answer.**

I stare at it long and hard, because... *damn.* Then I almost throw it out, knowing Ellie's aversion to fortunes. Instead, I decide to leave it right where it is. Because maybe it's something Ellie needs to read too.

# Chapter Thirty-one

## Ellie

Blake comes back to bed, his nakedness silhouetted by the light from the living room. He puts a glass of water on my nightstand and hands me my phone. I look down at it.

> **Blake: Can we text now please? You've worn me out, woman. Between signing all night and working your delectable body with my fingers, I'm not sure my hands will be good for anything more than texting for a while.**

It's hard to argue with that, so I don't. I smile and nod. He crawls back into bed as if it's his own. And I'm not quite sure how I feel about the warm, fuzzy feeling that brings to me. I watch him in the dim light as he closes his eyes and sets his phone on his chest. He looks… peaceful.

Maybe that's because *his* head isn't spinning out of control with warning signals. Maybe it's because *he* knows that whatever this is has an expiration date. Because all of his—affairs? Conquests? Flings?—do. Or maybe it's just because he's accepted that he isn't capable of more.

*More.*

Now I'm back to the warm fuzzy feeling of him lying next to me, one foot most definitely *not* out the door.

Even if more with Blake was an option, deep down I know it couldn't happen.

*It could if you let it.*

I close my eyes and lie back, a war going on in my head like I'm in one of those cartoons with an angel on one shoulder and the devil on the other.

Warm lips kiss my neck. My eyes fly open. Blake is looking right at me.

I furrow my brow.

He traces the side of my jaw with his finger. "You're beautiful."

My insides melt. The angel—or maybe it's the devil—crosses his arms and gives me a disapproving stare.

> **Blake: Now that we can talk, I wanted to ask you something I was curious about earlier. You haven't said anything about going to Lucas's wedding. Not since the day Lissa invited you. You're going, right?**

**Me: I shouldn't. I know she misread the
situation.**

**Blake: You don't want to be my date?**

**Me: Aren't you the best man?**

**Blake: One of them, yeah. Doesn't mean I
can't have a date. Come on, it'll be fun. You
can meet Dallas. And if you want, you can join
in on the pool.**

I narrow my eyes.

**Blake: Don't tell me you haven't heard rumors
about him.**

After I shrug, he goes on to explain how Lucas has left several
women at the altar and another one only weeks before. Apparently
the entire town is betting on whether or not he'll go through with
it.

I shake my head disapprovingly and tap out a text.

**Me: I'm not going to bet money on whether or
not he breaks Lissa's heart.**

**Blake: El, are you a romantic?**

I'm pretty sure I let out an audible snort. "Hardly," I sign.
He looks at me blankly, so I fingerspell it.

He laughs and pulls me close, tilting his head so I can see his lips in the light from outside the door. "I think you are. Maybe you just don't want to be."

It wasn't a question, so I don't provide an answer.

**Blake: It's settled then. You'll come.**

Though I don't text him back, someone else clearly does. His eyes are glued to his phone. And he doesn't look happy.

I put a hand on his arm. "Okay?" I ask when he looks over.

He shakes his head. "No. Not okay," he signs. Then he hands me his phone.

My entire body clenches when I see who it's from. I recognize the name from when he told me Maisy's story.

**Unknown number: Blake, this is Lucinda Wilcox. I got your contact info from a social worker. I've been going back and forth on if I should do this, but my counselor seems to think it's a good idea. I'd like you to bring Maisy to the city on Sunday. It's family weekend. I've attached the address. Come between noon and four.**

Suddenly, I become protective. Of Maisy. Of *him*. She wants to see the daughter she neglected and the guy she kept her from all those years. The nerve of her to even ask.

"Sorry," I sign, handing his phone back.

**Blake: That's what SHE should be saying. Sorry I neglected our kid. Sorry I didn't tell**

you about her. Sorry I'm such a fucking loser. Who does she think she is texting me out of nowhere demanding I bring Maisy to see her?

"Do you have to take her?" I sign.

Blake: I don't know. Maybe not. My lawyer told me I'd have to wait for Lucinda to get out of rehab and go before a judge to see what would happen in the custody case. I had no clue she'd ask to see Maisy before then.

"If you take her, I could come. You know, to help Maisy communicate and to be an impartial party to your meeting." I have to fingerspell several words, but it seems he gets it, and I'm pleased.

Blake: Impartial, huh? Do you really think you could be impartial when it comes to Maisy? I'm just not sure what to do. She's been doing so well. I don't want it to mess with her head. Maisy doesn't ever ask about her mom.

"Maybe she doesn't know how to ask."
"Whose side are you on here?" he signs.
"Yours."
Blake touches my arm and looks out into the other room. He glances back. "Someone is at your door."
I bolt up in bed. *Someone is at my door?* At eleven o'clock on a Friday. One who's inside the building without me having to buzz

them up? Sickness paws away at my insides. Could it be Grant? Has he found Tara and come after me?

Blake squeezes my hand. "You stay. I'll get it."

I rear back, swiveling my head forcefully.

He looks down at his nakedness and laughs, thinking that's why I didn't agree. "I'll get dressed first."

I pound on the bed to get his attention. When he looks over, I sign, "No."

"Why not? Unless you think it's your other boyfriend."

At the moment, I'm too scared to unpack that sentence. His pants are already on when I get up to stop him, but then I realize I'm naked too. By the time I throw on a robe, he's left the bedroom. Almost on instinct, I race to my bedroom closet, quickly dial the combo on the lockbox, and retrieve the gun, checking to make sure it's loaded.

I stick my head around the corner, ready to defend both myself and Blake from Grant. My hand shakes a mile a minute, so I'm certain I would have terrible aim. But at least I'll be able to make a stand.

I almost accidentally pull the trigger when Blake comes back and runs right into me. Or more accurately, right into the gun. His eyes go maniacally wide, and he says something I don't make out, before he carefully takes the gun from my trembling hands, guides me back to the bed, and sits me down. He empties the chamber, sets the gun on my dresser, and picks up his phone.

**Blake: Why in the hell did you have a gun pointed and ready to fire?**

"Who was at the door?" I ask.

**Blake: Nobody. Food delivery. She had the
wrong apartment. Answer the question, El.
Why did you look so fucking scared just now?**

I don't answer. Mostly because I can't. Not without letting
him in on my secret.

**Blake: Is there an ex-boyfriend or ex-husband
you're not telling me about?**

I shake my head.

He paces the floor at the end of the bed, staring over at the
gun. His mouth is moving, but I get the idea he's talking to himself,
not me. It gives me time to come up with a plausible excuse.

"What's going on, Ellie?" he signs. "You almost shot me. I
deserve to know."

I nod, calm enough now that I've been able to conjure up a
believable lie.

**Me: Everyone who knows me knows I can't
hear a knock on the door. It couldn't have
been anyone but an intruder. Especially at
this hour.**

**Blake: Intruders don't knock.**

All I can do is shrug.

He stops pacing and sits next to me. Resting a hand on my
knee, he blows out a long, drawn-out breath. "Do me a favor. The
next time you get scared, call 911."

"Sorry," I sign.

**Blake: Promise me, El.**

I nod even though it's another lie.

"Shit," he says. "I promised Allie I'd be back by eleven. I'm late."

"You should go," I sign.

"I think I should stay," he signs.

"I'm fine."

He looks over at the gun.

I put a hand on his jaw and direct him to look back at me. "I'm fine," I sign again, hoping he believes it this time.

He nods, albeit reluctantly. "Put that thing away."

"Okay."

Once fully dressed, he leans down and kisses me. When he pulls back, he signs, "Show me perfect again," fingerspelling the word perfect. Then he says, "After all, the only time I ever get to use the word is when I'm with you."

How this man continues to wedge himself further inside my heart is something I've yet to be able to explain.

I show him the sign.

"Perfect night," he signs. Then he shrugs and says, "Until you almost killed me." He crosses the room, turning back to wave goodbye.

I wait a minute to give him time to get out the front door, then I hop up and immediately lock it. Back in my room, I secure the gun away, hoping I never have another reason to get it out. Then I head to the kitchen for a midnight snack.

On the counter sits two halves of an opened fortune cookie, a slip of paper between them.

I read it, wondering if he simply forgot to throw it away, or if he left it as a message to me.

# Chapter Thirty-two

## Blake

Ellie has a gun.

And we're going to see Lucinda.

It's no surprise I haven't slept much at all the last two nights.

I mean, it makes sense, I suppose, El being from the city and all. But to get it out and *draw* it just because I told her someone knocked on her door?

Something doesn't add up.

I'm stalling getting out of bed and I know exactly why. I've been dreading this day since Lucinda sent me the text Friday night. There's no way to tell Maisy where we're going and who we're going to see. I have no pictures of Lucinda. What if we walk in the place and Maisy sees her and runs away in fear?

On the other hand, what if she sees her and runs *to* her?

My hand works my jaw as I contemplate which of the two scenarios scares me more.

Light blinds me for a second. Then weight shifts on my bed as Maisy crawls into it. I can't help my smile. It may have taken well over a month and an errant cockroach on the wall by her bed, but last week after she ran into my room to escape the bug, we had our first father/daughter snuggle. Ever since, she's come into my room each morning, Bolt in her arms, and the three of us cuddle until someone's stomach growls. Today it's mine.

"Hungry?" I sign.

She nods.

"What do you want?"

She does the sign for pancake.

"You help," I sign.

She scurries out of the room ahead of me, Bolt on her heels. By the time I hit the bathroom and get to the kitchen, she has the box of pancake mix, a spoon, and a bowl all ready to go. Maisy is a good helper. I shove the suspicion from my mind that she's a good helper because she had to do so much for herself.

Ten minutes later, the kitchen island is a mess with powder and stray dollops of batter, and hot pancakes are steaming on a platter—two smiley faced ones for her and two snowman ones for me.

The faces on hers are remarkably crooked. She has learned how to drizzle batter for eyes and a smile. The ones she made today look more like Hannibal Lecter than emojis.

She giggles as I slip the creations onto her plate.

Maisy's giggle has become one of my reasons for living. She can't even hear it and has no idea what it does to my heart.

She dips a sliced banana into the syrup. The syrup drips off, leaving a trail of sticky dots on the table in front of her. I dab a finger on one of the drips then touch it to her nose. Then I dab another and touch it to her cheeks. She wipes her face, making it one big sticky mess. I laugh, wet a napkin, and get on my knees next to her, wiping her clean.

She smiles, dabs her finger in the sole remaining drip of syrup, then smears it on my nose and cheeks.

I wipe the tip of my nose then lick my finger, making a silly face afterward.

She giggles again. Then she does something that changes my world. She points to herself then crosses her arms over her chest then points to me.

My heart fucking stops. She signed "I love you."

Tears come to my eyes, but I quickly wipe them away, not wanting her to misread my reaction. I've been signing the words to her for a week, even though I'm not sure she knows what they mean.

*I love you* can be signed in different ways. I chose the 'me love you' way which has me pointing to myself, crossing my arms over my heart, then pointing at her. The ILY sign that is a combination of the three letters just doesn't seem as emotional and expressive, and I need her to know that I don't just love her casually, I love her fiercely. And forever.

I think I smile so big, my face just might split in two.

As I take in her delighted reaction to my expression, it dawns on me that her eyes are no longer dark and distant. Hell, they're almost sparkling. There's been a fundamental shift in both of us with her declaration. I feel like we've turned a corner and there's no going back. And my heart has never been so full.

"I love you," I sign emphatically, then pull her in for a hug, knowing no truer words have ever been signed. "I love you so fucking much," I whisper, nestling her against me.

As she rests her head on my shoulder, her arms wrapped around my neck, I wonder why in the hell I'm about to put someone I love in a position to see Lucinda if I don't even know if she wants to.

Pulling back slightly, I try to hide the change in my mood from her.

"Let's clean up," I sign, dreading how this day may turn out.

~ ~ ~

"Change of plans," I tell Ellie, when she arrives a few hours later. "Can you watch Maisy?"

"Why?"

"I'm going alone."

Ellie's eyebrows knit together.

> Me: You're always telling me to let Maisy help decide what's best for her. I know nothing about Lucinda. What if she's Mommy Dearest? I can't do that to Maisy. So until we can have a conversation about it and I know where she stands, I'm not going to put Maisy in a position to be scared or hurt or even just confused. But I'm going. I have questions for Lucinda. Lots of them.

Ellie looks at me like a proud mother.

> Ellie: Wow... you've come a long way from the man who I accused of neglect.

> Me: You have no idea. We had a breakthrough today. She did a new sign.

"Which one?"

I consider showing her, but then think of who's standing in front of me. When I sign 'I love you' to Ellie, it's damn well going to be because I'm saying it to *her*.

*Aaaaaand* why *haven't you done that yet?*

**Me: She told me she loves me.**

Ellie's hand covers her heart, her eyes becoming glassy as she smiles as brightly as I did.

Maisy runs out, dressed for the day, sees Ellie, and squeals.

Ellie signs, "You and me play?"

Maisy thinks on it, walks to the dining room table, peruses the drawings until she finds what she's looking for, and brings it over. She holds out a picture I drew of the park near McQuaid Circle, complete with the playground.

Ellie signs, "You want to go to the playground?" She shows us the sign for playground then points to the one in the picture.

Maisy signs, "Yes," then grabs my hand and tries pulling me toward the door.

When I resist, she looks up. "Just you and Ellie," I say as I point to myself and shake my head.

I'm not sure if she understands, because it's always been the three of us. This is the first time they're going on an outing without me.

But my smart and trusting daughter simply blows me a kiss then takes Ellie's hand and drags her to the door.

I get out my keys, take the house key off the ring and hand it to Ellie before they're out the door.

"Good luck," she signs.

~ ~ ~

Ninety minutes later, I'm walking up to the rehab center. I hesitate before going inside, debating why I'm even here. Wondering if she'll even tell me the things I need to know, while at the same time feeling terrified of hearing them if she does.

I'm aware that one of the steps in addiction recovery is to make amends. Is that what she's trying to do? Or was she simply strongarmed by her therapist into summoning us here?

After checking in at the front desk and being issued a visitor name tag, I'm escorted through the building and out back to a courtyard. There are quite a few groups of people occupying the various seating areas. I scan the faces, wondering if I'd even recognize Lucinda after all these years.

"Ms. Wilcox is over there," the staffer says, pointing to a woman seated by a fountain of water cascading into a koi pond.

"Thanks."

The guy nods before he turns to go back inside.

Lucinda doesn't see me. She's working her hands anxiously, wringing them over and over as her left knee bounces up and down.

She's clearly nervous.

I'm also stricken by how thin she is. Then again, drugs can do that to a person.

When she looks up and sees me, I almost gasp. Her eyes are sunken. Her face gaunt. She's pale, her skin almost yellow. She immediately looks behind me, surely scanning the area for Maisy.

"Where is she?"

"*Where is she?*" I bark. "That's all you have to say? Are you fucking kidding me? Do you even know what I've gone through these past few months?"

Seeing her this way, her body screaming with the evidence of years of drug use, has me seething even more. I lose all sense of self control and everything that's been percolating inside me comes spewing out.

"You almost ruined her. What in the hell did you do, keep her locked up in your apartment because you were ashamed of her? Why didn't you get her checked out by a doctor? Why didn't you learn how to communicate with your own daughter? And why in God's name didn't you try to find out who her fucking father was? Look at you, Lucinda. You're a pathetic excuse for a human. People like you shouldn't be allowed to have children."

Lucinda's face is stoic, which somehow pisses me off even more.

"If you think you can do all the shit you did to Maisy, dump her on me, go to rehab for a few months, then get her back, you'd better think again. Because guess what? Despite your criminal neglect of her, she's thriving. She's going to school. She's learning how to sign. She's fucking happy. For the first time in her miserable life, she's happy. She calls me Dad, for Christ sake. Tell me, Lucinda, did she ever once call you Mom? And you wanted me to *bring* her here? You look like death warmed over. You'd have only scared her. Thank God I left her at home."

I'm not swayed in the least when her eyes become misty. She doesn't deserve my pity. "Oh, *you're* sad," I say, laughing incredulously. "You want me to feel sorry for you after what you did to her?" I throw up my hands, completely exasperated. "Jesus, why did I even come?" Then I remember why. For answers. So instead of spinning around and walking out after saying my piece, I sit and stare daggers. "Do you have *anything* to say?"

"I'm dying."

*Ah, shit.* Of all the things I thought she'd say, and all the excuses I was sure she'd spout; this was definitely not what I was expecting. "You're… dying?"

She nods. "It's amazing what clarity is brought to your life knowing you're going to die."

"I'm sorry to hear that. But did you really think having Maisy see you like this would be good for her? Or are you just wanting to make amends so she doesn't forever remember you as the monster you were?"

My words are harsh, I know. But being sick doesn't excuse her past actions.

"I guess it was a bad idea. It's one of the steps."

"Maybe normally it would be. But nothing about this situation is normal. Maisy didn't even know her name. She didn't even know people *had* names. She didn't know one goddamn thing until she came to live with me. You expect a child like that to understand why she's been brought here? I mean, you do know she's deaf, right? How could you not?"

Guilt crosses her face. "I never had her tested. I know it happened because of me. My drug use. I didn't want to admit it was my fault. Having her tested would mean I'd have to accept the blame. So I chose to ignore it.

"When I found out I was pregnant, I got excited at first. I thought having a baby was going to save me. Be my way out of drugs. It was going to be me and her against the world. The first few months after I had her were amazing. But then she didn't act like other babies. She didn't look at me when I came into a room. She didn't react to sounds. I knew something was wrong. I thought maybe she was autistic or brain damaged. I guess… I guess I didn't want to know."

I shake my head in disgust at her selfishness. "If she had gotten early intervention it would have changed everything. She's doing well, but it's been a struggle. Every day is a challenge. She's almost five and we can only have simple conversations. It took a long time for her to adjust. For her to understand I'm her father. How could you have been so goddamn self-centered? What did you think was going to happen to her as she got older?"

"I don't know!" She covers her face with her hands. "I'm a drug addict, Blake. My number one priority was how and where I was going to score my next high."

Seething over her admission, my brain is at odds with itself knowing she's going to die. I'm not a complete jerk, after all. "What's going on with you?"

"Cancer." She laughs sadly. "I deserve it after what I've done. It's my punishment."

Even though I don't share her view that she's somehow being punished by the universe, I'm not about to argue with her. I will agree, however, that it's a good dose of karma.

"Are you really dying or are you just saying that to get sympathy?"

"Do you know anything about stage four pancreatic cancer?"

I don't know much about cancer, but I've heard that's a really bad one. "Not really."

"They call it EOPC—early onset pancreatic cancer. I was fifteen when my mom died of the same thing. It was horrible for her at the end. I guess it must have been hereditary. Or maybe it was just fate."

"They can't treat it?"

"By the time they found it, it was too late. I missed all the signs. When I was using, the drugs masked the symptoms. And then when I came here, we all assumed the lack of appetite, the weight loss, and the fatigue were all part of withdrawal. Last month, when I wasn't showing any signs of improvement, I was given a full workup."

"How long do you have?"

She shrugs. "A few months maybe. It doesn't really matter. As soon as they kick me out of here I'm going to go out *my* way."

"What does that mean?"

"Exactly what you think it does."

I look around at the expansive gardens. "Why even stay here if you're going to use again when you leave?"

"Because there's nothing for me out there," she says, staring off in the distance. "Here, I have friends for the first time in a long time. Addiction is a lonely disease, Blake, when your primary relationship is with drugs. These people get me. They're just like me. I'm staying here until my ninety days are up, then I'm going to go out on my own terms. End stage pancreatic cancer is unforgiving. Even if I deserve every bit of pain and suffering. But I can't go through it. Not after watching what it did to my mom."

"Wait, you don't have a mom? Then who hired the PI to find me?"

"My dad and his new trophy wife."

It almost makes sense now, why they didn't want Maisy. The guy has a drug addict daughter and a 'difficult' grandchild his new young wife probably wanted nothing to do with. I scold myself for being one of those men who lets their cock make decisions for them. Or I used to be anyway.

"Do you... have a picture of her?" She looks guilty for asking.

I hesitate to do anything for this woman. But she is dying. So I get out my phone and scroll through until I find one. It's now when I realize all of my pictures over the past few months are of Maisy. Her alone. Her and Ellie. Her and Bolt. There are even a few selfies I took of the two of us together. It's a far cry from what my photo album looked like before Maisy.

I hand over my phone, showing her a picture I took of Maisy in one of her favorite dresses. Lucinda's hand flies to cover her mouth. "Oh my God. I've never seen her look like that." She touches the photo. "She looks so different. And she looks like you, but with my hair." She swipes the screen and scrolls through more. "You have a cat? She always carried around an old stuffed cat."

"I know. It's why I got her one. She loves him. He's got a disability."

Lucinda looks up at me, surprised.

"Don't look so shocked. Maisy is the one who chose him. She's an amazing little girl."

"And she's... *talking?*"

"She's signing. She only knows about two hundred signs at this point. That's not a lot, but it's enough to be able to communicate her needs. She's learning more every day."

"Two hundred seems like a lot."

"It's not. The average four-to-five-year-old will know twenty-five-hundred signs."

She nods, still scrolling through the phone. She stops and studies a photo of Ellie and Maisy. "Is this your wife?"

"That's one of Maisy's teachers."

She scrolls more. "She looks like more than just a teacher." She closes her eyes and hands me the phone. "I'm glad she's with you. She's where she belongs."

I scrub a hand across my jaw, knowing I have to ask. "You wanted me to bring her here to say goodbye, didn't you?"

She looks down at the ground, her eyes focusing on weeds coming through the cracks in the sidewalk. It's strange for me to have a conversation with someone while not looking into their eyes. Oh, how things have changed.

"That was the plan. But I'm not so sure anymore. I know now that seeing her would only be for me. And I guess I don't deserve it."

"If she were older and could understand what's happening, I'd give her the choice. I'm just worried it might cause a setback. But I'm also worried she'll hate me later on if I don't let her say goodbye, even if she doesn't understand. I mean what would I tell her? I'm not sure what the right answer is."

"You don't have to tell her anything. She never loved me. I know she didn't. All I was to her was someone who provided food and a warm place to sleep. She had a better relationship with the maid my dad hired to clean my apartment once a week. I know what I did. I wasn't high *all* the time. I yelled at her as if she could hear. I expected her to understand. I shoved her in front of the television when she was awake. I was the worst kind of mother. And I was selfish to want you to bring her here. I'm nothing to her."

She picks her phone up from the bench, searching through her own pictures, then texts me one. Finally, I see the resemblance to the woman I hooked up with in college.

"If you ever want to tell her about me, you can show her that picture. But it's okay if you don't. The lady in the pictures looks at Maisy as if she could be her mother. Maybe you should let Maisy think she is."

Jesus, this whole situation is truly fucked up.

"I'd better go," she says. "I'm really tired and nauseous."

It's strange to be looking at someone and think this person won't be alive soon. What am I supposed to say to her?

I stand. "I'm sorry you're going through this. I wouldn't wish it on anyone, no matter what they did."

She nods. "Thanks."

I walk away, having no idea what I'm going to tell Maisy. I guess the good thing is, I have time to figure it out.

"Blake?"

I turn and look into her sunken eyes.

"If you do tell her about me one day, tell her I'm sorry."

"Yeah, okay."

"And, Blake?"

I raise a brow.

"Thank you… for everything."

I nod and walk away.

Samantha Christy

# Chapter Thirty-three

## Ellie

An exhausting afternoon at the park leads to naptime for Maisy. She snuggles Bolt in her arms. He's a happy recipient of her attention. The two of them are inseparable. Standing in the doorway, I watch her drift off. When I'm certain she's out, I walk back down the hall, passing Blake's office. He wouldn't mind if I checked out his wine collection, would he?

It's a lie I tell myself to assuage the guilt for entering his private space. I do look at the extensive wine rack, but then I slip into the large office chair behind his desk. I sink into the comfortable leather, imagining him typing away on his laptop or having remote meetings with... whoever he does that sort of thing.

He's the heir to a successful winery. That means Maisy is too. That may make her life easier in some ways, but, like me, she'll still be the deaf child of hearing parents, which comes with its own obstacles.

Suddenly my mouth goes dry. What if Lucinda has changed? What if she not only wants Maisy back, but wants to give it a go with Blake? After all, isn't the best thing for a child to be with both biological parents?

I sigh, thinking of the monster who is my own biological father. No, it's definitely not always best.

Without even thinking, I get up, leave his office, and turn the corner into Blake's bedroom. I've never been in this room before. I inhale and get bombarded with his cologne. My eyes close and my mind wanders as I bask in the scent. Before I know it, I'm making his bed. Then I'm sitting on it. I'm sitting on it wondering how many women have sat here before me. How many has he—

My phone vibrates.

> **Sierra: He's buying it, hook, line, and sinker. I've been texting Mom's old phone for two weeks, sending pictures of me in New Zealand. After a week, I started acting worried, asking her why she wasn't responding. Then today she did. I mean, he obviously did for her. Ellie, he doesn't want me to know she's gone. He probably thinks I'd assume he hurt her again, or worse. So he's pretending everything is copacetic knowing I won't be back in the states for months.**

I lie back on Blake's pillow, enveloped by the scent that has pleasurable memories bombarding me.

**Me:** That's a relief. She's doing well in her new job. I check on her a lot. She's shy and reserved and keeps to herself, but she seems to be doing okay. I doubt she'll truly be happy until she's totally out from under his control.

**Sierra:** Do you think he'll just give up eventually?

**Me:** I don't know. Men like that need to win.

**Sierra:** I was afraid you were going to say that.

**Me:** We'll think of something. In the meantime, have a great season. Don't worry about your mom. I've got an eye on her.

**Sierra:** I can't thank you enough. I can already tell a difference when I talk to her. She was never able to text so freely. She knew he would read them. It's like I have a new mother.

**Me:** Just wait until she's completely free of him—that'll be a day for celebration.

Movement out of the corner of my eye surprises me. Blake is leaning against the bedroom doorway, a smug smile dancing across his face.

I sit up quickly, text Sierra goodbye and... *well, shit,* there's just no way to recover from this predicament.

I throw an embarrassed hand across my face, feeling my cheeks heat up.

"Sorry," I sign.

He laughs. "Don't ever feel sorry for being in my bed. In fact, I think you should be here more often."

I swing my legs over the side, stand up, and straighten the wrinkles. Then, shaking my head at my stupidity, I head for the living room.

I turn and sign, "How was it?"

He sighs and sits on the couch as if gathering his thoughts. My entire body tenses as my worst fears linger.

It takes him a good five minutes to text me the complete details of their meeting.

*She's dying?*

She won't be in Maisy's life? Or Blake's? I scold myself for the fleeting sense of relief that courses through my body. I should be sad, not relieved. I'm disgusted with myself after processing how awful that must be for such a young woman. No matter how pitiful a parent she is, I vow never to be okay with another person's misery.

**Me: What are you going to do?**

**Blake: What do you think I should do? Do you think it would mess with Maisy's head if I took her there?**

**Me: I'm not a psychologist, but I do have a lot of experience with deaf children and what they do and don't understand, although Maisy has proven to be the most interesting by far.**

"You mean the most difficult."

> **Me: That's not what I said. And I don't think of it that way. To answer your question, I'm not sure. From what you told me, it seems that Lucinda and Maisy's relationship may have been nothing more than warden and prisoner. She was neglectful to the point of it being a criminal offense, one she only got away with because she went to rehab instead of jail. Becoming sober has shown her the error of her ways. But that doesn't mean Maisy will understand. How could she? It took a long time for her to understand you're her father. One thing is for sure, Maisy will be confused. She may think you're taking her back to live with Lucinda.**

Blake's jaw drops and he sits heavily on the couch, as if the weight of the situation finally hit him.

"What?" I sign.

After resting his forearms on his knees and taking some deep breaths, he texts.

> **Blake: I've been so consumed over what to do about this situation that I forgot what it means. Maisy is mine. I'll have sole custody. She'll live here with me. Forever.**

I can see the battle in his eyes. He wants to jump for joy over the fact that there won't be a custody battle. There won't be visitation schedules and co-parenting arguments. No back and forth from here to the city. No frustrations if Lucinda doesn't up her parenting game. At the same time, however, it's only happening because Lucinda will be gone.

"Maisy is yours," I sign. "She'll live here with you forever." I teach him the signs and watch his reality sink in even more as he does them back to me.

"The grandparents?" I sign.

> **Blake: They didn't want anything to do with her before. I'm not sure they would now. Besides, no judge would hand over custody from a loving father to people who left her with a stranger to go on a world cruise.**

His head slumps and his hands scrub across his face. Finally he looks up. "She's mine," he says, glancing back at the bedroom where his daughter is napping after a long day at the park. "She's all mine."

> **Me: I'll reach out to our school psychologist. He knows Maisy. But in my opinion, I'd leave well enough alone. Lucinda said it herself, Maisy had a better relationship with the maid. Trying to explain to Maisy that Lucinda is her mother but she's dying and that's the last time she'll see her—it could do more damage and potentially cause setbacks.**

"My thoughts exactly," he signs. "But I figured I was just being selfish." He fingerspells *selfish* and I show him the sign.

**Me: Blake, you are the most selfless man I've ever met.**

He looks up, a smile finally crossing his face. He grabs the back of my knee, urging me closer. I've no choice but to sit on his lap or fall over the edge of the couch. He swipes a piece of hair behind my ear. "You are the most beautiful woman."

He got the 'most' sign wrong, but with the way he's looking into my eyes, now is not the time for a lesson.

"What time did Maisy go to sleep?"

"Twenty minutes."

His smile widens. "We have at least an hour then. Stay?"

I feel his erection beneath me as I contemplate his invitation.

"Stay, Ellie," he signs, with as much emotion on his face as I've ever seen.

I don't answer. Or maybe I do. My lips lower to meet his. As we kiss, a thousand things go through my head. How I wasn't lying, he's the most selfless man I've ever met, right up there with my father.

There are so many things about this man that I'm drawn to. Almost all of them have to do with his daughter. His resilience. His ability to adapt. His larger-than-life heart. Not to mention his smile, and... well, other parts of his anatomy.

I pull away. I can't fall in love with a man who goes through women like frat boys through beer.

Even if I could put aside all the stories, rumors, and flat-out facts I've heard about him. Even if he has miraculously changed because he's now responsible for another human. I have to see this for what it is.

My phone vibrates for the third time. I hold it up, using it as the excuse I need to roll off his lap.

**Brooke: I was wondering if you'd like to meet for dinner. I can pack up something from the cafeteria and we could meet in the park.**

Blake taps my shoulder. "Is that the same lady as before?"

I momentarily panic and try to remember what I told him when he caught her texting me last time. This is exactly why I hate lying to people. In my experience, secrets never stay secrets for long. Someone always makes a mistake. In this case, I hope it won't be me.

I hesitate long enough that he answers his own question. "She's a client, right?"

I nod.

He shuffles off the couch, then leans down, caging me against the backrest with his arms. "As long as you aren't accepting dinner invitations from male clients."

He stares at me long and hard as if to punctuate his point.

I raise my eyebrows at his possessiveness. Then I grin and shake my head.

"Good. Because the only man I want you having dinner with is me."

The intensity of his stare makes me wonder if he wants more. They say eyes are windows to the soul, and right now, his are likely revealing much more than he wants me to know.

He thumbs to the back, breaking the moment. "I should check on Maisy."

# Chapter Thirty-four

## Blake

For the rest of the afternoon, I wonder about this Brooke she's having dinner with. She said she's a client. I'm a client and we text all the time. But something about this Brooke worries me. Ellie seems on edge every time she texts. And more specifically, when I ask about it. And she looked away. It may have been only momentarily, but she did it. She's hiding something.

Then again, who am I to think Ellie Stone owes me any kind of explanation? We're not a couple. We go out sometimes. Sleep together occasionally. But other than the way she looks at me, I don't have any solid evidence she wants something beyond that.

I suppose she could be waiting for me to say something. But somehow I get the idea the enigmatic Dr. Stone waits for no man to take the upper hand. In fact, she's more the kind of person who says what she means and means what she says.

But, fuck, I'm falling hard.

I keep thinking about what Lucinda said. That 'the woman in the picture' should be Maisy's mother. I look down at Bolt, sleeping at my feet while Maisy plays a game on her iPad. He purrs in response when I reach down and give him a pat. "A match made in heaven," I say to no one.

I'm just not sure which match I'm talking about: Maisy and Bolt, Maisy and Ellie, or Ellie and me.

Maybe it's all three. Which makes me wonder why in the hell I keep procrastinating.

I should call someone for advice. The question is, who? Dallas and I were always the closest. But asking him for advice might be like a punch in the gut. Then there's Lucas. I get that he loves Lissa and all, but he also swore he loved Kaitlyn, Simone, and Veronica. Of course he'd say to go for it. I mean, when has he *not?*

Dax would know precisely squat on the subject. That leaves Cooper. After everything he went through, he's exactly the one. He and Serenity getting together made the most unlikely pair. Some people in this town thought it was disgusting the way he ended up marrying his dead brother's fiancée. Me—I say it was fate.

I shake the table to get Maisy's attention. "Go see Grandma?" I ask.

Her face lights up. She loves going to Mom and Dad's house. I get it. It's a veritable mansion. It's the only house I remember growing up in. I know they had one before the winery took off, when I was very young, but *Montana Manor*, as Allie dubbed it when we were teens, is every kid's dream. It's great for playing hide and seek. It has a theater room that rivals any commercial cinema. The wine cellar wasn't appreciated until we got older, but was still impressive to walk through, and always reminded me of the catacombs I'd seen in video games. Our pool was the envy of all high school pool parties, of which we had many, and the full-size basketball court made my brothers and me very popular with the jocks.

Maisy loves the elevator the most. Which is both amusing and sad. Sad because I know she lived in a tall building with an elevator, yet it seems a novelty to her. Did she *ever* leave the apartment?

After dropping her off, I head to Donovan's Pub, where Cooper works. It's not quite dinner time so there are few customers. I get his attention and point to a corner booth. A minute later, he walks over, two beers in hand.

He slides one my way. "What's up?"

I take a drink and look down into the beer, watching a bead of condensation roll down one side. "I found out I'm going to be a full-time dad today."

He raises his glass. "Hey, that's great. I know that's what you were hoping for. Congrats."

I don't tell him it's only happening because Maisy's mom is going to die. "Yeah, thanks. I'm still wrapping my head around it. The real reason I'm here is that…" I look in the booth behind me to make sure nobody is close enough to hear the conversation. "Uh… when did you know you wanted to be with Ren, like not just fool around with her, but *be* with her."

"Ahhh." He nods, a wrinkle cutting across the expanse of his forehead. "So this isn't so much about Maisy as it is her teacher."

"I… shit, I've never felt this way about anyone. How do I know it's not just because of Maisy? Ellie has helped her in more ways than I ever could. Is this like a patient falling for a nurse or whatever?"

Cooper snorts laughter. "Blake, I'm not sure the universe cares how you met or what you are to each other. I'm the perfect example of that. I mean, all signs pointed to Ren and me being a horrible idea. But sometimes, you look at someone and you just know."

My eyes snap up to his. "Yes. That's exactly how I felt when I first saw her. We didn't even talk." I snort. "Obviously. And I swear even if she didn't turn out to be Maisy's teacher, I'd have found her somehow. But I have to ask... did you and Ren end up together because you had something in common? Because you both lost that one person you loved more than anything?"

"Are you asking me if I think you and Ellie would be together if she and your daughter weren't deaf—the one thing that brought you together?"

I fold my arms across my body, perhaps an indication that I'm protecting myself from the answer. "I don't know. Sometimes I wonder if we'd have anything in common if it weren't for Maisy."

The sharp dip of his brows challenges my proclamation. "So Maisy is there when you and Ellie go on dates? How about when you do the deed?" He winks.

I don't laugh at his weak attempt at a joke. "Of course not."

"So you and Ellie *do* spend time alone without your kid?"

"Yeah."

"And how is it?"

"It's..." I think of the dinners we've had. The dancing. The no-speaking night that was more than incredible. I think of her kisses. What her lips do to me in bed. How she makes me feel. "...fucking amazing, Coop. I can't even put it into words."

He holds his arms out wide. "What's the problem then?"

"I'm not sure she feels the same way. She was dealt a pretty shitty hand as a kid. Not because she's deaf, but because her birth father wanted nothing to do with her. What if she's incapable of"—I wave a hand around— *"this.* What if I bring up the L word and she runs for the hills before I can break her heart too?"

"Or." He points the neck of his bottle at me. "You could get everything you want plus the perfect stepmom for Maisy. What have you got to lose?"

I take a drink, digesting what he said. "I suppose it's time to man up."

He reaches across the table and claps me on the shoulder. "That's the spirit."

"Maybe I'll do it next week, after all this wedding business with Lucas is over. Which reminds me, are we all set for the bachelor party here on Friday?"

"You bet."

"How's Lissa? She quit her job yet?"

"Nah. She's happy but guarded. She just doesn't want to be made a fool out of, you know?"

"I guess I can't blame her. But they've been together for years," I say. "Much longer than any of the others. I think this one's going to stick."

A worker behind the bar calls for Cooper.

"You good?" he asks. "Can I have Kelly whip you up something to go? Maisy too?"

"That would be great." I nod my appreciation. "Thanks for the talk."

While I'm waiting for the food, I watch one of the many televisions hanging from the ceiling. It's tuned to some home renovation show. I read the closed captioning scrolling across the bottom—a habit I'm starting to become accustomed to—as a couple tries to make more space for their growing family.

Huh, I think, wondering what kind of makeover I could give my house. I'd love to have a playroom for Maisy. A big pool for her class parties. A craft room to display all her drawings. By the time I'm done dreaming up renovations, I come to a realization: I'm going to have to move.

Then I come to a second one: I want the quiet, blonde-haired doctor to move *with* me.

# Chapter Thirty-five

## Ellie

I open my door and hold it for Beth as she walks through carrying a half-dozen dresses.

She takes them to my room and lays them on the bed. "What's the huge clothes emergency?" she asks.

"I'm going to a wedding."

Her eyebrows rise. "Making friends here. Nice."

"It's not one of my friends. Blake's brother Lucas is getting married."

Her mouth opens wide enough to catch flies. "Big step, Ellie. You're going as Blake's date?"

"Sort of. Not really. I don't know." I slump down next to the pile of clothes and momentarily cover my face. "What am I doing? I shouldn't go."

"Which is it? Not really, or sort of?"

"Lissa—that's his brother's fiancée—invited me a few weeks ago when I was at a restaurant with all of them. She thought we were a thing."

"You're not?"

I stare her down. "I've told you about him."

"Leopards can change their spots, Ellie."

My mouth clenches into a defiant pucker. "No, Beth. Leopards cannot change their spots."

"Has the man given you any indication he's interested in anyone else?"

I shrug. "I don't know what he does when I'm not around."

"Yeah, but have you heard anything?"

I sigh heavily. "No, Beth. I haven't *heard* anything."

"Jeez, why so touchy?" When I don't come back with a snarky remark, she adds, "Oh my god, you really like the guy. Ellie, are you in love with him?"

"Of course not," I say audibly, the vibrations in my chest alerting me to the increased volume of my voice.

She gives me the side-eye. "Me thinks you doth protest too much."

"Shut up and help me pick a dress."

Her mile-wide smile tells me she'd totally be on board if Blake and I became… more. The question is, *would I?*

Finally, after the fourth dress, I settle on one. It's light blue. Spaghetti straps. Above the knees but not inappropriately short. And it has a matching pashmina in case the venue is chilly.

"You are going to stop traffic in that thing," Beth signs.

I do a little hip wiggle in appreciation of her comment. Then I look down at my bare feet. "What shoes should I wear? Heels or wedges?"

"Heels," she signs. "Definitely heels. I'll pick out a pair. I'm thinking silver if you have any."

I'm going through my drawer of small handbags when I'm tapped forcefully on the shoulder. *Ouch.* I turn to see my sister glaring at me while holding the small gun lock box.

"What the hell is this?" she fumes.

I can tell by the angry look on her face that she was most definitely shouting. I reach for it, but she pulls it back, points to the engraving on the front, and signs one-handed as she yells some more.

"G. Lucas?" Her eyes blaze into me. "As in your idiot of a birth father? *That* G. Lucas? Ellie, what the fuck are you doing with a gun that belongs to him?"

My mind scrambles. Is this the moment when I have to come clean? "It's um… it's Sierra's. She couldn't take it to New Zealand, so I said I'd keep it here for her."

Beth studies my face. I don't break eye contact. I don't waver one little bit. *Believe me,* I implore.

She relaxes. "Well, Dad would kill you if he knew you had a gun here."

She puts it back on the shelf in my closet and comes out dangling a pair of stilettos on her fingers. They were tucked away in a box and I forgot I even had them. I've only worn them once, when I was 'Miss November' for a fundraising calendar my school did four years ago.

"No," I say emphatically.

"Yes." She nods, equally insistent.

"Beth, I'll probably be chasing Maisy around all afternoon. Those are so impractical."

"Are you going as Blake's date or Maisy's babysitter?"

"His date, but—"

"There!" She pumps a fist. "You said it, not me."

I roll my eyes. "Fine, so maybe technically I'll be his date. But he's in the wedding party. And so is his sister, and his parents have duties. It makes sense that I sit with Maisy."

"Excuses, excuses." She shoves the heels in my face. "Wear them. He'll go nuts."

I purse my lips.

"What?" she says and signs, motioning at the pile of dresses on the bed. "You didn't go through all of this to impress a four-year—"

One of the big advantages of being deaf is I can simply turn away and end any conversation. It goes both ways, however. When we were young, if Beth and I were fighting and she didn't like what I was signing, she'd turn off the lights. It was super annoying. As I'm sure the adolescent behavior I just displayed is.

Beth follows me to the kitchen, waiting while I get a Diet Coke from the fridge and lean against the counter. She doesn't talk, she just stares. Then something catches her eye, and before I can get to it, she's holding the tiny slip of paper in her hand. It's the fortune Blake left that night. For some reason, I couldn't bring myself to throw it away.

"Your heart knows the right answer," she says, reading it. She looks up. "Mom and Dad rubbing off on you?"

I snatch the slip of paper and throw it in the trash, annoyed that I know I'll be fishing through garbage to find it as soon as Beth is out the door.

"You're unbelievable," she pouts. "You are totally in love with him and you're so stubborn you won't admit it. He's not like the guys in high school, Ellie."

For the second time, I turn away, not wanting to have this conversation.

A gentle hand lands on my shoulder. She walks around me so I can see her, the depth of her warm gaze tells me the third degree is over and she's back to being my supportive little sister. "Come on, I'll do your makeup."

~ ~ ~

I gape at the limousine Blake sent for me. I told him not to pick me up since he has best man duties to contend with, but he insisted on sending a car. I thought he meant an Uber. It's not that I haven't been in limos before—I've been in plenty when going to the premieres of Uncle Chad's movies—but still, it's surreal that he sent it just for me.

Looking out the window as we approach the vineyard, I'm amazed at the wedding decorations. They begin all the way at the sign out on the main road. Tulle and bows adorn every fence post lining the long winding driveway leading to the events venue. It makes me wonder if they went all out for Lucas's first two weddings.

Lissa must be beside herself wondering if she's going to be just another name on his long list of failed relationships. But from what I've picked up, most of the town believes this is the one that will stick. Lissa seems nice and is someone I'd like to get to know. For her sake, I hope they're right.

Maisy, Allie, and Sarah are standing out front. Maisy loves wearing dresses, but this one takes the cake. She looks like a complete angel, straight from the gates of heaven. I'm not even sure she understands what today is, but she seems excited nonetheless.

I get out of the limo and she skips over, wrapping me in one of her usual all-encompassing hugs. I smile down at her and sign, "Beautiful Maisy."

She points out the big pink bow on her hip and twirls around. Then she touches the sequins lining the hem of my dress. "Beautiful Ellie."

"Thank you," I sign.

"Ellie, you're simply gorgeous," Sarah gushes.

"Wow," Allie says. "My brother is going to flip."

I feel the heat creep across my face as the two women share a look.

A very attractive and somewhat familiar-looking man comes out of the building. Blake trails behind him, stopping dead when he sees me. It's almost comical the way his eyes bug out, like a cartoon even, and it does nothing to tamp down my blush.

"Ellie," he says, winking as he uses my name sign. "This is Dallas."

No wonder the man looks familiar. "Nice to meet you," I sign.

I'm taken aback when he signs it back to me. When he sees my expression, he signs, "Deaf niece. I practice."

"Very good." I smile, pleased to see Dallas eager to learn. I know Blake was worried about how he might react to his niece. But he seems to be handling it very well. On the surface anyway.

Blake steps forward, takes my hand as if it's the most natural thing, then drops it almost immediately, looking down at Maisy. It's like he forgot we're surrounded by people. But his little girl is very observant. She noticed. Her eyes are staring at our hands, almost willing them to join again.

She scampers inside. When she comes back out again, she hands me a drawing. It's one we did together when I was trying to explain marriage. I did a decent job of drawing her uncle and Lissa, but I'm no artist. She shoves the picture at me and points to Blake then me then the picture.

It takes a moment for the crowd around us to catch up with what I understood immediately. She thinks Blake and I are getting married. My throat lurches with a hard swallow. I move my head from side to side, wishing Lucas and Lissa were somewhere near so I could correct her.

Allie's shoulders shake and laughter dances in her eyes. "Oh my gosh, she thinks the two of you are getting married."

My face is so hot that not even a snowball could lower my temperature.

When Blake's eyes meet mine, it's apparent he doesn't think it's so funny. I'm familiar with the expression though. It's the same one I saw when our eyes first connected months ago in Truman's grocery. And the one that was on his face the first time he made love to me.

Two things happen simultaneously: a rush of emotion flows through me, and a bolt of terror.

I break our stare and look around at the four dumbstruck onlookers.

"Come on, Maisy," I sign. "We will go watch."

We step inside to where guests are being seated. I'm touched from behind a moment before Blake comes around the front of me. "Sorry about that," he says. "Kids." He rolls his eyes. "I'll find you after. You and Maisy can sit in the second row, right behind my parents." He thumbs to the hallway. "I have to go make sure Lucas is still chained to the desk where I left him." He laughs at his joke and walks away.

As Maisy and I are escorted to the second row, I take in the event hall. I've only been in here once, the day I had a tour of the winery. It's been transformed into a stunning wedding venue. A hundred padded wooden chairs have been draped with white chair sashes and decorated with greenery and flowers. The aisle is a beautiful lattice-patterned runner that must be thirty yards long, extending from the doors to the altar. And the altar... wow, it's an archway made up of what must be thousands of flowers that complement the ones on the chairs. It's a truly magical sight.

But what delights me the most—what has my chest tightening and my eyes misting—is not any of the decorations, it's the person standing off to the side of the altar. It's Hannah. Blake hired an interpreter.

Hannah waves and tells me I look pretty.

"How many deaf here?" I ask.

"Just you."

*Just me?* He hired an interpreter for *me?* Well, for Maisy and me. But really, for me. A four-year-old wouldn't get much out of a wedding ceremony. I'm not sure why this surprises me. This is Blake Montana we're talking about. Despite his reputation, he's got the kindest heart of anyone I've ever met. Of course he hired an interpreter.

My mind goes back to the way he was looking at me outside. I tell myself it's a wedding. Weddings always make people emotional. It's one of the reasons I probably shouldn't have come. People already have the wrong idea about what I am to Blake. And I'm not about to make the same mistakes as any one of Lucas's long string of exes, who each had false hope of a happy ever after.

Putting those thoughts aside for now, I watch the string quartet in the far corner, imagining they're playing some sort of love song. I just know Maisy is itching to run over and put her hand on one of the violins. She loves instruments of all kinds. Each one produces different vibrations. Feeling sounds has become one of her favorite things. She does it as obsessively as teenagers check their cell phones. Blake's workout room has become home to a small set of drums, an electronic keyboard, a guitar, and Dallas's old saxophone, which apparently he played in middle school. There are plenty of deaf musicians. Will *she* want to be one?

I regard Maisy as she stares at the quartet, wondering just who and what she'll be in twenty years. And a wave of sadness washes over me when I realize I might not ever know. No—not a wave. A tsunami.

Heads turn, so I look behind us to see Blake escorting one of his grandmothers to the front row. Dallas is behind him escorting the other. Their sole living grandfather follows. Blake winks at Maisy, then me, as he passes and circles back around to the rear.

Next, Allie and Sarah are escorted by Blake's dad, and they all take the remaining empty seats in front of us.

The minister comes out of a side door and takes his place behind the flower altar. If I could hear, I'd bet there is a collective moment of breath-holding as people await Lucas to come from the same door and take his place. I find I'm holding my own breath when seconds pass without anyone coming through the door.

Seconds become minutes. People start whispering to each other.

Allie says something to her mom and when her mom turns slightly, I can see worried lines etched in her forehead.

I look behind me. I'm annoyed to see a few people laughing. I can only hope they're doing it silently. A guy a few rows back hands money to the man sitting next to him.

I stare at the altar. Surely he's going to show.

Blake's dad stands and rushes to the door we all expected Lucas to emerge from. When the door is opened, I catch a glimpse of Blake and Dallas, who appear to be arguing.

Allie turns. "It's not looking good," she signs.

My shoulders slump. *Poor Lissa.*

The next few minutes are some of the longest, most uncomfortable minutes I've ever experienced. Is Lissa out front on her father's arm waiting to be walked down the aisle? What must she be thinking? Is she thinking the day of her wedding just turned into a nightmare? Is Lucas dumping her as we sit here? Or did he simply disappear? Or maybe he's just having cold feet and his brothers are talking sense into him.

The side door opens, and I feel a momentary sense of relief. But only one person comes through. Blake's father. He walks to the minister and whispers something, then turns to the crowd.

"I apologize," Hannah interprets. "It looks like there's not going to be a wedding today." Chris's eyes grow dark with anger, making me think there was laughter or chatter at his declaration. "For any of you who think this is funny, please remember there is an amazing woman who thought this day was going to be the best day of her life. And for those of you wishing ill for my son, I hope you can find it in your heart to forgive him yet again. We all thought this one was going to be it. I offer no excuses except to say that... maybe he just hasn't found his true soulmate. I'm sorry." He motions to the opposite door. "I know this isn't a day of celebration, but I invite you to eat and drink and try to enjoy what's left of the day as we try to find our son and console Lissa."

Nobody moves for a good ten seconds. Then there is a parting of ways. Most of Lissa's friends and family leave while most of Lucas's go through the door to the reception hall. I guess they're used to this.

When I stand, Maisy looks up in confusion. Oh, boy. How do I explain this? Instead of trying, I just sign, "Let's go. We'll eat and dance."

At the word dance, I see excitement in her eyes. I know the first thing she'll do is find a speaker, wrap her body around it as tightly as she can, and then release it, staying close to feel the music as she dances like only a four-year-old can.

Once through the doors, waiters stand at the ready, handing out champagne. I reluctantly accept a glass. It's hardly a celebration. Allie scoops up two and sidles up next to me. Then she realizes she can't sign with her hands full and deposits them on the nearest table. "Might as well make the most of the night. There's all this great food and wine." She signs as much as she can, and I lip read the rest. "Besides, this wasn't entirely unexpected."

"I'm sorry," I sign. "I know you were hoping Lissa would be the one."

Blake walks up next to me, a sad smile on his face. Dallas accompanies him.

I catch bits and pieces of the conversation between the three siblings. It doesn't escape me how Blake keeps encouraging them to face me while speaking so I can feel more included.

"Where is he?" Allie asks.

Dallas shrugs then shouts angrily at Blake. They have a disagreement and Blake says something about it not being his fault.

"Can you stay with Maisy?" Blake asks, begging me with his eyes. "I want to see if I can find Lucas."

"Yes. Of course. You should be with your family."

"Thank you," he signs, then downs a shot being handed to him right before he and Dallas take off through the front door.

# Chapter Thirty-six

## Blake

"That motherfucker," I say for the tenth time since we hopped in Dallas's Ford F-150 Raptor.

"Don't say I didn't tell you," he grumbles.

I stare daggers into the side of his head. "Do you have no compassion? He just ruined Lissa's life. Maybe his own. She was the best thing that ever happened to him. I get that you've been gone for the past few years and haven't seen them together, but they're fucking perfect. If he can't marry *her* there's zero hope for him."

Stopped at an intersection, he turns toward me, eyes narrowed. "Are we talking about Lucas?"

"Of course we're talking about Lucas," I huff.

"Because I saw the way you were looking at Ellie."

"This isn't about me."

"Uh huh. Blake, listen, I have to say I was thrown by your phone call that day. Not just because you're a dad, but the way you talked about Ellie. And now, six weeks later, you still have a boner

339

for her—that's just not like you. And now it's like you're taking it personally that Lucas ditched."

"Whatever," I say as we pull up to Lucas's building.

We ride up to the fifth floor where there are two penthouse apartments. Lucas's is on the right. His spare key is still hidden under the ornate flower vase on the table between the two apartments where he stashed it back when I was in college so I could use his place for a sex den.

I shake my head at the thought. It seems like forever ago when I brought a girl here. But it's not. Last fall I brought... *ah, shit*, I can't even remember her name.

I don't even knock. If he's here, he's probably balls-deep in a bottle of whiskey. I whip open the door, not even thinking that maybe Lissa could be here instead. After all, she's lived here for over a year now.

"Lucas!" I shout, entering the place.

"Yo, Luke!" Dallas adds with much less gusto.

"Lissa? Are you here?" I ask.

We look through all five bedrooms. No one is here. The only trace of Lucas having been here is his discarded clothes he was wearing at the groom's brunch at Mom and Dad's house earlier.

"He hasn't been here," I say.

Dallas points to their huge walk-in closet. "But it looks like someone has."

I run a hand through my hair when I see Lissa's wedding dress in a pile on the closet floor. Drawers are half-opened, having been riffled through. Hangers are empty. Most of Lissa's clothes are gone. And it looks like she did it in a hurry. Hell, the whole thing only went down less than an hour ago. She must have high-tailed it back here and moved her shit out.

"Jesus," Dallas says. "She's not fucking around. Looks like she means it."

"Can you blame her? She probably moved back in with her folks."

"Let's head over to Mom and Dad's house. Maybe he went there instead. And they're probably stuck at the winery dealing with all the guests."

We have to drive down McQuaid Circle and through a residential neighborhood to get to our childhood home. I jerk against my seatbelt when Dallas stops his truck in the middle of the road.

"Fuck!" he barks.

I look at Dallas. He's staring down the street. In his haste to get to Mom and Dad's, he turned down his old street. The street with the house Phoebe and DJ died in.

A car honks behind us, but Dallas doesn't move.

I roll down the window and wave them by. Dallas doesn't even notice when the teen driving an old Camero flips him the bird. I think it might have been a Calloway, one of Cooper's cousins: Colt, Grey, or Storm.

"You could turn around," I say, stating the obvious when he seems frozen in place.

He ignores the suggestion, staring without even blinking. After I wave a few more cars past, he finally asks, "Do you know who bought the place?"

Dallas took off right after the funeral. He had Dad handle the sale on his behalf. I gather this is the first time he's driven down this street since.

"A retired couple I think. They moved from the city."

I can almost see his relief that a young family didn't move in and are living the life he was robbed of.

"When do you think you'll move back?" I ask, seeing an opportunity.

He looks away from the house like I asked him when he was going to eat nails. "Never."

"Come on. *Never?*"

"That's what I said."

"Dallas, it's been—"

"Don't fucking tell me how long it's been. Because I already know. It's been two years, one month, and twenty-six days. Do you think just because it's been that long that I'll magically get over it? Get over the fact that my twenty-six-year-old wife and six-month-old baby died in this town. In that house? That when I left for work that morning and kissed Phoebe goodbye it would be the last time I ever touched her? That when I held DJ, I had no way of knowing he'd never live to see his first birthday, crawl, or call me Daddy?"

His voice cracks at the last word, and I feel my heart breaking in a way it never would have before I became a father myself.

"What the hell don't you understand? That DJ died first, alone in his crib, and Phoebe had no idea what had happened when she succumbed herself, crumpling to the kitchen floor in convulsions before she died? Don't you get that every fucking day of my miserable life, I wonder what would have happened if I'd gotten home from work on time instead of staying late to earn brownie points from our father? That if I'd been there, I could have done something. Or at least died with them."

I'm not sure I can even speak. That was a lot of shit to unpack.

"Jesus." I scrub a hand across my face. "I'm sorry."

He backs into a driveway, turns in the other direction, and drives five minutes out of the way to get to our parents' house.

"His car isn't here," I say. "Let's check anyway."

It takes a lot longer to go through Montana Manor than it did Lucas's penthouse. It doesn't matter, though. It's empty as well.

"Should we check the bars?" I ask.

"He's not going to go anywhere with people. Everyone in this town knew today was his wedding." He looks out the back window in thought. "How about the back forty?"

"Right," I say. "Let's go."

He looks at me strangely.

"What?" I ask.

"Are you aware you just did sign language?"

I replay the last five seconds in my head. Huh, I guess I did. Well, *that's* never happened before.

We hop in his truck and head back to the winery. When we pass the main complex, there are still a few dozen cars there. I guess people stayed for free booze and food. And maybe to collect on bets they'd placed. I silently wonder if Ellie and Maisy are still inside.

Dallas drives to the far end of the property where there are a few acres of land Dad could never get vines to grow on. It became our playground when we were kids and came to work with our parents. We'd play tag out there. Kick the can. And when we got older, my brothers and I would have jousting fights on the ATVs used to drive through the vineyards. Mom and Dad would have killed us if they knew about that. It's surprising the three of us survived with little more than bruises and scratches.

It's the only place Lucas could go where no one would think to find him.

No one but us, that is.

"Christ, he's here," Dallas says, spotting his car in the distance.

Lucas drove right over the green space and may have even sideswiped some trees to park where he did.

I send a quick text to Mom to let her know we found him so she won't worry. But I don't disclose where. This is one of those times you just need your brothers.

It's like Lucas doesn't even notice when we walk up next to him. There's a half empty bottle of whiskey sitting on a tree stump, and he's smoking a cigarette—a habit he gave up in his early twenties. But I get now is not the time for a lecture.

He looks up, unhappy to have been found, and takes a long drag. Smoke comes out along with his words. "Don't fucking start with me. I know what I did. I know I'm a lowlife prick."

I hold out my hand for the bottle. "Can we join you?"

He shrugs. I take a pull then hand it to Dallas. We both left our jackets in the truck, and now we loosen our ties and take a seat on nearby stumps.

Neither Dallas nor I talk. We just take turns sipping whiskey. Lucas will talk when he's ready. If we know anything about our oldest brother, we know that.

He smokes three more cigarettes, flicking the last one—half-smoked—across the grass, and winces. His face is a greenish hue. I guess when you haven't smoked in a while it can make you ill. He takes a long swig of whiskey, then turns and vomits behind him. Then, he takes another drink and lights another cigarette as if punishing himself.

"I was going to go through with it," he says between clenched teeth. "I swear to God I was. Then I heard the violin music, and you guys left to go walk the girls down the aisle and I just... *Fuck!*" He kicks the stump with the back of his heel, putting one hell of a scuff on his eight-hundred-dollar Allen Edmonds Cap-toe Oxfords. "What the hell is wrong with me?"

All Dallas and I can do is look at each other. Because there's just no way to answer that.

The first time Lucas left a girl at the altar, it was almost understandable. They were young and they'd rushed into it far too soon. The second time surprised us all, especially considering Simone was one of his best friends. *Was.* Not anymore. He broke things off with his third fiancée just weeks before the wedding. He said it was because he knew he was going to bail and didn't want to hurt her.

But with Lissa, we thought things were different. Even after they'd been engaged for over a year, and he insisted he was ready to finally get married, she wouldn't do it. She just wanted to stay perpetually engaged. She agreed to move in with him, something he'd never done with the others. But she always told him she wasn't about to be another casualty of Lucas Montana's doomed love life. It took a long time, but after living together went so well, he finally wore her down and they set a date.

I, for one, am wishing she stood her ground. I could see them as one of those couples who never get married but who have a better relationship than most married couples.

And he went and screwed it all up.

"What the fuck do I do now?" he asks. When neither Dallas nor I speak, he says, "Seriously, what the fuck do I do?"

"That depends," I say, figuring Dallas isn't the one who's going to offer advice about anyone's love life. "Are you done with her?"

"No, I'm not done with her. I fucking love her."

Dallas scoffs, looking like he has something to say, but Lucas shuts him up.

"Don't start. I know I left her there and she probably hates me for it. She was fine with the way things were. She never wanted to get married. I promised her this time would be different. And she... she fucking believed me. And now I've gone and fucked up the best thing that ever happened to me."

He empties the bottle, shaking every last drop into his mouth before tossing it across the grass to join his pile of cigarettes.

"How long do you think she'll be mad at me? When do you think it'll be safe for me to go home?"

Dallas and I share a look.

"What?" Lucas asks.

"We, uh... just came from your place," I say. "It sort of looked like she moved out."

His drunken eyes snap up in surprise. "Moved out? It's barely been a few hours."

"It looked like she was in a hurry."

"Let's go," he says, fishing keys out of his pocket.

I take them from him. "Oh, no. You're not driving. I'll follow Dallas in your car. Neither of us had very much."

Thirty minutes later, Lucas is standing in his bedroom, staring into his closet, his face devoid of color. "She took almost everything." He picks up a few of her shirts off the floor. "Except these." He holds out the Donovan's Pub work shirts. "Why wouldn't she take these?"

He goes to the bathroom where half the vanity has been cleared off. Back in the bedroom, he sits on the end of the bed, looking over at Lissa's side. "She took her family photos." He shakes his head, staring at the one photo she *didn't* take. The one of the two of them taken on the day of their engagement. The one with the cracked glass I can only assume wasn't cracked this morning. "Fuck," he says, scooting across the bed and gathering it in his hands. "Do you think she's done with me?"

"I think you need to give her some time, Lucas. She needs to decide if she can be with a guy who doesn't want to be married to her."

"What do you think she'll do?" He looks from Dallas to me as if we have all the answers.

"I don't know. But she was willing to be in a relationship with you knowing your past. And she was the one who didn't want to get married. Maybe when she thinks about it, she'll come around. But what I do know is that you have to let her know you still love her. That you want to go back to the way things were before you talked her into all this."

"Yeah, okay. I can do that. She's probably at her parents' house. How long do you think I should wait?" He looks at his watch as if he's asking how many minutes or hours.

"I'd say at least a day or two. She's probably still pretty miffed. Let her cool off."

He walks out of the bedroom straight to his bar, bypassing the whiskey and going for a beer. "Might as well get shitfaced then. It is my wedding night after all."

Three hours later, Dallas and I carry our passed-out brother to bed.

We turn out the lights and let him sleep it off, vowing to meet back here in the morning.

On our way out the door, we run into Craig Monroe, Lissa's father.

"Ah, hey, Mr. Monroe."

"Dallas," he says. "Nice to see you back in town. You doing okay?"

Dallas shrugs.

"Is your brother here?" Craig asks.

"Passed out," I say. "After the bottle of whiskey he drank earlier, I doubt a nuclear explosion could wake him. Listen, if it means anything, he's feeling all kinds of stupid. He loves Lissa. He wants to work things out. He just doesn't want to be married is all. We told him to give Lissa some space."

"Is that so?" He crosses his arms. "Well, too little too late. He hurt my daughter. For years she was afraid of this happening. After they moved in together, she changed her tune. She felt *he* had changed his. I think we all did. And I'm not going to sugarcoat things and tell you I don't want to thwap some sense into him for doing this to my baby."

I chuckle. "You'd have to get in line."

"Yeah, well, as much as I want to see him in as much pain as she is, I'm not here to stir up a fight. I'm here to deliver a message."

"I'm afraid it'll have to wait. We can deliver it for you if you want."

He nods. "Okay then. Be sure to tell him all of it. Every word. Lissa is done with him. He humiliated her. She said he will never change, and after all the chances he's had to show what a real man he is, he failed her. She wants nothing to do with him. No contact whatsoever. She never wants to see or speak to him again."

"But…" I look at Dallas before I state the obvious. "This is a small town. How will that work?"

"Thanks to your brother, my daughter has decided not to live in Calloway Creek anymore." His hands ball up into fists. "Just another reason I'd like to thump him. He robbed me of my own goddamn daughter. You should tell him he might want to steer clear of me for a while."

"She's moving?" I ask. "Where? When?"

"She's already gone. As to the where, well, that's between Lissa, her mother, and me. And calling her will do no good. She left her cell phone. We helped her load her car. She pulled out of town about an hour ago."

"Wait, so she isn't going to give him a chance to make things right?"

"Son, your brother has left how many women now? There's no making things right. He used up all his chances. And now he has to live with his decision. You go ahead and pass that on."

"Yes, sir. And on behalf of Lucas, I'm really sorry."

"Hopefully you can prove you are by not following suit."

I nod. Because there's really nothing more to say. To him anyway. There's a hell of a lot I want to say to someone else, however.

Mr. Monroe turns and gets back on the elevator. Dallas and I watch the doors close then give each other a look as if asking *what now?*

Dallas drops his keys on the entry table and moves to park himself on the couch.

"Dude, he's not waking up anytime soon," I say, walking in after him.

"Yeah, but someone has to tell him when he does. I'll do it. You have a kid to go home to."

"How long are you going to stay in town?"

"Long enough to tell him. Then I'm gone."

I know it's pointless to ask him to reconsider. He's more stubborn than anyone I've ever known. He started asking Phoebe out when they were thirteen years old. He never even noticed other girls. Finally, when they were seventeen, she said yes. They were inseparable after that.

I sigh. Dallas had everything and lost it. Lucas had everything and fucked it up.

Knowing how it could end up, I'm not going to waste another minute without going after what I want. I reach out, shake his hand, then give him a hug. "I'm here if you ever need anything."

"I know, brother." He crosses his legs at the ankles and picks up the remote. "I know."

# Chapter Thirty-seven

## Blake

It's after dark by the time I get home. On one hand, I feel guilty having asked Ellie to stay with Maisy all day. On the other, I'm more than a little eager to see her.

I park in the garage, step inside, and flash the lights several times. I've learned my lesson more than once about how not to sneak up on the deaf.

Two people come around the corner. Neither of them is Ellie.

My sister and her friend Mia Cruz are both waiting, wide-eyed, to hear the news. I tell them everything.

"That stupid fucker," Allie says.

"I've been saying that myself all afternoon."

"She's really gone?" Mia asks. "Like for good?"

"That's what her dad said."

"I say good for her," Allie gruffs. "And I don't blame her. She doesn't want to be the laughingstock of Cal Creek. No woman should put up with that shit. He deserves to live the rest of his life as a miserable bachelor."

"Hey, now. That's a little harsh, don't you think?"

"You think our brother deserves a pass? You know the definition of crazy, right? Doing the same thing over and over and expecting a different result?" Her hands land on her hips. "I hope this sends a message to everyone who might consider dating him in the future. He's not going to change. And any woman who thinks he will is crazy."

I get a beer from the refrigerator and sit at the bar in the kitchen. There's a drawing on the countertop. I recognize it as one of Ellie's creations. I pick it up and run my finger along the edge.

"She left a few hours ago," Allie says.

I look up.

She nods at the picture. "Ellie. She left when Mia and I got here. I invited her to stay for a drink but… she didn't."

I put the picture down and take a long pull from the bottle.

"You really like her, don't you?" Allie asks.

I nod, staring into my beer.

"Maisy called her 'Mom' earlier."

My eyes snap to hers. "What?"

"When Mia and I first got here and Ellie went to leave, Maisy signed, *Mom, stay.*"

I scrub a hand across my prickly jaw. "Jesus, is that why she left?"

"I don't think so. But it is why she drew the picture."

I study the drawing again. It shows Maisy and me holding hands inside the house, and Ellie standing outside the house. She was trying to explain that she's not her mom and this isn't her house. Christ, it's the exact opposite of everything swirling around in my head.

Mia laughs. "Well, damn. It looks like *one* Montana brother may be off the market soon."

"Honestly, if I had it my way, yeah." I glance at the drawing again. "It's obvious she doesn't feel the same."

Allie blurts, "What? Because she was trying to explain to your kid that she's not her mom? It's true, she's not. That doesn't mean she's not hot for you, Blake. Or that she doesn't *want* to be inside the house in the picture. Everyone can see how she looks at you. When the two of you are in a room together, it's like you're the only ones there even if you're surrounded by people. Of all my brothers, I never expected you'd turn out to be the hopeless romantic. The two of you, I can't even explain it, you just seem to fit. It sort of gives me hope for humanity—especially after what happened today."

I sip my drink and contemplate her words. *You just seem to fit.*

"I was thinking of looking for a new house now that we know Maisy will be with me permanently. Do you want to go look at some with me?"

Allie cocks her head. "I think you're asking the wrong person, Blake." She kisses my cheek. "We're taking off. See you at work on Monday."

Mia signs, "Good night."

I smile, loving the way everyone in Maisy's world is making an effort.

After they're gone and I check on Maisy, to see her sleeping peacefully with Bolt, I go into my office and open my laptop. I search houses for sale. Calloway Creek is a small town. There aren't a lot of houses on the market at any given time, but there are two or three that might fit the bill. The bill being lots of bedrooms, a big yard, and either a pool or room for one.

**Me: Now that I'm a full-time dad, I need a bigger house.**

**Ellie: THAT'S what you got out of today?**

I laugh, because yeah, from her perspective, that did kind of come out of left field.

**Ellie: And your house is plenty big, Blake.**

**Me: I want her to grow up with everything I had. Big yard. Lots of room to run. Maybe a pool. Will you go house hunting with me?**

**Ellie: I don't know Calloway Creek nearly as well as you do. Maybe you should take Lucas.**

**Me: Lucas has been swimming in a bottle of whiskey since three o'clock. I doubt he'll be any good to anyone for a while. He's pretty torn up.**

**Ellie: Why didn't he marry her then?**

**Me: IDK. I guess some guys just have an issue with commitment.**

I re-read the text, the irony not being lost on me. I was one of those guys with commitment issues. Until now.

**Ellie: What about Allie, or your mom? I'm sure they'd be much better at picking a new place.**

**Me: I'm sure they'd be happy to do it. But they aren't nearly as pretty as you.**

The delay in a response clues me in on her hesitation.

**Me: Come on. I'll throw in dinner after.**

**Ellie: You're bribing me? I don't need a man to pay for dinner, Blake.**

**Me: Fine, then I'll throw in ME, all six-foot-two of naked me.**

I hold my breath waiting for a response. Is she thinking about what Maisy called her earlier? Is she thinking I'll toss her aside as easily as Lucas did Lissa? I suppose propositioning her with sex was the wrong move. I should grow a pair and tell her how I feel. Not over a text, however.

I walk into the dining room and peruse the drawings on the table. So many of them have Ellie in them. She already feels like family. She's a part of this. She's a part of *me*. But if I put it out there and tell her how I feel and she doesn't feel the same way, I'll ruin everything.

**Ellie: Well when you put it that way, how can a girl refuse?**

My knees almost buckle with relief.

*You're in as deep as an elephant in quicksand*, Dax would say. And he'd be right. I'm totally fucking deep. Way over my head deep. I shred the drawing of Ellie outside the house and toss it in the trash.

# Chapter Thirty-eight

## Ellie

After looking at the first two houses, I have little hope that Blake will find the perfect one. His expectations are high, and his wants, many. A large open floor plan. Gourmet kitchen. More bedrooms than he and Maisy could ever use. And number one on his list: a large, safe yard. In this small town, he may be looking for a unicorn.

He's got enough money that he could build his dream home. But I get the idea he's not keen on waiting the year or so it might take to make that happen.

When we follow his realtor, Dennis, to the final property, I sit a little straighter in the passenger seat of Blake's car. This house is in a cul-de-sac. At first sight, it looks promising. Three-car garage. Privacy fence surrounding a back yard, the top of a play structure peaking tall above it.

Then we pass a sign. A *road* sign. Blake and I look at each other in both excitement and surprise.

## DEAF CHILD AREA

It makes sense. This neighborhood backs up to the far end of the Deaf school property where the athletic fields are. He could walk her to school—that is, if he's going to continue sending her there for kindergarten. I know he's weighing the pros and cons of public school. Both schools have their merits. Though, in Maisy's case, with her being behind in all language skills, I believe she'd be better served at my school. Then again, I may be a bit biased. More importantly, though, *he* has to make the decision. I'm not here to influence, just inform.

The added bonus to this house, assuming the deaf child in the area isn't the one moving, is that Maisy could have a playmate. It could be exactly what Blake had hoped for and more.

He doesn't say anything. Maybe he's trying not to jinx it. I can tell he has high hopes for this one. After all, if this one doesn't work, he either has to search outside the town, build a house, or wait for more to come on the market.

We park behind Dennis on the street in front of the house. He has a conversation with Blake, but his bushy mustache makes it hard for me to read his lips. Blake's vocabulary has expanded so much, and he does his best to sign when he can. The man must study ASL like it's his second job.

"Lots of renovations," Blake says directly to me, obviously impressed with what he's hearing.

I see movement in the yard to the left. In front of a slightly smaller house is a boy and either his babysitter or mother. He's laughing as the woman tickles him. She kisses him on the head. Hmm... mother then.

When I turn back to Blake, he's still talking to the realtor. But then he stops abruptly, his head tipping sideways and his jaw hanging open as he gazes behind me. He touches my arm. "Look," he signs.

My heart catches in my throat, and I one hundred percent know he's going to buy this house before even setting foot inside as Blake and I watch the little boy sign with his mother.

She tells him to stay away from the street, especially since there are cars right here. When she sees us staring, she waves.

I smile and sign, "Your boy signs very well."

Now it's *her* jaw on the pavement. For a few seconds, it seems her head is trying to wrap around the situation. She takes the boy's hand and walks over.

"I'm Kelly Freeman," she signs, fingerspelling her name slowly. "This is Brayden."

"I'm Ellie," I sign.

"Deaf?" she asks, her lips not moving as she signs.

"Yes," I sign.

Her smile is a mile wide. "Me too." She turns her head slightly and shows me her cochlear implant. "Brayden too. My husband is hearing. Yours?"

Heat crosses my face. "This is Blake Montana. We're not married. The house would be for him."

Her eyes meet the ground for a moment, all excitement having left them.

"This is Kelly and Brayden," I sign slowly to Blake. "They are both deaf."

Blake's eyes seem to dance between them before settling on Brayden, who is half standing behind his mother. "How old are you?" Blake signs.

The boy looks up at his mother who gives him an encouraging nod. Then he holds up five fingers.

I have to bite back tears. Because I couldn't have scripted anything more perfectly. I mean, Blake might as well sign the contract now, sight unseen. I know anything inside the house he doesn't like, he can change. But having neighbors like this... it could mean all the difference for Maisy.

"My daughter is four," he says and signs. "She's deaf."

Brayden's eyes sparkle and he seems to come out of his shell. He tugs on his mom's shirt to get her attention. I can tell she's almost as excited as her son. He asks her, "Are they going to live in Mike's house?"

Kelly signs, "Mike was one of the children who lived here. He and his family moved out last week. We were hoping for another family. But this is beyond our wildest dreams."

I look at Blake, impressed that he seems to have understood some of what she signed. She's signing quickly, obviously not knowing Blake's limitations.

I want to tell her that we haven't even seen the house yet, but I don't. I don't because I know based on Blake's expression that it won't matter if it's covered in dinosaur wallpaper and has a disco ball in the bedroom.

"Is it just the two of them?" Kelly asks.

I nod. I don't miss the scowl on Blake's face. Maybe he thinks we're getting ahead of ourselves.

Brayden tugs on Kelly's shirt again and signs, "Will she play with me?"

Kelly explains to him that Blake hasn't bought the house, that he's just looking. That maybe he will, but he might not. Brayden looks at Blake with determination and marches over to him, signing much faster than I know Blake can keep up with. "You live here," he signs. "She can play with me. Mommy bakes cookies. She can eat them."

I go to tell Blake what the boy said, but he stops me. "I got this," he says. Then he signs to Brayden, "You sign very well."

Brayden beams with pride.

"I don't sign very well," Blake signs slowly. "I'm learning. My daughter, Maisy, is learning too."

"I can teach you," Brayden signs with enthusiasm.

"We'd like that."

Blake excuses himself to have a short conversation with Dennis, then motions to the house. We say our goodbyes to Kelly and Brayden and make our way inside. I let Dennis give his spiel to Blake and leave them in the kitchen as I wander the place by myself. It's completely empty, meticulously clean, and… ticks every single one of Blake's boxes.

A few minutes later, Blake snakes an arm around me as I look out over the expansive deck, summer kitchen, and back yard that puts all others to shame. There's no pool, but plenty of room for one. A play structure sits in one corner of the yard. A fire pit in the other. And at least a half-acre of grass in between. I can almost see Maisy and Brayden kicking around a soccer ball.

He squeezes my waist. "Did you see the bedroom at the top of the stairs?" he asks.

"Mike had a sister," I sign. "And she loves pink as much as Maisy."

The bedroom is just one more sign on a long list of signs that makes this the perfect place for them.

"If you don't buy this house, you are crazy," I sign.

"I don't know. I think I need more time to decide. Wait here."

He goes into the kitchen where Dennis is typing away on his phone, giving us space. They have a conversation and then Dennis waves at me and walks out the front door.

My brows sling low, curiosity getting the better of me.

"I suggested he go to Donovan's for a cup of coffee while we stay here and think about it." He pulls me close, wraps me in his arms and kisses me.

"What are you doing?" I sign.

"You remember what I said you'd get if you looked at houses with me? If I'm going to buy it, we might as well - - - it."

I shake my head, not having understood.

"Christen," he fingerspells. Then he does the sign for sex.

Butterflies dance in my stomach and my heart begins thrumming wildly. I glance around the empty house. "Here? Now?"

Before he can answer, his shirt is off. Then his shoes. Then his pants and boxer briefs. And as promised, he's standing gloriously naked in front of me. All six-feet-two of him.

I'm a guarded person. I rarely take the bull by the horns. Except when it comes to him apparently, because my entire body is humming in anticipation. Because he's got good… *horn*.

His penis hardens as he stares at me, and my mouth waters as if it's a juicy steak. Without breaking eye contact, I unbutton my blouse and unclasp my bra, letting both flutter to the floor. I expect him to look at my breasts, but he doesn't. His eyes don't stray from mine. Not even when I toe off my shoes and then slip off my jeans and underwear.

We're both naked, two feet of nothing between us. His gaze is intense as he continues to stare at me. It's as if the two of us have adopted a third language, one that has us speaking only with our eyes. And what his eyes are saying both scares and excites me. I melt under his perusal. Heat flushes my center. Tingles work up and down my spine.

He steps forward, closing the gap between us, and presses his body to mine until we're nothing but skin on skin. His penis throbs against my stomach, as hungry and demanding as his lips when they capture mine.

I spring myself up and into his arms and he holds me tightly, his hands under my butt. He groans something into my mouth. I think it was words. I lean back and focus on his lips, but all he does is shake his head, almost like he said something I wasn't meant to hear. I try not to let it bother me, and I get over it quickly when he lowers us onto the living room carpet and takes one of my breasts in his mouth.

Oh my God. I can't believe we're doing this here. What if Dennis comes back? What if another person comes to see the house?

When two fingers sink inside me, I decide I don't care. And when his tongue finds my clit, I come instantly, amused at just how quickly it happened.

Blake laughs as he climbs my body. "Someone likes… danger." He doesn't know the sign for danger, so I show him.

Then I crane my neck toward the front door. "Better not push our luck."

He reaches for his pants and gets a condom from his wallet. "I'll be quick then. Not as quick as you." He chuckles again.

I tug on his penis a few times, then guide him inside me, savoring the feeling I've been missing every night when I go to bed and dream of him. I've never dreamed of a man like I do Blake. When I wake up, though, reality always hits me.

Beth keeps telling me men can change. But she doesn't get it. None of them do. I know exactly what this is, and I've resigned myself to enjoying it as long as it lasts. The fact that I love him is an inconsequential detail. An unfortunate realization I'll have to deal with.

I couldn't help it. I'm not even sure exactly when it happened. Maybe the first time I saw him, even though I denied it for so long. But you can't help your feelings. You can't choose who you fall in love with. And I'm in love with him—a man I know I can never be with in the long run.

But I have this. Today. Now. And maybe tomorrow too. And I'll enjoy him. His smile. His body. His daughter, for at least another day.

His thrusts become more forceful, keeping up a punishing rhythm that tickles the very spot that has me moaning with pleasure once more. Maybe he's right. Maybe the thought of being caught has heightened my senses. Because my insides coil and burn with another impending climax, this time without him even pinching a nipple or touching my clit. My hips buck as I explode with a violent orgasm as he grunts into my shoulder, shuddering with his own release.

He rolls off me and stares at the ceiling, his chest rising and falling quickly with each breath. He removes the condom and sets it aside, but he didn't tie it, so it leaks. I point to the glob on the newly cleaned carpet.

His chest bounces with laughter. "Well, I have to buy the house now."

I laugh too, feeling vibrations in my throat that let me know it's audible.

He stares at me. He likes when I make noise. I sigh and turn to look out the window, but he tugs me back against him and cuddles me in the middle of this huge empty house.

His arms snake around me and he signs in front of my face, "One thing missing here."

I turn and face him, motioning at our surroundings. "This house has everything," I sign. "What else could you need?"

"You," he signs silently, pointing a finger between my breasts.

My eyebrows collide above the center of my nose.

"You're what's missing," he says. "Live here with me. With us."

My heart pumps uncontrollably, wondering if I read his lips correctly. "Sign it," I request.

"You live here," he signs as my heart stops beating altogether at his suggestion.

He looks nervous now. More nervous than I've ever seen him. I watch his Adam's apple bob as he swallows. Then, without moving his lips, he points to himself, crosses his arms over his heart, then points to me.

I blink over and over, because I'm sure this isn't happening.

When I don't move, because I'm literally frozen, he does it again, this time using words along with signs. "I love you, Ellie."

My heart soars and breaks at the very same time.

Finally, I move, reaching for my clothes and gathering them against me as if they will somehow protect me from his words.

I dress quickly. He doesn't. He just watches and waits. He waits for me to say it back. But I can't.

I want to.

But I can't.

All I can do is turn and stare into the back yard knowing this is the inevitable moment I've dreaded. I just didn't know it would come with a declaration of love. One that has knocked the wind out of me. But I knew this moment would happen sooner or later. A part of me, okay *all* of me, hoped it would be later. Much later.

I look back at him and shake my head sadly, my eyes lying to him as much as my thoughts are lying to me

# Chapter Thirty-nine

## Blake

She just stands there, looking lost. The shake of her head scares the hell out of me. I jump up and put on my clothes. There's so much I have to say to her, but I just don't know all the signs and I can't risk her misreading my lips.

> **Me: Dallas lost his family. And now Lucas screwed up his life. It made me realize everything I want is right in front of me. You are what I want. You and Maisy. I want us to be a family. I know it's only been months and we haven't talked about a future together. That's my fault. I don't know how to do this. This is new territory for me. I don't even know if you love me. But I think you do.**

As she reads it, her breathing accelerates. Fuck, I wish I could know what's going on inside her head right now.

> Ellie: I thought… Blake, I thought this was a
> fling. With your past, and the way we hide it,
> how could it be anything else?

"What? No!"

Guilt pierces my soul knowing all along she was thinking this
was just friends hooking up. My heart clambers in my throat as I
type quickly to explain.

> Me: El, my God, I knew from the first day we
> met that this would be different. That YOU
> would be different. I was sure you felt it too.
> Jesus, you thought I was going to use and
> discard you?

> Ellie: You don't even know much about me.

> Me: I know enough.

> Ellie: You're wrong. If you knew me well,
> you'd know I could never be with someone
> like you.

I look up, pissed that she's holding my past against me after
everything I've confessed. "Someone like *me*?"

"You could never understand," she signs.

I drive out a harsh sigh as a bad feeling surges through me.
"Try me."

She closes her eyes and looks away. There's a war going on
within her. And based on her body language, I fear it's one I'm
going to be on the losing side of.

She looks back at me and signs something that sets off a chain reaction inside me. My jaw tightens, my spine stiffens, and knots form in my gut. I glare at her, my eyes burning like hot embers. "Did you just say because I'm *not deaf?*"

Her chin dips in a single affirming nod.

"What the fuck, Ellie?"

Then, as if to prove a point, she signs really quickly, going on and on fully knowing I can't keep up.

I step forward and grab her hands. "Don't do this. Talk to me."

**Ellie: I told you you wouldn't understand. Hearing men never understand. We don't belong together.**

"So you're going to end this because I said I love you? And then what, run back to that Seth guy—a guy you don't even want? One who doesn't make your heart pound and your panties wet whenever he's around? What the hell is wrong with you?"

She takes a step back, offended.

I reach out and touch her arm. "I'm sorry. I didn't mean there is something wrong with you. I'm confused. I know you have feelings for me. The way you look at me. The way your body responds to me. You fucking love me, El. And you're lying to yourself if you say you don't. You're using your deafness as an excuse not to have a relationship with me."

"I'm not," she signs as if completely offended.

"Bullshit. I think you clearly are. You need an excuse to end this because you're afraid I'll leave you like he did, aren't you? Grant broke something inside you, and you don't think you're deserving of love or some crap like that. At least have the decency to own up to why you're throwing this away." I close my mouth, my lips in a thin line as I sign, "Are you getting this?"

> **Ellie: You're wrong. It's not about Grant. It's about us. I can't be in a relationship with a hearing man. Don't you understand that our worlds are too different? You'll want me to fit into yours and that's not who I am.**

"I know who you are. And I don't expect anything of you." Her head shakes as she texts.

> **Ellie: You all say that. But eventually, you'll want me to change. You'll want me to speak.**

"Are you kidding me?" I sign in frustration. I turn away for a moment to gather my thoughts then look directly at her as I speak. "Because I asked you months ago if you ever spoke, you're holding that against me? It was a legitimate question. It wasn't a demand. I don't give a shit if you speak or not."

"You will," she signs.

"That's so fucking unfair. You can't presume to know what I will or won't do."

"You don't know what it's like to be deaf."

"No, I don't," I sign. I need her to understand me word for word, so I use my phone again.

> **Me: You know what else I don't know? I don't know what it's like to be a woman. No matter how much you try to explain it, I'll never fully understand what it's like to have a period,**

have cramps, or carry a child. And you'll never know what it's like to get an erection, have a male orgasm, or get kicked in the balls. So we're different. Who cares? Lots of people are. They come from different backgrounds, cultures, and ethnicities. Yet they still get together. How is this any different?

Ellie: You'll forget I'm deaf. You already did once when you called me. Even today, I'm pretty sure you spoke to me on the floor. Am I right?

*Shit.* I nod guiltily.

"What did you say?"

"I said I love you," I sign. "It just came out."

Ellie: So you verbally declared your love for me when you knew I couldn't hear you. You forgot. A deaf person would never forget.

I pace the floor, putting footprints on the freshly vacuumed carpet by the wall.

Ellie: And you said once that you wanted me to scream your name.

I try to remember a time when I said it. "Jesus, El. I was making a joke about having sex. I didn't mean it literally."

**Ellie: All hearing men are the same. Eventually my silence will get to you, and you'll want more.**

All at once, things begin to make sense. For the second time, she's said something about *all hearing men*.

"What happened to you, El? Did a hearing man hurt you?"

Her silence is all the confirmation I need.

I take her hand. For a second, she lets me, but then she pulls away.

"Talk to me!"

She scolds me with her blazing hot stare.

I throw up my hands in frustration. "It's a figure of speech, Ellie," I say far too loudly. I use my hands and sign silently, "Talk to me."

When tears flood her eyes, I think the worst.

"Were you raped?"

Relief courses through me when she shakes her head.

"Then what?"

**Ellie: Nobody had to rape me. I let them do whatever they wanted.**

Her text hits me square in the chest. We've never talked about our sexual histories. I knew she was aware of my past. And I just assumed—based on her admission that she dated but didn't have relationships—she was afraid of being abandoned.

I step up to her, doing her name sign. "Ellie, tell me."

She sits down and leans against the wall. I sit next to her and wait as she types out a text. It's long. And with every second that passes, more bad feelings surface. All kinds of scenarios are swirling around in my head. I swear I'll hunt down and kill anyone who hurt her. All I can think of right now is protecting her in every way.

> **Ellie: People have always made fun of me. Being different, you have to have thick skin. But as a kid, it's not that easy. I used to speak. I grew up with hearing parents. A hearing sister. Yes, everyone signed, but I also spoke. It wasn't until elementary school that I understood that when I spoke, I didn't sound like everyone else. And that because I was born deaf, my accent was even more pronounced than most. The bullying got really bad in middle school. Kids were downright mean. They called me stupid and worse. When I was twelve, I stopped speaking altogether with the exception of when I was with my family.**

"El, I'm so sorry. No kid should have to go through that."

I swallow hard, tamping down the anger because I'm beginning to understand all the hurdles Maisy has in front of her.

> **Ellie: That's not all. When I went to high school, there were a lot of new people who didn't know me. I was the pretty blonde girl with the big boobs. Boys were attracted to me. Hearing boys. One boy sent me flowers on Valentine's Day when I was fifteen. It was the most special I'd ever felt. So I let him do**

things with me. Sex was a language everyone could speak, and almost instantly, I noticed I was becoming popular. Not with the girls, but I had Beth, so I didn't care about having friends. For the first time in my life, guys were seeking me out. Boys were fighting over me. And I let them. By senior year, I'd slept my way through the starting lineup of the varsity baseball team AND the football team.

I close my eyes at the thought of her being used by so many guys.

She taps my leg and signs, "I said you didn't know me."

"None of that matters. We all did stupid shit in high school."

"There's more," she signs.

Ellie: I knew the girls were all mad, calling me a slut, talking behind my back, but the attention from the boys outweighed it. Until homecoming senior year. I was named Homecoming Queen. It was like a dream, until it became a nightmare. At the dance, I was called on stage with Danny McVeigh, the Homecoming King and, at the time, the boy I was sleeping with. Everyone was staring at me. Danny told me as Homecoming Queen I had to give a speech. I didn't want to, so I just signed 'thank you' and started to walk away. He pulled me back and insisted. He said everyone was waiting and if I wanted to keep the title, I had to talk. I threw my crown at him and ran off stage. Everyone was laughing at me. Girls were high fiving each other. I'd fallen from grace, which was exactly what they wanted. It wasn't until the next week, when I was being shunned by everyone, that a brainy girl who always kept to herself told me everything. She said the boys all had a bet going to see which one of them could get me to talk first. Danny had conspired with a bunch of girls to get me elected queen. A lot of the girls were girls I went to middle school with. Girls who had heard me speak and who had made fun of me. They wanted everyone to hear the stupid deaf girl. They were tired of the way the popular guys were looking at me and ignoring them. Well, they got their wish. I never dated another hearing guy again. Until you.

"Jesus, Ellie. That's fucked up. Did you ever see the movie *Carrie?*"

She nods in understanding. "I wanted to kill them all," she signs.

Ellie: Instead of killing them, I just kept my head down and finished out the year. Then I went to Gallaudet, where everyone was like me. No one ever made fun of me. And no one tried to force me to speak.

I put both of our phones down and turn to face her square-on. I let my hands do the talking. "Ellie, I don't want you to speak. You are perfect the way you are."

She shakes her head. "You may think that now. But it will change."

"You don't give me... credit," I sign, fingerspelling the last word. "I love you. Nothing else matters."

She picks up her phone, stands, and walks toward the door. Turning back before leaving, she signs, "Buy the house. It will be good for Maisy. Goodbye, Blake."

"Goodbye?" I yell, knowing she can't hear, but I shout it again anyway. "Goodbye?" I stand. "What the fuck?"

I take a few deep breaths and gather my thoughts. She's just like my brother, Lucas. She loves me. I know she does. But she's leaving anyway. Do I just let her go?

No. Fuck that. I race to the door, expecting to see her sitting in the front seat of my car. But she's not there.

She's not anywhere.

She's just... gone.

I physically feel my heart splinter into a million pieces.

# Chapter Forty

## Ellie

By the time I get home, my shirt is damp, my eyes are puffy, and my spirit is broken.

He said he loved me.

I throw myself on my bed and cry. I cry because I know exactly what I'm doing. I'm throwing away possibly the best thing to ever happen to me. But I just... can't.

When I'm all out of tears, I pad out to the kitchen, start brewing a jumbo batch of coffee, and place a video call to Mom. When her face fills the screen, she cocks her head, and sadness overcomes her.

"Oh, baby," she signs, "What happened?"

Mom and I have always been close. I tell her almost as much as I tell Beth. I take her through the entire day, leaving out details about making love in the empty house.

"Ellie." She gives me a look only moms know how to give. "The fact that you're in the state you're in and you're calling me for motherly advice tells me everything I need to know. Sweetie, it's obvious you belong together. And I'm sorry to have to agree with him over you, but I believe he's right and you're making excuses."

I look away, pouting. It's the only thing I can do to stop the conversation. She's my mom. She should be on my side. When I finally look back, she's waiting patiently. This isn't the first time, or ever the hundredth, I've used my deafness to ignore someone.

"I've sat here and heard you out," she signs. "Now, you're going to listen to me. Okay?"

I nod.

"When I met your dad, and I mean Kyle, not Grant, I was a poor, pregnant girl from Chicago who walked dogs to make ends meet." She holds up a hand to stop me from cutting in. "I know you've heard some of this before. But it seems you need to hear it again. So listen."

I sit back and cross my arms.

"He was a doctor, and I was on the run from an abusive husband. We came from totally different worlds, yet we had an instant connection despite all those differences. He had loving parents and a solid support system. At the time, I had no one. And then, when he stepped up, declared his feelings and practically swept me off my feet, newborn and all, I left him for all the wrong reasons. He's the reason you're here, Ellie. If it weren't for him, I'd have probably miscarried in my dirty little apartment. He changed my life. But don't get me wrong, this wasn't just a damsel in distress story. I changed his life, too."

Tears collect in the corners of her eyes as she recalls the story. "Don't be me, Ellie. I almost lost him because I let my past control my actions. I was a stupid, stupid girl and threw away everything because... well, because I guess he loved me too much." She shakes her head in disbelief. "And I just didn't believe that over the course of a few short months, you could ever really know someone well enough to love them."

Those words physically hurt as if they'd punched me in the gut. I'd forgotten that it was just a short time they'd known each other, all while she was confined to a hospital bed.

She wipes away the tears that now coat her cheeks. "I was lucky. He took me back after I came to my senses. I can't imagine my life without him. You and I wouldn't be who we are today without Kyle Stone.

"So, sweetie, you better think long and hard about what you're doing here. Be honest with yourself. Can you imagine your life without Blake? Will you regret it next month, or next year, if he's moved on with someone else? And that adorable little girl you're always texting me pictures of, could you live with yourself if you cut her out of your life? She needs you. He needs you. You need him. That's why it works, Ellie. You all need each other. You all love each other. What else is there in life? It's not fair to punish him for things out of his control. So you're deaf. Who cares? I'm glad you're deaf, Ellie."

Surprised to see her say it, I can only stare at her in confusion.

"It took me a long time to admit it. But, yes, I'm glad you're deaf. You wouldn't be the amazing woman you are today if you weren't."

*She's glad I'm deaf.*

No one has ever said that. I mean, *I'm* good with it. Once I got past all the shit from high school and found my place in the world, I embraced it. But deep down, I guess I always thought everyone else in my life would be happier if I could hear.

But could my new place in the world really be with Blake? A hearing man? It would be a giant leap of faith I'm not sure I'm ready to take. Maybe Blake was right and Grant screwed me up so badly I'm incapable of truly loving anyone.

Mom's incessant waves get my attention and I look back at the screen. "Do you love him?" she signs.

Being stubborn, I shake my head. Mom just stares. I shrug. She stares some more. I sign, "Maybe." Then I momentarily close my eyes and sign, "Yes."

Her expression softens. "Then you need to ask yourself an important question. Would you think differently about all this if Blake were deaf?"

Immediately I know the answer. I know it because I've often wished it to be true. Sometimes in my dreams he's deaf and we have an amazing life and go on to have a gaggle of deaf kids.

"You don't have to answer," she signs. "It's written all over you. Ellie, you're punishing the man for the simple fact that he can hear. You, if anyone, should know how wrong that is. He loves you. His daughter loves you. Don't be afraid to be happy just because your idea of happiness ended up coming in a different package. The best things in life can be everything we didn't expect."

My eyes dart to the kitchen counter where the tiny slip of fortune cookie paper still sits where he left it.

*Your heart knows the right answer.*

I wipe my eyes. "Mom, I have to go."

She smiles. She doesn't have to ask where I'm going. Like mother, like daughter, I guess.

"Go find your happiness, baby. And when you get it—don't ever let go."

"Love you, Mom."

"I love you too, baby."

The screen goes blank and I can see my pitiful reflection in the glass. Red eyes. Streaked makeup. And I probably smell from the run home. Quickly, I shower and dress and fix my face. I'm contemplating where I can find Blake when a text comes in. *Is it him?* My heart flutters. *Is he coming after me?*

But when I look at my phone and see Sierra has been texting me for the last twenty minutes, my world comes to an abrupt halt.

> **Sierra: Ellie, I really messed up. I need to talk to you.**

> **Sierra: Are you there?**

> **Sierra: I'm at the airport on standby. Please answer me. Oh, God. I have to know you and Mom are okay.**

My heart pounds as I respond.

> **Me: I'm here. What's wrong?**

> **Sierra: Oh, thank God. You have to go find my mom. She's not responding. Then you both have to go somewhere safe.**

> **Me: I'll find her. But what happened?**

> **Sierra: It's my fault. I made a horrible mistake. I accidentally texted Mom's old phone instead of her new one. I did it 2 days**

ago. I didn't realize it until today when I got concerned that she hadn't texted me back. Ellie, he knows. I asked how her job was going and if she'd seen you and if she knew any gossip about you and Blake. I've put everyone I love in danger. You have to find her, Ellie.

Me: I'll find her. If you didn't mention where she worked, I'm sure she's okay.

Sierra: It'll take me at least a day to fly back, and that's assuming I catch a flight out today. I feel so helpless just sitting here. I caused this. I may have messed everything up. And I can't do a damn thing.

Me: You might be overreacting. It's been a while. Maybe he's given up on finding her.

Sierra: He hasn't. He's still reading the fake texts I send every week. He responds as if he's her. And I can see he read the accidental one shortly after I sent it.

Me: Okay. Don't panic. He's a long way away.

Sierra: It was 2 days ago. I made it to Chicago in half a day, remember?

**Me: I'll leave right now. I'm sure everything
will be fine. Text me when you get a flight. I
promise to let you know when I find her.**

I stash my phone in my pocket and replace my dress shoes
with sneakers. It'll be faster to run to the school than to wait for an
Uber. I open the door and freeze because someone is blocking the
way. Relief courses through me when my brain processes that it's
Tara.

Then relief turns to terror as Grant steps behind her, pushes
her through my doorway, and locks the door behind them.

# Chapter Forty-one

## Ellie

I don't even hesitate. He's holding onto Tara, so I run into my bedroom, lock the door behind me, and go for the gun in my closet.

Something hits the back of my leg. It's part of my door. Grant kicked it down. I'm fumbling with the code when I'm slammed to the floor. My head hits something and I see stars. When my eyes regain focus, Grant is standing over me, a fistful of Tara's shirt in one hand and his gun in the other.

He's yelling, but I can't make any of it out.

He kicks my foot and yells again.

He turns to Tara and I see her say, "She's deaf," as if he didn't already know. But it's like he doesn't know, because he continues to yell. *At me.*

"I can't hear you," I sign, knowing good and well he doesn't understand, but those basic signs are fairly intuitive.

"Stop doing that," he says, as I'm finally able to read his lips now that he's not yelling. He looks at my hands in disgust. I think he says, "You look ridiculous."

"What do you expect me to do, you idiot? This is how I communicate." I keep signing all the shit I've wanted to tell him even though I know it's only for me.

He strides forward and kicks my right hand with his boot. I wince in pain as I look at my hand, fairly sure he dislocated my forefinger.

"I said stop it!" he shouts, nostrils flaring.

It pisses me off that I have to keep looking at him to assess the situation. His face is red, his temple pulses in anger, and his jaw is clenched in fury. He towers over me, tall and buff. His dress shirt is soaked with sweat stains, and he's sporting a police badge on his belt, as if he'd left work the second he saw Sierra's text. Another gun is holstered to his side. He has two guns now. *What am I going to do?*

Behind him, Tara looks ashen. And it's now that I see a bruise forming on her cheek.

"You monster," I sign with my left hand.

He tries to kick that hand too, but I pull away.

He goes for my arm, and I swat him away until he gets purchase on my bicep and hauls me up, about pulling my shoulder out of the socket.

He forces Tara and me into the other room and onto the couch, then he paces the floor, occasionally hitting himself on the forehead with the barrel of his gun in frustration. I silently wish for it to go off and shoot him.

Tara is frozen to the couch. She's stoic. She's not going to fight. I'm the one who has to get us out of this. But how can I if I can't talk to him?

He yells something at Tara and waves the gun around recklessly. He's acting like a maniac, and I wonder if he's high on drugs.

There's only one thing I can think of to do. "Grant!" I say in what I think is a shout.

His eyes snap to me in surprise.

"You don't have to do this. We can work this out."

His lips turn into a sneer. "Shut her up," he says to Tara. "She sounds like an idiot."

"I called the police as soon as I got Sierra's text. They're on the way."

Two steps forward and my face burns with the slap he delivers. When I recover and look back, he's got the gun to Tara's head. "Shut her up or I'll kill you."

Tara turns to me with terror filled eyes.

I don't speak again.

He backs up but keeps the gun trained on his wife. "Get her phone," he says.

I pull it from my pocket and hold it out.

His lip twitches and he leans close. "Type in the fucking code."

I can smell the alcohol on his breath and his pupils are pin pricks. He's totally bombed.

I do what he asks and hand the phone over. A minute later, he laughs. "You're a liar. Do you know what I do to liars?" He narrows his eyes. "Are you reading my fucking lips?" He turns to Tara. "Tell her what I do to liars."

Tara doesn't say anything, she shrinks into the couch.

"Just my luck," I think he says. "I'm stuck with Deaf and Dumb." He touches the gun to Tara's temple. "Make me some food. I was driving all night."

She gets up and goes to the kitchen as if his request was the most natural thing in the world. Grant doesn't look at her as she walks away. It's like he knows she won't try anything. Was this how it was with my mom? Does he beat them down and strip them of who they are until they just become robots?

He points the gun at me, motioning for me to follow Tara.

In the kitchen, Grant smirks and immediately moves the knife block to a top cabinet out of my reach.

I'm helping Tara get cold cuts from the refrigerator when I spy the large pot of coffee I brewed before. It's full and steaming hot. Without giving it another thought, I grab the handle, spin around and throw the hot liquid at him. He dodges most of it, but a good bit lands on his arm and I see him wince in pain.

"You bitch!" he yells. It's easy to read his lips. Bitch is often a word that gets yelled.

I'm certain I'm about to be shot. I brace for it. I inhale what could be my last breath as I think about what this will do to Blake. To Maisy. To Mom, Dad, and Beth.

Instead of putting a bullet into me and ending my life, Grant smiles. I can see a few blisters already forming on his arm, yet he's smiling. It's the most sinister smile I've ever seen. It makes my skin crawl and my stomach turn.

"Sit the fuck down," he says, motioning to a kitchen chair with the gun.

He has words with Tara that I can't understand, then he sits opposite me as she puts a sandwich down in front of him. She cleans up the coffee on the floor, retrieves the coffee pot that miraculously didn't break when it landed on the living room carpet, and goes to brew another batch.

Good. Maybe drinking coffee will sober him up and make him realize what he's doing. Because, seriously, what does he think he's going to do? Kill me and walk out of here with Tara? He'd be caught. It doesn't matter if he's a cop. We have evidence now. The texts will prove he knew she was missing. There are witnesses. Surely someone saw him take Tara from the school. Regardless of what happens to me, he'll be caught.

There is a chance he may realize all this when he sobers up, though. And that has the potential of making things worse. If he knows he's going down, he'll have no problem taking everyone in his way down with him.

But if he stays drugged up or drunk, he'll make poor decisions. Yes, he could decide to shoot me, but his aim might be off. And his reactions will be slower. I have liquor in the cabinet, but how can I get him to drink it without him suspecting it's part of a plan?

When he eats, he does it with one hand, using the other to keep the gun on the table, a finger on the trigger. But when he looks down at his food, I take the opportunity to use my eyes to motion to the liquor cabinet. It takes a few times for Tara to see me, but when she does, I bring my hand up to my face in a quick drinking motion and then wipe my nose in case Grant catches a glance.

He stiffens and says something to Tara when she goes for the cabinet. Then a smile spreads across his face when he sees my liquor collection.

He turns to me. "See what a good wife I have? She knows I like my coffee Irish."

Tara puts the bottle on the table. Grant unscrews the top, sniffs it, and takes a giant swig.

*My plan is working. Stay calm.*

Tara pulls a coffee cup from the dish rack and sets it before him. He eyes it, then her. "I'll make it, sweetheart." He gets up, puts his gun in the front of his pants, kisses Tara on the cheek, then crosses the kitchen and gets the freshly brewed pot of coffee. He turns back to me with the same sinister smile from minutes ago. "The coffee's for you."

Before I can wrap my mind around what's happening, he grabs my right arm below the elbow, forces it palm-down on the table and pours hot coffee on it. I'm screaming and thrashing around, but I'm no match for his strength. And just when I think I'm going to pass out from the pain, he does it again with my left hand.

When the pot is empty, he backs away. I'm shaking. My pants are wet; not from coffee, but the release of my bladder. My hands are a shade of red I've never seen, and the pain surrounds me like a heavy blanket I can't shed. Even my throat is burning, but that must be from my screaming.

Out of the corner of my eye, I see Tara jumping onto Grant's back. They tussle and he throws her to the ground, gun pointed at her. But I can't think about that. I can't think about anything but the pain. Death must be less painful, and right now, it's what I'm wishing for. It's the last thought that goes through my mind before my head swims in dizziness and I see the table come up to meet my face.

Then everything goes black and there's no more pain.

# Chapter Forty-two

## Blake

I've driven around long enough. Screw my idea to give her space and hope she comes around. What if she takes off like Lissa? I'm not going to let that happen. I'm going to get through to her.

I park in the lot of her building and look up at her window, trying to find the words that will break down her barriers. Because apparently, *I love you* wasn't enough. But the longer I sit here, the more anxious I get. I just need to man up and do it.

I exit the car and walk to her building. I think I hear someone scream. It alarms me, but when I don't hear it again, I continue to the outer door. I stare at the security keypad. Texting her won't work. She probably won't let me up. I tug on the door, wondering if with enough force, I can open it. I'm surprised when it opens immediately. Upon further investigation, the lock has been broken and the wood around it splintered. I guess someone else was in my same predicament.

I'm thanking my lucky stars until I hear a second scream. Okay, now I know I wasn't hearing things. My whole body is on high alert. It was definitely a woman. I doubt it's coming from Ellie's apartment, but I take the steps two at a time anyway.

When I get to her door and hear a blood-curdling scream that pierces the very center of my being, I try her door. It's locked.

Two neighbors come into the hallway, having heard the screams. "Call the police!" I yell. Then I step back and with all my might, I kick in her door.

"Ellie!" I yell out of sheer terror.

A big motherfucker of a man comes from the kitchen and points a gun at me, growling, "Who the fuck are you?"

"Where's Ellie?" I ask, my eyes darting around the room hoping to see her. Praying that whatever is going on here is one big mistake.

The guy scoffs as if amused, not seeming disturbed in the least that I just busted down the door. "You mean my cunt of a daughter who thought she could hide my wife from me?"

*Grant Lucas. Oh, holy shit.* And he's got a gun pointed at me. But that's not what worries me the most. What worries me is the silence. There are no more screams. *Is she dead?*

My heart stops cold, fear burning a trail throughout my body, and for one tortuous moment, I get a taste of what Dallas must have endured.

A flash of someone coming from behind him gives me hope. But it's not Ellie. I have no idea who the woman is who just threw herself on his back. As he attempts to buck her off, the gun fires, followed by a searing pain in my thigh.

The pain isn't enough to keep me from charging him and barreling him to the ground. The gun goes flying. But there's another holstered to his side. We each struggle to get control of it when he goes limp. My ears ring at the sound of another gunshot in close range. I quickly check myself for a second wound when I see blood pooling on the ground. But as the color drains from Grant's face, I know I wasn't the one shot this time.

The woman holding the gun drops it and collapses onto the ground into a fetal position.

"Where's Ellie?" I shout through a ball of sawdust in my throat. The seconds I spend waiting for the woman to answer are nothing but pure agony.

Sirens sound in the distance as the woman points to the kitchen. "I... I t-tried to stop it."

I brace myself for what I'm going to find when I go around the corner. Flashes of my life without Ellie bombard my mind.

"No!" I scream, when I see her lifeless body slumped over the table. I run to her, looking for a bullet wound, praying for her to wake.

A small amount of blood trickles from a cut on her head. I press my fingers to her neck and cry out in relief when I feel a pulse. Then I see her hands. Bile rises in my throat as I try to comprehend what I'm looking at. The entire backs of both of her hands are swollen and red with white patches and various sizes of blisters that seem to grow with every second.

"Oh, Jesus." I pick her up and carry her into the other room just as police arrive, guns pointed.

"Put her down and put your hands up!" one yells.

"Blake Montana?" I glance up to see Mitchell Graves, a guy I went to high school with. He does a visual sweep of the room and asks, "What the hell happened here?"

"Get an ambulance!" I shout. "She's severely injured."

With guns still drawn, a third officer uses his radio to dispatch an ambulance.

I lay Ellie on the couch and check her pulse again.

One of the officers puts a few fingers to Grant's neck then shakes his head.

"Blake," Mitchell says. "I'm sorry, but I need you to step away from her."

"You'll have to fucking shoot me, Mitch. I'm not leaving her."

"That's m-my husband," the woman says. "I'm Tara Lucas. Ellie helped me escape."

"Escape what ma'am?" Mitch asks.

"Escape him." She points to the lifeless bastard on the floor. "He hurt me. He hurt me for years. Decades. And I'm not the only one." She nods to Ellie. "He's her birth father. He hurt her mother as well. He did this to Ellie. I tried to stop him. I couldn't stop him." She rambles on as I cradle Ellie in my arms, willing her to wake up. "I did it. I fired the gun. It was me." She holds out her wrists. "You can arrest me. It's okay. He can't hurt me anymore."

The officers holster their guns just as EMS arrives.

Patrick Kelsey, one of the paramedics, goes to the body on the ground first. "Not fucking him," I bark, more acid rising from my belly at the very thought of Grant Lucas being deserving of any medical attention. "Help Ellie."

He checks Grant's pulse anyway, wasting precious seconds in my opinion, then he and his partner ask me to move aside. "Jesus, Blake. What the fuck happened here?"

I can't answer, because I don't know.

"He poured an entire pot of boiling coffee on her hands," Tara says.

I turn and vomit at her words.

They put an oxygen mask on Ellie's face, a collar around her neck, and load her onto a backboard. Patrick puts rolled towels under both her hands, elevating them above her heart before wrapping them in gauze.

"Will she be okay?" I crawl over and touch her hair before they lift her onto the gurney. "Please tell me she'll be okay. Why isn't she conscious?"

"The burns are bad, Blake. She probably passed out from the pain. She's got a gash on her head that could be from a fall. We'll know more after we get her to the hospital."

"I'm going with you."

Mitch's strong hand clasps my shoulder. "I'm sorry, Blake. This is a homicide. We can't let you leave until we have full statements."

Patrick eyes my leg. "You're injured. Let me check it out."

"He shot me, but it's fine. It's Ellie I'm worried about."

"Sit down, Montana. I'm evaluating you while the others get her loaded in the rig." He leans down and looks right into my eyes. "Blake, I need to check your leg. Listen, I believe she's going to be okay. There's damage, but she can recover. There's protocol we have to follow." He nods at the officers. "If you try to leave, they'll restrain you. The sooner you cooperate the sooner you can go to her."

It takes everything I have not to plow him over and run to Ellie as her limp body is rolled into the hallway.

"Fuck!" I yell, then stomp into the kitchen, sitting on a chair as I stare at the coffee dripping off the table. *He burned her fucking hands.* If he weren't already dead, I'd kill him.

"Back up folks," I hear Mitch say in the other room. "It's over. Go back to your apartments."

Patrick cuts my jeans from knee to thigh. I brace myself to see a bullet hole, hoping I don't need to have surgery that will keep me from Ellie.

"It's a flesh wound," he says, rolling a swab of iodine over it then securing a bandage. "You were lucky. Had it been a few inches over, it may have hit an artery. You'd be as dead as that asshole in the other room."

Mitch interviews Tara in the second bedroom, presumably to get her away from the dead body. I can't hear them. He does it quietly, as does Henry, the officer who's grilling me. I suppose they want to make sure our stories match up.

I tell it three separate times, and he keeps asking more questions. I throw up my hands. "How many fucking ways can I say I walked into the middle of it, and then he shot me, and we fought until Tara shot him? Ask the goddamn neighbors. I mean, Christ, my girl is hurt. I have to get to her."

Mitch walks in. "The coroner is here. We're done for now. But you'll need to come to the station for an official statement. And, don't leave town."

I glare at him. "Where the hell would I go, Mitch? Ellie is in the hospital. That's the only place I'm going to be."

He nods and steps aside. "You're free to go then."

I'm walking out when it occurs to me that Tara is still here and is clearly shaken. I go to her. "Thank you," I say with the utmost sincerity. "That could have gone the other way. You saved Ellie. And you saved me."

"Too little too late," she says, tears streaming down her face.

I get my phone out. "I'm going to have my mom come over. She'll help you and get you anything you need. Her name is Sarah." I turn to Mitch. "Can you stay with her until she gets here?"

"Yeah, go."

I walk out of the room that's now filled with a dozen officers. Things like this don't happen in Calloway Creek. Grant's body is put into a body bag and lifted onto a gurney. Evidence tags mark bullet casings and other things they find important. A large pool of blood remains on the floor. It doesn't even turn my stomach to see it. He got what he deserved.

Questions from nosey neighbors are shot at me from every direction as I make my way down the stairs and to the car. I don't answer any of them. I call Mom on the way to the hospital. I call Allie, who's still with Maisy, and give her the gist. I drive as fast as I can, knowing most of the town's patrol cars are back at Ellie's place. I even run the one traffic light in town, once I'm sure the coast is clear.

I'm at the hospital in less than five minutes.

I park on the grass next to the ambulance bay, not caring if my car gets towed, and race inside, the whole time praying she's okay.

Her hands. I can't stop thinking about them. What if her body went into shock and her heart stopped and I wasn't with her? What if the injury to her head is severe? What if I've lost her before we even have a chance to be... *us?*

Holly Overton sits behind the desk in the ER. She looks up with sad eyes. "I know why you're here, Blake. But I have to follow the rules. Family only."

"Are you fucking serious?"

"I can't let you back. I'll lose my job."

"She doesn't *have* any family here yet. I'm the only one." I run a hand through my hair. "Shit. I have to contact her parents."

"I can do it if you'd like."

I shake my head. "No. It has to be me." I look past her to the locked doors leading to the back. "Holly, I have to know if she's okay. Please. I love her."

Her face is filled with empathy. "No promises. But I'll see what I can find out. Wait here."

"Believe me, I'm not going anywhere."

As she disappears through the doors, I sit and let my head fall back against the wall. My leg is throbbing. Has it been this whole time, or am I just now noticing?

I stare at my phone, wondering how I'm going to tell her parents. I don't have their contact information, but a quick search has me finding the phone number of Dr. Kyle Stone from New York City. I press the phone to my ear, hoping I don't have to leave a message. When he answers on the third ring, though, my heart lodges in my throat, because I know he's about to be as devastated as I am.

# Chapter Forty-three

## Ellie

*Ugh.*

My head is pounding. And my tongue is fuzzy.

I reach up to feel my head, and, *oh my God,* my hands. Hurt doesn't even begin to describe the pain. My eyes fly open. I'm disoriented by the overhead light. Someone… a nurse?… comes in, looks at a machine to my left, fiddles with something, and then I feel a rush of euphoria that dulls the pain.

It hurts to raise my hands. They're bandaged from my fingertips to my wrists. *Why?*

The nurse talks to someone in the corner then leaves.

It's Blake. He's the someone in the corner.

I look around frantically. I'm in a bad dream. I can't sign.

Blake rushes over, grinning with all his teeth. "Hey." The relief on his face is palpable. And the bags under his eyes tell me he's probably been sitting in that chair for a very long time.

I look from his eyes to my hands then back at him.

"It's okay. You're going to be okay. You'll have to wear the bandages for about a week, but the doctors think you'll heal up just fine."

I look at him in confusion. Why am I here? And after the way I left him, why is *he* here? And what the hell happened to my hands?

"Ellie, do you remember anything?"

When I don't answer, because I still feel as if this is a dream, he pulls a chair over, signing what he can but also speaking. "You've been in and out of it all night. The pain medication has kept you asleep mostly. The doctor came in earlier but said you might not remember."

I shake my head, hoping to wake up, but then the pain around my temple throbs.

"You hit your head. It's not bad. No concussion." He fingerspells *concussion*.

Though it hurts, I lift up a bandaged hand and tap it to my head then my chin. He immediately understands.

"Your parents have been here all night too. Once you woke up and they knew you'd be okay, they went to help Tara. I guess she and your mom have a lot in common."

As soon as the words come off his lips, everything comes rushing back. Grant bursting into my apartment. Threatening Tara. Holding us at gunpoint. Pouring hot coffee all over my hands. I lean over the side of the bed and vomit. Not much comes out. My head pounds again.

"It's okay," he signs then holds a cup of water with a straw near my lips. "You're going to be fine."

Reluctantly, I drink, but only because my throat feels like sandpaper.

Now that I've concluded this isn't a dream, I wonder how any of this can be okay with Grant still out there? And how are my parents helping Tara?

I go to ask him, but the bandages and the dull ache remind me I can't.

"You have questions," he says. "I'm here to answer all of them. I was there. And once you're not so drugged, the police will want to interview you."

The tip of my right middle finger sticks out of the bandage. I wiggle it at him.

"Why was I there?" he asks.

I nod.

"I came for you, Ellie. I wasn't about to leave things the way we did. When I got there, I heard screaming. I burst into your apartment and Grant shot me."

My eyes widen, searching his body for injuries. He stands and opens a slit in his jeans, showing a bandage. "Don't worry, it's just a scratch."

I shake my head, terrified. Grant shot him? And he's still out there? I look to the door.

He waves a hand to get my attention. "You don't have to be scared. He's gone. After I broke down your door, he and I tussled, the gun he was holding came loose, and Tara got hold of it and shot him. Grant is dead, Ellie. Tara saved us. He'll never hurt anyone again."

He's dead. Grant is dead. He shot Blake and mutilated me. But now it's over.

I close my eyes and blow out a long, relieved breath.

He puts a gentle hand on my arm, and I look up at him. "What were you thinking trying to help Tara without telling anyone?"

I look down at the covers.

He puts a finger under my chin and guides my face back up. "I'd have helped. Don't you know I'd do anything for you?"

Tears come to my eyes. There's so much I want to tell him.

"Beth is here. Do you want me to send her in?"

I shake my head.

"Is there anyone else you want me to call?"

I shake my head again. All I can do is stare at him. He came after me. And because he did, Tara and I are alive, and Grant can never hurt anyone again.

He. Came. After. Me.

Emotions I can't even explain flow through me.

"You want to tell me something," he says. He doesn't arch his brows. It wasn't a question.

I gently raise my bandaged hands and set them back down.

"It's okay. You don't need to sign. I know what you want to say." He sits on the edge of the bed, careful to avoid my hands. I move one up to my stomach to give him room, and he puts a hand on my leg as he looks directly into my eyes. "You want to tell me you thought about it and changed your mind. You changed your mind because you realized how stupid it would be to throw away what we have. You know we're perfect together. You know we don't need words or signs to talk to each other. You knew it from that first day in the market when we saw each other from across the store. We're perfect together because I can read your eyes like I'm doing right now. And you know what they tell me? That you love me." He signs, "You love me, Ellie." He brushes a hair off my forehead. "I don't need you to sign it. I don't need you to text it. I don't need you to write it down. I don't need any of that, because I know it's true."

I swallow. I swallow hard. And it hurts. Because the tears caught in my throat sting so much, I almost forget about the pain in my hands. But this hurt, it's a good one. He's right. He does know me. And we don't need words.

Which is why I decide to give him some.

I lick my lips. Then I speak.

"I love you, Blake," I say, hoping I'm clearly enunciating the first words he's ever heard me speak.

I thought he'd be surprised. Pleased, even. But strangely enough, he doesn't seem to be. His teary eyes look into mine as he puts a finger to my lips. "I don't need you to say it, either. All I need you to do is look at me."

So I do. I look at him. And we stare at each other just like we did that first day. We're connected on an almost telepathic level. He doesn't sign. He doesn't talk. But his eyes speak volumes. And it's everything I've ever wanted to hear.

# Chapter Forty-four

## Blake

*Three months later...*


Maisy and I put the finishing touches on her new room then stand back and admire our work. Her princess bed sits in the middle, the four-poster bed with a canopy on top and sheers along the sides making it look like something out of a Disney movie.

Bolt has his own bed in the corner, also pink, which as a boy I think he should protest, but I get the idea he'd put up with anything for Maisy.

I know the feeling.

"Perfect," I sign.

"I love it," she signs, and hugs me. "I love you, Daddy."

"I love you too."

Exchanging those words has become an everyday occurrence for us, and it warms my heart every single time.

Tapping her shoulder to get her attention as she organizes her toy ponies by height, I motion to the hallway. "I'm going to finish dinner."

"Celebrate," she signs.

"Yes, we're celebrating. Big day."

Her eyes light up. "You show me the room tonight?"

I smile and nod. "Yes. Later."

"We surprise Ellie?" she signs.

"That too. After the room."

I go downstairs and pass the one room that's been off limits to Maisy and Ellie as we went through the remodel. Both of them have had a hand in the renovations even though Ellie doesn't even live here. But it was fun to see her put her own touch on things as if she would one day. Which we both know she will. We know it without saying it. We know it without signing it. We just know.

Ellie never went home to her apartment. She moved into a rental house she's been sharing with Sierra and Tara. Ellie's boss gave Tara a legitimate job at the Deaf and Blind school, and Sierra has made the house her home base between ski instructor gigs.

On my way to the kitchen, I stop and look at the wall of pictures. I never thought I—Blake Montana—would have a wall of family pictures. But I do. And it's just one more testament to how my life has changed since Maisy and Ellie came into it.

I run a finger across the frame smack in the middle. I had to rearrange all the others to add it earlier today, but it's the most important picture by far. The bottom half of the frame has a picture of Maisy and me. It's my favorite photo of the two of us. One day at the winery, Maisy and I were holding hands walking through the vineyard. Ellie was trailing behind. She clapped her hands to get my attention, and when Maisy and I turned and looked over our shoulders, she started snapping photos.

Maisy is wearing one of her favorite princess dresses, her spiral blonde curls blowing in the light breeze as she smiles back at Ellie. I'm not wearing anything special, but it's not what we're wearing that makes this particular picture so extraordinary, it's how I'm looking at Maisy.

When Ellie showed me the photo, she had tears in her eyes. She said she'd never seen me look as much like a father as I did in that moment. Which is why it's only fitting that this be the photo in the same frame as Maisy's new birth certificate. The one that came this morning. The one that displays her new name and makes her officially a Montana. The one that bonds us for life.

The paperwork was filed months ago, right after I got word that Lucinda had passed. I went to see her once more after the first visit. I didn't take Maisy that time either. We both agreed it would be better that way, but we did make amends. Despite the way Lucinda treated Maisy, I wouldn't have Maisy if it weren't for her. And I didn't think she deserved to die without knowing how far Maisy had come. I showed her all kinds of pictures and told her stories. Lucinda just sat with a smile on her face. Two days later, she was gone.

One day, I'll tell Maisy about Lucinda. But not today. Today I have other things planned.

In the kitchen, I check on the short ribs that have been cooking all afternoon. I put a bottle of wine on the table and start on the potatoes and the other vegetables. Everything has to be perfect. It's our first night in the house and there's so much to celebrate.

Jonas, Brayden's dad, sees me in the kitchen window from his yard and gives me a wave. We've become fast friends with the neighbors. Even though we didn't move in until today, ever since our kids started kindergarten together a few weeks ago, I've been driving Maisy over and Jonas and I have been walking the kids to school. Those kids are like two peas in a pod. I swear Brayden's mom already has them betrothed.

Maisy loves school. She's even started learning English. Her signing improved by leaps and bounds after the two of us went to Seattle over the summer for a two-week intensive ASL camp. At this point, she may know more signs than I do.

An hour later, the house lights flash in rapid succession. Maisy comes bounding down the stairs. "Now?" she asks.

"Not yet."

She's impatient to get on with things, but gets over it quickly when I let Ellie in the front door.

"You can use your key," I sign.

She shrugs. "Not my house."

"Yet," I sign, capturing her eyes with mine.

She laughs, then her eyes close as she inhales. "What's that heavenly smell?" she asks.

"We made your favorite," Maisy signs.

I ruffle Maisy's curls. "Oh, *we* did, did we?" I tease.

"I put milk in the potatoes," she signs.

Ellie touches her shoulder. "That's the most important step."

Maisy beams at her then tugs at my shirt. "Now?"

I shake my head. "Eat first."

We go into the dining room and sit at the table. Ellie immediately spots the bottle of wine I'd set near her plate. She picks it up and her eyes sparkle with amusement.

She runs a hand over the label that reads:


**EL**

**Merlot**

**Montana Winery**

**Limited Edition**


She looks up with misty eyes. "You named a wine after me?"

"I did. Look closer."

She studies the label. Behind each English letter is the shadow of the corresponding ASL letter. "Oh, my God. I love this. I don't even care if it tastes like crud, I'll drink every last drop."

I laugh. "Believe me, it doesn't. I spent months working with our vintner"—I fingerspell the word because I seriously have no idea if there's an ASL sign for winemaker—"and I think you're going to go crazy over it."

She pushes away the corkscrew. "I'm not sure I want to open it. It's one of a kind."

"Actually, it's one of a hundred. I have the other ninety-nine under lock and key, and they will only get better with age."

"In that case." She holds out her glass, waits for me to pour it, inhales the robust fruity scent with a hint of oak, then closes her eyes and takes a sip. "Wow." Her eyes pop open. "If I didn't already love you, this would have done the trick."

I smile. "I'm glad you approve."

She sets her glass down. "I have a little surprise for you too."

I raise a brow in question.

She positions her right hand in the ILY sign, then, keeping the sign, taps her heart twice with her thumb.

I tilt my head, unfamiliar with the combination. "What does that mean?"

Her bright smile lights up the entire room. "It's your name sign."

I point to myself. "Mine?"

Ellie nods as Maisy claps. "It was Maisy's suggestion that we give you a name sign. Of course she'll still call you Dad, but she insisted you have one. When we secretly discussed our options, and I asked what she loves the most about you, she said it's your giant heart and the way you love us. I think it's the perfect sign because the ILY sign is similar to the sign used for alcohol—and everyone who knows you knows you're all about wine. Not to mention there are three fingers used in the name sign signifying—"

I grab her gorgeous hands and complete the thought myself. "Us," I sign and motion around the table.

These girls. These quiet, beautiful, amazing creatures who make my life worth living. I pray that I never take for granted their kindness, love, and unwavering zest for life.

After dinner, Ellie helps clean up as I deal with my very impatient daughter who is nearing the end of her rope.

Ellie emerges from the kitchen and signs, "Done."

I chuckle and tell her she left the faucet running. *Again.*

She rolls her eyes and signs, "Deaf problems."

I figure I've made Maisy wait long enough, so I announce, "I have a surprise for both of you."

Maisy jumps up and down, signing, "Room. Room."

Ellie's eyebrows go up. "The big reveal?"

I smile and nod. "Follow me."

We walk to the door at the end of the lower hallway. I've kept it locked so little prying eyes wouldn't see the surprise.

"Close your eyes and hold my hand," I sign. "You'll know when it's time to open them."

Maisy loves this game, and overdramatically squeezes her eyelids shut and holds out her hand.

Ellie glares at me.

"You too. Please? I promise it'll be worth it."

She plays along. I unlock the door, take Ellie's hand, guide them through, and shut the door with my foot. I lead them to the center of the room, drop Ellie's hand, and pull the remote from my pocket. I hit a few buttons and brace myself for it.

Sound assaults my ears as it bounces off the walls. Lights of varying colors flash along to the beat of the music. Both of my girls open their eyes when they feel the vibrations under their feet.

Maisy falls to the floor and puts her hands on the ground, absorbing the vibrations in both her hands and feet. The smile on her face is a mile wide as she watches the lights flash.

Ellie's jaw is on the floor as she turns in a circle and takes it all in.

It took a lot of ingenuity, but with the help of some others in the Deaf community, along with the best sound engineers money can buy, I created a sound room.

I rebuilt the walls with extra layers of drywall and four additional inches of insulation. The door hermetically seals to make it soundproof, so even if you stand right outside, you can't hear anything. At the front of the room is a built-in state-of-the-art sound system hooked up to a complex arrangement of lights hanging from the ceiling that have been programmed to flash along with the music. Different colors signify different tones, warm colors for bass, cool colors for treble. I have to admit, it's pretty amazing. You can almost *see* the music. And you can definitely *feel* it. Each of the walls has multiple floor-to-ceiling speakers, and I even special ordered some to be installed in the floor, which is why Maisy is sitting on it right now.

"This is the most incredible thing anyone has ever done for me," Ellie signs. Then her cheeks redden. "Not that it's for me."

I pull her close. "Of course it's for you. It's for the two most important people in my life."

She smiles and puts her head on my shoulder, swaying to the music in my arms.

I revel in the unexpected benefit of the room. Dancing with Ellie. Although I'm going to have to invest in some high-tech earplugs if I spend much time in here.

Maisy squeezes between us and joins in our dance.

This—this right here—might be my favorite moment in time. Then I laugh at myself, because I think that very same thing at least once a day when Maisy learns a new sign. Or when she runs into my arms after school. Or… basically anytime Ellie looks at me.

I tap Maisy on the shoulder and tell her, "Now."

She claps her hands and runs from the room.

Ellie narrows her eyes at me, but she barely has time to ask about it when Maisy trots back in the room, beaming, carrying two small boxes.

She hands the pink box to Ellie.

"For me?" Ellie asks.

Maisy bounces. "Open it."

Ellie carefully opens the long slender box, her hand covering her heart as she looks down at the platinum necklace that spells M-O-M in ASL letters. Maisy tugs on Ellie's hand then signs, "Will you be my mom?"

Tears flood Ellie's eyes. Before she can say anything, however, I open the second box and show her what's inside. Because there's more than one question she needs to answer.

When Ellie sees the ring, tears fall.

I take the ring out, drop to a knee, and sign amidst blaring music, "Will you be my wife?"

She doesn't need to reply. She doesn't need to sign or speak or even nod. Because I can see the answer in her eyes. Like Maisy, she's going to be a Montana. She's going to be one for the rest of her life and mine. She's going to raise Maisy with me and have more children to fill all the rooms in this house. She's going to love me as fiercely as I love her. She's going to be my forever.

Maisy however, is eager for an answer as she tugs at the hem of Ellie's dress, looking up at her expectantly.

Ellie sinks to her level and signs to my spunky, curly-haired, perfect daughter, "There is nothing I want more."

Maisy looks from Ellie to me, possibly confused by her answer.

I smile the biggest, brightest smile and sign, "That's a yes."

Maisy yelps and cheers and dances around before we all come together and hug as one. Because she understands.

She understands it all. Who *I* am. Who *Ellie* is. Who *she* is. And what we are together.

A family.

# Epilogue

## Ellie

*Two months later…*

On the arms of my parents, I walk down the aisle toward the man who becomes my husband today.

Blake has never looked more handsome. He's wearing a suit, something he rarely does, and a blue tie that he chose specifically to match my eyes.

His brothers are to his left, and on his right, my two sisters. Maisy is here, too, having practiced being our flower girl for the past eight weeks.

Hannah is off to one side, here to interpret the ceremony for all our deaf friends. I just hope I can read every single word that comes off his lips, because it's *him* I want to look at as he says his vows.

Blake takes both my hands in his as the minister says a few words. I don't bother watching, I know what the officiant is saying. Blake and I scripted the entire ceremony. The only thing we don't know are each other's vows. I tamp down my nervousness and get lost in Blake's eyes as the time comes for him to say his.

I'm surprised when his lips don't move. They don't move at all. Instead, he drops my hands and begins signing. A huge lump forms in my throat when I realize he's going to sign all his vows.

"Ellie," he signs, "I may never completely fit into your world, and you may never completely fit into mine. But it doesn't matter, because we fit with each other. We're the perfect fit. The only fit. You complete me in ways I didn't think were possible. You've taught me how things most people think are a hindrance can actually be a gift. Being able to communicate with you without spoken words somehow enhances our connection. What some call broken, I call beautiful. What some pity, I've come to celebrate.

"Your silence has opened my eyes. I'll never look at things the same way again. You've taught me that love isn't just saying I love you. It's showing it. It's living it. It's feeling it. Love is much more than just words. And it's something I never would have known if I hadn't met you. Today is not the best day of my life. That day was the day I first saw you. It was the same day I found out about Maisy. Today is just the day that solidifies us as a family—something that has surely been fated in the stars since the beginning of time."

I can't move. I can't breathe. The fact that he learned all those signs and did them to near perfection is just another testament of his love for me.

He reaches out to wipe a tear from my cheek. "It's your turn," he signs.

I blow out a long deep breath and swallow my anxiety. It's my turn to surprise him.

"Blake, my love," I sign as well as say, at a volume I hope is acceptable for the venue. I have to clear my throat before continuing, because when you don't speak for a long time, it's actually a bit hard.

His chin quivers at my spoken words. He quickly puts a finger to my lips right before signing, "You don't need to do this. You know by now that I love you exactly how you are."

"I know I don't need to," I sign. "I know I don't have to. And that's what makes me want to. Now, do you mind?"

He laughs, tears coating his lashes as I say, stutter, and sign my way through my much-shorter-than-his vows. Speaking publicly for the first—and most likely last—time in my adult life, I declare to him and everyone present my unwavering love for a man who accepts me exactly the way I am and who *never* expects me to be more. Which is why I will be more. For him. For them. For us.

When we're pronounced husband and wife, we kiss and gather Maisy into our arms. As a family, we turn and face the entire room of two hundred people. A room I'm stunned to see is silent. Because instead of clapping… they're all doing jazz hands.

# Bonus Epilogue

## Maisy Montana – 21 years later

I walk up to the podium, calm and confident. After all, I didn't work my ass off for the last decade to sit in the shadows. I scan the massive crowd in the arena and find my parents sitting in the front row to the left of the stage. Of course they're in the front row—they've always been my biggest supporters and loudest cheerleaders.

Before I start my speech, I lock eyes with another one of my biggest supporters, Brayden, who is sitting in the third row among my other fellow graduates. His face beams as he signs, "You got this."

I nod, because hell yes, I do.

Courtney, my ASL interpreter for the past eight years, stands off to the side, her body and mine being projected onto the split-screen jumbotron hanging from the center of the arena's ceiling.

I have my notes. All the names of the encouraging people in my life. I stare at the list and realize they might not be the only ones I should be thanking. In a matter of two seconds, I change my entire speech. I take a deep breath and begin.

"I'm not the smartest student in my class," I sign. "I'm not the valedictorian, the class president, or even on the student council. I'm not a hero. I'm just a girl from a small town who happens to be deaf. This doesn't make me any more special than the girl over there in the second row who comes from a large city and happens to have green eyes. But my peers chose to give me this platform, so I guess they think I have something important to say." I hold up my notes and wave them around. "I had this speech all written out. I know I'm expected to thank everyone who made this possible from my very first kindergarten teacher to my distant relatives. But I'm not sure that would be the best use of my time."

I spare a glance at Brayden, whose eyebrows are practically touching his hairline. I practiced my speech in front of him at least five times. I watch as a slow smile creeps up his face. He knows this isn't the first time I've gone rogue. And I imagine it's one of the things he loves about me.

"The people I really should be thanking aren't who you'd expect. To my very first dance instructor, Madame B, who assured me that a deaf girl couldn't dance—I'd invite you to my childhood home to see more than two dozen national trophies won by me and my high school dance team. To my sixth-grade band teacher, Ms. J—who said a deaf girl can't play an instrument and called a meeting with my parents when I insisted on playing the violin—I'd be happy to forward the email I received from Julliard, encouraging me to apply. And to my high school guidance counselor, Mr. G, who side-eyed me when I said I wanted to go into medicine. Deaf people can't be doctors, he said. Well, Mr. G, here I am, standing up on this stage, graduating from medical school." I lift one of my graduation cords and hold it up. "With honors."

Everyone claps. Brayden pumps a fist. Mom cries and rubs the necklace she's worn since I was four years old.

"Thank you to all the people who said I couldn't. Because I'm here to tell you I did, and I am."

More applause.

"And to all the people who assumed I'd go into medical intelligence to try and 'cure' deafness, I say this: deafness is not something that needs to be cured, fixed, or helped. I'm choosing to go into advanced technologies in medical robotics because of the soldier who lost a leg fighting for our country, the woman who lost a limb in a car accident, the baby born without ankle bones—*those* are things I can help. Those are problems worth fixing. Deafness isn't a sickness. And if you try to call me disabled, well, let's just say I'll put my trophies, accolades, and diplomas up against anyone, anyplace, anytime."

I pause until the audience stops clapping.

"I'm sure there are some who expected me to come up here and surprise everyone by giving my speech verbally, as if I've got something to prove." I shake my head. "Could I speak if I wanted to? Yeah, sure. But I don't need to. And I never have." I wave my hands around. "This is the only voice I need. I don't need to speak to be heard, and I don't need to hear to be whole."

I hope I'm not overstepping. I realize I might be soapboxing a bit. The massive smile on Brayden's face tells me, yeah, maybe I am… but that he loves it.

"Okay, okay, so I suppose I should thank some other people." I turn and look at my parents, signing directly at them. "Thanks Mom and Dad for always letting me be me. For allowing me to wear my best Sunday dresses to the playground. For looking the other way, never discouraging me, and always praying for the best when I insisted on doing things like skydiving, cave exploring, and scuba diving. For giving me two little brothers who, along with you, have championed me every step of the way without making me feel like I'm any different than any other person. For standing up to Ms. J, and quite possibly teaching an impressionable eleven-year-old a few more curse words than she already knew."

The faces in the audience indicate everyone is laughing. I wait a moment for it to die down, then I finish up, because, after all… life is waiting.

I turn to Courtney. "Thank you to my friend and interpreter, Courtney Granger, who probably deserves an honorary medical degree with everything she's learned by my side."

I try not to tear up before I thank the very last person to be thanked. "And to the guy down there in the third row. The little deaf boy next door who instantly became my other half. The man who has been by my side for the past twenty-one years and who I know will always be there. I can't wait to go on this next journey with you. To say you complete me is an understatement and far too cliché. We don't need each other to be whole, only to be happy."

Brayden's face fills with pride as I complete my speech, using the funny anecdotes I'd had in my notes. My eyes don't stray from his when the arena erupts in lengthy applause. And even though neither of us can hear it, I just know his clap is without a doubt the loudest.

I thank my lucky stars that Brayden and I matched into the same residency program. Because I can't imagine life without him. Well, that, and I'm pretty sure that tonight he's going to propose.

# Acknowledgments

This book has been a long time coming. Years ago, when I wrote Stone Vows, a baby was born. A beautiful, strong, deaf baby. And ever since, you all have been begging for a book about Ellie. I hope I did justice to your expectations.

I'm not deaf. But that wasn't going to stop me from telling this story that needed to be told. However, I had to be certain I was representing the Deaf community with accuracy and social awareness. To accomplish this, I put together an amazing team of deaf sensitivity readers. I'm not exaggerating when I say writing this book took a tribe.

Without the following people, Ellie's story couldn't be what it is. So thank you from the bottom of my heart to my deaf sensitivity team: K.T. James, Desiree Dorsey, Mary Smith, Gina Marie Sciongay, and Christina Drury. And to Paul and Ann, thanks for answering so many questions for me.

If you are interested in reading more books that are either written about deaf characters or are written by deaf authors, please check out K.T. and Desi's book club on Instagram @DEAFinitelyreaders.

Additionally, a huge shout out to my incredible editor, Michelle Fewer, who always seems to squeeze me in precisely when I need her the most. Your support and encouragement mean the world to me.

And Julie Collier. Julie, Julie, Julie. Where do I even begin? Without you as my PA and friend, I would be running around like a chicken with its head cut off. You keep me grounded. You don't pull any punches, and for all that I'm grateful.

To my team of beta readers, Joelle Yates, Laura Conley, and Ann Peters, I value your continued support. And last, but certainly not least, to my influencers and ARC team, you have my undying thanks for always championing my books.

# About the author

Samantha Christy's passion for writing started long before her first novel was published. Graduating from the University of Nebraska with a degree in Criminal Justice, she held the title of Computer Systems Analyst for The Supreme Court of Wisconsin and several major universities around the United States. Raised mainly in Indianapolis, she holds the Midwest and its homegrown values dear to her heart and upon the birth of her third child devoted herself to raising her family full time. While it took time to get from there to here, writing has remained her utmost passion and being a stay-at-home mom facilitated her ability to follow that dream. When she is not writing, she keeps busy cruising to every Caribbean island where ships sail. Samantha Christy currently resides in St. Augustine, Florida with her husband and four children.

You can reach Samantha Christy at any of these wonderful places:

Website:     www.samanthachristy.com

Facebook:    https://www.facebook.com/SamanthaChristyAuthor

Instagram:   @authorsamanthachristy

E-mail:      samanthachristy@comcast.net